1

Transfer of Power

Also by Vince Flynn

Term Limits

Available from POCKET BOOKS

Transfer
of
Power

VINCE FLYNN

POCKET BOOKS

NEW YORK   LONDON   TORONTO   SYDNEY   TOKYO   SINGAPORE

POCKET BOOKS, a division of Simon & Schuster Inc.
1230 Avenue of the Americas, New York, NY 10020

Copyright © 1999 by Vince Flynn

ISBN: 0-671-02319-5

First Pocket Books hardcover printing July 1999

10 9 8 7 6 5 4 3 2 1

Designed by Nancy Singer
Map by Paul Pugliese

Printed in the U.S.A.

For Terence and Kathleen Flynn

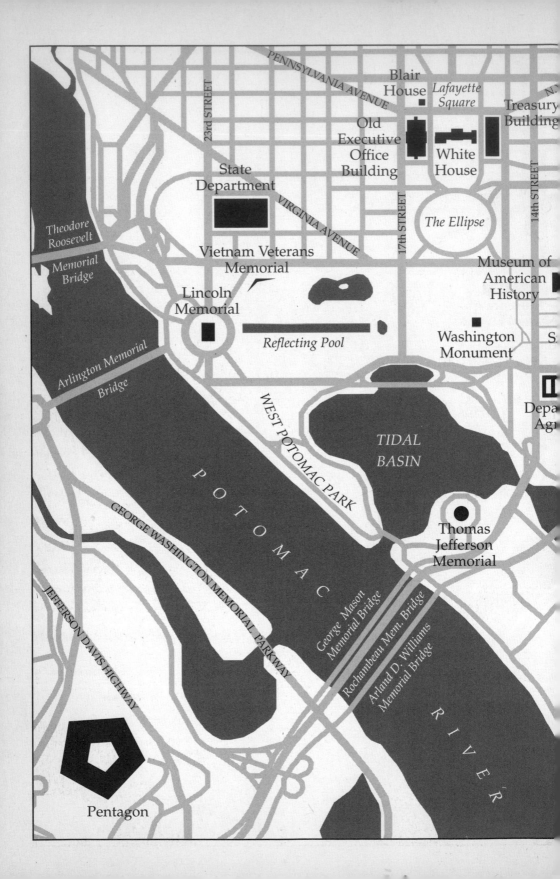

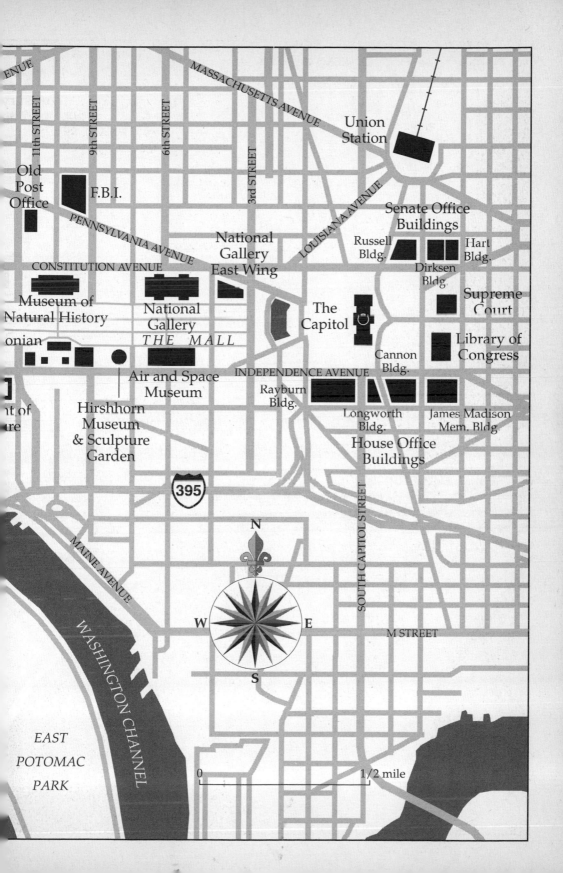

Out of respect for the United States Secret Service and the security of the president, certain facts regarding the layout of the White House and Secret Service tactics have either been changed or omitted.

Transfer of Power

1

Washington, D.C.

A FINE MIST fell from the darkening spring sky as the black limousine turned off of E Street. The armor-plated car weaved through the concrete-and-steel barricades at a speed suggesting urgency. As the limousine turned onto West Executive Drive, it slowed briefly for the heavy black gate to open, and then sped forward. After splashing through several puddles, the limo came to an abrupt stop in front of the ground-floor entrance to the West Wing of the White House.

The rear passenger door opened immediately, and Dr. Irene Kennedy stepped from the car. She walked under the long off-white awning that extended from the building to the curb and paused to let her boss catch up. Thomas Stansfield slowly climbed out of the limo and buttoned the jacket of his charcoal gray suit. At seventy-nine years of age Stansfield was an icon in the intelligence community. His career dated all the way back to World War II and the OSS, the precursor to the CIA. Stansfield had been one of Wild Bill Donovan's recruits almost sixty years earlier— a different war fought by a different breed. Stansfield was the last one. Now they were all gone, retired or dead, and it wouldn't be much longer before he turned over the reins of power at the much-maligned and embattled intelligence agency.

The CIA had changed during his tenure. More precisely, the threats had changed, and the CIA was forced to change with them. The old static days of a two-superpower world were long gone, replaced by small regional conflicts and the ever-growing threat of terrorism. As Stansfield closed out his career, this was what bothered him most. The threat of one individual bringing biological, chemical, or nuclear annihilation to America was becoming more and more plausible.

Stansfield looked up at the lazy mist that was falling from the early evening sky. A light spray dusted his face, and the silver-haired director of the CIA blinked. Something was bothering him, and he couldn't quite put his finger on it. Stansfield gave the darkening sky one last look and then stepped under the awning.

Kennedy continued through the double doors, where two uniformed

Secret Service officers were standing post, and started down the long hall. This was the first floor of the West Wing. The president's office was located on the floor above, but that was not where they would be meeting. Irene Kennedy sped ahead, while Stansfield followed at his always even pace.

Down the hallway, on the right, a U.S. Navy officer stood in his cleanly pressed black uniform with his hands clasped firmly in front of him. "Good evening, Dr. Kennedy. Everything is ready. The generals and the president are waiting for you." The watch officer of the White House Situation Room gestured to his left.

"Thank you, Commander Hicks," replied Kennedy as she walked past the naval officer.

They went down several steps, took a right, and came to a secure door with a camera mounted above it. To the left was a black-and-gold plaque with the words "White House Situation Room: Restricted Access."

The lock on the door buzzed, and Kennedy pushed the door open. She entered and turned to her left, into the Situation Room's new conference room. Director Stansfield followed her, and Commander Hicks closed the soundproof door behind them.

President Robert Hayes, dressed in a tuxedo, stood at the far end of the room and listened intently to the two men in front of him. The first, General Flood, was the chairman of the Joint Chiefs. Flood was six four and weighed almost two hundred seventy pounds. The second man was General Campbell, a half foot shorter than his superior and one hundred pounds lighter. Campbell was the commander of the U.S. military's Joint Special Operations Command, or JSOC. Before taking his most recent job, he had proudly commanded the famous 82nd Airborne Division and the 18th Airborne Corps.

President Hayes had been in office for only five months, and thus far had a decent working relationship with both the Pentagon and the CIA. Before being elected president, Robert Xavier Hayes had served as both U.S. congressman and senator. The Democrat from Ohio had been elected to the highest office in the land largely because he had a very clean personal life and was seen as someone who could mend the ever-deepening divide between the two parties. The previous administration had been rife with scandal, so much so that the American people had overwhelmingly picked someone whose personal life could pass the rigorous scrutiny of the press. Hayes was happily married and had three children in their thirties, all of whom had managed to stay off the tabloid covers and live relatively normal lives.

Kennedy set her briefcase on a chair near the end of the long table and said, "If everyone will be seated, we can get started." She felt rushed. Things were coming together at a frantic pace.

Director Stansfield greeted the two generals and the president. No one was in a talkative mood. The president worked his way around to the opposite end of the table and sat in his high-backed leather chair. All four walls of the room were covered with dark wood except a square section behind the president. That portion of the wall was white, and in the middle of it was the circular seal of the president of the United States.

With the president at the head of the table, the two generals sat on his right and Director Stansfield on his left. Kennedy handed each of the men identical folders that were sealed with red tape and marked Top Secret.

"Please feel free to open the files while I get the rest of the materials ready." Kennedy pushed some of her shoulder-length brown hair back behind her ear. After several seconds of digging through her briefcase, she found the right disk and inserted it into the A drive of the computer under the podium. About sixty seconds later the director of the CIA's Counterterrorism Center was ready to start.

A map of the Persian Gulf appeared on the large screen to Kennedy's right, and she began, "Mr. President, four days ago we inserted one of our people into the Iranian city of Bandar Abbas. Our man was operating on some information he received that Sheik Fara Harut might be in the city." Kennedy pressed a button, and the screen changed from the map to a grainy black-and-white photograph of a bearded man in a turban. "Fara Harut, shown here in this 1983 photograph, is the religious leader of the militant Islamic group Hezbollah. He has very strong ties to the religious conservatives in Iran." Kennedy glanced sideways at the president and added, "You may have noted some mention of him in your PDB." Kennedy was referring to the President's Daily Brief, an intelligence summary given to him every morning by the CIA.

The president nodded. "I recall the name."

Kennedy pressed a button, and a new photo appeared on the screen, this time of a much younger, clean-shaven, and handsome individual. "This is Rafique Aziz. It was taken in the late seventies, when Aziz was obtaining a degree in electrical engineering from American University in Beirut."

The president nodded reluctantly and said, "I am definitely familiar with this individual."

Kennedy nodded. "Well, you might not be familiar with this most recent development." The doctor pointed to the screen at the front of the room, and a series of photos played out showing charred buses and grotesque, bloody bodies. "These bombings have all been linked to the fundamentalist Palestinian group Hamas. Hamas has stepped up its attacks recently in an effort to derail the Middle East peace process. Hezbollah and Hamas have done very little to help each other's causes." Kennedy looked down the long table and added, "That is, until recently. Aziz and Harut have been looking for a way to continue their fight as things have calmed in Beirut. They found their opportunity after Israel assassinated Hamas leader Yehya Ayyash in 1996. Hamas turned even more militant, stepping up its efforts to drive Israel from the West Bank and Gaza Strip. In this most recent period, the Israelis have noted a marked increase in the sophistication of Hamas bombs and tactics. It is our belief that Rafique Aziz is responsible for this." Kennedy paused and got ready to drop the bombshell. "To make matters even worse, we have also learned that Saddam Hussein has offered to help fund some of the group's actions."

President Hayes shook his head slowly and scowled.

"It gets worse," Kennedy continued. "The stipulation that Saddam has put on the money is that it be used to attack the United States *domestically.*" Kennedy emphasized the last word.

The information caused Hayes's left eyebrow to rise a half inch. "Where did we get this?"

Kennedy looked to Stansfield, and the director of the CIA replied, "The NSA intercepted some communications, and we verified them through several of our foreign contacts."

"That's just great." Hayes shook his head. Looking to Kennedy with dread in his eyes, he asked, "What else?"

"Two nights ago our man in Iran informed us of a probable ID on Harut, and earlier this evening he made a positive ID."

The president folded his arms across his chest. "Can we be sure your guy has the right man?"

"Yes, Mr. President," answered Kennedy confidently.

Hayes looked from Kennedy to the map of Iran and then back. "I assume you didn't interrupt my dinner plans just to tell me you may have found this fellow."

"You are correct, Mr. President. We have been waiting for this chance for a long time. If we don't grab him now, we may never get another chance." Kennedy stopped to make sure the president understood the how serious she was. "General Campbell and I have put together a plan to grab Harut." Kennedy changed the main screen. A second map of the Persian Gulf appeared, this one with a half dozen new markings on it.

Kennedy looked to General Campbell and nodded.

Campbell rose from his chair, and with his ramrod posture, he marched to the front of the room. Once firmly in position behind the podium, he started. "Mr. President, Harut, like Saddam, never stays in the same place for more than three or four nights at a time. This is the first time in over a decade that we have been able to track his whereabouts for more than a day and be in a position to do something about it." Campbell gestured to the map. "We have two helicopters from the First Special Operations Wing that have left Saudi Arabia and are in the process of hooking up with the *Independence,* which is on patrol in the Persian Gulf." The general tapped the spot on the map that marked the location of the nuclear-powered aircraft carrier. "And over here"—the general moved his finger across the Persian Gulf to a spot just off the Iranian coast that was marked by a blue cigar-shaped object—"we have the USS *Honolulu.* As I'm sure you have already noted, she is no longer in international waters. Right now she is about two miles offshore and waiting for the orders to off-load her cargo."

While Campbell continued his briefing, President Hayes felt as if he were having an out-of-body experience. He had dreamt of this moment for years and loathed it. The idea of ordering U.S. troops into battle had no appeal, no mystique, no glory, and surely no satisfaction. People would die tonight because of the orders he gave. The enemy's men for sure and possibly some of his own.

President Hayes listened to the general intently and tried to be objective. Hayes was a student of history and knew that to never use force was foolish. If he did not act tonight, it might someday cost the lives of Americans. Terrorism had to be confronted. He could not pass on this decision.

Persian Gulf, 3:16 A.M. (local time)

IN THE IRANIAN seaside city of Bandar Abbas an elderly man shuffled down a dusty street in his dirty white djellaba, a simple robelike garment that flowed from his shoulders to his ankles. A brown turban covered his head and face; a pair of worn leather sandals, his feet. The wind blew in off the Persian Gulf, and the night sky was filled with thick clouds.

The decrepit old man mumbled to himself in Farsi, the native language, as he went. Like so many things in life, appearances could be deceiving. Underneath the ragged turban and djellaba was one hundred ninety pounds of solid, lean muscle. Mitch Rapp, a thirty-one-year-old American, hadn't showered in a week. His deeply bronzed skin was covered with a film of dirt, and his black hair and beard were spotted with streaks of gray dye that made him look twice his age.

During the late mornings and early afternoons, the American had slept in a tiny apartment. By afternoon and evening he roamed the streets with a brown canvas bag collecting discarded pop cans and bottles. While he played the role of street bum, he kept his posture slouched and his demeanor timid. But his eyes and mind were alert. He scanned doorways and windows and listened to conversations—waiting for a clue. Two days earlier he had discovered the telltale sign he had been looking for. Rapp was searching for a man, a man he wanted to kill.

His pursuit of this man had led him to some of the roughest and dirtiest cities in the Middle East, North Africa, and Europe. In the process Rapp had himself been shot, stabbed, and hunted, and every step of the way his quarry had managed to stay just out of his reach. Six months earlier, on a rainy Paris night, Rapp had had his chance and blown it. A moment of hesitation, of stupid indecision, had allowed Rafique Aziz to escape by the narrowest of margins. Never again, Rapp had sworn a thousand times. Next time he would pull the trigger—innocent bystander in the way or not.

Tonight, Rapp was determined to pick up the trail again. Nearing the house he had discovered two days earlier, Rapp scanned the rooftops and windows for signs of sentries he might have missed on his previous visits. The smell of the salty air mixing with the open sewage heightened his instincts. He was on enemy ground, walking straight into the lion's den. The streets he walked belonged to Hezbollah, one of several militant Islamic groups that dominated the underbelly of Middle Eastern politics. The terrorist group had killed thousands in their *jihad*—their holy war. This was their stronghold in the dirty seaside city of Bandar Abbas. Rapp had learned early in his profession that home was where his enemies were most vulnerable, where they were most likely to feel comfortable and let down their guard. Tonight he would come into their home—unannounced and uninvited.

Rapp adjusted his turban to conceal everything but his eyes. Then, he turned the corner and continued the shuffle of a man more than twice his age. Several doors down a man sat on a folding chair with an AK-47 resting on his lap.

Rapp mumbled to himself in Farsi, intentionally trying to alert the bodyguard to his presence. The bodyguard heard his approaching footsteps and aimed his gun in the direction of the noise. The babbling tramp appeared from the shadows, and the bodyguard relaxed, dropping his weapon back onto his lap. It was his crazy late-night visitor, just another worthless vagrant.

As Rapp approached the bodyguard, he pulled his turban away from his mouth. Smiling, he flashed a set of fake rotten teeth and greeted the armed sentry as he shuffled past. The large man nodded and then leaned back in his chair, resting his head against the wall of the house.

Rapp continued down the street, his alert eyes taking inventory of everything on the block. He noted every window and every doorway. He looked beyond the doorframes and the curtains, into the shadows. If this was a trap, that was where they would be waiting.

Rapp turned onto an even narrower street. Sixty feet down, the American ducked into an alley that had been built long before cars were envisioned. The tunnel-like passage was four feet wide and enclosed in darkness. Slowing his pace, Rapp stopped in the second alcove on his left and closed his eyes. He set his canvas bag of bottles and cans down and listened intently while squeezing his eyelids tighter, trying to speed up the process of adjusting to the near total darkness.

White House Situation Room

GENERAL CAMPBELL FINISHED the mission briefing and stood at the far end of the room with Kennedy. For the last twenty-four hours they had worked almost nonstop to get everything in place, and now they looked on somewhat helplessly as the president analyzed the pros and cons of the mission. After a minute of silence President Hayes looked at Director Stansfield and asked, "Who is this man we have on the ground?"

Director Stansfield closed his mission summary and placed it on the table. "He is one of our best. Fluent in three languages, not counting English, and he understands another half dozen dialects well enough to get by."

"Is he American?"

"Yes."

President Hayes nodded slowly, and then asked the million dollar question. "Instead of exposing ourselves by trying to grab Harut . . ." The president paused and formulated the most tactful way to say what he was thinking. "Why don't we have your man—" The president looked to Kennedy. "What is his name?"

"His code name is Iron Man."

"Why don't we have this Iron Man . . . eliminate Harut?" President Hayes looked cautiously around the room, nervously aware that what he had just suggested was against the law.

"We have looked at that as an option, Mr. President, but there is another issue we haven't discussed." Kennedy looked to her boss.

Stansfield sat leaning back in his chair with one leg crossed over the other. He removed his left hand from his chin and said, "We have just recently come into some information," Stansfield stated evenly, "that is directly related to this operation. Yesterday I received a call from one of my counterparts abroad. They informed me that Hamas is targeting Washington for a terrorist attack. When and where is not certain, but we have a corroborating source that can confirm this intelligence."

Hayes shook his head and uttered a curse under his breath. "Where did you get this information?"

"Our Israeli friends brought it to my attention several weeks ago, and it was corroborated by the British this morning."

"Elaborate, please." Hayes made a rolling motion with his index finger.

"The Israelis picked up a Hamas commander during one of their sweeps through the West Bank about a month ago. While they were interrogating him, he made several references to an attack that was being planned here in Washington. The Israelis couldn't get anything more out of the commander on this issue, except that the man behind the operation is none other than Rafique Aziz."

President Hayes swiveled in his chair and looked up at the smaller screen that vividly showed the carnage left from one of Aziz's bus bombings in Israel. The mere thought of the same thing happening in Washington, D.C., caused the president's blood to boil.

"This dovetails," continued Stansfield, "with the NSA's report that Saddam has offered to bankroll any terrorist attack that is carried out in the United States."

President Hayes looked at the director of the CIA and rose out of his chair. He reminded himself to stay calm. Saddam had become the unreachable thorn in America's back, and it was time to start dealing with him in a more ruthless manner.

With sarcasm dripping from his voice, the president said, "This is just wonderful." All Hayes could think about was the lunatic terrorism of the Middle East playing itself out in the streets of America. He knew there was no way he could allow it to happen, not if he could take the battle to them first.

Irene Kennedy half listened to the conversation between the two generals, her boss, and the president. At the moment, she was more concerned with Mitch Rapp. Rapp was her recruit, and she had grown very fond of him. There was nothing sexual about the connection; it was more in the nature of a bond between two people who had been through the wringer together.

Kennedy had spent more than half of her youth bouncing around the Middle East as her father was moved from one embassy to the another. As a State Department brat she saw nothing unusual in this, since most of her friends had gone through similar experiences. In fact Kennedy had loved growing up in the Middle East, but unfortunately all of those fond memories came crashing down in April of 1983 when a car bomb ripped through the U.S. embassy in Beirut. Kennedy's father was killed in the blast, and her life was forever changed.

The anger she felt in the wake of the tragedy had led her to the CIA, and it didn't take Langley long to make up their mind about Kennedy. She had spent twelve years of her life growing up in Middle East, she had a doctorate in Arabic studies, and she was motivated. Kennedy was earmarked from the very start for counterterrorism. Now, some sixteen years later, she was running the show at the Counterterrorism Center.

But that was only part of Kennedy's story—the part that was reported to the legislative oversight committees. A separate job that fell under Kennedy's purview was responsibility for the Orion Team, one of the most secretive organizations within the CIA. Only a handful of people knew of the group's existence, and it was to stay that way indefinitely. It had to. The group had been formed by Director Stansfield in response to another terrorist incident. The downing of Pan Am Flight 103 over Lockerbie, Scotland, in December of 1988. Irene Kennedy was given the reins and instructed to build a group with one single task—to hunt down and kill terrorists. As Director Stansfield had said at the time, "There are certain people here in Washington who have decided it is time to go on the offensive." Who those people were, Kennedy had never asked, and in truth, she never wanted to know. She only knew that she agreed with the strategy and was willing to risk everything to help implement it. That risk was very real, and by no means marginal. If the wrong people on the Hill, or over at Justice, ever got wind of the Orion Team, they would hold an inquisition, and Kennedy's head would be the first one on the chopping block.

The truth was, the American people would never be able to stomach the escapades of Mitch Rapp and the Orion Team. In the political grandstanding that would take place under a congressional investigation, everyone would forget the fact that it was a war. The team would be portrayed as a group of rogue operatives with complete disregard for the Constitution. Someone like Rapp, who was at this very moment putting his life on the line, would be eaten alive by the country-club liberals and conservative opportunists looking to make a name for themselves.

Kennedy felt the burden of responsibility for Rapp. She was the one that had gone to Syracuse University in the winter of 1988 and discovered him. He did not find the CIA—as she had done after her father's death—

they had found him. Thirty-five students from Syracuse had perished on Pan Am Flight 103, and one of them had been Mitch Rapp's high school sweetheart. Irene Kennedy had dangled the prospect of revenge in front of an anguished Rapp, and he had leapt at the chance without a moment's hesitation. Now, a decade later, they had turned him into quite possibly the most efficient and lethal killer in the modern era of the Agency.

President Hayes had heard enough. He pondered the ramifications for a long moment. If he chose not to act, the end result could cost American lives. Yes, he could lose men tonight, but these men had assumed a risk when they signed up. If he walked away, it could cost the lives of noncombatants. Hayes knew what he had to do.

With a no-nonsense tone, the president asked, "General Campbell, what do you think we should do?"

In his clipped military tone, Campbell replied, "I think it's an opportunity we can't pass up, Mr. President."

"Dr. Kennedy, I assume you think we should go in?" asked Hayes.

"Yes, Mr. President."

"Thomas?" Hayes looked to the director of the CIA.

Stansfield paused for a second and then nodded.

The president turned lastly to General Flood. "Jack, what do you think?"

The general folded his large hands and thumped them on the table once. "I think we should grab him."

President Hayes squinted at the map of Iran on the large screen while he thought about the potential risk. After about twenty seconds of silence, he said, "You have my authorization."

As soon as the sentence was completed, Kennedy and Campbell were on the phone giving the mission the green light to the various players and commands involved.

Stansfield slid two white sheets of paper across the table. They were identical. One was for the president's records, and the other was for Stansfield's. The president grabbed a pen from his breast pocket and put his signature on both sheets. The relatively bland document was a *presidential finding,* required by law whenever the president authorized any type of covert mission. These simple documents had been a source of much controversy in Washington over the years.

"When do you plan to notify the committees?" asked President Hayes.

By law, the chairman and ranking minority member of both the House and Senate intelligence committees had to be informed of the intended action before it took place. This, however, was an area that was grayer than the London sky and one that was abused often, and sometimes for good reasons.

Stansfield placed his signed copy in a folder and said, "Fortunately, the gentlemen in question all have plans for this evening. I will alert their aides that I need to speak to them in about an hour. If all goes well, they will not be able to make it out to Langley until after our people have safely completed their job."

"Good." President Hayes stood and pulled on his cuff links. "My wife and I will be attending an event at the Kennedy Center. Where are you going to monitor the mission?"

"At Langley," replied Stansfield.

"Keep me updated, and good luck." With that the president left the room.

2

Strait of Hormuz, Persian Gulf

THE WIND SWEPT across the surface of the dark water as layers of billowing, low-slung clouds raced overhead in a crisscrossing pattern. The higher cluster headed northwest toward the open water of the Persian Gulf, while the lower clouds moved inland from the island dotted Strait of Hormuz to the mainland of ancient Persia and present-day Iran. The moon peeked through an occasional hole in the clouds. With the howling wind, the rain came and went in varying degrees of strength. It was not a night to be on the water.

In the shallows of a five-foot swell, a mast broke the surface and continued to rise, slashing into the high side of the trough like the ominous dorsal fin of a shark. White foam churned behind the narrow object as it continued southward. Rising a full ten feet above the waves, it instantly began to search the night sky. The thin tiger-striped object was an electronic support-measures antenna designed to detect radar emissions. Seconds later the thin mast was joined by another. This mast scanned the horizon a full three hundred sixty degrees, and then both objects submerged as quickly as they had appeared.

Underneath the stormy surface, a very expensive piece of hardware silently stalked the coast of Iran. Unbeknownst to all but her crew, she had just released her lethal cargo. As the 688-class attack submarine turned for international water, two heads bobbed to the surface and then three more. The swells rose and fell around them as they converged in a circle. One of the men wrestled with a black bag, freed the strap that was holding it together, and then pulled a cord. The IBS (inflatable boat: small) began to unfold and fill with air. Less than a minute later the boat was fully inflated, and two of the men began the process of attaching a small outboard engine to the back, while a third readied the fuel bladder. The rough seas tossed the boat in every direction, but the men worked undeterred.

As soon as the motor was secured, the last two men climbed into the boat, their black wet suits making them nearly invisible against the dark rubber. The engine was primed three times, and on the second pull it caught. The man in back twisted the throttle, and they scooted forward up the side of a swell.

Lieutenant Commander Dan Harris held on to one of the straps at the front of the boat and checked the compass strapped to his wrist. Next he looked at his Global Positioning System. The small GPS device strapped next to his compass used eighteen satellites orbiting the earth ten thousand miles up in space to tell him his exact location to within four meters. The submarine had dropped off Harris and his men thirty meters from where he had requested. Harris grinned through his thickly bearded face at the professionalism demonstrated by those anal-retentive submariners. They were, from top to bottom, nothing if not perfectionists.

The muscular commander gripped the hand strap a little tighter as the boat crashed nose first into the shallows of a swell. Dan Harris, Annapolis class of '81, was somewhat of an oddity. He was both cultured and uncouth, temperamental and unflappable, angry and calm, emotional and logical, compassionate and ruthless—he was, in short, whatever the situation dictated. He had learned by watching the naval special-warfare commanders that had gone before him. The U.S. Navy was a huge bureaucracy, and if you wanted to be able to run your command your own way, you had to spend an awful lot of time stroking the egos of the admirals who wrote the orders. Lt. Commander Dan Harris had walked that fine line almost to perfection, and that was why he was about to head into action while his colleagues were sitting behind desks at Little Creek and Coronado.

The small rubber boat slammed into a wave, and a deluge of cool, salty water sprayed over the bow, drenching the five bearded members of the U.S. Navy's top secret counterterrorist force SEAL Team Six. Harris shook the water from his face, and his ponytail whipped from side to side in the air behind him. The five men crashing through the rough water on this stormy night were known in the covert-operations business as long-haired SEALs. They were allowed to break Navy regulations on facial hair and hair length for just this type of mission. They were the best shooters in the business, and hence, given the most clandestine and often roughest missions.

The men possessed many similar traits, but at first glance the most notable was their dark features. Lt. Commander Harris had handpicked the men, and for tonight's mission they were traveling extra light. Harris had brought along his best. There would be no room for mistakes.

Bandar Abbas, Iran

A LARGE WAVE crashed to the beach, its back end sending a spray of salt water into the air. Mitch Rapp adjusted his turban and wiped the salt water from his face. He looked up and down the coast checking to make sure he was alone. Walking toward the pier to the north, he stopped, picked up a pop can and dropped it into his canvas bag. He continued his hunched shuffle. When he reached the wood pier, he walked underneath and checked the other side. Next, he walked back under the pier and up the incline of beach to check the small recesses where the wooden structure was secured to its concrete foundation. For the next ten minutes Rapp methodically checked every part of the structure to make sure it was unoccupied. He had picked the landing zone, and it was his responsibility to make sure there were no surprises.

Rapp checked his watch while the wind whistled through the tangled web of wood pilings that supported the pier. Everything was on schedule. Rapp had given up almost ten years of his life for this moment, and he was not going to let it slip away.

Persian Gulf

THE NUCLEAR-POWERED aircraft carrier USS *Independence* pounded through the stormy waters. She and her battle group of twelve ships and two submarines had been on patrol in the northern part of the gulf for the last twenty-three days. Late the previous evening the group had been ordered to proceed on a sweep to the south and east, back toward the Strait of Hormuz.

Just three hours earlier, under the cover of darkness, the large gray carrier had taken on two U.S. Air Force helicopters, which now sat just amidships of the carrier's island structure. Both helicopters were painted a flat tan with stripes of a slightly darker brown. They belonged to the 1st Special Operations Wing—the people in charge of getting American commandos in and out the hairiest places on earth. The first and larger of the two helicopters, was a MH-53J Pave Low. With a price tag of close to forty million dollars, the Pave Low was considered the most advanced military helicopter in the world. It took a crew of six to fly this large and complex helicopter, and its navigational system rivaled those of the most advanced fighter-bombers in the U.S. arsenal. The Pave Low was equipped with the Air Force's Enhanced Navigation System, or ENS. Using twenty separate systems, such as Doppler navigation, automatic direction finders, attitude director indicators, GPS, and a bevy of compasses and gyroscopes, the ENS told the pilots exactly where they were at all times.

This system was what allowed the highly trained aviators of the 1st Special Operations Wing to fly hundreds of miles, at treetop level, in the worst of weather conditions and land exactly on a target within seconds of their stated extraction or infiltration time. Which, in the business of special ops, could mean the difference between success and failure, or more pointedly, life and death. It took an unusual aviator to handle this large, complicated helicopter and the Air Force made sure that only the most qualified pilots were given the controls of these technological marvels.

The second helicopter was only two thirds the size of the hulking Pave Low. The MD-5300 Pave Hawk was equipped with a reduced version of the Pave Low's Enhanced Navigation System. The smaller, more agile, helicopter would be riding shotgun for tonight's mission. Inside both crafts, the pilots and flight crews were methodically running down their preflight checklists. There would be no room for mistakes. The slightest mistake could result in death and if it happened over land, worse, an international incident.

Iranian Coast

LT. COMMANDER DAN Harris held a pair of night-vision binoculars up to his eyes and tried in vain to search the landing area. Even though they were only several hundred yards offshore, he could barely see a thing. The boat was being thrashed in and out of the stormy sea, which made it impossible to hold the binoculars steady. Just when he had an area framed, the boat would shift and he'd end up staring at the back of a wave ten feet in front of them.

Harris secured the night-vision binoculars in a waterproof pack and stuck his right hand into the neck of his scuba suit. The commando retrieved the earpiece to his secure Motorola MX300 radio and cupped it next to his left ear. Above the din of water and wind, he shouted, "Iron Man, this is Whiskey Five. Do you read? Over." Harris's throat mike picked up his words and broadcast them.

The crackled reply came over the earpiece. "Whiskey Five, this is Iron Man. I read you loud and clear. Over."

Harris turned his back to the wind in hopes that he could hear better. "We are in position, Iron Man. What's the status of our LZ?"

"Everything is secure."

"Roger that. We'll see you in five." Harris pulled at the neck of his wet suit with his left hand and stuffed the headset back inside. Turning to his men, he shouted, "Grab your gear, and let's get moving."

Each man checked his swim pack and put on his fins and dive mask. When everyone had given the thumbs-up sign, Harris gave the order to go over the sides. Once in the water the SEALs unsheathed their K-bars and punctured the sides of the rubber boat. Musty air hissed its way free. After ten seconds, the weight of the motor began to pull the deflated boat under the surface and to the bottom.

Seeing the pier from the boat was hard enough; trying to do it from the water was futile. Everyone took a compass reading, and then Harris ordered his best swimmer to take the lead. The five men swam in a tight formation, checking their heading as they went. After several minutes of rough swimming, they neared the pier, maneuvered around the south side of the structure, and lined up to catch a wave. In unison, the five SEALs rode a wave in on their bellies. One by one they gently landed on the beach, and like alligators they scurried their way along the wet sand until they were safely out of sight under the pier.

Without being ordered, each man moved into a defensive position of cover—their Heckler & Koch 10-mm MP-10 submachine guns already extracted from their waterproof packs and ready to fire. Attached to the threaded barrels of the weapons were thick, black water-technology sound suppressors that made the weapons extremely quiet. Two of the men crawled to the north side, two stayed at the south side, and Harris moved to the middle. All of them remained right at the surf line.

The waves continued to pound the beach—a clamoring of thunderous echoes reverberated from the tangled maze of the pier. The surf raced up the beach and enveloped all of Harris except his head and weapon. The frothing water subsided in a retreat, and then seconds later was replaced by another wave. Harris looked around the left side of a barnacle-coated piling and studied the wooden labyrinth before him. The roar of the surf and the howling wind made listening difficult. As Harris looked in and around the maze of wooden supports, the SEAL heard a faint whistle followed by another and then a third. Then, about thirty feet away, a man in a white robe stepped from behind one of the pilings and waved. Harris kept the thick, black silencer of his submachine gun trained on the man's head.

Mitch Rapp approached with his arms extended outward and his hands open. In a voice just loud enough to be heard over the crashing surf, he said, "Danny Boy."

Harris took his eyes off Rapp for a second and checked the areas to his left and right. Then rising to one knee, he said, "It's good to see you, Mitch."

Rapp was one of the few people from the intelligence community that Harris trusted. This trust was based on two facts. The first being that Rapp, like Harris and his SEALs, actually put his life on the line and got down and dirty out in the field. The second, Harris had seen Rapp in action, and he was efficient, lethally efficient.

"We don't have a lot of time to screw around, so let's get you and your men changed and get rolling."

Harris stood and whistled; then he motioned for his men to follow. Rapp led the five SEALs up into the recesses of the pier where it met with the road. While they changed, Rapp kept watch. Each of the SEALs folded up his wet suit once on his legs and again on his arms. Then they pulled djellabas, sandals, and turbans from their packs. Within minutes they were in disguise and ready to go.

Rapp pulled the group into a tight circle. He had worked with all of the SEALs on previous missions and greeted them individually. Harris had brought along four of his best. To Rapp's right was Mick Reavers, a big linebacker type who weighed in at about two hundred fifty pounds. Next to Reavers were Tony Clark and Jordan Rostein, both medium-built demolition experts who had been swim buddies since they went through Basic Underwater Demolition School, or BUDS, as it was known in the SEAL community. And lastly there was little Charlie Wicker, known by his friends as simply Slick. Barely five foot six, Wicker weighed less than one hundred fifty pounds, but what he lacked in size he made up for in talent. Wicker could climb, slither, and shoot better than anyone at SEAL Team Six or Delta Force. He was possibly the best sniper in the business, and with that position came a strange respect. Other soldiers tend to give snipers a wide berth. Their survival instincts tell them it's not a good idea to mess with someone who can shoot you dead in the head from a thousand yards.

Harris and his men had received continuous intelligence updates while onboard the *Honolulu*. Thanks to Rapp's intelligence from the ground and the high-resolution satellite imaging of Bandar Abbas, Harris and his men had been able to coordinate the formation of their plan with Rapp before leaving the boat.

Rapp, bent down on one knee, looked at the other five bearded Americans and asked, "Any questions before we get started?" Each of the men answered with a simple shake of his head. Rapp nodded and said, "Good. Harry, let's get things rolling."

Harris touched his lip mike and said, "Bravo Six, this is Whiskey Five. What's your status? Over."

There were several seconds of static, and then the reply came back. "Whiskey Five, this is Bravo Six. We are ready to roll. Over."

"What's your ETA for our extraction? Over."

"Three two minutes. I repeat three two minutes. Over."

Harris looked at his men and Rapp, who were all listening to the same conversation over their headsets. "Start the extraction countdown on my mark. Over."

"Roger."

All six men sitting under the dark pier synchronized their digital wristwatches accordingly. Harris spoke precisely. "Three, two, one, mark." Harris pressed the button on his watch and said, "We'll see you in thirty-two minutes, Bravo Six."

Looking to his left, Harris said, "Slick, you hit the road first." Then, jerking his thumb, he added, "Get going."

The wiry sniper rose and left the group without saying a word. Two minutes later Tony and Jordan moved out, and then finally Rapp, Harris, and Reavers made their way out from under the tangled wooden structure.

3

Persian Gulf

ON THE DECK of the USS *Independence* the rotors of the Pave Low and Pave Hawk started their slow drooping turn. Within half a minute the bend in the long blades was gone and they were spinning level, their rotor wash buffeting the shirts of the deck crew, who were pulling away the fueling hoses and readying the helicopters for takeoff. Another set of sailors scrambled under the desert-camouflaged helicopters and removed the bright yellow metal chocks from around the landing gear. In the back of the big Pave Low the three crew members checked their weapons. Bristling from the port and starboard hatches were two 7.62-millimeter miniguns, and a third was sling mounted beside the open cargo ramp. The two pilots, crew chief, and three flight crew members were all wearing night-vision goggles mounted over their flight helmets. Fifty feet away, in the sleek Pave Hawk, the same checks were being conducted. The two door gunners sat at the ready with their miniguns pointing out the open sides—the combination of their bulbous flight helmets and awkward night-vision goggles gave them the ominous appearance of modern technological warriors.

The pilot of the Pave Low gave the order to go feet wet, and a second later the large bird lifted ten feet off the fuel-streaked black deck of the supercarrier. The Pave Low immediately peeled to the port side of the moving ship and went nose down for the waves. The Pave Hawk mimicked the maneuver and pulled into formation one hundred fifty feet back and just to port of the Pave Low. The two helicopters raced eastward for the coast of Iran, skimming the water, their radar profiles nonexistent, the digital time display in their cockpits ticking downward.

Bandar Abbas, Iran

AS THEY TURNED into a narrow alley, a strong gust of wind smacked them in the face and snapped their flowing clothes against their bodies like a loosely trimmed sail. Rapp lowered his head and squinted as a wall of dust and sand peppered his face. Fortunately, the billowing clouds still filled the night sky, blotting out the moon. The three Americans, with Rapp in the lead, walked down the dirty streets with their weapons concealed. Rapp was lightly armed with only a knife and a silenced Beretta 9-mm pistol. The two SEALs had their submachine guns ready and gripped just under the folds of their robes. They traveled a circuitous route to move into position. When they reached an alley several blocks away from their objective, Lt. Commander Harris called the other SEALs for a status report, while Rapp used the time to check on the helicopters.

Everything was proceeding on schedule. Now all they had to do was sit and wait. Rapp looked down the narrow passageway and checked both entrances. They were well concealed. Harris tapped Rapp on the shoulder and held his watch in front of Rapp's face. The digital countdown read ten minutes and forty-one seconds until the choppers arrived. Harris asked, "When do you want to get moving?"

Rapp held up three fingers, and Harris nodded.

Leaning against the stucco wall, Rapp closed his eyes and focused on his breathing. He began to visualize what was to come. How he would take the guard out. What to expect when he got to the top of the stairs. He thought he knew how many people would be inside, but one could never be exactly sure. That was why Harris and his people were there. Rapp had seen firsthand during the day that almost every man in the neighborhood carried a gun or rifle. This was, after all, Hezbollah's own backyard. Rapp felt his chest tighten at the thought, causing a spike in his nerves. He reminded himself that a little bit of fear was a good thing.

At T minus four minutes Harris called for another status report, and everyone checked in by the numbers.

Harris gave Rapp the thumbs up sign, and Rapp pulled the arm of his lip mike down. "Slick, cover me as I come down the street, but don't shoot unless something goes wrong."

The wiry SEAL had picked a three-story clay house that sat atop a slight hill four blocks away and on the same street as the house they were going to hit. He had deftly slithered his way up a drainpipe and set up position on the flat rooftop. With a foam pad under his elbows and chest, the sniper peered through his night-vision scope at the street below. Tucked next to his right cheek was an Israeli-made Galil sniper rifle with a twenty-round magazine. Wicker loved his Galil. The SEAL had more accurate rifles, but none as rugged and compact. With its collapsible stock and attached bipod, the weapon was ideal for the mission.

Wicker listened to Rapp over his headset and moved the crosshairs of his optic-green scope until they were centered on the left temple of the guard sitting in front of Harut's. "Roger that, Iron Man. The guard looks like he's having a hard time staying awake. Other than him, the street is all yours."

"Roger that," whispered Rapp. He checked his watch, took a deep breath, and then looked to Harris. "Give me a ten-second head start, and then get moving." Harris nodded, and Rapp disappeared around the corner.

There was about a six-inch lip at the edge of the flat roof. Wicker had run all of his calculations. The wind was gusting at speeds of up to twenty knots and could potentially cause some problems, but most of that would be negated by the fact that he was only two hundred yards from the target. For Wicker, this was close.

Wicker saw Rapp appear at the opposite end of the street, one block away from the guard. The sniper licked his lips and took a slow even breath.

Rapp slid his feet in a gingerly shuffle, making a scraping noise to alert the sleepy guard to his presence before he was close enough to startle him. With his head down and posture slouched, Rapp mumbled to himself in Farsi, while his eyes checked the street.

As he neared, the guard looked his way and sat up a little straighter. The muzzle of the gun came up, but then upon recognizing the crazy old man, the guard let his weapon fall back to his lap.

The scene was developing in a casual, nonthreatening way, just as it had a dozen times over the last three nights. As he inched down the street, Rapp continued his mumbling, stumbling, and bumbling act. When he was about twenty feet away, Rapp greeted the guard and, without giving him a chance to respond, began talking about the weather. Deftly, Rapp noted the large man's weight location on the chair. His legs were stretched out in front of him, and his balance was back. He was in no position to spring to his feet.

At first it looked as if Rapp was going to pass right by. He gave no sign of slowing until he was right in front of the guard. Drawing closer, as if to ask a question, he zeroed in on the Iranian's eyes and pointed down the street with his left hand. At the same time his right hand slid underneath his robe in a smooth, almost undetectable motion. Gripping the hard rubber handle of his matte-black knife, Rapp extracted the weapon and stepped forward.

In one fluid motion, the sharp blade of the knife sliced deep into the neck of the guard just under the jawline. Rapp cupped his left hand over the man's mouth and drove the knife upward into the base of the brain. Then, with a quick twist of the handle, the guard's entire body went from rigid to limp in one convulsion as his brain stem was severed. Rapp propped the dead man against the wall and extracted the bloody knife. Looking over both shoulders, he wiped the knife on the guard's brown robe and covered the wound with the dead man's turban.

Silently, Rapp ducked into the doorway and crouched. A narrow hallway of worn wooden steps proceeded to the second-story apartment. Just as he had expected, there was no way of getting up the old rickety stairs without announcing his presence. Rapp scanned the steps leading to the second floor for trip wires and replaced his knife. From a thigh holster under his djellaba he retrieved his silenced 9-mm Beretta. Several seconds later Harris and Reavers joined him.

Rapp stood and motioned for them to follow. To the surprise of the two SEALs, Rapp coughed loudly and began climbing the stairs while complaining in Farsi of the cold night air. The two SEALs followed close behind, their suppressed MP-10s up and ready to fire. Rapp climbed to the top landing, checked to make sure Harris and Reavers were behind him, and then took one step back, brought his right foot up, and lunged forward. His kick splintered the doorframe and sent the unpainted door swinging inward. In a blaze of motion, Rapp rushed the room, his silenced Beretta up and sweeping from right to left.

The two men at the kitchen table looked up from their backgammon board with sleepy eyes. Before they had a chance to reach for their weapons, Rapp fired. The silencer coughed twice, sending a bullet into each man's forehead. As the bodies toppled from their chairs, Rapp rushed across the room and dove through the shabby curtain that served as a door to the bedroom. He hit the floor, did a forward somersault, came up on one knee, and began to search for his target. A thin wall of light from the kitchen now cut through the bedroom in a diagonal swath. Rapp saw an arm move through the block of light and fired.

Fara Harut was lunging for his gun, but before he could reach it, a bullet smashed through his right wrist, breaking it instantly and sending it jerking away from its destination. The elderly man recoiled in pain and clutched his wounded limb. His next reaction was to scream for help, but before he could do so, the words were sucked from his mouth.

Mitch Rapp, adrenaline pumping, had lunged from his spot on the floor and brought the butt end of the Beretta's grip smashing down across the Iranian's temple. Harut crumpled back dazed and bleeding.

Rapp heard Harris call "clear" from behind him, while Reavers did the same from the kitchen. With his left hand, Rapp retrieved a syringe from under his robe and pulled the protective plastic cover off with his teeth. Then he stabbed the needle into Harut's neck and pressed the plunger. The sedative would keep him out for the next two hours.

Carefully, Rapp put the plastic cover back on the syringe and placed it in his robe. Then he began searching the room for any documents that might be useful. In the nightstand he found a gun. He removed the clip, emptied the chamber, and tossed the gun into the far corner.

Harris was now at the bedroom window his MP-10 at the ready. Over his radio he said, "Give me a sit rep by the numbers." Turning to Rapp, he said, "Nice work, Mitch. I'm glad we could be here to watch."

"We're not out of here yet, Harry." Rapp continued searching for anything of value.

Harris kept his eye on the street and listened to his men report in. When they were done, he said, "All right. Jordan and Tony, get your asses up here. Slick, keep me posted on what's going on outside. We're heading up to the roof."

As Harris walked back into the kitchen, he pointed to the ladder on the far wall and said, "Reavers, get up on the roof and test the strobe . . . and make sure you check for wires on that hatch before you open it."

Reavers climbed the short ladder and looked at the edges of the square hatch that led to the flat roof. After he was sure there were no booby traps, he opened the hatch and climbed onto the roof.

Harris, in the meantime, opened the back door just in time to greet his two men who were climbing the rickety stairs from the alley. Pointing to the front and back stairways Harris said, "Booby-trap both of 'em." Then he spun and went back toward the bedroom saying, "Bravo Six, this is Whiskey Five. We are ready for pickup. What's your ETA? Over."

The reply from the helicopters came back. "We are seven two seconds out. I repeat, seven two seconds out. Over."

Harris checked his watch. They were within fifteen seconds of their planned extraction time. "Slick, what's going on outside?"

Down the street, Wicker rubbed the trigger guard of his rifle while he scanned the dark street with his night-vision scope. "Everything is quiet so far."

Back in the bedroom, Rapp had turned his attention to cuffing and gagging Harut. Harris came through the doorway as he was finishing up.

"Mitch, let's go. The chopper is on its way in."

"Roger." Rapp stuck a sheaf of documents in his waistband and threw Harut over his shoulder. He bounced the old man twice until he had him in the right position. Then he started for the ladder. As Rapp started to climb, he heard the first sign of trouble come over his earpiece.

4

Bandar Abbas, Iran

FROM ATOP HIS perch down the street, Wicker was keeping a careful eye on the street and humming a Bob Marley tune to himself. Peering through his optic-green night-vision scope, he kept his breathing shallow and smooth. Suddenly, the door from the downstairs apartment opened, and a man wearing a pair of underwear appeared with an AK-47 gripped in his hands.

"Harry," the sniper spoke into his mike, "you've got company. The guy from the downstairs apartment just came outside." Wicker watched through his scope as the man walked over to the slumped guard and shook his shoulder. The dead guard rolled from the chair to the ground, and the man stepped back quickly, bringing his AK-47 up to the firing position.

Wicker didn't have to think—from the moment the man had stepped outside, his head had never left the crosshairs of the scope. The SEAL squeezed the trigger of his riffle, the suppressor at the end of the barrel hissed with the expulsion of gasses, and the bullet was away.

The heavy round hit the man in the side of the head and propelled him to the ground, his body tensing as it was thrown and his index finger compressing on the trigger of the AK-47. A two-round burst of the loud rifle broke the predawn silence.

"Tango down," stated a calm Wicker as he began a sweep for other targets.

HARRIS WAS STANDING under Rapp, making sure he got up the ladder, when he heard what he instantly knew to be the distinctive sound of an AK-47 firing. There was a split-second pause, and then everybody kicked it into high gear. Harris stepped away from the ladder and listened as Wicker gave him an update. When he had heard enough, he yelled at Jordan and Tony, "Are you two almost done?"

Without looking up, Tony, the smaller of the two, said, "We'll be right with you."

Harris pulled the mike back down. "Reavers, any sign of our bird?"

Reavers had crawled to the edge of the roof to see what was happening on the street. He was looking down at the two dead bodies beneath him when his boss asked about the choppers. He looked up and scanned the horizon. The helicopters were nowhere in sight. "That's a negative, Harry," replied Reavers.

"Is the strobe up and running?" asked Harris. The strobe Harris was referring to was an infrared strobe light that was invisible to the naked eye but glaringly visible to anyone wearing night-vision goggles.

From his perch down the block Wicker did a quick check with his night-vision scope and noted the flashing light atop the house. "The strobe is active."

Harris looked at his watch and turned back to his two men booby-trapping the stairs. "That's it, everyone on the roof. Let's go!"

The two men connected one last grenade and then scooted up the ladder. Harris followed them up and rolled onto the dirty flat roof. With his MP-10 in one hand, he closed the hatch. Spinning to check where his men were, the commander grabbed his night-vision binoculars and looked to the northwest, scanning the sky for the choppers. As he searched the horizon, he heard Wicker call, "More Tangos on the move."

Wicker peered through his scope as two men, and then a third, appeared from the house across the street. All three were armed. Wicker maneuvered the scope and said, "Everyone stay down. I can handle it." As the first man approached the bodies of the dead men on the street, Wicker centered in on the side of his head and squeezed off a round. He slid the Galil to the left just a touch and framed up the second man, who was now standing in shock while he watched the man in front of him crumple to the ground. Wicker squeezed the trigger again and moved on. The third man was backpedaling for the door, waving his arms and screaming. He never made it.

Harris dropped to his belly and quickly crawled to the edge of the flat roof. With his MP-10 up and ready, he looked over the edge at the bodies in the street. The SEALs were already deployed around the perimeter of the roof. Two covering the alley, and two covering the front. Rapp knelt over the unconscious body of Harut and searched the sky for the helicopters.

"Boys," barked Harris, "shoot anything that moves."

THE COPILOT OF the Pave Low spotted the strobes when they were about a mile from the beach and alerted the rest of the crew. They had been directed to hit the northern strobe first. The Pave Low alerted the pilots of the Pave Hawk, which was flying in formation at just under one hundred fifty miles per hour and hugging the deck.

Simultaneously the two helicopters broke formation. The larger Pave Low banked to the left and began to slow, while the agile Pave Hawk broke to the right and began a full-speed run to the south.

RIGHT ABOUT THE time Harris detected the noise of the incoming helicopters, the night sky blew open. A sustained burst of machine gun fire erupted from the building across the street. All but two of the twenty-some rounds flew wildly over their heads. The two that hit the lip at the edge of the roof sent chunks of clay flying.

Lying on his side, Harris said, "Bravo Six, this is Whiskey Five. We are under fire! I repeat, under fire! The LZ is hot!"

"Roger that, Whiskey Five," came the reply from the Pave Low. "Where is the fire coming from?"

"Directly across the street to our west."

"Roger, Whiskey Five. We have your position marked and will be on top of you in about twenty seconds."

Harris stayed flat on the roof. Another burst of machine gun fire rang out with more of the rounds crashing into the side of the roof, and then a second and a third gun joined in. "Slick," the commander called out over the radio, "can you get these guys off my ass?"

"That's a negative, Harry. The angle is wrong."

Harris rolled onto his back as shouts were heard from below and a an-other volley of bullets rang out. "Reavers!" yelled Harris. "I'll draw their fire, and you bag 'em."

While lying on his back, Harris held his MP-10 over the edge and squeezed off four bursts at the house across the street. A second later Reavers popped up, saw a muzzle flash in the second-story window, and zipped the target with three shots to the chest. Reavers quickly ducked back down as a flurry of return fire rang out.

Wicker chimed in from his spot down the street. "I think we stuck our hands in the hornet's nest." More targets appeared, and Wicker went to work.

THE PAVE LOW came in much slower than a Hollywood director would have liked, but these big flying buses didn't stop on a dime. The roar of its powerful 3,900-horsepower turbine engines and churning rotors was deafening. As soon as he had targets in sight, the starboard gunner opened up with his 7.62-millimeter minigun—hosing down the building across the street. The Pave Low stopped just on the other side of the strobe, but did not touch down. Within seconds of coming to a stop, the smaller Pave

Hawk appeared from the south and passed directly overhead, her guns blazing.

Rapp grabbed Harut, threw him over his shoulder, and ran up the ramp of the Pave Low. Harris crouched at the foot of the ramp and picked up the strobe. He counted each of his men by slapping them on the ass as they ran up the ramp. When they were all in, Harris bounded into the chopper and gave the tail gunner a thumbs-up. One second later the helicopter rose ten feet and began lumbering above the rooftops, all three gunners laying down suppressive fire as they moved out.

Wicker continued to search for targets right up to the last second, but there were none to be found. The miniguns from the helicopters had cleared the street. As the Pave Low neared his position, the sniper saw the escort come screaming down the street for another pass. Wicker grabbed his gear, and as the ramp of the Pave Low neared, he jumped up and into the back of the cargo area.

The second the pilots heard the last man was onboard, they twisted the throttles to the stops and headed for sea. Twenty excruciating seconds later they were feet-wet hugging the water of the gulf, the Pave Hawk back in formation, heading for home.

Washington, D.C., Midnight

THE PLUSH ROOM was located on the southwest corner of the tenth floor. It was one of the Washington Hotel's finest rooms. A faint gray light from the street below spilled through the windows and reflected off the white ceiling and walls. The sole occupant stood in front of an ornate mirror and stared at his reflection, his fingers gently probing the tender areas around his eyes and then his jaw. He was a handsome man, strikingly so. Even more so since the surgical changes had been made. The more rugged features had been smoothed and refined. He had been looking at this new face for almost a month and had yet to grow accustomed to it. Pulling the cigarette from his mouth, he turned his head to the right and studied his profile. The red scar tissue had healed but was still sensitive in the areas where the skin was thin. The cheeks were more sallow, partially from the surgery but also because he had lost twenty pounds. He was pleased with the results. They were not perfect, but they would be good enough.

Exhaling a cloud of smoke, he stepped away from the mirror and turned. Through the haze of smoke he looked out the large window at the city before him. His posture was erect; his dark skin and short black hair stood out starkly against the handmade white dress shirt he was wearing.

To his left, the stoic Washington Monument jutted into the night sky, marking the center of the National Mall. Beyond that, the curved dome of the Jefferson Memorial shone just above the trees, while further to the west, marking the end of the mall, were the beautiful alabaster pillars of the Lincoln Memorial, and directly across the street lay the expansive Treasury Department. None of this, however, interested him. What did, sat just on the other side of the Treasury Department.

He inhaled and then extracted the cigarette with a slow, even motion, letting his hand and the cigarette come to a rest at his side. As the dark-eyed man took in the historic landscape, the corners of his mouth turned upward ever so slightly. It was an ominous smile. Rafique Aziz hated everything before him with more passion than any American could ever understand. The monuments and buildings before him were all symbols of America's imperialism, greed, corruption, and arrogance. The very things that had corrupted his homeland and pitted brother against brother. There were even those who were talking about peace with Israel, the Zionists who, with the aid of the mighty America, had plunged his Beirut into a hell on earth. It was time again, time for another revolution. It was time to ignite the jihad.

5

Washington, D.C., 6:55 A.M.

THE MAJORITY OF the United States Secret Service's five thousand plus agents were assigned to field offices around the country and focused their attention on catching counterfeiters. But the better known role of the agency was that of protecting politicians and, more specifically, the president of the United States. The Secret Service's presidential detail carried a roster of approximately two hundred special agents at any given time, and their positions were arguably the most competitive and sought-after jobs in all of law enforcement.

Secret Service agent Ellen Morton was one of the lucky few. Morton walked through the Executive Mansion and stopped at the detail's down room located on the ground floor of the White House. The tiny cramped room was officially designated Staircase; the name derived from the room's location, which was underneath the stairs that led to the First Family's private residence on the second and third floors of the mansion.

Morton poked her head through the open doorway. "Morning, Ted. How'd the night go?"

The agent leaned back and clasped his hands behind his head. With a yawn he gave his one word answer, "Quiet."

In order to give the First Family a certain amount of privacy, the Secret Service did not venture up to the second and third floors of the mansion unless called. They instead relied on a series of pressure pads installed in various areas beneath the carpet to track the president's whereabouts on the floors above.

"Is he up?" asked Morton.

"Yep. The steward phoned down and said he's putting on a suit."

On most mornings President Hayes went straight over to the West Wing at seven, but there were times, usually after he had been traveling, when he liked to work out in his private gym on the third floor and then walk over to the office at around eight. The agents on the detail usually had no idea what to expect until the Navy steward called down to tell them the president was wearing either workout clothes or a suit.

The security panel on the wall of Staircase beeped and a red light blinked, announcing that the president's elevator was moving. Morton nodded to the other agent and raised her hand mike to her mouth. "Horsepower, from Morton. Woody is on his way down." *Horsepower* was the designation for the presidential detail's command post located under the Oval Office.

The presidential detail's chief concern and focus was the president, while the actual security of the White House compound was handled by the Secret Service's Uniformed Division. There was a second command post located on the fifth floor of the Executive Office Building, across the street from the White House, that coordinated and monitored the two group's activities. It was called the Joint Operations Center, or JOC, and was built in the wake of an unauthorized attempted landing on the South Lawn by a single-engine airplane in 1994. JOC monitored the movements of both the uniformed officers and the special agents.

The doors to elevator opened, and President Hayes emerged wearing a dark suit, white shirt, and paisley tie. The president looked at the familiar face before him and said, "Good morning, Ellen."

"Good morning, sir." Morton moved out ahead of the president, walking down the long hall that led to the Palm Room. As shift leader, or whip, of the day detail, it was her responsibility to coordinate the movement of the president from the mansion to the West Wing. They entered the Palm Room, and Morton spoke into her hand mike. "Horsepower, from Morton. Woody is approaching the Colonnade." As Morton reached the double glass doors, she nodded to the agent on the other side and watched him move out ahead. Morton held the door for President Hayes, and then the two of them stepped out onto the fieldstone walkway of the Colonnade.

The president stopped and took in the bright spring morning. Feeling the warm morning sun on his face for the first time in weeks, he closed his eyes and smiled. After a long moment, he drew in a deep breath. Then opening his eyes, he looked out at the mist-covered grass of the South Lawn. Ellen Morton stood silently behind him, her hands clasped in front of her. Without turning, President Hayes said, "Beautiful morning, isn't it?"

"Yes, it is, sir." Morton grinned to herself. She was still not used to Hayes's private persona. With all of the security and pomp and circumstance, it was easy to forget that he was a real person—a husband, a father, and a grandfather.

"It makes me wish I was on the golf course." Hayes shook his head. "Well, it's off to the daily grind." With that he started down the stone walkway. Morton followed a step behind as they headed past Jefferson's pillars. When they reached the doors that led to the West Wing by the White House pressroom, they took a left, continuing past the French doors of the Cabinet Room and then around to the right. As they rounded the corner, Morton looked ahead at the agent by the Oval Office. He was getting ready to insert a key into the door. Over her earpiece Morton heard the agent say, "Horsepower, from Cowley. Authorized break on the Oval Colonnade door." The agent then stuck the key in the door and opened it, holding it for the president and Morton.

The president took a final look at the blooming flowers in the Rose Garden as he walked, and then greeted the agent holding the door. "Good morning, Pat."

"Good morning, sir."

President Hayes walked into the Oval Office first and Morton second. The president continued straight ahead, passing his desk and then going through the short hallway that led to his private study, bathroom, and dining room. Morton turned to the right and opened the door that led to the secretary's office. She closed it behind her and said into her mike, "Horsepower, from Morton. Woody is in the Oval."

On the other side of the Oval Office, in the main hallway, two Secret Service agents from the presidential detail relieved two uniformed officers and took up posts outside the door to the president's dining room and the main door to the Oval Office.

Inside the president's private dining room, Hayes took off his suit coat and handed it to a small Filipino man dressed in a white waistcoat and black pants. "Good morning, Carl."

"Good morning, Mr. President," answered the Navy steward. Carl closed the door and took the president's jacket, hanging it on an antique wooden valet in the corner.

A circular oak table for four occupied the center of the room. Hayes sat at the seat closest to the Oval Office and pulled in his chair. Folded and laid out in front of him were copies of *The Washington Post, The Washington Times, The New York Times,* and *USA Today.* The same four papers were laid out in the same order every day, Monday through Friday. The president began perusing the headlines.

The steward approached and placed a cup of black coffee next to the copy of the *Times.* "What would you like for breakfast this morning, Mr. President?"

Without looking up, President Hayes reached out for the cup of coffee. "How about a half a grapefruit to start with, please."

The steward nodded and retreated into the pantry while the president began reading an article in the *Post.* Before the grapefruit was served, there was a knock on the door. The Navy steward opened it and greeted the two visitors. Bill Schwartz, the president's national security adviser, entered the room with Dr. Irene Kennedy from the CIA.

The lanky national security adviser greeted the president's steward. "Good morning, Carl."

"Good morning, Mr. Schwartz. What would you like to drink?"

"My usual please."

"And for the lady?"

"Just a cup of regular, please," replied Kennedy.

Schwartz maneuvered his thin frame across the room and sat in the spot directly across from Hayes. Kennedy placed her briefcase on the floor and sat immediately to the president's right. The president looked up at his national security adviser and asked, "How was your trip?" Schwartz had just returned from Brussels, where he had attended three days of meetings on the further expansion of NATO.

Schwartz removed his small silver-rimmed glasses and began to clean the lenses with his tie. "It was slow, boring, and painful."

"It always is with NATO." President Hayes took a sip of coffee and placed the mug back on the table. "The only organization that's worse is the UN."

"That is true." Schwartz nodded his head slowly and watched Carl place a mug of coffee in front of Kennedy and then himself.

Next, the steward gave the president his halved grapefruit and put the other half in front of Schwartz, saying, "Eat this. I'm going to get you some pancakes too, and see if we can put some meat on your bones." The steward then winked at the president. Carl had worked in the White House for more than twenty years and was an expert at ribbing even the most powerful of Washington insiders.

With his hands clasped in front of his waist, Carl bent forward and, in a much more friendly tone than the one he had used with the national security adviser, asked, "May I get you anything to eat, miss?"

"No, thank you. I'm fine." Kennedy wrapped her hands around the warm coffee mug.

The steward turned to President Hayes. "If you need anything more, please ring."

"I will. Thank you, Carl." The president watched the steward leave and then leaned back. Looking to Kennedy, he said, "I got your message last night. I'm glad to hear everything went well."

"Yes. So far so good." Kennedy brought her coffee up to her lips and took a small sip.

"Bill, how much do you know about last night's activities?" asked the president.

Schwartz dumped a teaspoon of sugar onto his moist grapefruit and said, "Irene filled me in on the basics when I got in last night."

"What time was that?"

"Just after midnight."

The president looked to Kennedy. "Have we discovered anything yet?"

"Our man and Harut left Saudi Arabia around two this morning. They are supposed to touch down at Ramstein Air Force Base in Germany"—Kennedy looked at her watch and did the calculation—"in about thirty minutes. There they will be met by a team of specialists who will board the plane and start to interrogate Harut while airborne for Andrews."

The president thought about asking her what she meant by the term "specialists," but decided he was better off not knowing. "When can we expect some answers?"

"It's hard to tell. Sometimes the information is extracted easily, but the drugs don't always work the same way on everyone. There are certain precautions we need to take to make sure he isn't lying." Kennedy paused. Stansfield had told her from day one to always be on the cautious side. Especially when dealing with politicians. She looked to NSA Schwartz and then back at President Hayes. "We need to be thorough."

Hayes stacked the newspapers, one on top of each other, off to the side. "Are we talking hours or days?"

"We will start getting information out of him within minutes. Depending on what he knows and what kind of health he's in, we should have some answers within an hour. But let me caution you that it will take weeks to fully interrogate and debrief him."

"But our priority here is to find out if, when, and where they are planning this attack in Washington."

"Yes." Kennedy nodded.

Hayes looked to Schwartz, whose job it was to coordinate the efforts of all the intelligence agencies. "I want this to receive top priority, and I want a full briefing on the interrogation."

Kennedy nodded. "Yes, Mr. President."

Washington, D.C.

TWO MILES EAST of the White House a green-and-white truck backed up to the entrance of a dilapidated warehouse and stopped. Plastered in large white letters across the green side of the cargo area were the words "White Knight Linen Service." Two men in blue coveralls came out of the warehouse and hefted the rusting garage door up, its casters screeching as metal scraped on metal. The driver put the truck in reverse, and the two men guided the boxy vehicle through the narrow door with hand signals. When all of the truck was inside, the door was closed.

A hazy light filtered through the dirty windows near the roof of the building. Four men approached the rear of the truck, and a ramp was secured to the fender. The men began to unload the truck's canvas laundry baskets and boxes of fresh linen. After about five minutes the vehicle's cargo area was empty.

From an elevated glass office a man in green fatigues appeared. His closely trimmed beard grew from the top of his cheekbones down into his collar, and his hands and forearms were covered with thick black hair. In contrast to the rest of his body, the top of his head was bald—a shiny bronze oasis of smooth skin bordered by a horseshoe of black hair. Although short in stature, Muammar Bengazi was obviously strong.

Gripping the metal railing with his thick fingers, Bengazi watched his men work. They had come too far to make any mistakes now. Everything had to be done perfectly from this point forward. They had been given a summary from their benefactor that detailed the exact layout of the building. Bengazi was told the report had been compiled by the KGB some twenty years earlier. More recently, one of his men had got inside the building and given them a more up-to-date summary.

Bengazi whistled, and his men looked up. From his perch, he pointed to three objects sitting under canvas tarps located in the far corner of the warehouse. He watched his men walk over and yank the tarps back. Underneath sat three Kawasaki all-terrain vehicles painted in a drab tan-and-green camouflage pattern. The small vehicles were used by hunters for their maneuverability and power. Around the back of each vehicle a U-shaped cargo rack was attached. The cargo racks were stacked with metal trunks that were tightly secured by black bungee cords.

One by one the men started the ATVs. The musty smell of the warehouse was soon replaced with that of gas and oil. A small trailer, also loaded with metal boxes, was hooked to one of the ATVs and backed up the ramp and into the truck. The other two ATVs followed and were backed in tightly.

Bengazi walked down the metal stairs from the office to the floor of the warehouse. He was surprisingly light on his feet for a man of such girth. He approached a bright yellow forklift, climbed into the driver's seat, and started the engine. After the vehicle warmed up, Bengazi backed it carefully up the ramp and into the back of the truck. The forklift was missing its two metal forks that were normally positioned in front.

When Bengazi had the heavy piece of machinery exactly where he wanted it, he turned it off and climbed down. He jumped from the tailgate and moved off to the side. For the next five minutes he watched his men reload enough of the truck's original cargo to conceal the forklift and ATVs. He walked from one side of the tailgate to the other, attempting to peer around and over the boxes and baskets. Satisfied with the job, he nodded to his men and checked his watch. They were on schedule.

Ramstein Air Force Base, Germany

THERE WAS A slight jolt followed by a hydraulic whine. Mitch Rapp was yanked from his deep sleep and jerked forward in his seat, simultaneously reaching for his Beretta and looking to his left. He breathed a sigh of relief, and slowly his hand released the grip of his gun. Harut was still there, hands and feet cuffed, with a black hood over his head, lying strapped to the leather couch of the Learjet. His turban and robe had been replaced with a green flight suit.

Rapp rubbed his eyes and looked out the small window on his right, quickly realizing that the bump that had awakened him was the landing gear locking into position. They were almost level with the German countryside. A second later they cleared the trees, and the concrete runway was beneath them. The green fields were replaced by a rank of gray hangars and planes. First a row of large C-130s, then several flights of F-16s, and then finally they touched down. Rapp continued to rub his eyes with clenched fists. He felt almost as if he had been drugged. The past three nights had been marked by a total of six hours of sleep. Rapp checked his watch and estimated that he had been out for almost four hours. It was a good start, but he wouldn't mind getting a couple more hours of shut-eye as they crossed the Atlantic. There was no telling how quickly he would have to go out in the field again.

The plane taxied off the main runway and came to a stop next to a fuel truck and a blue van with blacked out windows. Rapp unbuckled his seat belt and got up. His appearance had changed since leaving Bandar Abbas. The unkempt black-and-gray beard was gone, replaced by a cleanly shaven face. With the beard gone, a scar was now visible on Rapp's left cheek. It was narrow, less than an eighth of and inch, and it started by his ear and ran straight down to his jaw—the pink scar tissue offset by his bronze skin. The doctors at Johns Hopkins had done a good job minimizing the knife mark. At first it was almost half an inch wide, but after the plastic surgeons were done, there was only a thin line. This scar, more than any of his others, was a daily reminder to Rapp that what he was doing was very real and very dangerous. A streak of gray could still be found in his long, thick hair, but most of it had been washed out during the fifteen-minute shower he took after the helicopters had landed in Saudi Arabia. Rapp had shared a quick Miller Lite with Harris and his men and then headed for the showers to wash a week's worth of dirt and grime from his body. He stood under the hot water and scrubbed every inch of his filthy skin three times. When he had finished washing the dirt and smell away, he stood under the hot water for another five minutes and savored a second Miller Lite.

By the time he was clean and dressed, the Learjet was ready. Rapp went back into the room where Harris and his marauders were already into their second case of beer and found Harut changed into a green flight suit, medicated, and lying on a cot in the corner. Congratulations were exchanged once again, and then Rapp threw Harut over his shoulder and headed for the flight line.

Now on the ground in Germany, Rapp looked down at Harut and yawned. Rapp would have just as soon put a bullet in Harut's head back in Iran, but if it meant finding out where Aziz was, the young American was willing to do almost anything. Rapp walked to the front of the jet with his head tilted to the side. When he reached the door, he grabbed the handle and twisted it clockwise. There was a slight hiss as the pressurized air escaped. Rapp let the door out and eased it toward the ground. Despite the overcast morning sky, he still had to shield his eyes from the light. His lean biceps bulged under the fabric of the black polo shirt he was wearing, and a brown leather shoulder holster held his Beretta securely to his side.

The door of the blue van opened, and a woman stepped onto the tarmac. Two men followed her. It wasn't often that Rapp felt uneasy, but as he watched Dr. Jane Hornig walk toward him, he found himself suddenly wishing he were elsewhere. Hornig, in her mid-forties, scurried toward the jet with one hand clutching the lapels of her blue blazer and the other holding her metallic briefcase. As Rapp watched her approach, he couldn't help but think of the scene from The Wizard of Oz when the mean neighbor, who turns out to be the Wicked Witch of the West, shows up on her bike to take Toto away. The music was even playing in the back of his mind.

Rapp was convinced that Hornig's face had seen neither sun nor makeup in over a decade. She had the classic demeanor of a scientist, disheveled and low-maintenance. Clothes and appearance didn't matter to Hornig; only her work did. Standing just a touch over five feet tall, she still wore her hair in a bun and dressed as if she had never found her way out of the sixties. On the one occasion that Lt. Commander Harris had met Dr. Hornig, he had, in his typical smart-ass way, dubbed her Dr. Strangelove, after the hilariously abused character played by Peter Sellers in the 1964 Cold War spoof.

Hornig, for all of her eerie qualities, was far more than just a psychologist. She also had advanced degrees in both biochemistry and neurology and was considered the foremost expert in America on the history and evolution of human torture. She had an interesting business relationship with the CIA. Langley provided her with guinea pigs for her experimental drugs and techniques, and in return she gave them what they wanted—information pulled from the deepest recesses of the human brain. This often included details that the subjects would not be able to remember on their own. Rapp had watched Hornig and her henchmen work on one occasion, and after about ten minutes, he decided he could wait for the Memorex version when they were done.

As Hornig approached the foot of the stairs, she looked up and said, "Hello, Mr. Kruse."

Very few people at Langley knew Rapp's real name. To them he was Mr. Kruse, a case officer who specialized in the Middle East. People in the intelligence business knew not to ask too many personal questions when dealing with field personnel. Indiscretion usually guaranteed an official reprimand from one's superior.

Rapp greeted the doctor and stepped back, allowing her room to enter.

Hornig looked to the rear of the plane. "How is he doing?"

"Fine. I gave him the exact doses you prescribed."

"Good." The doctor set a silver ballistic briefcase on the nearest seat and turned to the door. "These are my assistants, Sam and Pat."

Rapp looked at the two men and nodded. Both were carrying two larger silver ballistic briefcases. "There is a bedroom at the rear of the plane." Rapp pointed. "It's probably the best place to get set up."

Hornig agreed, and she and her two assistants continued single file toward the rear of the jet.

Rapp watched them move Harut into the bedroom and decided it would be a good time to get some fresh air. As he stepped down onto the tarmac, he felt the rare urge to smoke a cigarette. It was a nasty little habit he had picked up while working undercover, and from time to time he still found himself craving one. He looked to his left, where an airman was busy refueling the plane. Rapp almost made the stupid mistake of asking the man for a cigarette, but he saw the flammable insignia on the side of

the green truck. Rapp stood awkwardly next to the plane and looked to
his left and then right. The low gray skies and rows of sterile military
hangars gave the morning a depressing and dirty feeling.

Rapp sensed the oncoming downturn in his emotions and fought it.
There was the tinge of self-pity, triggered by either the dreary surroundings or the arrival of Hornig, or probably both. These little mood swings
had become more and more frequent over the last year. Rapp thought he
knew what was causing them. When you spent as much time alone with
your thoughts as he did, self-diagnosis became as normal as eating. He was
nowhere near the pain and anguish that he had suffered almost a decade
earlier. This wasn't like that; it was different. This was more like a warning
that if he didn't do something, he would be stuck on a certain path for the
rest of his life. A barren path marked by loneliness.

Before leaving on the most recent mission, he had talked to Kennedy
about it. His parents were both gone, and although he still had friends outside of work and a brother in New York with whom he was very close, it
wasn't as if he could pick up the phone and talk about his day at the office. He could talk about his computer-consulting business all he wanted,
but Langley was off limits. Officially, Rapp didn't even work for the CIA.
He was what they liked to refer to in the business asa private contractor.
Rapp lived a life completely separate from the Agency. With the help of
Langley, he ran a computer-consulting business on the side that just happened to do a fair amount of international business, which of course gave
him the cover to travel. His only passion in life, outside of work, was com-
peting in the annual Ironman competition in Hawaii—an event that the
former all-American lacrosse player from Syracuse University had actually
won once.

During these dark, brooding moments, Rapp had wondered how
screwed-up his life was or, worse, how screwed-up it might get. He would
continually ask himself if it was normal to want with such determination
to kill another human being. He knew this was the crux of his problem
and had once joked with Kennedy by saying, "Most people have lists of
things they want to do before they get to a certain age, like go skydiving,
travel to China, have a kid . . . not me. At the top of my list of things to
do before I turn forty is kill Fara Harut and Rafique Aziz. How healthy do
you think that is?"

Laughing and making jokes were all part of therapy for Rapp; without humor, he would never make it. In his job he needed to stay loose or,
like a watch wound too tight, he would explode. Rapp had studied it from
every angle, and he believed that his position was both moral and just.

The problem, however, lay in the fact that Rapp knew the hunt was

destroying him. He was increasingly losing touch with that segment of society that was labeled normal. His friends from college were all married
and having children, and for him there wasn't the hope of either on the
horizon. He knew that to have a normal life he would have to finish what
he had set out to do. He could not have a family and continue to work for
the CIA. The two would not mix.

Rapp thought back to how nice his life had been just ten years earlier
and to the weird twist of fate that had led him to this point in life, to this
dreary military base in Germany. "No one ever said life would be easy," his
father used to say. Rapp laughed at the thought of his father telling him to
"Suck it up," as he had done countless times throughout Rapp's youth. It
had gotten to the point where Rapp's father would say the three short
words with a smile on his face. The short phrase had grown from words of
criticism into words of encouragement.

The roar of a jet sounded in the distance, and Rapp stepped away
from the plane to search it out. Looking down the long runway, he saw a
lone F-16 racing in the opposite direction, its single engine on after-
burner, glowing bright orange. The agile jet lifted into the air, above the
mirage of dancing runway heat and instantly retracted its landing gear. As
the plane climbed, Rapp watched it gain speed. He followed it for a
minute or more until it was a speck in the expansive gray morning sky. A
second jet pulled onto the runway and screamed into the air, chasing after
the first.

Rapp gazed at the second jet and knew he was a possessed man. He
would pursue Rafique Aziz wherever he went, even if it led to his own
destruction. The trick would be to catch Aziz before he himself reached
the point of no return, and Rapp could sense that point nearing, hovering just over the horizon.

Rapp watched the airman detach the fuel hose and climb into the
truck. As the tanker pulled away from the Learjet, the plane's twin engines
began turning. Rapp took one last look at the dreary scenery and climbed
into the jet. As he pulled the door up and secured it, he smiled and whispered to himself his father's words of encouragement.

6

THE TAN, WELL-KEPT man was shown into the oak-paneled office of the chairman of the Democratic National Committee. The rotund and jovial Russ Piper stood from behind his desk and walked over to greet his wealthy visitor. Extending his hand, Piper said, "Prince Kalib, it is a pleasure to finally meet you."

Rafique Aziz extended his hand with the proper amount of aloofness and took Piper's hand in a light grip.

"How was your flight?" asked Piper.

Aziz looked around the room, gazing at the framed photos hanging on the paneled walls. "Fine." Aziz planned to keep conversation to a minimum. The real Prince Kalib was a recluse, and the characteristic fit his needs perfectly.

"I understand you're en route to the Mayo Clinic to visit your father."

"That is correct." Aziz nodded.

"How is the sultan doing?"

"He is fine." Aziz extracted a gold cigarette case from his jacket pocket. "The doctors at the Mayo Clinic are the best in the world." Aziz lit the cigarette with a matching gold lighter, exhaled a cloud of smoke, and walked over to the window.

Piper watched his guest light up with his mouth slightly agape, words of admonishment ready to spill forth. The chairman almost informed his royal guest that smoking was not allowed in the building, but after a brief moment he thought better of it. Piper ran his hand down his tie and checked to make sure it was straight. "Yes, we've treated many of our own presidents there," added Piper, getting back to the conversation.

Aziz continued to look out the window at the large rotunda of the Capitol. Then turning slowly, he said, "I assume you had no difficulty in arranging our meeting?"

"No difficulty whatsoever," Piper said proudly. "The president and I are very close."

"Good." While holding his cigarette with one hand, he reached into his jacket and pulled out a long blue check. "As per your instructions, I

had this written to your party through one of my American corpora-
tions."

Piper grabbed the check with both hands and looked at the all-
important box on the right side. The chairman of the Democratic National Committee smiled at the large number. "This is greatly appreciated,
Your Highness."

Aziz nodded benevolently.

"I can promise you that I will do everything within my power to help
your country obtain the proper defensive weapons that you seek."

"Kingdom," corrected Aziz.

"Yes, kingdom." Piper nervously rubbed his hands together. "My
apologies." Looking at his watch, he said, "Well, we should probably get
going. I have a limousine waiting downstairs to take us to the White
House. We don't want to be late to see the president."

"No, we don't." Aziz grinned. "I've been looking forward to this day
for a long time."

The White House

PRESIDENT HAYES SAT behind his desk in the Oval Office. His suit
coat was draped over the back of his high-backed leather chair, and in
front of him was a photocopy of his daily schedule. The schedule was
typed, but his nine A.M. meeting had been crossed out and his chief of
staff had written something in the margin. The president squinted at the
handwriting and tried to make out the small cursive letters. Hayes picked
up the paper and decided it wasn't his eyes that needed help; it was his
chief of staff's handwriting.

Without knocking, Valerie Jones entered the Oval Office through the
main hallway. She had a stack of folders under her left arm and a leather
day-timer in her right hand. "Good morning, Robert." Jones continued
across the room and set the folders on the left side of the president's desk.

Hayes held up the schedule for her to see. "What's this you wrote here
in the margin?"

Without having to look, Jones said, "Last-minute change. Prince
Kalib from Oman is on his way through town to see his father at the Mayo
Clinic."

Hayes tapped his capped Waterman pen against his cheek while
frowning. "And?"

"And . . ." Jones put her hands on her hips and smiled. "You don't
want to know. Just take my word for it. It'll be a worthwhile meeting."

President Hayes nodded slowly. Leaning back in his chair, he studied

Jones's outfit for a split second. She was wearing a yellow silk blouse that was almost dark enough to pass for gold. Hayes thought the bright blouse combined with the black skirt and scarf made her look like a bumblebee. Having a wife and two grown daughters of his own, he was smart enough to keep this opinion to himself. "What else do you have for me?"

"The First Lady left Andrews about fifteen minutes ago and will be on the ground in Columbus just before ten. Which reminds me . . ." Jones stepped to her left and placed both hands on the surface of the desk. "I still think you should go to Columbus. You can fly out tomorrow afternoon and make the party with no trouble at all." The president's fifth grandchild and his namesake, Robert Xavier Hayes, was celebrating his first birthday tomorrow.

Hayes shook his head. "I'm going to see little Robert in two weeks, and I'll celebrate his birthday then."

"I think you should go tomorrow," persisted the chief of staff.

"I'm not going. It costs a lot of money to fly everybody over there just for the evening."

"Fine." At the insistence of the First Lady, Jones had given it one more try. The chief of staff grabbed one of the folders she had brought and opened it. "I need your signature on about thirty documents. Some of them you'll want to glance over, and others you can just sign."

With a sigh Hayes began working his way through the stack of papers.

Washington, D.C.

THE WHITE KNIGHT linen truck pulled up to the cobblestone entrance of the underground parking garage at the Treasury Building. A uniformed Secret Service agent stepped out from his guard booth and smiled at the driver saying, "How *are* ya, Vinney?"

"Good, Tony." The driver stepped down from the cab. "You staying awake this morning?"

"Just barely." The officer handed him a clipboard and asked, "Did you watch the game last night?"

"Of course. I hate those stinking Yankees. I think I hate the Yankees more than the Red Sox." Abu Hasan took the clipboard and signed his fake name, Vinney Vitelli. Hasan had been working for the White Knight Linen Service for almost eight months. White Knight was in the middle of its four-year contract with the Treasury Department. Getting a job with the company had been easy, and passing the FBI background check had proved even easier. The only hard part was getting rid of the previous driver. The old driver had come down with an incapacitating case of food poisoning the day after he had dined with Hasan about five months ago. Hasan had conveniently stepped in and covered the man's route until he was better. Two weeks after that, when the man was killed in an attempted robbery near his apartment, Hasan was right there to step in and take over the dead man's route.

Hasan handed the clipboard back to the Secret Service officer. "I have two extra tickets to the Indians-Orioles game on Saturday if you want them."

The officer grabbed the clipboard. "That would be great. My kid would love it."

Hasan smiled. "Good." He had worked hard to get to know as many of the uniformed officers as he could. It was crucial to the mission. If they couldn't get the truck into the garage without being inspected, the entire plan would fail. "Are you working tomorrow afternoon?" asked Hasan as he turned to go back to the truck.

"Yep."

"Good, I'll bring them by."

"Thanks, Vinney. I appreciate it." The guard tugged on the brim of his cap.

Hasan climbed back up into the cab and released the emergency brake. As the heavy steel gates opened, the terrorist looked to his left at the fence that separated the White House from the Treasury Department. He grinned and bit down hard on his tongue, fighting back the urge to smile as he looked beyond the gate at the most famous house in the world. Hasan put the truck in gear, drove through the gate and down the ramp.

Washington, D.C.

THE TAXICAB CONTINUED south down Pennsylvania Avenue and crossed the intersection at Seventeenth Street. The driver pulled in between two large, circular concrete planters, turned to the left, and stopped. Only a block away from the White House, the road ahead was closed to all motor traffic. Anna Rielly sat in the backseat and looked out at the barricades the Secret Service had constructed in the wake of the Oklahoma City bombing. A row of concrete planters extended from each curb and stopped, leaving just enough room for a guard booth and a huge steel barricade with the word "STOP" emblazoned in white against a red background. The steel barricade was hydraulic and could be lowered to allow authorized vehicles to proceed to the next checkpoint.

Rielly paid the driver and got out of the backseat. She had a large black bag over one shoulder and a smaller purse over the other. While she

adjusted the large bag, she looked up at the gothic-looking Executive Office Building and frowned. Rielly tried to decide if she liked the building
or not. She studied the ominous structure and brushed her shoulder-
length dark brown hair back behind both ears. It was beautiful in its crafts-
manship but seemed out of place among the rest of Washington's
architecture.

The young reporter was wearing pleated black dress pants and a
matching jacket that were offset by a white silk blouse. Wanting to savor
every moment of this achievement, she took in the whole scene. Her skin
was aglow in the early morning sunlight, and Rielly beamed with pride as
she approached the guard booth. "Hello, I'm the new White House correspondent for . . ."

The uniformed Secret Service officer behind the bulletproof glass
pressed a button on his panel and said, "Ma'am, I only check motor traffic at this gate. You may proceed down another block to the northwest
gate, where they can check you in to the White House."

Rielly thanked the guard and walked in between two of the planters.
As she continued down the middle of Pennsylvania Avenue, she noticed
the Blair House on her left, the president's unofficial residence when he
could not stay at the White House because of construction or some other
problem. Rielly continued walking, taking it all in. At the next block she
stopped at another guard booth, identical to the first. Anna Rielly proudly
presented her credentials to the man behind the blue-hued bulletproof
glass. She had finally made it to the big leagues after serving as a reporter
and weekend anchor for the NBC affiliate in Chicago for the last five
years. NBC had picked her to be their new White House correspondent.

Rielly looked around while she waited for the guard to run her
through his computer. On the other side of the fence she could see all of
the tripods and equipment that the networks left on the White House
lawn for their live shots. Some were sitting under tarps, and others were
just laid out and covered with morning dew. Rielly couldn't begin to
count how many times she had imagined herself standing in that exact
spot giving the nation the inside story on what had just happened at the
White House. Since her first journalism class at the University of Michigan twelve years earlier, she had dreamed of this day, covering the White
House, the center of politics—important issues that affected world events.
No more boring chitchat about the weather, fronts coming off of Lake
Michigan. Sports, weather, and murders were ninety-nine percent of the
broadcast in Chicago. Rielly smiled briefly as she thought of her life there.
She would miss her brothers and parents dearly, but flights to Chicago
were cheap and frequent.

The uniformed Secret Service officer looked at Rielly through the glass and asked, "First day on the job?"

Rielly smiled, showing a set of dimples. "Yep."

The agent placed her ID and a badge in the metal trough under the glass and slid them to her. Through the speaker, he said, "Please wear this badge at all times while in the compound. You may proceed down the street here"—the guard pointed—"to that white awning on the left. They'll tell you where to go from there."

Rielly thanked the man, and she was buzzed through the first gate and then a second. She continued down West Executive Drive to the awning. As she stepped onto the curb, a limousine pulled up. Its back door opened, and she heard a familiar voice call her name. Rielly turned and saw Russ Piper, the former mayor of Chicago, struggling to get out of the backseat of the limo

Piper had one hand on the door and the other on the doorframe. The majority of his weight was in his belly, so he had to draw himself to the very edge of the seat before he had the leverage to stand.

Rielly, somewhat surprised, said, "Russ." She stepped forward and met Piper's hug.

Piper squeezed her tight and then stepped away, still holding her by the shoulders. "Dorothy just told me last night you were coming to town, but I had no idea it would be this fast."

Rielly's face twisted. "I didn't even know I was coming until two days ago. How did your wife find out so fast?"

"My guess would be that your mother told her, which of course means half of Chicago knows by now that you're the new White House correspondent for NBC." Piper gave her a big hug again. "Congratulations, Anna. I know how hard you've worked for this, and I think it's just fantastic." He kissed her on the forehead. Rielly's mother was very active in Chicago Democratic politics, and her parents had been close friends with the Pipers for as long as she could remember.

Piper released her again and with a frown asked, "When were you planning on calling us?"

"I just got in last night."

"Where are you staying?" Piper's brow furrowed. "I hope you're not staying at a hotel. Dorothy will be really upset if you don't stay with us."

Anna tilted her head. "Russ, I'm not on spring break." She looked away from Piper as a second man stepped from the limo. She noted that he was probably a foreigner, and one with a lot of money, judging by the clothes he was wearing.

Piper followed Rielly's gaze to his guest and said, "Oh, I'm sorry.

Prince Kalib, I would like you to meet a very good friend of mine, Ms. Anna Rielly."

Aziz looked at the stunning woman before him and was immediately drawn to her green eyes. Extending his hand, he took hers and bent forward, kissing the back of Rielly's soft hand. Standing straight, he said, "It is a pleasure to meet you."

Rielly retracted her hand, feeling somewhat uncomfortable with the forward gesture. "Likewise."

"Anna is the new White House correspondent for NBC."

"Congratulations." Aziz canted his chin, and while doing so, noted the two guards by the door.

"Thank you."

Piper looked at his watch. "Anna, the president is squeezing us in, so I don't want to be late. Do you have plans for dinner?"

"Ah . . ." Rielly shook her head while she thought about it. "No."

"Good. Call Dorothy and tell her we're on."

Rielly smiled. "I'll call right away."

"Good, we'll see you tonight."

Piper and Aziz walked under the awning and through the double doors that led to the ground floor of the West Wing. A uniformed Secret Service officer who was sitting behind a desk watched a monitor as they passed through the door. The monitor was connected to an X-ray machine and a metal detector that were built into the wood-framed doorway.

The officer rose to his feet. "Good morning, Chairman Piper."

"Good morning, Dick. I have one guest, and I'll vouch for him personally."

The officer checked his list and saw that Piper's office had called late the previous evening and scheduled a meeting with the president. "Is this Prince Kalib?"

"Yes," replied Piper.

The agent handed Aziz a visitor's badge and said, "Please wear this at all times while in the building, and when you're done with your meeting, return to this desk and turn it in before leaving."

Aziz took the badge, and Piper said, "Thanks, Dick," as he and the prince started down the hallway.

As Aziz clipped the badge to his lapel, he noticed his hands felt almost weightless. His whole body felt light. He was finally going through the real steps of something that he had played over and over in his mind countless times. This was it, and it all seemed so easy. As they continued down the hallway, Aziz reached down and pressed a button on his watch once. After doing so, he glanced over his shoulder and looked at the guards by the door.

Washington, D.C.

ONE BLOCK EAST of the White House a slight man in a white jacket and black pants was vacuuming the hallway on the top floor of the Washington Hotel. The man paused for a moment and looked out the French doors that led to the rooftop patio. Across the street he could see the roof of the Treasury Department and then just beyond that the White House. From this elevated position he could clearly see the guard standing watch on the roof of the Executive Mansion, less than two hundred yards away. The guard was wearing blue coveralls and a matching baseball cap. A pair of binoculars were slung around his neck, and from time to time he used them to scan different areas. On the far side of the roof was a small white guard booth.

Salim Rusan had looked out these doors five days a week for almost three months and watched the movements of the Secret Service. The guard on the roof would be easy to take care of. The young Palestinian shifted his eyes to the far end of the South Lawn, where the Rose Garden ran up to the edge of the Colonnade, just outside the Oval Office. A Secret Service agent was on post, not one of the uniformed officers. That meant the president was in the West Wing, where he was supposed to be. The agent by the Oval Office would be first, and the guard on the roof would be second. That had been Aziz's decision. Aziz had decided everything. Every last detail.

The pager on the young Palestinian's hip vibrated, and he jerked at the awkward feeling. Aziz was inside the White House. It was going to happen. Rusan started for the closet at the end of the hallway, licking his lips and noting the tightening sensation in his chest. It was time to get ready.

7

30,000 feet, Eastern Atlantic Ocean

THEY WERE AIRBORNE and sailing smoothly westward through clear skies. Rapp looked out the window at a blanket of cottony clouds that seemed to stretch forever. The young Virginian never tired of looking at the sight beneath him. It was always different; every cloud always had its own distinct pattern. Rapp had taken up flying a half decade earlier. It had not been his idea, but part of his continued training with Langley. He quickly found that nothing could clear his mind and relieve stress like flying. He would be asleep in minutes.

As Rapp settled into the comfortable chair, he heard a muffled scream from the rear of the plane. It was followed by what sounded like three long grunts. Rapp looked back at the small door to the bedroom and then leaned one ear against the bulkhead and covered the other with his hand. It did no good. He could still hear Harut's screams of pain.

Rapp stood and began to pace up and down the short isle. A feeling of restlessness gnawed at him. Near the forward bulkhead he found the previous week's issue of *Newsweek* and started flipping through the advertisement-laden front section until he found the Periscope page. As he scanned the columns, he sat on the couch where Harut had been tied during their journey from Saudi Arabia. There were more strange noises from the bedroom, and Rapp tried to drown them out by focusing on the magazine. He moved on to the comics and then flipped to the last page, hoping to find a column by George Will. Instead, it was Meg Greenfield's week. Rapp read the first two paragraphs and lost interest. He began flipping through the magazine in reverse, reading various articles that grabbed his attention.

Suddenly the door to the bedroom opened, and Dr. Hornig appeared with a panicked look on her face. "Mitch, you'd better get in here!"

Washington, D.C., 8:58 A.M.

THE WHITE KNIGHT linen truck eased its way down the long cobblestone ramp and into the parking garage of the Treasury Building. The truck turned to the right and pulled into the loading area. Abu Hasan put the truck in park and let it idle. He looked out the front window and then checked the side mirrors. No one was in sight, but he knew from his previous visits that three security cameras monitored this area of the garage. Hasan fumbled with his clipboard and tried to look busy until the signal was given.

Hasan looked in his rearview mirror at a nondescript gray metal door. The door marked the entrance of the Treasury tunnel, which led into the basement of the White House. Hasan had learned on his late-night visit to the White House that the door was referred to as the Marilyn Monroe door. The name derived from a certain president that used it to sneak women in and out of the Executive Mansion.

Hasan had handled his part of the mission brilliantly. Besides getting a job at the linen company, he had befriended someone that worked inside the White House. Hasan had moved into the man's neighborhood. He had followed the administration official closely, bumping into him at the grocery store, the athletic club, and the corner bar. Hasan had found out the man was a college basketball nut, so he became one. When the NCAA Final Four Tournament came around, Hasan was right there on the barstool, next to the man, cheering on the official's alma mater to a sweet sixteen appearance. After that they started hitting the nightspots on a regular basis, working as a team trying to pick up women. Then one night several months ago Hasan convinced the man that a little late-night tour of the White House might be the best way to seal the deal with a couple of attractive women they had been working. Hasan had timed it perfectly. He knew the president was out of town and security would be lax. The White House official had run with the idea, and the rest was easy.

In the back of the truck the air had grown musty and warm. Bengazi and his men were already sweating through their fatigues. Two men sat astride each of the three ATVs, none of them daring to move other than to wipe the rivulets of sweat that ran down their faces. All nine of them were dressed in dark green fatigues and tactical assault vests. Each man carried an AKSU-74 with eight high-capacity magazines and a half dozen hand grenades. The AKSU was the shortened version of the AK-74, Kalashnikov's replacement for the venerable AK-47.

The thickly bearded Bengazi sat atop the forklift and checked his watch. He looked around the cramped confines of the cargo area and decided it was time. He nodded to the only two men who were standing, and they went to work. Moving slowly, so as to not shake the truck, they shifted the boxes and laundry baskets to the side and created a path for the forklift and the ATVs.

When they were done, Bengazi turned and nodded to one of his men sitting on the back of an ATV. The man carefully popped the clasps on the trunk to his left and swung open the lid. From a foam cutout he extracted two rocket-propelled grenade launchers, or RPGs, and passed them forward. He then removed the first layer of foam and revealed four oblong armor-piercing grenades. One by one, he passed the grenades forward and then closed the trunk.

Bengazi felt his pager vibrate and looked down. He turned to his men and snapped his fingers twice. There was no quickening of the pulse for Bengazi. He was too battle hardened to get excited. Now well into his forties, he was unflappable. The rest of the men in the truck were half his age, still filled with optimism and grand dreams. Bengazi was a realist, and despite everything that Aziz had told him, he did not expect to see his beloved Beirut again. It was time for one final blow against the foreigners who had destroyed the peaceful and beautiful city of his youth.

Bengazi reached for the gas mask that was clipped to his web belt and secured it to the top of his head, leaving it perched above his thick single eyebrow until the final signal was given. The two men carrying the RPGs moved softly to the tailgate and waited.

30,000 Feet, Eastern Atlantic Ocean

MITCH RAPP STOOD over Harut, his eyes widening, not quite sure he was hearing what he was hearing or, if he really was, if he could believe it. Dr. Hornig asked the same question, worded in a slightly different way. Harut, his eyes glassed over, mumbled the same answer—an answer that seemed to stop time. Rapp was absolutely shocked, frozen with indecision as his mind tried to absorb the unbelievable.

He finally turned to Hornig and asked the only question he could think of, "Is he telling the truth?"

Hornig motioned to an array of equipment that one of her assistants was monitoring. "I'm pretty sure. All of his baselines match up. I have asked him the same question a half dozen ways"—Hornig looked down at her notes—"thirty-two times. He's telling the truth. The only way this information could be wrong would be if Aziz had lied to him with the forethought that he might be interrogated, and"—Hornig began shaking her head—"the odds of that would be astronomical."

"Fuck." Rapp ran a hand through his hair. "When is this thing planned? Do they have a specific date?"

Hornig brought her hands up, motioning for caution. "I haven't been able to pursue that specific line of questioning as far as I would like, but as of right now, it looks like it is planned for today."

Rapp lowered his chin. "You've got to be fucking kidding me!"

"I'm afraid not."

Rapp started for the main cabin and then stopped abruptly. "What type of an attack are we talking about?"

"All he keeps saying is, 'An assault.'"

Rapp cursed again and banged his fist against the doorframe while he tried to decide what to do. Incomplete information or not, he knew he had to make the call. Rapp left the bedroom and grabbed his backpack. Turning it upside down he dumped all of the contents on the couch. After throwing some clothes and papers to the side, he found his SATCOM unit and pressed the power button. Clutching the black object with both hands, he stared at the small screen and cursed the signal indicator. In frustration, Rapp squeezed the object tighter in an effort to speed up its link with the nearest U.S. satellite.

Langley, Virginia—CIA Headquarters

DIRECTOR STANSFIELD'S OFFICE was located on the seventh floor of the main building. The office itself was conservatively decorated. Stansfield was not one to display his awards and achievements, so his paneled walls were sparsely decorated with photographs of his deceased wife, their daughters, and his grandchildren. His desk was so organized that even the Post-it notes had their own place. Six of them were lined up symmetrically in the left-hand corner.

Stansfield sat in his chair with his elbows on the armrest and his hands folded under his chin. Irene Kennedy sat across from him in one of two chairs and wrapped up a summation of her breakfast meeting with President Hayes. Stansfield listened intently and nodded from time to time. He would wait until Kennedy was finished before he asked any questions.

After another five minutes, Kennedy closed the file on her lap and said, "The president stressed that he wanted compete cooperation by all agencies, and a full disclosure of information."

In response to the statement, Stansfield raised an eyebrow. "Hmm."

"How do you want me to handle it?"

Stansfield lowered his hands and thought about it. "Use your best judgment. I'm all for sharing information, as long as our sources and operations aren't compromised in the process."

"And, of course, as long as we get something in return." Kennedy smiled.

The right side of Stansfield's mouth turned ever so slightly upward. "Yes."

Kennedy nodded and handed her boss a red plastic folder. The white label on the cover was adorned with the requisite letters, or as Agency insiders liked to say, "alphabet soup." This particular string of letters told the director that the file contained signal intelligence and Keyhole, or satellite, imagery. The TS and SCI notations also told him the file was top secret and compartmentalized.

As director of the CIA's Counterterrorism Center, Kennedy was responsible for keeping Stansfield informed on all of the various threats against the U.S. On this particular morning the subject was North Korea. She had barely made it through the first page of the briefing when Stansfield's phone rang. Kennedy paused to see if he would answer it.

The director grabbed the handset and said, "Stansfield."

"Director Stansfield, we have a flash-traffic-priority call from Iron Man, for you or Dr. Kennedy."

"Patch him through." Stansfield hit the speakerphone button and replaced the handset.

There were several clicks on the line, and then Stansfield said, "Hello."

"Sir, we've got a big problem," started an agitated Rapp. "Is Irene there?"

"Yes. She's sitting right next to me." Rapp's frazzled tone did not go unnoticed by Stansfield and Kennedy.

"Aziz is in D.C."

"Say again."

Rapp repeated himself more deliberately. "Aziz is in D.C."

"Are you sure?" asked Kennedy.

"Yes. Dr. Hornig is positive. She's been working on Harut for close to thirty minutes and says there is no way he's lying. And that's only part of it." There was a brief pause on the line. "Harut says Aziz's target is the White House."

There was a moment of shocked silence while Kennedy and Stansfield looked at each other. After several seconds, Rapp asked, "Did you hear what I said?"

"Yes we heard you, Mitch," answered Stansfield. "It's just a little much. We need to be sure about this before we—"

Rapp cut him off. "Well, unfortunately we don't have that luxury. According to Harut, the attack is supposed to take place today!"

Kennedy stood and placed both hands on the desk. "What are we talking about here, Mitch? What kind of an attack?"

"All he keeps saying is an all-out assault. A raid."

"How?" Kennedy asked.

"I don't know. Dr. Hornig is trying to find out more."

Stansfield stood and joined Kennedy in looking down at the phone. "Is there anything else, Mitch?"

"Not right now."

"All right. We'd better get to work on this. We have to make some calls on this end. Call us back the second you find anything else out."

"Roger."

Stansfield punched the button and disconnected the call. He and Kennedy were face-to-face leaning over the desk. Stansfield looked out the window briefly and then back to Kennedy. "Call Jack Warch and tell him we have a strong reason to believe there is a terrorist attack planned against the White House, and tell him we think it's planned for today."

"What about the president?"

"Call Warch first. I need to think about a couple of things before we tell the president."

"And the FBI?" asked Kennedy.

"I'll call Director Roach." Stansfield pointed to his credenza, where a second phone was located. "Get Warch on the line fast, but stress that he take reasonable precautions. We don't want this to rattle too many cages until we're absolutely positive."

Executive Office Building

JACK WARCH, THE special agent in charge of the presidential detail, sat behind his desk located in room number ten of the Executive Office Building, directly across the street from the West Wing. Warch had served under four presidents and had been with the Secret Service for over twenty years.

The special agent in charge had that runner's look about him. In his early forties, he still jogged four to five times a week and expected the men and women who worked under his command to do the same. The presidential detail was the most visible aspect of the Secret Service, and posts in it were in very high demand. Over the previous decade, Warch had watched fitness take a backseat to an insidious wave of political correctness and an older, equally insidious, old-boys' network. When Warch took over the detail, he put everyone on notice by spreading the word that he didn't care who your dad was, what color your skin was, what sex you were, or who your patron was; if you couldn't pass your fitness tests, you weren't going to work on his detail.

Reaching out with his left hand, Warch took a sip of hot coffee and looked over the day's schedule. Things looked light, just the way he liked it. No visitors and no trips off premises. If every day was like this, he would be a bored but happy man. Warch's phone rang, and without taking his eyes off the schedule, he reached out and grabbed it. "Special Agent Warch speaking."

"Jack, it's Irene Kennedy."

Warch had sat in on dozens of briefings with Kennedy over the years and knew her well enough to know from the tone of her voice that she had something serious to say. "Hello, Irene. What's the problem?"

"I've got some bad news," started Kennedy. "We've just learned that there is a possibility that the White House will be the target of a terrorist attack." Kennedy paused to give Warch a second to digest the information before she dropped the other shoe. "And . . . we think the attack is supposed to take place today."

Warch closed his eyes and squeezed his forehead with his free hand. "Say again."

Kennedy repeated herself and then added, "Jack, we don't want you to overreact, but we've received this information from a very reliable source."

"What are we talking about, a car bomb, a plane . . . what?"

Kennedy cleared her throat. "We were told an assault. That's all the information we have, and we are trying to get more."

Warch pushed his chair away from his desk and stood. "What?" he asked incredulously. "An assault. That's impossible. They'd need a tank if they wanted to breach our outer perimeter."

"Jack, I don't know how they plan on doing whatever it is that they are going to do," started Kennedy in a calming voice, "and I'm sorry I can't give you anything else at this point. But the bottom line is we are taking this very seriously. For obvious reasons Director Stansfield wanted me to call you first. We suggest that you tighten things up over there without alerting the press, and as soon as we find more out, we will let you know."

Warch continued to squeeze his forehead. "Today. You think it's planned for today?"

"Yes."

Warch looked at his watch. It was almost nine A.M. "I've got to get moving." He grabbed his digital phone from the desk. "If you hear anything more, call me on my mobile." He gave Kennedy the number and then hung up. Warch, who was more entrusted with the president's life than any other person in the Secret Service, took every warning, no matter how small, very seriously. And a warning from the CIA's lead official on terrorism ranked about as serious as it could get. Leaving his office in a hurry, he walked quickly down the hallway and started to run through a mental list of options.

As Warch moved toward the exit, his mind fixed on the question of what type of assault could be planned. The Secret Service made it a priority to practice defending against different attacks on the president. They spent millions of dollars running their agents through their training center in Beltsville, Maryland, on a monthly basis. They practiced motorcade tactics, rope-line tactics, *Air Force One* and *Marine One* evacuations—almost every scenario one could think of. The analysis was in on truck bombs. With the barriers that were set up around the grounds, it would be impossible for a truck to get close enough. There would be a lot of broken glass, but the president would be safe. A plane, Warch thought. In every scenario they covered, an attack by a plane loaded with explosives represented the most lethal threat to the president.

As Warch walked out the door and onto West Executive Drive, he raised his hand mike to his mouth and said, "Horsepower, from Warch. Tell Hercules to look sharp, and tell them I want the stingers out and ready." *Hercules* was the call sign for the part of the detail that handled the rooftop. Warch hesitated for a second. He was tempted to put the entire White House detail on full alert but decided he should consult the president first. Hayes didn't like surprises, and despite Kennedy's intensity, this would not be the first time the Secret Service had been given a false alarm.

8

The White House

ANNA RIELLY POKED her head into her new basement office. The windowless room was smaller than the kitchen of her not very roomy one-bedroom apartment back in Lincoln Park. There were three desks against three of the walls and barely enough room for all of the chairs in the middle. A handsome man in his early forties, whom Rielly recognized from TV, stood to greet her.

"You must be Anna Rielly." The man extended his hand. "I'm Stone Alexander, ABC's White House correspondent. We've been expecting you."

Rielly shook his hand and looked dejectedly at her new office.

Alexander read the disappointment on her face and said, "It's not quite what you expected, is it?"

"No. I mean I didn't expect the Taj Mahal, but this is ridiculous."

"Don't worry. Look at the fringe benefits." Alexander grinned and held his arms out.

Rielly eyed his sculpted hair, handsome face, and waxed eyebrows. "And what would those be?"

Alexander smiled, showing a perfect set of bleached white teeth. "You get to work with me."

"Really?" said Rielly.

"Yeah, really." Alexander placed his hand on her shoulder and turned her out into the hall. "I was just on my way to get some coffee before you got here. Let's go get a couple of cups, and I'll show you around and introduce you to everyone." As they walked toward the White House mess, Alexander continued his small talk. "So, how long have you been in town?"

"Just got in yesterday."

"Has anyone shown you around yet?"

"No. I haven't even unpacked."

Alexander put his hand on her back and ushered her into the mess first. Rielly noticed that he let his hand linger on her back for an inappropriate amount of time. She looked around the cafeteria and was once again shocked by how small it was. There were probably twenty people sitting at the rectangular tables drinking coffee, eating, talking, and reading various newspapers.

"So are you married?" asked Alexander.

Rielly hesitated for a second and figured lying would do no good. "No."

Alexander grinned with optimism. "Maybe I could show you around tonight. I know a great new restaurant in Adams-Morgan."

"Thanks, but I have a lot of unpacking to do."

"A person has to eat," he said persistently.

Rielly realized Mr. Hormone would need to be dealt with a little more firmly and said, "Thanks, but I have a rule about dating reporters."

"And what would that be?" asked Alexander, his smile still plastered across his face.

"I don't," Rielly said as she continued to look around the room.

"And why is that?"

Rielly turned around and, with a sarcastic grin, replied, "I don't trust them."

Alexander laughed. "Are there any other rules I need to know about?"

"Yeah . . . I don't like to date men who are prettier than I am."

"THIS IS THE Roosevelt Room. It is called that because of the two portraits that hang on its walls." Piper stepped into the room and motioned to the two paintings. Aziz strained to remain calm as Piper stopped at every painting, statue, and room on the way to the Oval Office. Acting his part as a West Wing tour guide, Piper babbled on about the history of the building, and Aziz nodded politely.

"You'll notice that the portrait of Franklin Delano Roosevelt hangs above the fireplace mantel and the portrait of Teddy Roosevelt hangs over here to our right. It has become a tradition at the White House that whenever the sitting president is a Republican, Teddy's portrait hangs over the fireplace, and when a Democrat is in office, the portraits are switched and FDR's portrait hangs in the position of honor." Piper folded his hands in front of his robust midsection and smiled at the rendering of his party's icon.

While Aziz feigned interest in the artwork and historical rooms, he had marked and counted the exact position of every Secret Service officer and agent they had passed. It all seemed so easy as he casually walked among them. He was a welcomed and honored guest in a place he did not belong. All of the fences, high-tech security, and heavily armed Secret Service agents were there to stop him, and not a single one of them had the slightest clue that within their midst walked their greatest fear.

Piper rubbed a hand along the long shiny surface of the Roosevelt Room's conference table. "A lot of our guests get this room confused with the Cabinet Room. That however, is across the hall and on our way to the pressroom. I'll show you those when we're done meeting with the president." Piper walked to the fireplace and stopped. "I almost forgot." Gesturing to a small bronze sculpture on the mantel, he said, "This is something we are very proud of. Our previous First Lady, also a Democrat I might add"—Piper beamed with pride—"had this bust of Eleanor Roosevelt added to the room. She felt that the room was too much of a boys' club and felt that a woman needed to be added to the mix."

Aziz looked at the small statue and said, "In my country such an idea would be ludicrous." He turned and walked to the open doorway to his right. As he looked across the hall, Aziz felt both a wave of elation and tension rising up from within. He knew from studying the floor plans of the White House that the door in front of him was one of four doors that led to the Oval Office. It was open, and from where he was standing, he could clearly see the rich blue carpet and furniture arranged in front of the fireplace. He was so close.

Standing next to the door was a very large and serious-looking Secret Service agent. The agent's sandy brown hair was cut short around his ears, and his neck bulged underneath his white shirt and tie. Aziz did a quick inventory as his eyes met the agent's and slid downward. Before turning back to Piper, Aziz noted that the agent was left-handed. The bulge on the agent's left hip was caused by his Secret Service standard issue SIG-Sauer handgun.

Piper joined Aziz in the doorway and said, "Are you ready to meet the president?"

Aziz nodded and willed himself forward at Piper's side, his legs feeling rubbery as the adrenaline began to pump through his veins. Aziz stepped into the hallway, and for a split second he wondered if it could be a trap, if they might know who he really was. But before he could worry any further, they were at the door, and Piper was knocking on the frame.

Piper stepped into the executive office first, and Aziz followed. The chairman of the DNC stopped abruptly just inside the room and looked at the president, who was on the phone.

President Hayes placed a hand over the mouthpiece and said, "Take a seat. I'll be with you in a minute."

Aziz stood teetering on the balls of his feet, caught in complete indecision. He swallowed once to try to quench his quickly drying throat and then looked to Piper, who was whispering something to him. Slowly, Aziz took his focus off the president.

Piper motioned to one of the couches by the fireplace and in a hushed voice said, "Let's have a seat over here. He'll be with us in a minute."

Aziz followed Piper to the couch and calculated his chances of rushing the president. The door they had just come through was still open, and he knew that there were agents posted outside two of the room's other three doors. Aziz had also guessed that the president had security measures in and around his desk. With only a small composite knife as a weapon, he couldn't risk alerting the agents posted outside the office until the president was within reach. But he was so close. Aziz calculated that he could cover the twenty feet to the desk in two seconds at the most. It would take the agents almost that long to draw their weapons. Think fast, he told himself as a film of sweat began to form on his skin.

Piper plopped down on the couch and patted the seat next to him. Aziz nodded and stepped past Piper. It was time to sit or move. Aziz looked across the room at the president, who had just swiveled in his chair and turned his back to them. Hayes was looking out the window while he talked on the phone; his head was all that could be seen above the back of his black leather chair. In that split second Aziz decided to move.

He checked the underside of his belt to make sure the knife was there and then brought his left hand up toward his chest. Aziz looked down at the watch and selected the correct button that would send out the signal to the men waiting in the truck. He was about to make history, about to strike a blow for all of Islam. Piper said something from behind him, but Aziz did not hear the words. His attention was elsewhere.

Slowly, he brought his other hand up to the watch. Aziz brought his gaze down to his wrist to make sure he pressed the right button. His heart was pumping so fast he felt his temples begin to throb. A layer of sweat on his skin glistened, and his hands were clammy. So moist were his palms that he stopped short of pressing the button and decided to wipe the sweat from his palms one last time. He ran his opened hands up and down the thighs of his pants twice, reminding himself while he did it how difficult it was to hold the small knife. When his palms were as dry as he could get them, he brought the watch back up and went to press the button.

His right index finger poised over the button, Aziz sensed movement and stopped everything. He looked up. From the door to the right of the president's desk, a woman in a bright yellow blouse came walking quickly forward. She continued around the nearest side chair to where the president was sitting and deposited a stack of papers on his desk.

Aziz exhaled a deep breath, his body trembling in a release of energy as he did so. Piper said something again, and Aziz turned around to face him.

"Sit down, Prince Kalib."

Aziz looked back toward the president and the woman, and then sat. A bead of nervous sweat ran down his forehead, and he wiped it away with the back of his hand.

"Are you feeling all right?" Asked Piper. "You look a little warm."

Aziz turned and smiled. "It is a little warm in here, but nothing compared to my country."

"That's a good point."

Slowly, Aziz began to regain his composure. He reminded himself of how far he had come, and of how close he was to obtaining everything he had struggled for. He needed the president to come to him. He needed to be patient. Aziz had waited this long; another minute would be nothing. When the president went to shake his hand, it would begin.

SECRET SERVICE AGENT Warch walked into the president's secretary's office, which was sandwiched in between the Cabinet Room and the Oval Office.

"Sally, I need to see him ASAP."

Sally Burke finished writing something and looked up, smiling. "Good morning, Jack." The president's secretary could tell by the tone of Warch's voice that he was in a hurry, but he could take a number with all of the other people who daily streamed into her office in an attempt to get some face time with America's highest elected official. "He's in with someone right now. It'll probably be twenty minutes to a half an hour."

Warch shook his head. "It can't wait that long. I have to see him right away."

Burke had had many dealings with Warch over the last five months, but she had never seen him look quite so concerned.

"I don't know what you want me to do, Jack. He's meeting with a foreign dignitary. We can hardly go bursting in."

"He's meeting with what?" asked an angered Warch. "I didn't see anything on his schedule."

Burke sat up a little straighter, somewhat surprised by the agent's tone. "It was a last-minute change."

"Who is he meeting with?"

"Russ Piper and ah—" Burke looked down at her desk. "Prince Kalib."

Warch's forehead creased. "I don't remember seeing a Prince Kalib on the WHAVS list." *WHAVS,* pronounced "waves," stood for White House Access Visitor System. The uniformed division used the system to screen guests for any criminal and/or mental history that could be threatening to the president.

Burke looked up sheepishly. "I don't know what to say. The DNC added him to the list late last night."

"Goddamnit," cursed Warch through clenched teeth. "How many times do I have to tell you people that no one gets in to see him unless we've done a complete check?" Warch backed away from the desk and thought about his options. If he barged in on a meeting with a foreign dignitary and everything turned out to be a false alarm, Hayes would have his ass. Warch looked back to the president's secretary. "Where is Prince Kalib from?"

"Oman, I think." Burke nervously checked her planner. Warch was acting very out of character. "Yes, he's from Oman."

Warch's suspicion doubled at the mention of the tiny Persian Gulf state. In a quick clipped voice, Warch asked, "Has he ever been to the White House before?"

"No." Burke shook her head. "Not that I know of."

Warch had to decide, and he had to decide fast. His mind quickly scrolled through a list of possibilities, and all the while his conversation with Irene Kennedy loomed larger and larger. Warch paced back and forth in front Burke's desk, and then finally his instincts kicked in. He turned for the door that Special Agent Ellen Morton was standing next to, and his left hand snapped up to his mouth. He was about to make the best or the worst decision of his career. Into the hand mike, the special agent in charge of the president's detail barked out the command, "Warch to detail. Harden up on the Oval Office!"

PRESIDENT HAYES FINISHED writing a note to himself and said, "It was good talking to you, Harry. I appreciate your help on this. Thanks." Hayes hung up the phone and stood. From the back of his chair, he grabbed his suit coat and put it on. The president tugged at each sleeve once and then buttoned the top button of the dark coat. Smiling, he stepped out from behind his desk, and with Valerie Jones at his side, he said, "Prince Kalib, it is an honor to finally meet you."

Rafique Aziz rose from the couch and smiled his first honest smile all morning. Subtly, he crossed his hands in front of his waist, letting his right hand fall on the wrist of his left. Aziz felt for the button, not wanting to take his eyes off the president. He had practiced it so many times and dreamt about it thousands of times more. This was how he had always thought it would be. The so-American gesture of shaking hands. It was the perfect opportunity to strike. He had been right to wait for the president to come to him. Aziz's smile broadened even further as his index finger circled the face of the watch once, searching for the proper button. He found it and pressed it twice. Then his hand moved casually to his belt, a feeling of ecstasy washing over him as his hostage approached.

The Treasury Building

IN THE CAB of the White Knight Linen truck Abu Hasan felt the vibration on his hip and tossed his clipboard onto the floor of the cab. While his left hand jerked open the driver's door, his right grabbed a small bundle. Hasan leapt from the cab in his green pants and white shirt. As he hit the concrete pavement of the parking garage floor, he heard a roar erupt from the cargo area of the truck as the forklift and ATVs were fired up. Hasan sprinted for the plain gray door and dropped to one knee, placing the small canvas bundle on the ground in front of him. He opened it and threw the thick sheets of cotton to the side, grabbed the preformed piece of plastique explosive, and attached it to the door. Hasan smacked the gray claylike material with the side of his fist twice to make sure it was secured and then stuck a blasting cap into the explosive material. Grabbing the reel of yellow Primacord, he ran along the same wall for twenty feet and hunched down. Hasan pressed the detonator, and a split second later there was a short, loud bang.

The tailgate of the truck flew open immediately, and two men jumped to the ground. On the right-hand side, against the wall of the truck's cargo area, the ramp lay on its side. The men yanked it from the vehicle and secured it just as Bengazi moved the forklift to the edge. The heavy machine teetered forward until the majority of its weight was on the ramp. Then Bengazi released the brake and let the machine carry itself to the concrete floor. As soon as all four wheels were on solid ground, Bengazi stepped on the gas and roared for the blown-away door. The two men with the RPGs ran alongside and jumped onto the side steps.

Hasan yanked open the remnants of the Marilyn Monroe door. A cloud of cordite filled the air, and Bengazi and his men pulled their gas masks all the way down. The forklift lurched forward, the two men carrying the RPGs clinging to the sides, as Bengazi gunned the powerful engine. The heavy yellow machine thundered into the concrete tunnel as the agile ATVs raced down the ramp one by one, their knobby rubber tires squealing as they turned hard for the tunnel.

The Washington Hotel

ON THE TOP floor of the Washington Hotel, in the cluttered janitor's closet, Salim Rusan was waiting patiently. Laid out before him on a clean white towel was a Russian-made SVD sniper rifle. The SVD fired a powerful 7.62-mmx54 rimmed cartridge and could achieve accurate kills at ranges of up to a thousand yards in the right hands. Rusan did not plan to use even a quarter of the rifle's range. On top of the long rifle, almost fifty inches from shoulder butt to muzzle, was a PSO 1 x 4 scope. A ten-round magazine was inserted in the rifle, and a second magazine was in Rusan's pocket. That was all the ammunition Aziz had allowed him to take. Aziz had been adamant that Rusan was to stay for no longer than two minutes and then leave the hotel. There were other things that he would be needed for later.

The pager began its vibration, announcing that after almost a year of planning it was time for action. Rusan reached down and turned the pager off with one hand while grabbing the light nine-pound rifle with the other. He burst from the closet into the empty hallway and walked quickly for the rooftop's patio doors. Rusan counted to himself slowly to help keep his heart rate low, a trick his Soviet trainers had taught him while he had stalked the burned-out buildings of Beirut as a teenager.

With his sniper's rifle clutched in one hand, he opened the door to the patio and dropped to his stomach. Quickly, he crawled the thirty feet to the edge and stuck the long black barrel through the railing. Hugging the rifle tightly against his shoulder and cheek, he looked through the scope and acquired the large South Portico of the White House. From there, Rusan followed the edge of the building to the Oval Office and prepared to fire. When he reached the door that was just outside the president's office, he found nothing. Rusan searched the patio quickly and again found nothing. Not having time to waste, he moved on to his secondary target. The scope quickly found not one, but four Secret Service agents standing near the guard booth on the roof of the White House. Rusan picked the agent on the far left, centered the crosshairs on the man's head, and squeezed the trigger.

The White House

THERE ARE VERY few things, short of a gunshot, that can get a Secret Service agent's heart beating faster than the phrase "Harden up." Those two little words, heard so often during training exercises, are rarely uttered while on duty at the White House. Just outside the main door to the Oval

Office, the two agents standing post drew their weapons without hesitation. The shorter of the two also pulled out a set of keys and opened the door to a seemingly benign wooden credenza. A second later a third agent appeared from around the corner with a gun clutched in both hands. The agent who had opened the credenza quickly extracted three Uzi submachine guns, passing one to each of the other two agents and keeping the third for himself. The entire process took less than five seconds.

One floor below, in Horsepower, the detail's command post, the agent sitting at the security console rose and walked quickly across the room. He bolted the door shut and returned to his seat without speaking. Two more agents, at the far end of the room, unlocked a metal cabinet, revealing a cache of weapons. Each man took an MP-5 submachine gun. They both chambered a round and walked to the room's other door, which led to a hidden staircase to the Oval Office.

Upstairs Jack Warch entered the Oval Office with his suit coat open and thrown back over his right hip. His right hand was wrapped around the grip of his still holstered weapon. Warch quickly approached the president's side, not taking his eyes off the dark-featured man standing by the fireplace.

"Excuse me for the intrusion, Mr. President, but I need to talk to you for a second." The president stopped in his tracks, alarmed by the forceful entrance. He looked to Warch and then his chief of staff.

There was a moment of uncertainty. As Warch eyed the president's visitor, he couldn't quite discern the intent of the well-dressed man he was staring down. Then he saw it, something in the other man's eyes. Gripping his gun tighter, he pulled it up a half an inch out of the smooth leather holster. The president was saying something, but Warch wasn't listening. He was waiting for one more sign that this man standing in the Oval Office was not who he said he was.

Back downstairs in Horsepower, the young agent sitting at the security console looked intently at the array of surveillance monitors before him. His eyes searched for anything that could be even remotely construed as a threat. Midway through his sweep, his focus was broken by the beeping of his computer. The agent's eyes snapped from the monitors to his computer screen to find four capitalized words flashing. Grabbing the arm of his headset the agent blurted out the words, "HORSEPOWER TO DETAIL! WE HAVE A SECURITY BREACH IN THE TREASURY TUNNEL! I REPEAT, WE HAVE A SECURITY BREACH IN THE TREASURY TUNNEL!"

Up in the Oval Office the stream of words blared into Warch's right ear like Klaxons. His gun was out of his holster and aimed at the president's guest in a split second. His left hand snapped to his lips, and he barked into his hand mike, "WARCH TO DETAIL. HARDEN UP ON WOODY IMMEDIATELY!"

Three of the four doors to the Oval Office burst open instantly, and four agents rushed to surround the president, their weapons drawn and ready. As the wall of agents closed around the commander in chief, the next sign of danger came blaring over their earpieces. "AGENTS DOWN! AGENTS DOWN! HERCULES IS UNDER FIRE!"

With his SIG-Sauer aimed at Aziz's forehead, Warch screamed, "EVAC, EVAC!"

Ellen Morton was standing directly behind the president when the evacuation order was given, and in a tribute to her training, she didn't waste a second. Morton reached up and grabbed President Hayes by the back of his shirt collar and yanked him to the left. Two more agents rushed through the main door with their guns drawn and joined the scrum that was moving toward the president's private study. Morton kicked a chair out of the group's way as they moved in unison. The president's chief of staff was caught up in the wave of bodies and was rushed out of the room with them. Jack Warch stood his ground and covered the evacuation, his eyes still locked in a stare with Aziz.

The Treasury Tunnel

THE HEAVY FORKLIFT screamed down the smooth concrete tunnel, gaining speed as it went. The two men riding on the sides wrapped their inside arms around the cage and aimed their armor-piercing shells at the door in their path. Both men sighted in on the hinges and fired. There was a loud swooshing noise marked by a white trail of smoke as the warheads raced forward in unison and then slammed into the steel door.

The ensuing explosion was deafening as debris, smoke, and fire erupted back down the throat of the narrow passageway. Bengazi closed his eyes and kept the accelerator to the floor. The forklift maintained its speed, passing through the bright showering debris and then into total darkness. There was a moment of silence, and then a foundation-cracking collision as the forklift thudded into the steel door, knocking it off its twisted hinges and lurching to a stop inside the basement of the White House.

The collision had jolted Bengazi forward, knocking his foot from the gas pedal and sending his two men flying from the vehicle. His ears were ringing from the explosion, and he couldn't see past the cage of the forklift due to the thick smoke and dust. By the time he had righted himself in the seat, his two men were back at his side and climbing back onto the vehicle. Bengazi pressed the gas pedal to the floor, the engine roared, and the forklift lurched forward.

The heavy machine continued through the thick smoke, finding its way down the main hallway of the White House's first basement. Without warning, the butted front end of the forklift slammed into what Bengazi knew to be the first set of double doors. The center bar and two doors peeled away from the frame as if they were tin. On the other side of the double doors, there was no smoke. Bengazi's men immediately opened up with their AK-74s on full automatic as three uniformed Secret Service officers, rushing to head off the security breach in the Treasury tunnel, were caught in the open. The bullets cut them to the ground instantly, and what little life may have been left in them was squeezed away as the forklift rolled over them.

The White House

WARCH STEPPED BACKWARD to cover the president's retreat. With his gun still leveled on the man across the room, he listened to the frantic radio traffic coming over his earpiece and tried to decide where to take the president. A decision had to be made, either evacuate him from the compound via the south ground's limo or stash him in his new bunker. Right as Warch reached the doorway to the study, the building was rocked by an explosion.

Aziz had been waiting for the explosion and sprang. Taking a quick step to the side, he grabbed Chairman Piper around the throat with one arm and drew his knife with the other. Aziz stuck the tip of the knife into Piper's throat, breaking the skin and drawing blood. Careful to keep his head shielded behind Piper's, Aziz yelled, "Order your men to stop with the evacuation, or I will kill him!"

The request fell on deaf ears. Warch's primary, immediate, and only concern was the president. Nothing else mattered, especially not the political operative who had brought this snake into the White House. Warch took one final step backward into the study and closed the door to the Oval Office.

Seconds earlier Special Agent Morton had pressed a hidden button in the short hallway. There was a hydraulic hiss, and an entire section of the wall lurched inward, revealing a hidden staircase. Morton started down the steep stairs first, followed by two agents who had the president sandwiched in between them. Valerie Jones, caught up in the human freight train, was grabbed by one of the last two agents and thrust forward.

Warch was now at the top of the stairs yelling, "BUNKER! TAKE HIM TO THE BUNKER!" Warch then stepped into the hidden passageway and sealed the wall behind him. As he started down the stairs, he raised his hand mike to his mouth and said, "Horsepower, from Warch. We are moving Woody to the bunker! I repeat, we are moving Woody to the bunker!"

The group clambered down to the first landing. Waiting for them at the bottom were two Secret Service agents who had just come out the side door of Horsepower. They had already opened the heavy steel door to the tunnel that ran underneath the Rose Garden and over to the mansion. One of them took the lead and started down the next flight of stairs, while the other one waited to cover from the rear.

The caravan, now totaling eleven people, continued into the tunnel. The wide passageway was covered with an ugly brown carpeting. The group raced ahead at a full speed, the agents almost carrying the president. When they reached the far end, they had two choices. They could proceed either up a set of stairs and into the first basement of the mansion or down a short set of stairs on the right. The lead agent hustled down the steps on his right. He came to an abrupt halt at a riveted steel door and punched an access code into the control panel. As soon as he heard the metallic release of the lock, he threw his shoulder into the door and burst into a large anteroom. The first two agents into the room fanned out to the left, and with their guns leveled, they covered a second door to the twenty-by-ten-foot anteroom. As soon as the last agent had cleared the tunnel, the door to it was closed and locked.

Jack Warch pushed his way through the group, grabbing the president firmly by the upper arm. The two large agents who had been glued to Hayes on the way down the stairs and through the passageway moved forward, staying with their charge.

A dazed President Hayes looked to Warch and asked, "What in the hell is going on?"

Warch decided not to answer the obvious and proceeded forward. At the opposite end of the anteroom, Warch approached a large, smooth vault door. The special agent in charge of the presidential detail flipped open the cover to the control panel and punched in a nine-digit code. There was a brief moment of silence and then a hissing noise as the rubber airtight seal on the door contracted. Next, the locking stems retracted and an electric motor began to whine as the two-foot-thick solid steel door swung open, revealing the president's newly completed bunker.

The White House Mess

ANNA RIELLY WAS standing near the center of the White House mess holding a paper cup of black coffee and listening to Stone Alexander explain why the room was called a mess instead of a dining room. Apparently it had something to do with the U.S. Navy. She was only half listening to Alexander as he rambled on. Two men in dark suits, sitting at a nearby table had caught her eye. They had a police-officer look about them that was common to most of her father's friends and more than one of her brothers. Almost simultaneously, the two men brought their hands up to their ears and held them there. Rielly guessed from the gesture that they must be Secret Service. She was about to turn her attention back to her tour guide when the two agents abruptly stood and raced across the room with their weapons drawn.

Oblivious to what had just transpired not more than twenty feet away, Stone Alexander continued with his oral dissertation on the West Wing. Being new to the job, Rielly wasn't sure if what she had just witnessed was normal, but common sense told her that law enforcement officers didn't draw their weapons unless there was a good reason. Rielly looked around the room and concluded from the some of the faces she saw that she wasn't the only one who had noticed the brandishing of firearms.

Rielly set her coffee down and looked at Alexander. "I think there's something going on."

Alexander looked down at her and smiled. "Don't worry; I have that effect on a lot of women. You'll get used to it." It was apparent from the full-fledged grin on Alexander's face that he found himself quite amusing.

Rielly shook her head. "Jesus, do you ever give it a rest? I'm talking about those two guys who just ran out of here with their guns—"

An explosion rumbled from somewhere in the building and stopped the young reporter in midsentence. The noise was so startling, and out of place, that Stone Alexander flinched and spilled half of his coffee down the front of his shirt. The next brief moment seemed like an eternity. Everyone in the White House mess froze with the same wide-eyed look, and then the silence was shattered by loud cracks of gunfire.

The Executive Mansion

MUAMMAR BENGAZI slammed on the brakes, and the forklift came to a skidding halt in the first basement of the Executive Mansion. He could hear the higher pitch of the ATVs' engines not far behind. Bengazi swiftly jumped to the ground and ran through a door to his left. Bounding up the stairs two at a time, he kept his AK-74 aimed upward as he climbed. The two men who had fired the RPGs followed close behind. When they reached the first landing, the door above them opened and two uniformed Secret Service officers rushed into the stairwell with their pistols drawn. Bengazi unleashed a quick burst of bullets, striking both men in the chest and sending them backward. The fallen officers blocked the door from closing, and as Bengazi reached the last step, he rolled a smoke grenade and then a fragmentation grenade into the hallway.

The double explosion was followed by a chorus of screams and falling debris. Bengazi and his men burst from the stairwell through the thickening gray smoke and began firing their weapons in all three directions. With their gas masks secured, they moved unhindered by the smoke toward the South Portico. Bengazi grabbed another grenade from his vest and yanked the pin. Fifty feet ahead, directly down the hall, was the Palm Room—the same room the president walked through every morning on his way to the Oval Office. Bengazi threw the grenade forward and ducked into an alcove on his right, while his men took shelter in a doorway on the left. There was a clinking noise as the grenade hit the tile floor and then a glass-shattering explosion as it detonated. Bengazi rushed forward again; every second was precious. As he reached the Palm Room, he turned the corner and almost tripped over a bloody Secret Service officer, who lay dying on the floor, his body eviscerated by shards of glass. Bengazi looked through the shattered windowpanes out onto the South Lawn and saw four black-clad men running toward him, their machine guns searching for a target.

They belonged to the Secret Service Uniformed Division's Emergency Response Team or ERT, and they had been expected. Bengazi raised his weapon to take aim at the lead man, but before he had a chance to dispose of him, the officer was struck by a high-velocity round that separated a large chunk of his head from the rest of his body. Within seconds the other three Secret Service officers were all lying on the ground, either dead or dying.

Bengazi was happy to see that Salim Rusan was doing his job. From his spot on the roof of the Washington Hotel, Rusan was to cover Bengazi and the others as they broke out into the open for the West Wing.

Bengazi yelled over his shoulder, "RPG!"

While he searched the South Lawn for more targets, one of his men stepped to his side with a rocket-propelled grenade launcher steadied on his shoulder and dropped to one knee. The man sighted in on the double doors at the other end of the Colonnade. The clicking of the trigger was followed by a low swooshing noise and another deafening explosion.

Bengazi broke into a full sprint along the Colonnade, his AK-74 aimed at the burned and smoking entrance to the West Wing.

The Oval Office

THE FLOOR SHOOK, and several chunks of plaster fell from the ceiling of the Oval Office. Rafique Aziz had his back pressed against the fireplace and was holding Russ Piper tightly at knifepoint. The loud cracks of rifle fire told him his men were close. Aziz was enraged with himself for letting the president get away. He had been so close.

Seconds later Bengazi burst into the Oval Office, sweeping the smoking muzzle of his rifle from one end of the room to the other and back. The only two men in the room were Aziz and Chairman Piper. Bengazi's other men joined him within seconds and covered the hallway. Not daring to ask the obvious, Bengazi lifted his gas mask and retrieved a pistol from his thigh holster. He extended the grip toward Aziz.

Aziz threw Piper to the side. The chairman of the DNC stumbled over a chair and fell to the ground. He propped himself up on one elbow, still not quite sure what he had done.

"What are you doing?" Piper yelled with a look of utter shock on his round face. "This can't be happening!"

Without hesitation, Aziz pointed his weapon at Piper and squeezed the trigger. The bullet struck the chairman right between the eyes and sent his heavy head thudding to the floor. A pool of crimson blood flowed from the Piper's head and began to work its way across the plush blue carpet and onto the presidential seal.

"I have been waiting to do that all morning," growled Aziz. Then extending his hand, he said, "Give me your radio." Bengazi turned his back, and Aziz withdrew the small radio from Bengazi's combat vest. Aziz unplugged the headset jack and brought the radio to his mouth. With the gun in one hand and the radio in the other, Aziz started for the doorway. "The president has made it to his bunker. Cut the communications immediately, secure the building, and take as many hostages as possible."

9

THE SMALL JET cleared the dark expansive water of the Atlantic, and within minutes the jagged shoreline of the Chesapeake Bay came into view. Mitch Rapp looked down at the familiar body of water with a determination and focus that had been missing just hours earlier. When Irene Kennedy had called and recounted the startling events at the White House, Rapp found himself awash in a sea of shock. For a decade he had followed, more closely than any other individual, the actions of Rafique Aziz. There had been the kidnappings in Beirut, Istanbul, and Paris; the bombings in Spain, Italy, France, Lebanon, and Israel; and the event that had led Rapp into his unusual occupation, the downing of Pan Am Flight 103.

Despite Kennedy's insistence that Aziz was, in fact, in control of the White House, it took several minutes for the sheer scope and gravity of the situation to sink in with Rapp. As more of the morning's events were relayed, the fog hanging over Rapp's mind began to dissipate. Instead, Rapp saw before him, in this turmoil and tragedy, an opportunity to bring the destructive chase to an end. He was sick of showing up to count the bodies and look at the evidence. He was sick of chasing Rafique Aziz, always missing him, sometimes by months and days, or even seconds.

As the plane descended toward Andrews Air Force Base, Rapp looked out the window at the rolling Maryland countryside with a clear and precise plan in his mind of what he needed to do. In Paris he had hesitated because of a single innocent bystander. At the time, he did not know it, but he had traded the lives of all the people who had died this morning for the life of that one woman. The logic was irrefutable. If he had pulled the trigger in Paris, none of this would have happened. Never again, he told himself. This would be the end of the road for one of them.

The Learjet set down gently and taxied to a portion of the base the CIA leased from the Air Force. As the plane approached a brown hangar, the large doors were opened, inviting the jet out of the sunlight and away from prying eyes. Once inside, the doors were closed and the pilots shut down the engines.

Rapp peered out the small window and saw a group of a half dozen people waiting in the hangar's glass office. He immediately recognized Irene Kennedy and Director Stansfield. Rapp grabbed his backpack and started for the door while Jane Hornig appeared from the bedroom. Rapp lowered the door and took one large step to the ground. Out of habit he turned and offered his hand to Hornig. The two of them walked across the spotless concrete floor to the fluorescent-lit office. Rapp opened the glass door, and the loosely hung venetian blind swung away and then back, clanking several times.

Director Stansfield stood in the sparsely furnished military office, the handset of a secure mobile phone held firmly against his ear. His SPO, or security protection officer, was standing next to him holding the rest of the unit, which was roughly the size of a camera case. Stansfield looked up at Rapp and said into the receiver, "He's standing right in front of me." The director's gray eyes then looked to the ground, and he nodded several times. "I was planning on it. We should be there in about twenty minutes."

Stansfield handed the phone to his SPO and said, "Would everybody excuse us for a minute?" The four other people who had been waiting in the office with Kennedy and Stansfield filed out of the room, leaving the director and Kennedy alone to talk with Hornig and Rapp.

Irene Kennedy grabbed a garment bag from the back of one of the chairs and handed it to Rapp. "You need to get changed. We have a meeting at the Pentagon in twenty minutes."

Rapp took the bag and looked to Stansfield. He didn't like the idea of showing his face to a roomful of politicians and bureaucrats. "Who was that on the phone?"

"General Flood. He wanted to make sure I was bringing you to the meeting."

"Why?" asked Rapp as he started to take off his holster.

"He didn't say."

Rapp looked at Stansfield with some concern. "Am I giving a briefing?"

Kennedy fielded the question by pulling a leather wallet out of her purse. "Your credentials? Same cover as always. Mitch Kruse, Middle Eastern analyst on my counterterrorism team. You have been with the CIA for five years, et cetera, et cetera. . . ." Kennedy handed him the wallet. "You know the routine. We want you there if the need arises. We would, of course, prefer it if you kept a low profile."

Rapp took the wallet and set it on the desk next to his holstered 9-mm Beretta. He quickly stripped down to his boxers while Kennedy and Stansfield began to question Hornig. A small pinkish scar was visible just above his left hip, about the size of a quarter, the mark left by the bullet of an overzealous and confused FBI agent. On his tanned lower back was a scar left by the knife of the surgeon who had removed the bullet.

"Have you got an exact number out of him yet?" asked Kennedy of Jane Hornig.

"Yes"—Hornig shrugged her shoulders—"at least we think so. Remember that everything we get out of him is what he thinks to be the truth. As far as Harut knows, there are twelve of them, counting Aziz." Hornig folded her arms across her chest and assumed a wider stance.

"What type of weapons?"

"Besides your standard firearms"—Hornig looked to Rapp, who was pulling on his dress pants—"a lot of plastique explosives. Mitch?"

Rapp grabbed a white T-shirt and said, "More than enough to blow the whole place to kingdom come."

Stansfield shook his head and asked, "What about his demands?"

"I haven't had the chance to get around to that yet, but I'll start as soon as we get him moved."

Stansfield nodded. "We have arranged to transfer you to one of the safe houses in Virginia. You are to talk to no one other than Irene, Mitch, and me. Very few people outside of our immediate circle know we have Harut, and we would like to keep it that way. I need you to focus your questioning in the area of demands. We need to know what Aziz is going to ask for, before he asks for it."

Hornig accepted her orders with a nod and cautioned, "If he knows what the demands are, I will find out."

"And," started Kennedy, "it would help if we got as complete a list as possible of the men Aziz brought with him."

Hornig made another mental note. She was prepared to extract every last piece of information from Harut, and if they had a shopping list, she was more than willing to oblige.

"Mitch, can you think of anything else?" asked Kennedy.

Rapp shoved the tails of his white dress shirt into his pants and buttoned them. "Yeah. I'd like to know how long he plans on hanging around, and how in the hell he plans on getting out of there. If I know Aziz, he has a timetable, and he's planned this entire thing down to the last minute."

Stansfield nodded in agreement and said to Hornig, "You know how to get ahold of us. We'll try to stay out of your way, but I want to be updated the moment you find anything of consequence."

"I'll get to work immediately." Dr. Hornig pushed her glasses up on the bridge of her nose and nodded.

"Good. Mitch, let's go. You can finish in the helicopter." Stansfield started for the door with Kennedy and Hornig on his heels. Rapp grabbed the garment bag and the rest of his stuff and followed. As he stepped out of the office, he saw a gurney being wheeled across the smooth floor toward an ambulance. Harut was strapped to the top under a gray blanket.

A small outer door to the hangar was opened, and a stream of bright sunshine shot across the floor. Rapp could now hear the spinning rotors of a helicopter waiting on the tarmac. He paused for a second and watched as the gurney was shoved into the ambulance. Jane Hornig and her two assistants climbed in, and the doors were closed. Rapp was now frozen in thought as he looked at the ambulance pulling away.

Irene Kennedy appeared in the small door with her sunglasses on and her hair blowing in the wind. "Come on, Mitch. We're going to be late."

Rapp, his concentration broken, turned to his boss and blinked several times. Kennedy waved for him to hurry, and Rapp jogged to the door, still wondering what it was that he was missing.

VICE PRESIDENT SHERMAN Baxter had returned to Washington from a fund-raising trip to New York as fast as his entourage could pull up stakes and ship out. *Air Force One* had landed at Andrews about forty minutes before Rapp and Dr. Hornig had set down.

Baxter sat in the back of the tanklike presidential limousine with his chief of staff, Dallas King, and Attorney General Margaret Tutwiler. As the motorcade of Secret Service vehicles raced through D.C., Dallas King laid out their strategy. The Stanford Law grad and San Diego native ran a hand through his signature bleach-blond hair.

"This crisis presents us with a unique opportunity." King paused for emphasis and then looked at Attorney General Tutwiler. "Your job in this is going to be crucial, Marge. We need to let the FBI know that Sherm is in charge. We can't have them withholding information from us, and we definitely can't have them trying any rescue operations without our approval." The thirty-two-year-old rising star smashed his fist into the palm of his hand for emphasis. "Nothing goes down without our approval. Am I clear on that?"

Marge Tutwiler was just starting to get used to Dallas King's ambitious style. Vice President Baxter's lap dog was a charmer. He had good looks, a sharp mind, and good sense of humor. The only thing he lacked was a sense of his place in the pecking order. Marge Tutwiler—California political activist, self-anointed law enforcement critic, and former USC law professor—was not used to anyone speaking to her in such a tone, let alone someone not much older than her not-so-former students.

With a tired expression, Tutwiler said, "Dallas, I was dealing with the

FBI when you were still riding around your little San Diego neighborhood on a Big Wheel. Don't worry; I can handle them."

Dallas smiled and reached across the back of the limo, gently placing his hand on the attorney general's knee. "I'm sorry, Marge. I didn't mean to imply you didn't know how to handle the FBI." The perpetually tanned chief of staff released her knee and held both hands up in a token form of surrender. "I just meant we need to strategize together." Dallas flashed his wily smile and thought to himself, *This bitch's ego is bigger than her ass.*

Sherman Baxter the Third, former governor of California and current vice president of the United States, cleared his throat and interjected, "No matter what our titles are, we are outsiders in this town, and don't forget it. Dallas is right, Marge, and it doesn't hurt to remind us that we need to keep the FBI on a short leash." Sherman Baxter, like most politicians, had two very distinct personalities. Behind closed doors Baxter was extremely demanding and prone to fits of rage. The fifty-four-year-old Californian had grown to look at the Oval Office almost as if it were his birthright. In his mind, he deserved it a hell of a lot more than his running mate. If it hadn't been for Baxter and his California connections, President Hayes would never have made it to the White House.

In public they were the perfect picture of cooperation, but behind closed doors Baxter's contempt for his boss could not be concealed. In his eyes, Hayes was a complete simpleton who had managed to stumble into the White House because he had a cleaner sexual past than any of the other candidates—and, most important, because Sherman Baxter had delivered California. When Baxter had decided to run with Hayes, he had looked upon the endeavor as a stepping-stone to the presidency.

After a grueling campaign and just five short months in office, Baxter was already tired of playing second fiddle to Hayes. Sherman Baxter the Third, heir to one of California's finest family wineries, did not take kindly to receiving orders from a man whose family had made their money manufacturing radiator hoses. Three more years would be hard enough to take, and seven was absolutely unthinkable.

As King and Tutwiler continued to talk, Baxter gazed out the window. His black hair was thinning, and he wore it slicked back. Baxter folded his left arm over his slightly bulging midsection and remembered something that King liked to say when they discussed the agony of another three years underneath Hayes the simp: "Don't forget, you're one heartbeat away from the presidency, boss. You never know when some nut might punch Hayes's ticket."

How prophetic Dallas could be, Baxter thought to himself. As the motorcade pulled onto the George Mason Memorial Bridge, the tightly wound Baxter allowed himself a moment to relish the fact that for now, he was for all intents and purposes the president of the United States.

SPECIAL AGENT SKIP McMahon of the FBI looked down at the White House from the Secret Service's Joint Operations Center on the fifth floor of the Executive Office Building. From his vantage point he could count the bodies of nine Secret Service officers. He had been told there were more on the other side of the building, but an accurate number was impossible to ascertain. Even now, four hours after the attack, information was sparse. No one knew what was going on inside the building.

McMahon was a twenty-six-year veteran of the FBI who had seen it all, or at least he thought he had. He had started with the Bureau right out of college and after doing a four-year stint investigating bank robberies in Las Vegas, he was moved back to Washington, where he started working counterintelligence cases. After almost a decade of chasing spies he was moved into the FBI's violent crimes unit. It was a transfer that led to the downfall of his marriage and almost his career. The former defensive tackle for Penn State had quickly found that he had a knack for getting inside the twisted minds of the individuals he was charged with catching. Six years of sloshing through the septic tank of American society had taken its toll. McMahon had been asked one too many times to step into the shoes of a serial killer and visualize how some sick pervert had abducted, raped, tortured, and then killed an innocent little girl.

Fortunately for McMahon he had seen the writing on the wall and gotten out before the job destroyed him. McMahon had recently been put in charge of the Bureau's Critical Incident Response Group, or CIRG, which was the lead organization in resolving hostage situations. The FBI's elite Hostage Rescue Team, or HRT, was under his command along with another half dozen investigative and support units. But not once in the hundreds of meetings that McMahon had attended on urban terrorism had he ever heard someone postulate that the White House was vulnerable to a full-scale assault.

McMahon shifted his attention from terra firma to the horizon. On a more immediate note, he was not happy with the current command-and-control situation. Both FBI and Secret Service sniper teams occupied every rooftop within a block of the White House. Each team reporting to and taking orders from its own agency. In short, it was not the way to handle a crisis, and it was something that needed to be rectified immediately.

A female agent standing next to McMahon held her watch in front of his face. "You'd better get moving. The meeting is in twenty minutes."

McMahon nodded. With sagging shoulders, he looked at the fallen officers on the South Lawn and asked, "What's the body count?"

Special Agent Kathy Jennings looked at a small notebook and said, "We have it at eighteen, with God only knows how many more inside the building."

McMahon shook his head as he took in the carnage. He looked tired, and the crisis was only in its infancy. After a moment, he turned and headed for the door. McMahon dreaded attending meetings with the bigwigs. On his way out, he thanked several of the Secret Service agents for allowing him to take a look from their vantage point.

Jennings followed a half step behind, and as soon as she was sure no one could hear, she said, "I don't think they were too happy to see us. Do you think they know we're going to be running the show?"

"I don't know. They've lost at least eighteen men . . . probably double that, and the White House is their baby." McMahon turned for the stairs and started down.

"But they're not set up for this kind of thing. This is clearly . . ." Jennings stopped talking for a second as they passed two Secret Service officers who were on their way up the stairs. In a lower voice, she continued, "This is clearly the Bureau's territory. It's a domestic terrorist activity."

"A lot of people are going to want to stick their hands in this pie before it's over."

"Like who?"

"Like the United States military, and again, the Secret Service."

The confident young agent shook her head in disagreement. "The military is forbidden from . . ." started Jennings.

McMahon raised his hand and stopped her. "Save the lecture for one of your law-school buddies." The senior agent was very proud of the fact that he was one of the few people in the Bureau without an accounting or law degree. "I'm talking reality here, and I'm talking from experience. Why do you think this meeting is being held at the Pentagon?" McMahon let her think about the question while they descended another flight. "If we're so clearly in charge, why isn't this meeting being held at the Hoover Building or over at Justice?"

Jennings slowly started to see his point and nodded as they reached the first floor. While they continued toward the Seventeenth Street exit, McMahon said, "While I'm at the Pentagon, I want you to get the mobile command post in order. Get the shift changes set up, and don't take any crap from anyone." With his voice raised an octave, he added, "And you tell those clowns I'm in a surly mood, and that when I get back from this stupid dog-and-pony show, I'm going to be looking to blow a little steam." McMahon's temper was well known among his fellow law-enforcement officers at the Bureau. "No one works longer than an eight-hour shift unless I authorize it, and I don't want people loitering around when their shifts are over. We could be here for weeks, and I don't want burned-out people sitting at the controls."

"Anything else?"

"Yeah. Make sure HRT gets priority on everything. I want them in position ASAP."

THE EXPENSIVE SUIT was gone, replaced by drab green military fatigues, a holstered pistol, and a gas mask that was secured to his web belt. Rafique Aziz sat at the head of the long table and stared at the bank of television sets located on the far wall of the Situation Room. Three of the six TVs were tuned to the major networks, and a fourth was tuned to CNN. All of them were covering the White House crisis from their studios in New York and with live shots from across the street at Lafayette Square.

Much of Aziz's original anger at missing the president had dissipated. With typical thoroughness, Aziz had prepared for this contingency, and if given enough time, everything could still be achieved. Now he had to at least allow himself a moment of satisfaction. He had done it. He controlled the most famous and decadent symbol of the West. He had taken his *jihad,* his holy war, to the heart of the enemy, and once he pried the president from his bunker, he would be able to complete his plan. No longer would America meddle in the affairs of the Arab world.

There was a knock on the door, and without turning, Aziz said, "Enter."

The usually stoic Muammar Bengazi walked into the room with a smile on his face, an AK-74 slung over his shoulder, and a notepad in his left hand. He approached Aziz and said, "We are in complete control of the building. As you ordered, all outer walls and points of entry have been wired with explosive charges." A gleam appeared in the terrorist's eye. "And as you predicted, we also have control of the Secret Service's weapons and security system." Bengazi stepped forward and placed his hands on the back of one of the table's chairs. "As ordered, I have taken their perimeter system off-line. We are using only their rooftop-mounted cameras and have disconnected the computers from their modems. They are no longer feeding their headquarters with images."

"Good. I do not trust them. With all of their technology, who knows how they might have tried to trick us."

Bengazi nodded in agreement. "As you requested." He handed Aziz the notepad that was under his left arm. "Here is a list of all the hostages by name and position. I circled the most important ones."

Aziz leaned back in the chair and flipped through the pages, his chin resting on his chest. "Seventy-six total hostages."

"That is correct."

Aziz found what he was looking for on the third page—it was the name of the first person he would kill. He tapped the name with his finger and then asked, "How many Secret Service agents?"

"I did not include them with the seventy-six hostages. They are on the next page. Nine alive, four of whom are in need of medical attention. We also have several marines and other military types mixed in with them."

"Do you have them separated from the others?"

"Yes. They are upstairs, as you planned."

"Bound and hooded?" Aziz asked with a raised eyebrow.

"Of course."

"Have any of the civilians tried to distinguish themselves as leaders?"

"None so far."

Flipping the notebook back to the first page, Aziz said, "When the first one stands up"—he held up his forefinger—"and tries to show bravado, I want you to come and get me. I will deal with him personally. We are spread thin enough as it is. I do not want to have to worry about some cowboy giving us trouble from within."

Bengazi nodded and suggested, "I think it might be a good idea to let the civilians go to the bathroom."

Aziz looked at his watch. It was a reasonable request, and one that would help calm them. "Fine, but leave the Secret Service agents and the marines to wallow in their own excrement."

"Yes, Rafique. Do you wish to inspect the explosives?"

"No. I trust that you have done your job. Now I have to make a phone call." Aziz pointed at the TV. "They are getting ready to meet at their Pentagon."

Bengazi nodded. "If you do not need me for anything else, I have some details to attend to."

"One more thing," said Aziz, as he tilted his chin upward. "How is our little thief coming along?"

"All of his equipment is in place, and he has started work." With a shrug, Bengazi added "He tells me he is on schedule."

"Good. Keep an eye on him." Aziz lowered his chin. "He is, after all, not one if us."

"I told him not to go anywhere other than the bathroom unless he calls me first," Bengazi said with a smile. "I told him there are booby traps everywhere and I wouldn't want him to accidentally set one off."

With a smile, Aziz placed a flat hand on his radio and said, "If I need anything, I will call." He watched Bengazi start for the door and said, "Muammar, relax. They will not be coming tonight. The politicians are in charge right now. They will keep the FBI at bay until we are ready."

Bengazi nodded. "I know; you told me how things would proceed, but the time for them to attack would be now, before we get settled in. The hostages are still strong and fresh. They could give us trouble. In three days we will have them weakened and confused. If I were them, I would attack now."

Aziz grinned at his friend. "You have to understand how Washington works. The military will advise to move quickly and with overwhelming force, but the politicians will want to move with caution."

"What about the FBI?"

"They will stay in the middle and take orders like they always do. Relax, my friend, they will not be coming for a while. . . ." With a look of amusement, Aziz added, "In fact, I will probably have to provoke them into attacking."

Bengazi raised his thick eyebrows. "When the time is right."

"Precisely. You are wearing the special clothes I gave you?"

Bengazi shook his head. "No."

"Why not?" asked Aziz with a touch of anger.

"I don't feel right abandoning the other men if it comes to that."

"The plan will not work if everybody is in on it, Muammar. I am ordering you put them on. If the Americans come, it is our only chance."

Bengazi nodded reluctantly and then left. Aziz watched him go and thought about his plan for escape. It had a chance of working. Some things had to go their way, but at the very least, it gave them a fighting chance. If he could just get his hands on the president, none of it would matter.

Aziz returned his attention to the TVs, where the networks were now talking to their Pentagon reporters. He grabbed the remote and turned up the volume on the TV carrying CNN. Aziz listened as the correspondent announced that the vice president and other federal authorities were holding an emergency meeting at the Pentagon. The terrorist smiled as he looked around the opulent Situation Room. Such meetings were usually held in the very room he occupied.

10

THE JOINT CHIEFS briefing room is located in the inner sanctum of the monolithic five-sided building that houses the United States Department of Defense—the E Ring. The wide hallway that cuts in front of the modern crisis center is cluttered with more stars and bars than any other government building or military base in the world. Colonels and captains that walk the corridor find themselves saluting as often as a private fresh out of basic training. The E Ring is not known for being a lighthearted, casual workplace, and on this particular day the mood had taken on an even more serious tone.

Two marines stood post by the wide double doors as Washington's biggest players filed into the soon bristling room. With aides in tow, the president's entire cabinet trickled into the room until it was filled almost to capacity. The secretary of the interior was first, followed by the secretary of health and human services, and then the secretary of state. Within five minutes the entire cabinet had arrived, minus the attorney general. The room quickly took on the sound of a crowded bar as aides talked to their bosses and prepped them on the most recent news.

When FBI Director Roach and Special Agent Skip McMahon entered the room, they were hit with a flurry of questions. Fortunately for Roach and McMahon, General Flood entered the room with the other members of the Joint Chiefs just seconds later. Flood walked to the far end of the table and placed a large black ceramic coffee mug on the table.

"Everyone take a seat." Flood's commanding voice carried through the large room, and the talking was instantly reduced to a trickle. "Let's go, people." Flood clapped his hands together and pointed at the chairs arranged around the forty-foot rectangular conference table. "We have a lot of work to do."

As the attendees took their seats, Vice President Baxter entered the room with Attorney General Tutwiler and Dallas King. The three of them proceeded to the opposite end of the table from General Flood, where chairs had been saved for them. The secretary of state, a close friend of President Hayes, leaned over and immediately began asking Baxter just what in the hell was going on. While he was doing so, CIA director Stansfield entered the room with Irene Kennedy and Mitch Rapp. Flood pointed to three seats near his end of the huge table and then motioned for one of his aides to close the doors. An Army major walked over to the tall double doors and swung them closed with a finality that let everyone know the meeting was starting.

"People," announced Flood, "I'm not going to pussyfoot around on this. There are a lot rumors going around about what happened over at the White House this morning—some of them scratch the surface, but most of them are way off base. Here is what happened. At approximately oh-nine-hundred a group of terrorists attacked and took control of the White House."

Before Flood could continue, the room erupted into a series of fragmented conversations and expletives. "People!" bellowed Flood, restoring order. "We have a lot of ground to cover, so keep a lid on it." Flood angrily eyeballed the group, daring someone to defy him. After making sure everyone understood implicitly that his patience was thin, the general continued. "As I was saying, this group is in control of the White House and holds an unknown number of hostages. The only good news we have in all of this is that President Hayes was safely evacuated to his bunker during the raid. Communications have been cut, but we know the president is safe. This brings us to our first point of order. It is obvious that President Hayes is not in a position to discharge his duties as commander in chief. So, according to the Twenty-fifth Amendment, the powers of the president of the United States have been transferred to Vice President Baxter until such time as President Hayes may resume his duties. I have been informed that the majority of the cabinet has agreed to this, and I apologize to those of you who could not be reached earlier, but things have been rather hectic."

The general brought his hands together and clasped them tightly in front of his chest. "Let us be clear about this. For the time being, Vice President Baxter is the acting *president* and the *commander in chief* of our armed forces." Flood again looked around the substantial table, giving the group a moment for thought, and then added, "However, for reasons of clarity, we will continue to refer to him as Vice President Baxter. Are we all clear on this?"

General Flood waited a brief moment to see if anyone was crazy enough to draw his ire and then looked to his left at the director of the Secret Service. "Director Tracy is now going to give us the specifics on what transpired this morning. Again, hold all questions until he is done."

A solemn-faced director of the Secret Service stood and walked to the podium located at General Flood's end of the table. Alex Tracy was a squat man with a sizable head and the standard amount of intensity required to run one of the world's finest law-enforcement agencies. Tracy walked toward the podium with the enthusiasm of a man being sent to the gallows. He set a file on the top shelf and placed his hands on the sides.

With a look of exhaustion and a shaky voice, he started. "Late last night DNC Chairman Piper called over to the White House and obtained a meeting with the president. That meeting was scheduled for this morning at nine. White House staff broke with Secret Service policy and granted Piper and his guest a meeting without giving us time to run a background check on the chairman's guest. We now know that guest to be Rafique Aziz, the world-renowned terrorist." Tracy looked up at no one in particular and then continued. "It appears that Aziz approached the Democratic National Committee under the assumed identity of a Prince Kalib of Oman. Aziz gave a five-hundred thousand-dollar check to the party and, in return, requested that he meet with the president personally." This time when he paused, the director focused his look more precisely on the group of politicians at the far end of the table.

Almost every cabinet member was a Democrat, and a murmur broke out as they shot each other anxious looks. This little nugget of information had "congressional investigation" written all over it.

Tracy continued after about six seconds. "Aziz and Chairman Piper arrived at the White House this morning at about the same time that we received a tip from the CIA that the White House was targeted for a terrorist attack. While Aziz and Piper were entering the White House, a locally contracted linen truck arrived at the Treasury Building, as it does every morning, Monday through Friday. In a complete breakdown of security, the truck was allowed admittance into the underground parking facility by a uniformed Secret Service officer without being properly inspected." Tracy forced himself to straighten his posture. Out of sheer embarrassment he paused and looked down at his notes. Aziz getting into the White House could be blamed on Chairman Piper, but the truck was the Secret Service's fault. "It appears the back of this truck was loaded with an unknown number of terrorists and equipment that was used to breach the security of the Treasury tunnel. This was a major breakdown on the part of my agency, and we have already started an internal investigation." Tracy looked down the length of table at Vice President Baxter. "We will have a preliminary report ready by this evening."

Looking back to his notes, he continued, "After receiving the tip from the CIA, Jack Warch, the special agent in charge of the president's detail, left his office in the EOB and went over to the West Wing to consult with President Hayes. When Warch arrived, Piper and his guest were already in the Oval Office. As soon as Warch found out about the unauthorized visit, he entered the Oval Office to check on the president. After that things happened very fast. A sniper on the roof of the Washington Hotel opened fire on the Secret Service officers posted on the roof of the White House. Within seconds the outer door to the Treasury tunnel was breached, and Warch ordered the president's evacuation to his bunker. As many of you know, the old bunker at the White House dates back to World War Two and is really nothing more than a reinforced tunnel. Construction of a new bunker, located in the third basement of the mansion, was completed this past January. The Army Corps of Engineers did the work. They used the standard military design that has been incorporated into all of our command-and-control centers. . . . Excuse me." Tracy turned his head to the side and coughed.

"This new facility is not, however, fully operational. The actual construction of the bunker is completed. Its biological, chemical, and radioactive filtration systems are in place and operational, but its communications package has not been installed. That was to take place this summer. The bunker has been stocked, however, with rations and other necessities." Tracy was slowly gaining back some of his normal confidence. "We know with one hundred percent certainty that Special Agent Warch succeeded in evacuating President Hayes, Valerie Jones, and eight other Secret Service agents to the White House's basement bunker. Up until approximately nine-fifteen we were in contact with the bunker via our encrypted radios, and then all communication was severed. My technical advisers have informed me that the terrorists are using a jammer to block the radio signals.

"We have confirmed that eighteen secret service agents and officers have been killed and fifteen are unaccounted for." Tracy's voice wavered slightly. "We assume that the fifteen have either been killed or are being held hostage." Tracy felt a lump forming in his throat and paused to collect himself. After thumbing through his notes for several seconds, he continued, "Our best estimates are that Aziz and his men hold somewhere between eighty and one hundred hostages, with an unknown number of fatalities. We have secured the perimeter of the White House, and our counterassault team is in place and prepared to retake the building if and when you ask them to do so." Tracy closed his file and again looked down the length of the table at Vice President Baxter. He finished by saying, "The only good news I have to report is that the president is safe. I have spoken to the engineers who built the new bunker, and they say there is no way Aziz can get to him."

Vice President Baxter sat leaning back in his chair with one hand under his chin and the other dangling from his armrest. He and Dallas had rehearsed this next part. As a newcomer to the unique power circles of Washington, he needed to let everyone in the room know he was in charge. An example had to be set, and Tracy's head was on the chopping block. Baxter kept his eyes on Tracy, as he uncrossed his legs and let his chair tilt forward. In a voice devoid of compassion, he asked, "Director Tracy, would you mind explaining to me how in the hell something like this could happen?"

Tracy stood silent at the podium, a little caught off guard by the bluntness of the question. Vice President Baxter looked at him while drumming his fingers on the table. After a long moment, Baxter said, "Director Tracy, your agency has failed our country miserably. You have put us in dire straits, and now you stand before us with nothing to say." Baxter looked around the table trying to build a mood of consensus. "I have decided that the FBI will relieve your people as soon as Director Roach can have his agents in place." Baxter turned to look at FBI director Roach.

Secret Service Director Tracy's embarrassment was quickly replaced by anger. "Sir," he protested, "the White House falls under the Secret Service's jurisdiction. We are—"

Baxter raised his voice and cut Tracy off. "I have been advised by the attorney general that although the White House normally falls under the purview of the Secret Service, it is still a federal building and that makes it the FBI's territory."

"But my men have an intimate knowledge of the building and its grounds," stated Tracy in earnest. "We have agents that are being held hostage . . ."

Baxter shook his head vigorously. "Director Tracy, the Secret Service had its chance, and they have failed . . . miserably, I might add."

The humiliating public rebuke caused Tracy's cheeks to flush. He couldn't believe it was happening. He had worked in Washington for twenty-nine years and had seen countless others thrown to the lions in situations far less serious than this. He should have seen it coming, but everything had happened so fast. He had spent the last several hours worrying about the men he had lost, not the political fallout of the crisis. Tracy stood a little straighter and tried to salvage some honor. "We saved the president's life today and lost at least eighteen of our own men. . . . I would hardly—"

Baxter slammed a fist to the table, and with a rage no one in the room had witnessed before, other than King and Tutwiler, he cut Director Tracy off in midsentence.

"You have lost the White House, and you have embarrassed the entire country!" Baxter glared at Tracy a moment longer and then sat back in his chair. After taking a deep breath, he reined himself in a notch and continued in a quieter but equally firm voice, "I have consulted with Treasury Secretary Rose and have decided I want your resignation on his desk before I address the nation tonight." Shaking his head, Baxter added, "It is entirely beyond me how you could have let this happen."

Rather than cowering, the tenacious director stood his ground. The combination of the murder of his people and becoming the sacrificial lamb to satisfy the media sent Tracy's blood pressure shooting upward. Baxter had no idea what it was like to devote one's life to the pride-sucking job of guarding men such as him, some of whom had fewer scruples than a pimp. Tracy's complexion reddened as he stared at Baxter. In the briefest of moments he had to decide if he would bow to protocol and be dismissed like a servant or stand and fight. He decided on the latter. He owed at least that much to the men and women who had died under his command.

"I'll tell you how it happened. It happened because you and all of your esteemed colleagues have ignored every request the Secret Service has made for increased security since I have taken over the agency." Tracy raised his voice. "It happened because in your obsession with raising money for your beloved party, your chairman sidestepped Secret Service procedure and invited the most notorious terrorist in the world to the White House!"

Baxter shouted, "That will be enough, Director Tracy! You may gather your things and leave!"

Tracy stared down the long table with a look of flagrant disrespect. In a voice dripping with contempt, he said, "You go ahead and blame all of this on the Secret Service when you address the nation tonight, and when I hold my press conference tomorrow morning, I'll be sure to remind everyone of your comment regarding the Secret Service during the last election." Tracy shook his head. "I remember it verbatim because it seemed rather inconsiderate of you to be taking a shot at the very people who were putting in one-hundred-plus-hour weeks protecting you. You said that 'the Secret Service is comprised of a paranoid group of people, who, although well-meaning, have an inflated sense of self-importance.' I'm sure those words, combined with your and President Hayes's recent refusal of a request for an increase in our budget, will go over just great with all of your voters. And let's not leave out the fact that while my people were being killed, you were getting ready to attend a five-thousand-dollar a plate breakfast with all of your network buddies in New York."

Tracy turned his rage on the secretary of the treasury. "And let me remind my boss of his response to my request to expand the security perimeter around the White House. In a letter this last February, Secretary Rose refused, saying that the White House is one of the securest buildings in the world and that any further requests to expand the building's security perimeter will be denied."

Tracy grabbed his file from the podium. "How dare you call into question my commitment and professionalism! I have spent twenty-nine years of my life protecting presidents and their families!" He started for the door and then stopped abruptly, turning to look at the assembled crowd. "Right now we need to be worried about saving the men and women who are trapped inside the White House . . . not worrying about our careers."

Having spoken his piece, Tracy turned for the door, and with a stiff arm, he slammed it open and disappeared into the hallway.

Director Tracy's exit left the room in a shocked silence. After several moments the attendees began to whisper comments to one another, and then the room broke into a series of regionalized conversations. At the far end of the table Dallas King asked his boss if he had, indeed, made such a comment, and all Vice President Baxter could do was nod in frustration. King then turned to Treasury Secretary Rose and asked him if he had put his words in writing. Rose confirmed that he had, and Dallas King turned back to his boss and stated the obvious, "We're screwed."

Baxter shot his chief of staff a look of irritation and then turned his attention to General Flood at the far end of the table. The vice president twirled his finger in the air, signaling to the general that he wanted to get things moving. The general nodded, and with his baritone voice, he quieted the room. Flood then nodded to Irene Kennedy, who rose from her chair and made her way to the podium.

RAFIQUE AZIZ LOOKED at the Situation Room's TVs and then his watch. It had been almost twenty minutes since the vice president had arrived for the meeting. *The timing should be about right,* he thought to himself. Aziz studied the large phone next to him and looked at the twenty or so labels that marked preprogrammed telephone numbers. Most of the labels Aziz didn't recognize, but some were familiar. Not far down the first column he found the one he was looking for. It was marked Pentagon JCBR, which he understood to be the Joint Chiefs briefing room. Aziz went over his scripted words one more time, and then picked up the phone and pressed the button.

*   *   *

GENERAL FLOOD WAS listening to Kennedy give the background briefing on Aziz when he heard the quiet ring of the phone next to him. Flood glanced down and looked to see where the call was coming from. The screen at the top of the phone read, "WH SIT ROOM." Flood raised one hand to stop Kennedy from talking, and with the other, he snatched the handset from its cradle. "General Flood here."

"I hope I'm not interrupting your meeting."

Flood squeezed the phone and asked, "Who is this?"

"That is none of your concern. Put me on speakerphone so I can talk to the entire group. I do not want to have to repeat myself."

Flood considered the demand for a moment, and then reluctantly gave in and pressed a button. He then placed the handset back in its cradle and folded his arms across his chest. "You are on speakerphone. Go ahead."

Aziz's voice came pouring down from the room's overhead speaker system. "I have complete control of your White House. Any attempt to retake it will be futile. The United States currently holds fourteen point seven billion dollars in frozen assets that belong to the country of Iran. You illegally seized this money when the corrupt government of the Shah was overthrown by the people of Allah. If you return all of this money to Iran by nine tomorrow morning, I will release one-third of the seventy-six hostages I currently hold. This is nonnegotiable. If this demand is not met precisely as I have stated, I will kill one hostage every hour until it is met. I will remind you one more time, any attempt by you to rescue the hostages will be futile. The FBI's vaunted Hostage Rescue Team is no match for my men; just as your highly touted Secret Service was no match. In fifteen minutes I will place all of the wounded and dead outside of the West Entrance. Medical technicians in short-sleeve shirts and pants will be allowed to come in groups of two, one stretcher at a time, to pick up the bodies. No equipment or bags. Only two men at a time and a stretcher. Anything unusual and we will open fire."

The voice paused for a second and then said more firmly, "The account numbers that the money is to be transferred to are as follows . . ."

IT TOOK AZIZ a little over a minute to give all of the numbers. Then, without giving them a chance to ask any questions, he repeated the demand one last time and hung up the phone. Aziz leaned back and took in the moment. Keep it short, keep them off balance, and most important, let them know who is running the show. Aziz knew what would happen at nine tomorrow as sure as if he had a crystal ball. He had read all of the books that had been written by former FBI agents on hostage negotiations, and most important, he knew Vice President Baxter was in charge, and with Baxter came Attorney General Tutwiler.

Aziz had done his homework on Tutwiler. Via the Internet he had obtained copies of her speeches and lectures. She had been an outspoken critic of the FBI's techniques at Ruby Ridge and Waco. In Tutwiler's opinion the FBI should have worn the captors down over time and obtained the incremental release of hostages through negotiation and actually giving in to some of the group's smaller demands.

What a fool she was to speak in public and give him the chance to study her, Aziz thought. These Americans were fat and lazy. He knew what her every move would be. He would break her within two days, and when Baxter finally realized he should listen to his generals, it would be too late. Aziz would have the president, and everything would be in position for his final demand.

PRESIDENT HAYES LOOKED at Valerie Jones and asked, "What in the hell happened?"

The two of them were sitting next to each other on the couch. Jones looked very uncomfortable. Hayes had finally got around to asking the obvious question, and his chief of staff didn't know how to answer it.

Shaking her head and looking at the ground, she replied, "I don't know."

Hayes had met Jones years ago when she worked on his congressional staff. After that, the Ivy League–educated New Yorker had gone to work for CBS and risen through the ranks. Jones was bright, hardworking, and at times a little pushy. If she were a man, she'd be called a hard-ass, but because she wore skirts, she was referred to by some as a real bitch. Jones knew this and didn't let it bother her. As gatekeeper to the president, it worked to her advantage. Every day she received dozens of requests for the president's time. If she were patient and nice with everyone that called, those requests would double within a week. The very definition of her job required that she be blunt and firm. Not enough time. Not enough energy.

"Valerie, you have to have some idea who in the hell that was." Hayes watched her for a response. He got none and expanded his questioning. "What did Russ tell you?" Hayes asked, referring to the chairman of the Democratic National Committee.

"He said the man was a wealthy Arab prince who wanted to make a donation to the DNC."

"A foreigner making a donation to the DNC." Hayes shook his head in anger.

"Russ said it would all be legit."

Hayes frowned. "I thought I told all of you people, 'No funny stuff.' I want everything to be aboveboard." Hayes kept his voice low, but it was obvious he was angry.

Without looking up, Jones replied, "It was a lot of money, and it was going to be legal."

Hayes almost lost it. This was something he had been adamant about since the day he had decided to run for president. The expression on his face told his chief of staff that the amount of money would not make the transgression any easier to take.

Jones realized it had been the wrong thing to say.

"'Sorry' might not be good enough for this one."

Jones looked up with a fair amount of fright. "What are you trying to say?"

"Exactly what I said. 'Sorry' might not be good enough. People have died, Val, and there are a lot of questions that are going to have to be answered." President Hayes stared at her, making sure she truly understood the gravity of the situation.

Across the bunker, near the door, Special Agent Jack Warch was sitting on his bunk, sprawled against the cool concrete wall. The usually rigid Warch had removed his tie and jacket, both of which were neatly folded next to him on the hinged navy-style bunk. The thirty- by twenty-foot room had eighteen sturdy bunks. Two sets of four, one lower and one upper, were bolted along each of the long walls and two more on the wall by the door. The bunks were of the no-frills military style. One side of the bed was attached to the wall by two hinges, and the outer corners were each attached to a three-foot chain that was bolted to the wall. When not being used the bunks could be swung up and out of the way. The floor and the first four feet of the wall were covered by the same plain brown carpet that adorned the floor and walls of the evacuation tunnel. At the opposite end of the bunker there was a small bathroom and kitchenette. In the middle of the room was a square arrangement of two couches and two love seats, all four made of brown vinyl trying to disguise itself as leather. The seamless ceiling and walls were painted an off-white that helped to soften, just slightly, the room's bleak appearance.

The special agent in charge of the presidential detail reached out and picked up his black Motorola encrypted radio. His flesh-toned earpiece and hand mike lay uselessly coiled on the bunk's pillow. Not more than ten minutes after they made it into the bunker the expensive little radio had dropped code—the Secret Service's euphemism for the radio not working. It was not just Warch's radio. All ten agents had looked at each other at the exact same moment, knowing instantly that they were cut off. The terrorists had gotten to the digital encryption system and crashed it, taking all of the radios off-line. Warch had switched to his digital phone, and for five minutes he tried frantically to reestablished contact with the Secret Service's joint operations command. The phone was working, but they weren't answering. Then the line went dead.

They were completely cut off from the outside and could only assume the worst. If the Secret Service had fended off the attack, they would not still be siting in the bunker. With or without communications, his people knew the codes and could simply come and open the door. The worst had to be assumed. They had lost the White House. Warch looked across the bunker at a disheveled President Hayes and his chief of staff. They were sitting on one of the couches talking in whispers. It was time to tell him the truth.

11

AFTER AZIZ'S ELECTRIFYING phone call, chaos had once again broken out in the Pentagon's Joint Chiefs briefing room. To Mitch Rapp's left, his bosses were conferring with the Joint Chiefs, and to his right, Vice President Baxter was holding court with the cabinet. Rapp, having a fairly good idea how most of the people to his left would handle the situation, decided to focus his listening on the politicians to his right. After several minutes, Rapp concluded that no one in Baxter's group knew their head from their ass, and in the process of coming to this conclusion, he also discovered a correlation between their opinions and the conviction with which they stated them. It seemed that the less someone knew, the more forcefully he tried to state his case.

Words like "caution" and "prudence" crept into every sentence, and every time Rapp heard them uttered, he couldn't help but think that these men and women had no idea whom they were dealing with. On more than one occasion, Rapp fought the urge to interject his frank opinion and correct the neophytes to his right. Twice he actually started to come out of his seat, but caught himself in time. Kennedy was right. It was best for him to keep a low profile.

The fragmented conversations continued for several more minutes, and then Vice President Baxter began snapping his fingers and calling for the group's attention. The discussions trickled to a stop, and then Baxter said, "Attorney General Tutwiler has a plan, and I would like everyone to hear her out."

All eyes went from Baxter to the attorney general as she pulled her chair forward. Tutwiler took off her glasses and held them in both hands. "Treasury Secretary Rose has confirmed that this money does in fact exist, and as most of us know, it was frozen by our government when the Shah was overthrown. There is a case to be made that this money is not ours." Tutwiler set her glasses down and centered them on her leather briefing folder. "I strongly believe that as a sign of good faith and willingness to negotiate for the hostages we should release part of the money at nine tomorrow, and in return, we will ask Mr. Aziz to show his good faith and release some of the hostages."

In unison her end of the table turned to see how the idea would be received by the other end, which was anchored by the representatives from the Joint Chiefs, the CIA, and the FBI. Admiral Nelson, the chief of naval operations, was the first to speak.

With his bald head and gaunt face, Nelson said, "I would advise against giving them anything! It will set a horrible precedent! Our policy on terrorism has always been zero tolerance and no negotiation. Zero!" Nelson brought his hand up and formed the number with his thumb and fingers. "The entire world is watching. . . . Now is not the time to reverse our course."

Vice President Baxter looked at his military advisers. He had known this would be their position, but now he needed them on board. He needed to build some consensus. That way if everything blew up, he wouldn't be the only one holding the bag. Baxter decided to play up the compassion factor. "Let me remind everyone that we have hostages in there. American citizens. Yes, the president is safe, but we still have to do our best to get our people out of there alive. These are troops we left behind, and if we have to pay a little money . . . that isn't even ours"—Baxter looked around the room nodding his head—"to get some of them out . . . then that is what we are going to do." The vice president focused his attention on the opposite end of the table, looking each of the military officers in the eye, one at a time. He would call them later individually to shore up support where it was needed.

After finishing his Dale Carnegie personal-eye-contact maneuver, the vice president moved on to his conclusion. "In light of the recent news, this is what we are going to do." Baxter pointed at Director Roach of the FBI. "I want you and your people to take charge of the entire area surrounding the White House. If you need to use any of the Secret Service's people in an advisory role, feel free to do so."

Director Roach leaned forward. "I assume you would like us to draw up plans for rescuing the hostages?"

"Of course, but no action is to be taken unless I say so. If we have to go in, I want to have secured the release of as many hostages as possible beforehand."

Baxter then turned to Attorney General Tutwiler and said, "Marge, please fill us in on how things will proceed tomorrow."

Tutwiler inclined her head forward so she could see all the way down the table. "At nine tomorrow we will call Mr. Aziz and inform him that we are prepared to transfer part of the money into his accounts. This will be fairly easy to do. Secretary Rose tells me the money is in a dozen separate banks, so we will simply transfer the proper amount of money from one of the banks to Iran. The sum will be around a billion dollars. We will tell him we are working on getting the rest of the money, but it would help if, in a sign of good faith, he would release some of the hostages." Tutwiler paused for a moment, distracted by a man halfway down the table who was shaking his head vigorously.

Tutwiler started speaking again but kept her eyes on the man. "I have done quite a bit of research on hostage negotiations and have found that in these situations if you can get the captors to acquiesce to even the smallest request, you have significantly increased your chances for freeing the hostages." Tutwiler stopped speaking as she watched the man shake his head one last time and then drop his face into his hands. The attorney general was not the only one who noticed.

Rapp couldn't take it anymore. Every time Tutwiler uttered a word, he felt as if someone were driving a nail further and further into his temple. As Rapp buried his face in his hands, he said to himself, *This can't be happening. Please tell me this isn't happening. I have put in all of this work, and I'm so close.* Rapp squeezed his head in his hands and thought to himself, *This woman has no idea what the fuck she is talking about.*

At least half of the people at the table were looking back and forth between Marge Tutwiler and the unknown dark-haired man who seemed to be in danger of suffering an aneurysm before their very eyes. That the others were watching also did not go unnoticed by the attorney general. Tutwiler cleared her throat loudly and asked, "Excuse me, is everything all right?"

Rapp didn't hear her at first, and then he felt Irene Kennedy touch his arm. Slowly, Rapp let his hands fall from his face and looked up, to find the attention of everyone at the table on him. When Tutwiler repeated her question, Rapp looked at her and said, "I'm sorry, I didn't hear you."

In an extremely impatient tone, the attorney general asked, "Is there something you would like to add, or should we get you some aspirin for your . . . headache?"

Rapp turned briefly to his bosses, who gave him no signal one way or another, and then directed his attention back to the attorney general. As he registered the condescending expression on her face, something told him now was not the time to be meek. This was it. For the first time in this shitty journey, he knew where Rafique Aziz was and where he would be for the immediate future. Cover or no cover, there was a good chance this was going to be the last battle, and there was no sense in going home with a lot of unused ammo.

Rapp straightened himself and said, "I would most definitely like to add something. . . . Actually I would like to add a lot." He paused briefly and then said, "First of all, if you only give him part of the money and ask him to release some of the hostages, he will blow his screwy lid. He will take one or more of the hostages right to the window, so all of the cameras can watch, and he will kill them. He will blow their heads off on national TV."

Tutwiler threw her head back and, with a disapproving look, said, "Is that right, Mr. . . ."

"Mr. Kruse."

"And what exactly is your expertise in regards to negotiating with terrorists, Mr. Kruse?"

Rapp found the question so ridiculous, he shook his head and laughingly replied, "None."

Tutwiler, not used to being treated in such a manner, turned to Baxter and said in a loud enough voice for half of the room to hear, "What is this man doing here?"

Her arrogant question drove Rapp up and out of his chair with Irene Kennedy's hand gripping at his forearm. Rapp pried his boss's fingers loose, saying firmly, "I've put way too much into this."

Rapp began walking toward the podium. His suit, white shirt, and tie did a decent job of helping him blend in, but to anyone who cared to notice, it wasn't hard to figure out he was more than an analyst. When Rapp reached the podium, he repeated Tutwiler's question to the group. "What is this man doing here?" Rapp stared up at the ceiling as if mulling the question over. "You know, I've asked myself that question a lot of times over the last decade, and I'm afraid I can't answer it for you." Rapp turned back toward Tutwiler, a look of feigned wonderment on his face. "But I can answer your other question . . . the one about negotiating with terrorists." Rapp paused and then said casually, "I don't negotiate with terrorists, Ms. Tutwiler. I kill them." Grabbing the podium, Rapp looked down the length of the table and said, "I hunt them down, and I kill them."

Tutwiler sat up a little straighter, attempting to appear unfazed by the unusual admission. Trying to gain some composure, she asked the first question that came to mind. "Who do you work for, Mr. Kruse?"

"I'm afraid that's on a need-to-know basis, ma'am." With his smart-ass grin, Rapp gave the standard spycraft reply, "And you don't need to know."

"Well, Mr. Kruse, if we decide it's time to kill these terrorists," said Tutwiler, repeating his words in a mocking tone, "we will make sure we give you a call. Until then, we would all appreciate it if you would take a seat so we can get on with the business at hand."

Tutwiler's smugness was really starting to irk Rapp, and his temper was dangerously close to reaching a level that he couldn't control. He studied her for a second and then asked, "Ms. Tutwiler, have you ever been to Beirut?" Rapp waited a moment for her response and then said, "I didn't think so. Just in case you were wondering, that's where Rafique Aziz is from. How about Iran? Have you ever been there?" Rapp gave her less than a second to answer. "I didn't think so. I was in Iran last night," Rapp added casually. "Actually, I spent most of the last week there. And since we don't have an embassy in Iran, you can probably figure out that I wasn't on official government business. Do you by chance speak Farsi or any Arabic dialects?" Rapp shook his head, answering the question for her. "I didn't think so. How about the Muslim faith, the jihad? Are you up to speed on the customs of Rafique Aziz and his people?"

"What's your point, Mr. Kruse?" asked a defiant Tutwiler.

Rapp looked down the long table at the smug attorney general and growled in a voice that was barely beneath a shout, "The point is, Ms. Tutwiler, you don't have the slightest clue who you're dealing with!" Rapp pointed at her with each word. "While you were running around on the talk-show circuit criticizing law-enforcement officers, who have done more in one week to stop crime than you will do in your entire academic-theory-laden lifetime, I was crawling around in the gutter of every hellhole in the Middle East trying to find Rafique Aziz." Rapp watched Tutwiler fold her arms tightly across her chest and roll her eyes.

The last gesture did it, and in a voice intended to shake up more than just the attorney general, he yelled, "Hey, lady, this isn't a game! This isn't about who has the most master's degrees or the biggest job title. People have died, and before this thing is over, more people are going to die!" Rapp turned his face to the side, showing the pinkish mark that angled downward across his bronzed face. "Do you see this scar? Let me clue you in on a little secret. It isn't a paper cut. It was given to me, in person, by none other than Rafique Aziz. So when I offer my opinion about a man who you have never met . . . who you know nothing about, you should sit up and listen." Rapp tightly gripped both sides of the podium. "The man we are talking about here isn't a bank robber, and he sure as hell isn't some hack like David Koresh. He's a religious zealot who also happens to be a very highly trained and intelligent killer. Your little plan for tomorrow might stand a chance if we were dealing with some pissed-off employee who had taken over a bank or a post office, but this is the big leagues." Rapp zeroed in on Tutwiler. "Aziz isn't some two-bit criminal. When you jerk his chain tomorrow, by only giving him part of what he's asked for, he's going to take a bite out of your ass, and he's going to bite hard." Rapp leaned forward, elbows bent, poised over the podium, looking for even the smallest sign that he was getting through to the politicians at the other end of the room.

The expressions on their faces said it all. Everything he said was falling on deaf ears. The men and women at the opposite end of the table were looking at him as if he were speaking a foreign language. Rapp couldn't believe it. Rafique Aziz was *his* cause. It had become *his* personal crusade; he'd devoted a full third of *his* life to hunting this one man. And that was only the start. It had grown to be much more than that as the death toll mounted. It had turned into a race to stop him from killing again. There was no one in this room, and probably no one in the world, who understood the mind of Rafique Aziz better than Rapp, and after all that he had given, how was he being repaid at the exact moment when they should be listening to him most? He was being regarded as if he were some crazed idiot.

Rapp bit down hard on his tongue and fought back the urge to scream at the top of his lungs. At that moment he realized he had one course of action. If the smug Marge Tutwiler wanted to put her little theories to work and these idiots wanted to follow her, then so be it. Tutwiler had given herself more than enough rope to hang herself with, and Rapp knew that as sure as the sun would rise tomorrow, she would be swinging from the gallows in the morning.

Rapp shook his head and said, "I've given you fair warning." As he started for the exit, he yelled over his shoulder, "Call me after you're done playing games, and I'll come in and clean up your mess." With that Rapp opened the door and disappeared into the hallway.

General Flood watched Rapp leave the room and then swiveled his chair away from the table, beckoning one of his aides over with a discreet wave of his forefinger. When the general had asked Director Stansfield to bring the young operative, he had not envisioned the scene that had just unfolded, but he was happy somebody had stepped up to the plate. An Air Force captain bent to the general's ear and Flood whispered, "Please detain Mr. Kruse for me, and have him wait in my office until we're finished."

ALL OF THE hostages, with the exception of the Secret Service agents, had been moved to the White House mess. The tables and chairs that normally occupied the room had been thrown into the main hallway that led out onto West Executive Drive and now formed a tangled blockade. The hostages were seated on the floor, bunched in a tight circle like corralled cattle. Anywhere from one to four terrorists were watching over them at a time, and they came and went with no apparent pattern, often stopping to kick and scream at the hostages.

Anna Rielly was relieved as she sat back down on the blue carpet of the White House mess. She had made it to the bathroom and back without being hit or kicked. The woman in front of her had been slapped for daring to look up at one of the terrorists. Rielly had kept her eyes down with only one exception. One of the terrorists had followed her into the stall and to her complete humiliation had watched her go to the bathroom. Rielly was frightened by the expression on his face. He had stared at her intently while she relieved herself, and when she stood to pull her pants up, his eyes had followed her every move. The thought caused Rielly to clutch the neck of her blouse and shudder.

After the World Trade Center bombing Rielly had done a piece on Islamic terrorism for the NBC affiliate in Chicago. That two-week project had given her enough insight into the minds of radical Islamic fundamentalists to know that they were crazed in a way that was difficult even for the daughter of a Chicago cop to understand. In her captors' minds women were objects to be owned or discarded, no different than a piece of livestock. Women who were not "of the faith" were deemed impure and evil, another way of saying, "fair game."

What a first day on the job, she thought to herself. Rielly had wanted to be in the thick of real news, and now she was an actual part of one of the biggest stories in decades. She brushed a strand of her brown hair behind her ear, and with her head tilted toward the ground, she looked up toward one of the guards. The guard turned in her direction, and she quickly averted her eyes. *Don't make eye contact,* she told herself. *Look submissive and try to blend in.*

Anna Rielly was blessed with a healthy sense of street smarts. Having grown up in the heart of Chicago, she had been exposed to the seedier side of life at an early age. Her mother, a social worker, and her father, a Chicago cop, made sure their five sons and only daughter understood that life was much different from what was shown on TV. All of this exposure had given the young woman a very strong survival instinct. Several years earlier in Chicago it had saved her life, and here in Washington she was hoping to repeat the performance.

Rielly had already removed all of her jewelry and as much of her makeup as possible. She knew that the less attention she attracted to herself the better. There had already been two men who had had their noses split wide open, and there was another woman who had been slapped so hard on the side of her head that her ear had started to bleed. Rielly kept repeating to herself, "Just keep a low profile, and you might make it out of here alive."

Less could be said for Rielly's new office partner, Stone Alexander, who was sitting at her side. He hadn't wandered more than several feet from her since the onset of the attack. Not that he was protecting her—if anything, it was Rielly who was protecting him. Alexander leaned closer to her and asked, "How long are they going to make us sit here?"

Without moving her lips, Rielly whispered, "The only thing I know is, if one of these guys sees you talking, he's going to come over here and crack his rifle over your surgically altered nose. . . . So for the last time, shut up."

Alexander shrank away and dropped his head onto his folded hands. He had already cried twice. *Pathetic,* Rielly thought to herself. Her father had always said people show their true colors in a crisis, and Alexander had shown his. It was yellow.

Out of the corner of her eye, she saw someone new enter the room, and she glanced up at the man, careful to keep her head down. Rielly had not seen this one before. He looked different from the others. He was wearing the same green fatigues, but his hair was well styled and he lacked any facial hair. Rielly noted that the man was actually quite handsome.

That was when it hit her. It was the same man that Russ Piper had introduced her to. A Prince somebody or other. *Oh, my God,* Rielly thought. *Where is Russ?* With her head down Rielly scanned the mass of people, looking for her parents' friend. Piper was nowhere in sight, and she could not remember seeing him since this morning.

Rielly scrutinized the man again. This man was the leader. It was obvious by how the others spoke to him and looked at him. When this supposed prince had entered the room, the other three terrorists had done everything short of snapping off salutes. The bald terrorist, who Rielly had originally thought was the leader, entered the room and approached the prince. He began whispering in the leader's ear, and Rielly instantly noticed a change in the prince's eyes.

RAFIQUE AZIZ STOOD with a demeanor that looked to be teetering between confidence and rage. As Muammar Bengazi whispered in his ear, the scales began to tilt in favor of rage. Aziz had known this moment would come. The fact that he had already played it out in his mind a hundred times would not take away from his performance.

Bengazi finished relaying to his friend the information that had been requested. Without hesitation, Aziz yelled, "Where?"

Bengazi pointed to a hostage sitting near the edge of the group, and then followed Aziz as he walked briskly toward the man. Aziz stopped five feet from a man in a white shirt and loosened tie. Pointing to the man, Aziz asked Bengazi, "Him?" Bengazi nodded.

Aziz looked down at the man and commanded, "Stand!" The man did as he was told and rose to a height several inches taller than Aziz. The man looked to be in his early to mid fifties with short brown-and-gray hair. In a voice loud enough to make sure everyone heard him, Aziz asked, "You have a request?"

"Ah," the man started out somewhat nervously, "we have a pregnant woman in the group, and several other people who are older. I had asked . . . ah . . . your man"—the White House employee pointed to Bengazi—"if we could get some blankets and food for . . ."

Aziz cut him off with a loud, "No!"

The man took a quarter of a step back. "But"—he gestured with an open hand to a woman on the floor—"she's pregnant."

Aziz looked at the bulging stomach of the woman on the floor. She was lying on her back with her head resting on an older woman's lap. Without taking his eyes of the expectant mother, Aziz slid his right hand to his thigh and found the grip of his gun. He pulled the pistol from his holster and turned to the man standing before him. Without saying a word, without the slightest expression on his face, Aziz raised the gun to the man's forehead and, from a distance of one foot, pulled the trigger.

The loud crack of the gunshot caused everyone in the room to jerk involuntarily. Before the report of the gun had died, the man was propelled backward and into the huddled mass of hostages—his blood, brain matter, and skull fragments showering a half dozen shocked individuals.

As the room erupted, Rafique Aziz turned and marched for the exit. His cold expression masked a perverse satisfaction in completing another chapter in his plan. Aziz left the room to the noise of his men screaming at the hostages. As he walked down the hall to the Situation Room, a smile creased his lips. When the time came, the hostages would give him no trouble. From this point forward, they would be as docile as a flock of lambs.

12

AS THE CHAIRMAN of the Joint Chiefs, General Flood was the highest-ranking officer in the U.S. military. The size and opulence of his office, located just down the hall from the Joint Chiefs briefing room, was fitting for a man who wielded such power. The walls were covered with photos and plaques that documented his rise through the ranks of the Army. In typical military fashion the show was arranged in order—starting in one corner with a photo of a young plebe at West Point and then documenting his ascension through the ranks until he reached his current and final post.

The room was set up in thirds. At the far end was a rectangular conference table that seated twenty. In the middle of the room was the general's substantial Thomas Aquinas–style desk. The expansive wood surface curved so the desk literally wrapped its way around the general's healthy midsection. This allowed Flood to swivel in his chair and go from project to project without having to exert too much effort.

The last third of the office was dominated by an assortment of couches and chairs arranged around a long glass coffee table. Mitch Rapp sat in one of the chairs facing the office's entrance. General Flood's aide had escorted him into the room almost thirty minutes earlier. Since then, Rapp had been eyeing an expensive bottle of Booker's small-batch bourbon that was sitting behind the general's well-stocked wet bar on his right. Rapp was tired and edgy. He hadn't worked out in almost a week, and since he was used to putting in at least two hours a day, six days a week, his body was rebelling. The sleep he had gotten had been minimal, the food had been awful, and now it had all come down to this. His expertise was being called into question by someone who had been teaching law students for the last decade while he had been putting his ass on the line. Rapp had never felt such frustration. Aziz was right across the river, sitting in the White House, and there was nothing he could do about it but sit and wait.

After another ten minutes or so, General Flood returned to his office. He was accompanied by Rapp's two bosses and General Campbell, the commander of the Joint Special Operations Command. Rapp stood to meet them and tried to get a read from Director Stansfield as to whether he was going to have him taken out and shot. Rapp quickly realized it was a futile effort. Trying to gauge Thomas Stansfield was like trying to read the expression of the Sphinx. The longer you observed the more you thought you saw. But in reality you saw nothing. In the case of the Sphinx, it was because there was nothing, but in the case of Thomas Stansfield, there was a lot.

General Flood began to undo the gold buttons of his military blouse almost immediately. "Well, Mr. Kruse, you sure as hell caught a lot of people's attention in there." Flood pulled his jacket off and threw it over the back of one of the chairs.

"I'm sorry if I . . ."

Flood cut him off with a flip of the wrist. "No need for apologies. It was exactly what they needed." The general continued for the bar. "Who needs a drink? I sure as hell do." Flood turned over a glass tumbler and grabbed a bottle of twenty-five-year-old McCallan single-malt scotch. The general poured in three fingers' worth and then added a handful of ice. After swirling the cubes around in the glass, he brought the drink to his lips and took a long pull. He closed his eyes and set the drink down, savoring the taste. After a moment of silence, he opened his eyes and exhaled, a look of satisfaction on his face. "Irene, what would you like?"

Kennedy was not a big drinker, but from past experience she knew that with the general it was not important that you drank your drink; it was just important that you had one in front of you. "Vodka, please."

Flood knew what Stansfield and Campbell drank and had already begun pouring their drinks. "Mr. Rapp—" Flood looked up. "I assume it's all right that I call you by your real name." Rapp nodded. "What's your poison?"

"Bourbon. Booker's, please."

Flood glanced up from his bartending duties with a raised eyebrow. Rapp wasn't sure if the general was impressed or thought him crazy. Flood finished with the drinks and brought them over to the group, saying, "As I was saying, Mr. Rapp, you really got their attention in there. Dallas King, Vice President Baxter's chief of staff, came up to me after the meeting and wanted to know who in the hell you were." Flood handed Kennedy her drink. "Here you go, Irene."

"And . . ." asked Rapp.

"And"—Flood snorted—"I told him he needed to get a higher security clearance if he wanted to discuss such matters. I could hardly tell him you were an analyst after your little performance." Flood finished delivering the drinks and took the chair opposite Rapp at the long end of the coffee table. Kennedy and Stansfield were seated on one couch, and General Campbell faced them on the other.

Rapp looked to his bosses and said, "I'm sorry if I was out of line, but I've come too far to watch a bunch of hacks screw this up."

The director of the CIA held his glass of scotch with both hands. After a moment, he nodded his head slowly and said, "I would have preferred you to have kept quiet, but you did say some things that needed to be said." Stansfield took a sip and then added, "And in a way that none of us could have."

General Flood nodded in agreement. "And more importantly, you have made it very clear what's at stake. Right now Baxter has put all of his chips behind Marge Tutwiler, and thanks to your blunt critique of her game plan, her position is fully exposed. If her strategy backfires tomorrow, Baxter will drop her in a heartbeat, and he will have to listen to us."

Rapp sat back. "So we sit around and wait for this to blow up in Tutwiler's face?"

"Nope." General Flood shook his head. "I never like to sit around and wait. There are always preparations to be made before one goes into battle." Flood shifted his ample frame and placed his drink on the end table to his right. "The four of us here"—Flood motioned to Kennedy, Stansfield, Campbell, and himself—"are in agreement that in all likelihood there is only one way this crisis will be resolved. We will have to retake the building by force. Aziz will string Vice President Baxter along until we're in an untenable situation . . . a situation where we cannot and should not meet his demands. When that time comes, we have to be in a position to move, and as I said before, I don't like sending men into battle unless I'm prepared."

Flood paused and took a sip of scotch. "Now, you people are in the intelligence-gathering business"—Flood gestured to Stansfield, Kennedy, and Rapp—"so I don't have to explain to you that a battle plan without good intel is iffy at best. So the bottom line is we need real, hard intel, and we need it now."

Leaning back, Flood crossed his legs. "Someone has to get inside." Looking at Rapp, Flood added, "We need a volunteer. Someone who is willing to take some risks. Someone who understands Rafique Aziz. Someone with unique talents such as yours, Mr. Rapp."

The general's words felt like warm sunshine after a cold swim. Rapp couldn't keep himself from grinning. With confidence, he replied, "I'm your man."

Flood smiled. "I thought so." Then turning to the director of the CIA, Flood asked, "Thomas?"

Stansfield thought about it for a second and nodded. "I think it's a good idea, but it might be tough getting approval for it. The FBI won't like it."

"I could give a damn," growled the general. "This is war, and in war we fight by a different set of rules. Now, I like Brian Roach," said Flood, referring to the director of the FBI, "but he needs to understand that we cannot afford to play by one set of rules while Aziz plays by another. We need our A-Team on the front line, not the junior varsity, and"—Flood pointed to Rapp—"Mitch here is the A-Team." Flood took a sip of his drink, and then leaning forward, he placed his big hand on Stansfield's shoulder. "You find a way to get him in, and I'll make sure we get approval."

Stansfield thought a moment and then nodded his head in agreement.

General Flood withdrew his hand and sat back. Looking around the room, he asked, "Now, does anybody have any ideas on how we're going to get him in?"

After a while Stansfield said, "No, but I have a good idea where to start."

THE SUN WAS setting as Vice President Baxter left the Pentagon. Attorney General Tutwiler had gone back to the Hoover Building with FBI Director Roach and Special Agent McMahon. Baxter sat alone with Dallas King in the backseat of the armor-plated limousine. The vice president looked languidly out the window as Dallas King babbled on about what should be covered when Baxter addressed the nation—a move they had decided was both necessary and an opportunity that couldn't be missed. Baxter would be guaranteed the largest audience in the history of presidential addresses. The only question for King right now was whether they should do a scripted address, with Baxter reading from a TelePrompTer, or hold a more natural and impromptu press conference.

Baxter was only half listening to his subordinate. King was rambling on about focus groups and polling data while the vice president's mind kept drifting back to the dark-featured gentleman from the CIA. The terrorism specialist, Baxter reminded himself.

Baxter held his hand up and motioned for King to be silent. The vice president let his well-manicured fingers fall to his knee while he struggled to pin down what exactly it was that was bothering him. After a moment he pursed his lips and said, "Call our contacts over at the National Security Agency and see what you can find out about that Mr. Kruse fellow."

"I'm already on it," replied King as he typed a note into his palm-top computer.

"Find out what he really does for the CIA." Baxter looked out the window again. "If he's right, and we have to take the building back by force . . ." Baxter shook his head.

King looked up from his computer and said, "We will lose hostages, and the American people will never vote for a trigger-happy presidential candidate that ordered the death of seventy-six Americans."

Baxter added an eye roll to his head shaking. "This no longer appears to be the opportunity that you originally thought."

King closed his palm-top and placed it in the breast pocket of his suit coat. "I never said it was going to be easy. With this much on the line, it's never easy. The trick, as always, will be to navigate our way through the minefield."

"There may not be a path through this particular one," Baxter sighed.

"I haven't come across a minefield yet that I couldn't get through." King flashed his confident grin. "Your job is to sit back and let everybody else look for the mines. Tomorrow, for instance, we let Marge take the lead on this negotiation angle. If it works, we're all one big happy family. If it doesn't, she takes the fall all on her own."

"What if we have to storm the place and we lose thirty . . . forty . . . hell, maybe all of the hostages?" Baxter pointed at himself. "I'm the only one who can order that. You said it yourself. The American people will never vote for a president who has the slaughter of that many hostages hanging around his neck." Baxter shook his head. "Shit, I just thought of something else. What if I order the assault and it doesn't work? What if the nation sits down for dinner and they're treated to footage of FBI agents getting killed while trying to storm the White House? My career would be over, and yours too." Baxter's defeatist head-shaking continued, and with gritted teeth, he added, "We're screwed almost any way you look at this thing."

"Not true," replied King. "If we pull this off, you'll be a hero." King pointed at his boss. "You'll be the next president of the United States of America. We just need to play our cards very carefully, and we need to start with Director Tracy. We miscalculated how he would handle your public reprimand. We can't have him holding a press conference tomorrow. If he reads the comments you made when you were campaigning, it would make us look like shit. I think I should go see him. Offer him the olive branch and tell him we want him to stay in charge of the Secret Service and help the FBI. I'll tell him it was Tutwiler's idea to can him, and you went along with it because you were so upset about the attack. I'll tell him you weren't thinking clearly, and that you're grateful for the service he has given this country . . . yada . . . yada . . . yada. You know the gig. I'll stroke him."

Baxter thought about it for a second and with a tired sigh said, "Go ahead. Do whatever it takes to keep him quiet."

13

THE WHITE HOUSE was silent as the clock approached midnight. Aziz left the Situation Room and walked down the hall to Horsepower. The door was open, and Aziz entered without knocking. Sitting in a swivel chair, Bengazi was keeping an eye on a bank of black-and-white security monitors. The monitors showed different areas of the grounds around the White House and shots of all the main entrances. Normally the system also kept an eye on areas within the White House, but Bengazi had disabled the cameras for fear that the FBI might find some way to pirate the images and spy on them.

Aziz placed his hand on the back of the chair and asked, "How does everything look?"

"Nice and quiet."

"Good. Have you been getting sleep?"

"Yes."

"How about the men?"

"They are doing fine."

"And the hostages?"

"Asleep."

As Aziz looked at the monitors, the walkie-talkie on his hip squawked and his name barked forth.

Bringing it to his mouth, he said, "Yes."

"Rafique, I have made progress. I think you should come see."

"I'll be right down." Aziz had been not-so-patiently waiting for this update. Having succeeded beyond all of his people's wildest dreams, he was still not content, and would not be until he wrestled the cowardly president from his bunker. He held the White House hostage and the entire government of the United States had come to a grinding halt, but that wasn't enough.

Aziz reached the third basement and headed for the bunker. When he rounded the corner, he found his man sitting on a toolbox, drenched in sweat, and smoking a cigarette. The short, fat man looked up with a large grin, his nicotine-stained teeth topped by a pointy nose and a graying mustache. Goggles hung from his neck and a pair of orange ear protectors were perched atop his head, giving him the appearance of a plump rodent.

The man placed his large and thick horn-rimmed glasses back on his face and waved toward the outer door to the bunker with a smile. "Open sesame."

Aziz stepped forward and pushed on the steel door. It swung inward, revealing a room and a shiny vaultlike door at the other end. A rush of emotion swept over him as he thought of the president and his body-guards sitting on the other side of the door, thinking they were safe. Aziz walked slowly across the concrete floor and stopped just in front of the vault door. Extending his hand, he placed his palm flat on the smooth sur-face. Clenching his fist, Aziz hammered on the door twice. No sound re-verberated. Spinning away from the door, Aziz looked at the last minute addition to his cause. The frumpy man before him was a gift from Aziz's newest benefactor. A man who had a very personal stake in how Aziz's mission turned out. The slovenly safecracker standing in the doorway had come complete with his own tools and unique talent. As it was explained to Aziz, the door that was installed on the president's bunker was of the same type that the U.S. military used for all of their command-and-control bunkers, and was designed to withstand large blasts, not drills and acetylene blowtorches.

Aziz looked at the man and asked, "How long will this door take?"

The safecracker exhaled a cloud of smoke and said, "If I push it and risk burning out one of the drills, I could probably have it open in thirty hours."

"What happens if you lose one of the drills?"

"Then we are in trouble." The little thief shrugged. "It could end up taking three to four days."

"And if you play it safe?"

"I can have it open in forty-eight hours."

Aziz put his hands in a prayerful grip and bounced them off his chin twice. "Forty-eight hours will suffice." And with a wave of his finger, he cautioned, "But no longer than that." Aziz walked past him and slapped him on the shoulder. "Good work, Mustafa." Aziz left the room, leaving his little thief to retrieve the crown jewel. As he walked down the hallway, he thought, *All I have to do is keep them at bay for two more days.*

THE LIGHTS WERE off in the bunker, and everyone was trying to get some sleep. Warch was lying on the bunk closest to the door. The Secret Service agent was wide-awake. He could hear President Hayes snoring at the far end of the room, and every minute or so squeaking springs could be heard as someone turned on the narrow beds.

Warch wondered how his wife and children were doing. His family would be afraid, but that couldn't be helped. Being married to someone who was trained to throw himself in front of an oncoming bullet was a little nerve-racking, but Sara was strong. She would have the kids to keep her busy, and her parents were in Baltimore. The Service would tell her and the kids that he was all right.

Warch's thoughts turned to the other wives and husbands that weren't as fortunate. Over and over again, Warch had replayed the frantic radio traffic that had barked out over his earpiece while they rushed the president to the bunker. "Agents down! Agents down!" And then there was the explosion and the machine gun fire. And now, over twelve hours later—nothing. Everything added up to one conclusion: Aziz and his terrorists were in control of the White House. Warch ran down a list of the faces and names of his agents who were on the day shift. He couldn't help but wonder which ones had made it out alive and which ones were dead.

Still, despite what was undoubtedly the worst day in the history of the Secret Service, they had at least saved the president from the talons of Aziz. Warch savored that one accomplishment as he felt sleep coming on. He rolled toward the wall and let out a yawn. When most of the air was expelled from his lungs, he froze.

Warch had not heard the noise before; he was sure of that. Craning his neck toward the door, he tried to listen. It was a clanging noise, metal on metal. There were several more clanging noises and then a low whine, almost like an electric razor. Warch listened for another moment and then sprang out of bed, throwing his blankets to the side. The concrete floor felt cold to his feet. In his white T-shirt and boxers he knelt on the floor and pressed his left ear to the door, and then it hit him. It was a drill. They were drilling through the vault door, which meant they had already broken through the outer door. Warch's palms became sweaty on the cool metallic surface, and he swore out loud. Standing, he turned on the light and said to the room at large, "Wake up, people. We have trouble."

14

A FAINT METHODICAL beep could be heard in the distance. Rapp felt as if he were swimming upward for it, out of a deep black hole. The noise became more pronounced with each kick and downward stroke. It was getting lighter; he was nearing the surface.

Suddenly, Rapp sat up in bed, his thick black hair sticking out in Medusa-like fashion. It took him a second to realize he'd been dreaming. It was the same damn dream he'd been having for as long as he could remember. Drowning, it was always drowning. He was always swimming for the surface, gasping for air.

Several shakes of the head later, Rapp realized where he was. The faint gray light of early morning was spilling through his bedroom windows. He turned to make out the red digital numerals of his alarm clock. There was a four followed by another and then a five.

God, it was nice to be home, Rapp thought. Without looking, he reached over and swatted the snooze button. Then he flopped backward onto the crisp white sheets and stretched out, kicking the blanket to the side. Not quite ready to get out of bed, he allowed his mind to drift. Outside the bedroom window, he could hear the gentle waves of the Chesapeake lapping against the rocky shore. They were calling his name, tugging at him to get out of bed. Rapp turned diagonally across the queen-size bed and stretched his arms way above his head, letting out a drawn-out yawn.

He had forced himself to go home and sleep after a meeting at Director Tracy's house. There was nothing else to do. Dr. Hornig had promised a full report on the results of her interrogation with Fara Harut in the morning, and until then it was a waiting game—something Rapp wasn't very good at.

Now, as he rolled onto his side, he suddenly remembered the events of the day before and of the little crisis that was taking place thirty-some miles to the west. A small voice in the back of his head screamed something, and Rapp was on his feet instantly. Naked, he walked across the hardwood floor of his bedroom and stopped in front of a set of French doors. They were open, and through the screens he could now hear birdsongs filling the still morning air. Across the bay, on the treelined horizon, the sky was brightening. The sun was coming up over the Atlantic, and a memorable day was about to begin, whether he liked it or not.

The lapping water continued to call his name, and with more enthusiasm than any sane person would have had, Rapp turned and headed across the worn and creaky wood floor of his beach house. Once he'd finished negotiating the precipitous staircase that led down to the main floor, he walked to the kitchen and then the mud room. Hanging on a brass hook by the backdoor was a faded, salt-stained blue swimsuit that looked as old as its owner.

Rapp put the worn trunks on, grabbed his goggles and a towel, and headed out the backdoor. The thermometer on the deck railing told him it was a comfortable sixty-two degrees. Just cool enough to wake him up, but not so cold as to dash his enthusiasm. With several shakes of his arms, he continued across the brand-new deck to the stairs that led down to the water. Rapp had bought the house the previous year, and his only home improvement to date was to tear down the rotted wood deck and stairs and replace them. After a thirty-foot descent, he put on his goggles and picked up the pace. Rapp ran across the long, flat section of dock that jutted out into the water. On the right was a twenty-four-foot Boston Whaler, and at the end of the dock was a bench that sat atop an eight-foot section that turned at a ninety-degree angle to the left. By the time Rapp reached the bench, he was at a full jog. Without breaking stride, he tossed the towel onto the bench and dove into the salty water.

He found his rhythm within six or seven strokes and settled in for the one-mile swim up the coast. Rapp no longer competed professionally, but just three years earlier he had been one of the world's top-ranked triathletes. In the Mount Everest of triathlon competitions, the Ironman in Hawaii, Rapp had posted three top-five finishes and a first place. But his work with the CIA had picked up considerably in the last five years, and the hectic and unpredictable schedule had forced him to give up competition.

Rapp returned to the dock in front of his house at twenty to six feeling fresh and loose. After toweling off, he made it back up to the house and into the shower. Fifteen minutes later he was shaved, dressed, and out the door, with a cup of piping hot coffee in his hand. Rapp slid behind the wheel of his new black Volvo sedan and eased it out of the narrow garage. He took it slow as he drove down his crumbling asphalt driveway. That was another project he would have to tackle before winter came. When he reached a sturdier surface, he increased speed and began to enjoy the performance of the new sedan. It felt good to be back in civilization.

Several minutes later he was on Route 50 and on his way to a meeting at Langley. Dr. Hornig was to give a briefing at seven A.M. on everything she had learned from her session with Fara Harut. Rapp was not overly excited about sharing breakfast with Dr. Strangelove, but considering the information she would provide, he was willing to bite the bullet.

Twenty-two minutes later, Rapp caught the Beltway and took it around the northern part of D.C. Traffic was picking up, but at this early hour it still moved along at a brisk ten miles per hour over the posted speed limit. Fifteen minutes after reaching the Beltway, Rapp pulled through the first security checkpoint at Langley and parked his car. After passing through the main security checkpoint of the old building, Rapp took the elevator to Director Stansfield's office on the seventh floor.

Stansfield's administrative assistant reported his arrival over her headset, and a moment later Irene Kennedy appeared. Kennedy escorted Rapp into the director's inner sanctum, where the man himself was seated behind his large desk, a pair of bifocals perched at the edge of his nose, his attention focused on an open file.

Stansfield took another moment to finish and then closed the file. Before standing, he grabbed a stack of documents, opened one of the drawers behind his desk, inserted them, closed the door, and locked it with a key.

Stansfield left his suit coat hanging on the coatrack and came around the desk, pulling up his suit pants another notch. "Good morning, Mitch. I hope you got some sleep last night."

"I did, sir. And you?"

Stansfield placed his fragile hand on Rapp's shoulder. The DCI was almost a full head shorter than Rapp. "When you get to my age, Mitch, sleep becomes a very elusive thing." Stansfield turned his young specialist away from his desk and started walking him across the office. "I've set up a meeting for you this morning, but we'll talk about that later. Dr. Hornig is waiting for us, and I'd like to hear what she's found out before we get into anything else."

As Rapp followed Stansfield and Kennedy through a door and into a windowless conference room, he wondered who his mystery meeting was with. Dr. Hornig was already seated on one side of the table and was looking over her own handwritten notes. Stansfield took his seat at the head of the table, and Rapp and Kennedy sat across from Hornig. Rapp noticed she was wearing the same clothes as the day before. It appeared as though she had not slept.

Taking off her black horn-rimmed glasses, Hornig set them on top of her notes and rubbed her eyes, saying, "We have a lot of information. An incredible amount, really." She lowered her hands and shook her head. "It's going to take months to sort through all of it. But having said that, I know you are more interested in information involving Mr. Aziz and the current White House crisis."

Hornig looked down at her notes. "I apologize for the lack of summaries and transcripts, but I was working on Mr. Harut right up until I left for this meeting."

"No explanation needed, Dr. Hornig," stated Stansfield.

"To start with"—Hornig grabbed a piece of paper—"I have the names of the other ten terrorists who are with Mr. Aziz at the White House. It was very difficult to get this information out of him." Hornig handed Stansfield the sheet.

The DCI looked at the yellow piece of paper for no more than five seconds and then handed the sheet to Irene Kennedy, who studied it with Mitch Rapp looking over her shoulder. Stansfield gave them about ten seconds and asked, "Irene?"

Kennedy looked up and brushed a stand of brown hair back behind her ear. "This will be a big help. Off the top of my head, I know about half of them. I can run the rest through our data banks, and any of the ones that we don't get a profile on, we can ask MI-Six or Mossad."

"Good. I want full traces and profiles prepared on each and every one of them as soon as possible." Stansfield turned back to Hornig. "Now, what do we know about the demands?"

Hornig looked down at her notes and flipped through several pages. "Mr. Harut knew in detail about the first demand, involving the return of the frozen assets to Iran. We can infer, since Mitch took him before those demands were made public, that he has intimate knowledge of what Mr. Aziz is going to ask for—up to a point, that is."

Rapp ignored the first part of Hornig's comment—the part involving the rookie detective work—and asked, "What does 'up to a point' mean?"

"I'll get to that in a minute," replied Hornig. "His second demand involves the lifting of all UN sanctions against Iraq." Hornig looked at her audience to gauge any reaction, and then continued. "The third demand involves the U.S. recognizing a free and sovereign Palestinian state."

With a furrowed brow, Rapp asked, "Where?"

Hornig cleared her throat and said, "The West Bank and the Gaza Strip."

Rapp set his coffee down. "The Israelis are going to shit their pants."

"I would concur." Stansfield looked to Hornig. "What else?"

"There's one more demand . . . one final demand, but Mr. Harut doesn't know what it is."

Rapp tilted his head skeptically. "Come again?"

"I really don't think he knows," replied Hornig a touch defensively. "I spent almost two full hours delving into this specific subject. I pushed as hard as I felt I could."

"Maybe you need to push harder," stated Rapp.

Hornig leaned back slightly and folded her arms. "I plan on it. Just as soon as Mr. Harut gets some rest."

"As soon as you both get some rest," interjected Stansfield. "I don't want you burned out, Dr. Hornig."

Hornig was slightly frustrated by all of the unsolicited advice. She didn't tell them how to do their jobs, and she'd appreciate it if they would return the courtesy.

Stansfield, oblivious to Hornig's issues, turned his attention to Kennedy. "Any thoughts on what the final demand might be?"

Kennedy stared off into space for a moment and then said, "A few, but I'd like to do a little research before I come to any conclusions."

Looking at one of his most trusted advisers, Stansfield thought of pressing for more information and then decided it was better to let Kennedy develop her theories in time. With some of his people he had to engage them in a game of mental gymnastics to get the best out of them; with Kennedy she was best left alone. Stansfield turned his chair back toward Hornig, who was once again shuffling through her notes. "What else do you have for us, Dr. Hornig?"

Hornig began reading down a long list of information that would be sifted through by Agency analysts for months, possibly years, to come. Rapp listened intently, gathering more and more insight into how Aziz had put his master plan together. Hornig covered the selection of the men Aziz had brought and where they were trained. She discussed how several of them were sent to America almost a year earlier to start their cover and avoid drawing the attention of the FBI or the Secret Service. She even provided the name of the South American clinic and doctor who had given Aziz his new face. Rapp made a mental note to talk to Kennedy and Stansfield about paying the plastic surgeon a little visit at a later date. The man would live as long as he agreed to cooperate and inform for the Agency. A plastic surgeon who kept company with men like Rafique Aziz could be a very valuable informant, if Aziz hadn't already killed him.

Hornig was providing a bevy of facts that on their own held no great significance, but as they were pieced together, they would hopefully provide a very valuable map of Aziz's final intent. Hornig shared her information for almost a full thirty minutes. Rapp and Kennedy took notes while Stansfield sat back and listened. As the clock neared eight, Hornig moved on to something she had discovered just before leaving the safe house.

"Early this morning, Mr. Harut kept mentioning a certain name. He was slipping in and out of consciousness and was often incoherent. Despite this state of mind he kept repeating the word 'Nebuchadnezzar.'"

As if on cue, Stansfield, Kennedy, and Rapp all leaned forward. Hornig, looking surprised by the unified reaction, asked, "You all know what, or I should say, who Nebuchadnezzar was?"

"Was and is," answered Kennedy. "Nebuchadnezzar was the king of Babylonia from 605 to 562 B.C. His great claim to fame in the Arab world is that he destroyed Jerusalem in 586 and then enslaved the Israelites. Saddam Hussein fancies himself the second coming of Nebuchadnezzar. He feels that it is his destiny to unite all of the Arab people and destroy Israel."

"He doesn't really believe it," added Rapp with a frown. "He just uses it as a PR ploy to get all of the religious zealots whipped into a frenzy."

"And it works," added Kennedy while leaning forward. "Tell me more about the context in which he mentioned the word."

"I was asking him about the financing for the operation. And again he kept mumbling this word. I looked it up and found out who the historical Nebuchadnezzar was. I had no idea he could have been referring to Saddam Hussein."

"Where was Matt Shipley when all of this was being said?" Shipley was one of the two hundred plus employees who worked for the Counterterrorism Center. His specialty was Arabic languages, and Kennedy had sent him out to the safe house the previous evening to help with the interrogation of Harut. Kennedy didn't show it, but she was irritated that Shipley had missed such an obvious reference.

"I had sent everyone to bed around five this morning. We'd been working nonstop since the previous afternoon." Hornig shrugged her shoulders. "We needed to give the subject some rest, and I needed to get my notes organized for this meeting. This oversight was not Mr. Shipley's fault."

Kennedy accepted the explanation. "How did you stumble across this reference if Harut was asleep?"

"I was in the room with him, organizing my notes. Someone has to keep an eye on his vitals, so I was sitting near him when he began to mumble about Nebuchadnezzar. It is not at all unusual for my subjects to continue to talk while they are sleeping."

"Was this recorded?" asked Kennedy.

"Of course. The recording equipment is always running."

"Good." Kennedy jotted herself a note to call Shipley and tell him to review the tapes immediately.

"What," began Stansfield, "was the general context of his ramblings about Nebuchadnezzar?"

"Money—he kept talking about Nebuchadnezzar and money."

Kennedy finished her note. "This corroborates what we heard from our other sources—that Saddam was funneling money into Hezbollah and Hamas."

Looking at his watch, Stansfield said, "Dr. Hornig, do you have anything else for us?"

"No, but I should have more for you this afternoon."

Stansfield looked at Rapp and Kennedy. "Any other questions?"

"Yeah," said Rapp. "How does Aziz plan on getting out of here when it's all over?"

Hornig blinked her eyes as an expression of embarrassment spread across her face. "Ah . . . I haven't got around to that yet."

Rapp looked at her harshly. "You might want to move that one up to the top of your list."

"Yes." Hornig jotted herself a note.

Stansfield again looked to Rapp and Kennedy. "Anything else?" They both shook their heads, and then Stansfield looked to the other side of the table. "Nice work so far, Dr. Hornig. Now, if you'll excuse us, I need to discuss a few things with Irene and Mitch."

Hornig gathered her papers and stood. After she'd placed her notes in a tan canvas shopping bag, she left the room.

Rapp noticed the canvas bag and, after the door was closed, said, "I hope you have somebody baby-sitting her."

"I do." The director nodded. "But we might want to bring it up a notch." Stansfield looked to Kennedy. "Irene, I think we need to get some more bodies out there to keep a close eye on things. Around the clock. I want someone from CTC in that room with Harut every second of the day. And I want them awake."

Kennedy shook her head and said, "I apologize. I already made a note to take care of it."

"Now, Mitch." Stansfield turned his focus back to Rapp. "Irene and I are heading downtown. Considering how the meeting went at the Pentagon yesterday, I think it would be best if you did not join us."

Rapp had expected this, and in truth, he really didn't want to be there to see his predictions come true. There were times when there was no joy in being right, and this would be one of them. "What would you like me to do?"

Retrieving a piece of paper from his shirt pocket, Stansfield unfolded it and slid it across the table. "That is the address and phone number of Milt Adams. The man we discussed with Director Tracy last night. He is expecting your call."

"How do you want me to handle it?"

Stansfield's eyes narrowed while he thought about the question. After several seconds, he said, "Go ahead and use your cover, and tell him you're with Langley. Mr. Adams is a very patriotic individual. We can trust him, but there's no need to tell him anything more than he needs to know."

Stansfield got up, and Kennedy and Rapp followed. As they walked back into the director's office, Stansfield said, "Mitch, it's impossible to overstate how important this is. If you find a way in, General Flood and I will do everything we can to make it happen. Just make sure you give it to me straight. I want realistic odds on whether or not it can be done. Am I understood?"

Hiding his excitement, Rapp replied with a simple, "Yes, sir."

15

RAFIQUE AZIZ LOOKED at the computer screen to his left and smiled. *They are so predictable,* he thought to himself. The laptop computer to his left was hooked up to one of the Situation Room's secure modems. He was staring at the account balance of the Swiss bank that would receive the money before it was to be safely transferred to Iran. The account was at a little over a billion dollars and holding. With about forty-five minutes to go, he doubted that they would transfer the remainder of the money.

The second laptop, to his right, was for a special purpose. Every time Aziz looked at it he beamed with pride. It had been a stroke of genius. Aziz had no doubt that the Americans would come. If he got his hands on the president, his chances might improve, but in the meantime the second laptop was his fail-safe. Studying American counterterrorism tactics, he understood that above all they loved their technology. They would try to jam his ability to remotely detonate the bombs, and in the process they would start a countdown to destruction.

Each of the twenty-four bombs he had brought contained a digital pager that acted as both a receiver and a detonator. Hooked up to the laptop was digital phone. Every two minutes the computer would dial the group paging number for all twenty-four bombs and then send a five-digit number. If that code wasn't received every two minutes, the pagers would go into a sixty-second countdown mode. If the countdown reached zero, the bombs were ignited.

Aziz also carried a pager and a digital phone as a backup measure. If the pager beeped and the countdown was started, it meant only one of two things. Either the Americans were attacking or the computer had malfunctioned. If the computer malfunctioned, he could abort the countdown with his own phone. If that didn't work, it meant the Americans were coming.

THE CRITICAL INCIDENT Response Group's crisis management unit had set up their command post on the fourth floor of the Executive Office Building in a conference room that overlooked the West Wing of the White House. The large wood conference table had been pushed against

118

the inner wall and was covered with a half dozen phones, two radio-charger trays, and several laptops. The rest of the room's furniture had been removed with the exception of about half of the chairs. Against the two side walls, portable tables had been set up and were cluttered with more laptops, phones, televisions, and fax machines. Many of the phones had masking tape on the handsets and were labeled with black felt-tipped marker. Almost half of the phones were dedicated to the FBI's Strategic Information Operations Center, or SIOC. The SIOC, which fell under the purview of the Bureau's criminal investigative division, was charged with handling almost all of the Bureau's high-profile cases. Maps of the White House compound and blueprints of the inner structure were pasted to the walls, and men and women in blue FBI polo shirts were busy pecking away at computers and talking into phones. Two negotiators who were fluent in Arabic were on-site and ready to man the phones for as long as the siege lasted.

Special Agent Skip McMahon stood at the window and glared at the spectacle taking place in Lafayette Square, across the street from the White House. He was fuming; actually *pissed* was the word he had been using repeatedly since around five A.M. Within hours of the terrorist attack on the White House the media had moved in and set up shop smack dab in the middle of Pennsylvania Avenue. They began broadcasting their live reports from right in front of the White House's north fence. When McMahon had arrived on the scene, one of his first orders was to have the media moved back, way back.

Hours earlier, in the predawn darkness, McMahon had been attempting to steal some sleep on the couch in his office at the Hoover Building when one of his agents came in to inform him that a federal judge had intervened on behalf of the networks. Now, as McMahon looked down at Lafayette Square, the media circus was omnipresent. On the north end of the park, a mere hundred yards from the White House, the three networks and CNN were all broadcasting live from atop elevated platforms, and FOX was scrambling to join the group. They were all there with their morning shows as if it were a goddamn state fair. *Good Morning America, Today, CBS This Morning*—all of them.

For the last two hours, McMahon had been fighting the urge to pick up the phone and start chewing ass about the judge's ruling. He had instead decided it was a better use of his time and energy to wait until all of the big shots were together. McMahon looked down at his watch. It was 8:34, and they should be arriving any minute.

*   *   *

SHE HAD MADE it through the first twenty-four hours without getting hit. Anna Rielly felt pretty good, considering what she had been through. Her back was a little stiff from sleeping on the floor or, at least, trying to sleep on the floor. The terrorists had made sleep next to impossible by waking them at least once an hour from sundown to sunup. And to make matters worse, they also pulled people from the group and beat them in front of everyone.

For the women, there was something else to be afraid of. Sometime after midnight, a young blond woman had been yanked from the group by the terrorist that had followed Rielly into the bathroom. Rielly could not say for sure how long the young woman had been gone—the terrorists had taken everyone's watch in an effort to further disorient them—but it seemed to be at least several hours. When the woman finally returned, her clothes were partially torn and she had a look in her eyes . . . a look Rielly had once seen in her own eyes.

Rielly glanced down at Stone Alexander, who was lying crunched up in a fetal position, his jacket neatly folded under his head for a pillow. She was grateful that he had stopped crying. The less attention drawn to them the better.

Brushing a wisp of hair back behind her ear, she looked around the room, careful to keep her head down. Two guards were by the door talking to each other. Rielly knew she wasn't the only one who had to go to the bathroom, but no one dared ask after what had happened the night before.

Folding her legs Indian style, she glanced over her shoulder and then quickly turned her head back. The terrorist, the one with all of the jewelry and slicked-back hair, was staring at her with a cigarette hanging from his mouth—the same man who had plucked the young blond from the group the night before.

Anna Rielly had been through that nightmare before, and she had sworn to herself that she would rather die than let it happen again. Four years earlier, Rielly had taken the Loop from the TV station in downtown Chicago to her apartment in Lincoln Park. It was late when she stepped off the train. When she reached the street, two men jumped her from the shadows and dragged her into an alley and raped her.

That harrowing event had left her bruised and battered, but her physical wounds were easy to overcome compared to the deeper mental scars. Even these were starting to heal, though, thanks in no small part to Coreen Alten, Rielly's therapist. Rielly had been going to Alten twice a week for almost four years. Before the rape she had been a fun-loving, outgoing young woman who very much enjoyed male companionship.

The rape had given her a hard edge and an understandable distrust of men. With the help of Alten she had again grown to enjoy the company of men who were interested in her, but the physical boundary still had not been crossed. When she took her new job in Washington, Rielly thought it was the perfect chance for a fresh start.

One of the only benefits of the personal disaster was her hyperawareness. Rielly had already had street smarts, but the rape had raised her awareness to an almost paranormal level. It was hard to imagine how her current situation could get any worse, but Rielly sensed that when nightfall came, it would.

IRENE KENNEDY WAS almost run over as she attempted to enter the FBI's command post. Two stocky men in SWAT uniforms came barreling out the doorway. The first almost butted Kennedy in the forehead with the brim of his blue baseball cap, but stopped just shy, grabbing her by the shoulders. He apologized without realizing whom he had almost knocked down, and then recognized Kennedy.

"Oh, Irene, I'm sorry." Sid Slater, aka the Jewish Terror, was still holding her by the shoulders.

"Sid," said Kennedy, also surprised, not used to seeing the commander of the FBI's Hostage Rescue Team in full SWAT gear. Slater had the physique of a bricklayer. Several inches shy of six feet and in his midforties, he had a barrel chest and strong, thick hands attached to Popeye-like forearms. Slater wasn't built to run marathons, rather, he was more suited to run through bolted doors.

"Where are you off to in such a hurry?" asked Kennedy.

"I'm trying to get some last-minute intel before they start talking." Slater pointed with his thumb over his shoulder and shook his head. "And I sure as hell don't want to be in there when the shit hits the fan."

Kennedy looked into the room. "What's going on?"

"I don't have time to talk about it; Skip can fill you in. Are you gonna be at the planning meeting this afternoon?"

Kennedy nodded. "I'll be there."

"Good. . . . We can talk then. I have a lot of questions for you." With that, the Jewish Terror headed off down the hallway.

As Slater and the other man marched away, Kennedy watched them for a second, the bright yellow letters on their backs and their dark SWAT uniforms announcing to all that they were on the front line, that they would be the ones to storm the White House. Kennedy considered all the explosives Aziz had brought along and felt overwhelming dread as Slater moved off.

Kennedy entered the FBI's command post, which was buzzing with the activity of radios, phones, faxes, and people. She had just left the conference room on the other side of the building where Vice President Baxter was gathered with select members of the cabinet and the intelligence and federal-law-enforcement communities. From there that group would monitor the conversation between Aziz and the FBI negotiator and make any decisions if needed. At McMahon's request, Kennedy was to stay with him in the FBI's command post to offer any insight.

Across the room, by the windows that overlooked the West Wing, Skip McMahon was talking to a seated Attorney General Tutwiler and motioning to a group of phones. Kennedy walked across the room and stopped several feet away so as to not interrupt. She listened to what Skip was saying and quickly grew alarmed. Kennedy began to look around the room, and she did not like what she saw, or didn't see. It was getting close to nine, and she did not see anyone who appeared to be the FBI negotiator.

A short while later McMahon finished explaining to Tutwiler how the different phones worked and then turned to face Kennedy. With his back to the attorney general he rolled his eyes in frustration. "Morning, Irene."

"Good morning." Kennedy nodded to Tutwiler and then looked back at McMahon. "Where is your negotiator?"

Before McMahon had a chance to answer, Tutwiler said, "I'll be handling the negotiations."

In as passive a tone as Kennedy could muster, she replied, "No offense, Madam Attorney General, but I don't think that is the most prudent course."

"And why is that?" asked Tutwiler aggressively.

"Because Rafique Aziz will take it as an insult that we have chosen a woman to negotiate with him."

"I am here, Ms. Kennedy, because I am the top-ranking law-enforcement officer in the land. I am *here*"—Tutwiler stressed the word and pointed at the ground—"to send a clear message to these terrorists that we are extremely serious about this situation."

Kennedy's thoughts drifted back to Mitch Rapp's words at the Pentagon the day before. They gave her the strength to state her opinion a bit more firmly. "And I am here to advise you as the director of the CIA's Counterterrorism Center, you are making a grave mistake. I respect your accomplishments, Madam Attorney General, but Rafique Aziz will not. He will make you pay for what he will see as a blatant insult to his manhood."

Tutwiler defiantly crossed her arms. "I have encountered chauvinists all my life, and I have found that there is only one way to deal with them . . . head-on."

"Again, I respect your accomplishments, but you couldn't be more wrong. You have absolutely no idea who you're dealing with." Seeing that Tutwiler was not going to budge, Kennedy left the room and started down the hallway to explain the new development to Stansfield. Midway down the hall she heard McMahon call her name.

A second later McMahon pulled up alongside her and placed his hand on her shoulder. "Irene, it's not worth it. I already went all the way to the top. For now, she gets her way."

Kennedy stopped, her cheeks slightly flushed. Murmuring more to herself than McMahon she said, "Now I know why Mitch got so mad yesterday."

McMahon didn't quite get Kennedy's comment and decided to ignore it. "The way I figure it, Irene, is that Tutwiler's ass is hangin' out pretty far on this one. After she screws up this morning, she'll be out of our hair." McMahon studied Kennedy's tense face, not used to such a reaction from the almost always unflappable protégé of Thomas Stansfield. "Take a deep breath, Irene; it's not going to do you any good to get upset right now."

Kennedy looked up at McMahon and bit down on the bottom corner of her lip. "I'm usually the one giving you this lecture."

"What can I say; I'm a quick learner." McMahon gave her a fake smile and turned Kennedy back toward the command post. "I need you with me during this call, all right?"

Kennedy nodded and went along reluctantly.

HIS FINGERS TAPPED the shiny surface of the conference table of the White House Situation Room and his eyes stayed transfixed on the computer screen. Rafique Aziz sat in the president's leather chair, rocking slightly. Aziz brought his wrist up and checked the time. The balance of the Swiss bank account hadn't changed in almost half an hour. Two more minutes and the spectacle would start. Aziz's eyes lifted an inch above the top of the computer screen and looked at the bank of television screens that dominated the far wall.

The three major networks and CNN were all broadcasting live from the other side of Lafayette Park. NBC and CBS were interviewing family members of the hostages; ABC was talking to a psychiatrist who had written a book on hostages identifying with their captors, the so-called Stockholm syndrome; and CNN was talking to a retired FBI agent, whom Aziz thought to be typically smug.

A thin smile creased his lips as Aziz thought about just how predictable these Americans were. The smile widened even further. Aziz put his hands behind his neck and rocked back and forth in the chair. A mailbox icon appeared on the second laptop, and an electronic voice alerted him to an incoming E-mail. Aziz quickly tapped the proper keys, and a second later the message was up on the screen. As Aziz read the message, he moved closer to the screen, reading the first line over and over, unable to get past the shock of it. It couldn't be. How could they have gotten their hands on him? Why now?

The message read, *"Fara Harut abducted in early morning commando raid yesterday. Group suffered heavy casualties. Harut assumed taken alive. Do not know who conducted operation, but assume either America, Britain, or Israel."*

ACROSS THE STREET in the Executive Office Building, Vice President Baxter was holding court in a separate conference room down the hall from the FBI's command post. As always Dallas King was sitting next to Baxter, General Flood was on the vice president's left, and farther down the table FBI Director Roach, CIA Director Stansfield, and Secret Service Director Tracy had taken their seats. The secretaries of state and defense were also present, along with a dozen aides and several Secret Service agents from the vice president's detail. The door was closed, and each occupant stared expectantly at the black speaker placed in the center of the table. After twenty more seconds of silence the black box announced the ringing of the phone in the Situation Room.

AZIZ WAS STILL staring at the message when the phone started to ring. He was furious, outraged that such a thing could happen, and now of all times. His eyes burned a hole in the screen as his mind raced to calculate the potential damage this catastrophe could inflict on his mission. All the while Aziz tried to keep emotion out of it. Fara Harut was his mentor, the man who had wooed him from the classroom to the battlefield, the man who had shown him the evil of the Zionists. Harut was the reason he was where he was today, and now, he was gone.

The phone continued its irritating noise, and Aziz had to catch himself from answering it—not now, not until he calmed down and put himself in the proper mind-set. There was the plan, and he had to stick with it. After he had more time to think, he could deal with this calamity. Laying his hands flat on the table, he forced all of the tension from his body and immersed himself in his role. Finally, after the phone had rung at least a dozen times, he reached out and slowly brought the receiver to his mouth.

"Yes."

"Mr. Aziz," stated a calm and confident female voice, "this is Attorney General Margaret Tutwiler. We are having some problems getting together all of the money." There was a pause on the line and then, "So far we have managed to transfer—"

"One point three billion dollars." Aziz gave her the sum as he stood abruptly. Anger coursing through every inch of his body. This was too much. He had done his research on the Americans. He knew who all of the players would be. He knew that with Hayes out of commission the transfer of power would take place, and with Vice President Baxter came an increased role for the already important attorney general. But to insult him in such a way was inconceivable. It was such a blatant affront that there was no way it could be anything other than intentional.

A slightly surprised Tutwiler said, "Yes, one point three billion." She stammered for a second. "It's going to take some time to gather all of the money. . . . It would be a big help, as far as expediting the transfer of the remainder of the money, if you could show us a sign of your good faith."

Aziz closed his eyelids tightly, commanding himself to continue forward with the plan. In a pained voice, he asked, "What would you propose?"

"The release of several hostages would go a long way in showing us you are sincere."

This was beyond belief. In a voice that was near breaking, Aziz asked, "How many would you like me to release—ten, twenty . . . maybe thirty of them?"

Tutwiler, unsure of how genuine the offer was, tentatively replied, "Um . . . thirty would be great . . . and after they are released, we can work on getting more of the money transferred."

Aziz stood looking down the length of the table, staring at everything and nothing at the same time, his instincts sharp, his anger funneling into a direct beam of energy. Plan or no plan, this had moved into the realm of the personal. They were trying to insult him by sending this woman to talk with him. They were testing him to see how far he would go. Was it a trap? He thought not. It was too early for an attack, it was broad daylight, and the media was right across the street. If they wanted to test his resolve, he would show them just how strong and determined it was.

It was all too much. First the news that Fara Harut had been taken, and now this stupid woman insulting him. Finally, unable to hold it in anymore, he yelled, "What did I tell you yesterday? I said all of the money by nine! I didn't say part of it; I said all of it! Don't insult me by talking to me of the difficulty of transferring the money! Your Treasury Department could transfer ten times the money I asked for in one hour if they wanted to! I think it is time to teach you stupid Americans a lesson! Look out your windows, and I will show you what happens when you play your idiotic games with me!"

ANNA RIELLY SAT on the floor uncomfortably, her stomach growling. She seriously wondered if she'd be able to make it another hour without wetting her pants. Several of the other hostages had already done so, and the room was beginning to reek of urine. Rielly heard the sound of heavy boots approaching, and then the head terrorist entered the room. The entire group cowered at the sight of the obviously enraged man.

Aziz walked right up to the edge of the hostages and pointed to a man. "You! Stand up right now!" Whoever he was yelling at didn't respond fast enough, and Aziz yelled even louder, "Now!"

As the hostage stood, Rielly immediately recognized him. It was Bill Schwartz, the president's national security adviser. The terrorist screamed at the woman who was clutching Schwartz's leg and said, "You too! Come!"

The woman also did not move fast enough, and Aziz reached down and grabbed her by her hair, yanking her to her feet like a rag doll. With the help of another terrorist he led them out of the room.

Aziz pushed the two hostages in front of him up the stairs to the first level of the West Wing. Then, before stepping out underneath the small portico on the north side of the building, Aziz pulled a mesh hood down over his face. He took a small remote control from his drab green combat vest and punched in a code, disarming the explosive device that was attached to the door.

Aziz kicked open the double doors and marched outside. All alone in the morning sunlight, he crossed the narrow driveway and stepped back onto another sidewalk near the edge of the small portico. Aziz defiantly looked around at the dozens of guns that were trained on him. The long barrels of sniper rifles could be seen bristling from every rooftop in sight. He knew they wouldn't shoot, they couldn't shoot, not in America. That command had to come down through layers of bureaucrats, and it was far too early for that. Aziz raised his AK-74 in the air and unleashed a loud eight-round burst. Defiantly, he cradled his weapon across his chest and stood his ground, showing the Americans that he was not afraid. After he had made his presence felt, he marched back into the building and looked at his watch. He had decided he would give the media thirty seconds to get their cameras focused on the entrance.

Aziz was following his script precisely, with one exception. The rage. It had been his plan from the start to kill the national security adviser. But now, he decided to deviate slightly from his plan and allow himself some personal satisfaction in retaliation for Harut. In an almost spastic flurry, Aziz wheeled and slapped Schwartz across the face.

His face within inches of Schwartz's, he yelled, "How does is feel to be terrified, you dog?"

The national security adviser's eyes welled up with tears, and the woman standing next to him began to sob. Schwartz wrapped his arms around his secretary. He knew what was happening, he knew it was the end, and there was nothing he could do to stop it. Aziz continued to scream and taunt him with questions.

"How many times have you ordered the death of my Arab brothers? How many times?" Aziz's eyes were maniacal with rage. Schwartz gave no answer, and Aziz slapped him again; then, grabbing him by the collar, Aziz forced the national security adviser toward the door with his secretary's arms still wrapped tightly around her boss's waist. As they reached the door, Aziz placed his boot on the woman's butt and shoved.

Schwartz and the woman tumbled out into the light and fell to the pavement. Aziz stood in the doorway and yelled through his mesh hood for them to get up. The woman was crying harder now, and Schwartz's tears were flowing freely down his cheeks. The presidential adviser stood and pulled his secretary to her feet. Aziz screamed at them to start walking, and after several seconds they began to do so, though slowly.

Standing in the doorway, Aziz watched the two hostages walk toward the north gate. When they reached the halfway point, when they were within clear view of the news cameras, Aziz raised his rifle and took aim.

"Stop!" he yelled. When the president's national security adviser turned to look over his shoulder, Aziz had Schwartz's face in the center of his sights. He squeezed the trigger once, the powerful rifle bucked, and he brought it right back to level, the woman's head now framed in the cold black sights. A quick squeeze of the trigger and the second body was tumbling to the pavement just behind the first. As the woman came to rest on top of Schwartz, Aziz zeroed in and unloaded another dozen rounds. The loud clacking of the Kalashnikov rifle reverberated across the pristine north grounds of the White House.

When Aziz was satisfied, he closed the door, the smoking muzzle of his AK-74 hanging at his side. Before starting back for the basement, he rearmed the booby-trapped doorway and then started down the hall, his eyes full of hate, his breaths deep, and his pace quick. When he reached the staircase, he ran down the steps, through the hallway, and into the empty Situation Room. Grabbing the phone, he yelled, "Are you still there?"

*   *   *

SKIP MCMAHON HELD the phone to his ear and looked down at the two bodies lying in the driveway. The man he recognized. He then turned to Marge Tutwiler, who sat motionless at the table, staring out the window. McMahon then looked at Irene Kennedy, who sadly shook her head.

"I'm here," answered McMahon.

"Who is this?" shouted Aziz.

"Special Agent Skip McMahon of the FBI."

"Good! Don't ever insult me by putting that woman on the phone again. My demands are unchanged! I will kill one hostage every hour until all of the money is placed in the account I have given you! When you do that, I will release one-third of the hostages! One hostage every hour! Am I understood?"

"I understand you very clearly, but one hour might be pushing it."

Now was the time to shift gear. "Listen to me, McMahon." Aziz now spoke calmly, in an almost professional tone. "I know your rules of engagement. I just killed two hostages, so now you must send in your Hostage Rescue Team." Aziz stopped and then added in a grave tone, "That will be a big mistake, and I will tell you why. If you attempt such a stunt, I will blow this great building of yours to kingdom come and all of the hostages with it. My men and I will gladly become martyrs for our cause, and you know it." Aziz paused for a moment. "It does not need to come to that, however. The only reason why I killed those two hostages was because of the stupidity of your attorney general. If you and I play by the rules, no one needs to die. You hand over all of the money in one hour, and I release a third of the hostages. It is as simple as that. Have I made myself clear?"

"Yes."

"Good. From now on, McMahon, I talk to you and only you. Now I will await the rest of the money." Aziz calmly placed the phone back in its cradle. He knew exactly how to play them.

16

THE VICE PRESIDENT and the others sat in silence around the conference table. There was a knock on the door followed by a slight pause. Then the door opened cautiously and McMahon and Irene Kennedy entered. The men sitting around the table were sullen. FBI Director Roach looked up and asked, "Who did they kill?"

Irene Kennedy answered. "We don't know who the woman was, but the man was Bill Schwartz."

Every person in the room lowered his or her head. They had all worked with Schwartz at one time or another, and he was well liked. After a long period of silence, Vice President Baxter asked, "If we give him the money, will he release a third of the hostages?"

The question was greeted with shrugs and uncertainty by all of the men sitting at the table. Eventually all eyes turned to Kennedy. She was the expert. Slowly, she nodded her head and then said, "I think he will keep his word."

The vice president took in the analysis with pursed lips. It was what he wanted to hear. Dallas King leaned over and cupped his hand over his boss's ear. Whispering, he said, "If he starts killing a hostage every hour, we are in some serious trouble. I don't care how much it costs, or what they do with the money, if we can free a third of the hostages, I say we do it."

Baxter nodded as King eased away and back into his seat. King was right. They were boxed in, and there were only two ways out. As far as Baxter was concerned, one of them wasn't even an option. The vice president looked at FBI Director Roach and said, "Brian, would you start the wheels in motion for transferring the rest of the money into the account? It is my decision that we will wait until he releases one third of the hostages, and then we will proceed from there. Any questions?" Baxter looked around the room and everyone shook their heads. Baxter then looked back to the head of the FBI. "Let me know if you run into any problems, and make sure it's done within the hour. We don't need to see any more hostages gunned down."

Roach nodded, and he and McMahon left the room.

The aged director of central intelligence sat in his chair and observed. He hadn't had a lot of face time with the vice president prior to the crisis and was still trying to get a good read on him. Baxter seemed to despise the fact that he had been put in this situation. That worried Thomas Stansfield. Great leaders rose to the occasion. They almost thrived when confronted with a crisis. This man seemed to shrink from it.

Turning in his chair, Stansfield got back to the business at hand. "Mr. Vice President, we need to make some contingency plans."

Baxter nodded. "I know . . . I know, but let's just take it one step at a time. Let's get some of the hostages released, and then we'll deal with the next demand."

"I'm afraid we don't have that luxury, sir." Stansfield paused. "What if his next demand is untenable?" Stansfield had decided to wait until he had a full report from Dr. Hornig before he briefed the vice president on what they knew from Harut.

"I really don't want to think about that right now."

General Flood leaned forward, miffed at Baxter's reply. "We have no choice but to think about it. We have to be ready to move if this thing gets out of control."

Baxter squirmed. All eyes in the room were on him, and he desperately wanted to avoid making a decision. Why would he have to be the butcher? Finally, reluctantly, he let out the difficult words, though they didn't exactly ring with confidence. "Get everything in place, and if the time comes, I'll be ready to give the order."

The large warrior turned to Stansfield, and the two men exchanged knowing glances. Baxter did not have what it would take. He was in over his head and would blow in the wind until the last possible second.

The vice president placed his elbows on the table and rubbed his eyes. Without looking up, he said, "Let's take a break and meet back here in thirty minutes. I need some time alone . . . to think."

Everyone, with the exception of King, rose and started for the door. Baxter looked at his chief of staff and said, "You too, Dallas. Go check on Marge, and see how she's doing." King nodded and left with the others.

IT HAD BEEN an absolute bear to get from Langley to Capitol Hill. Traffic was horrendous due to the street closures and the large crowds around the White House. Rapp turned his black Volvo from Second Street on to Pennsylvania Avenue and gunned it to get around a cabbie who was driving like he had his head shoved up his ass. The farther Rapp traveled away from the Capitol, the worse the neighborhood got. The mix of homes went from nicely restored to run-down and dilapidated eyesores.

Several blocks later, Rapp took a left and found the home he had been looking for, an immaculate turn-of-the-century Victorian with fresh paint and ornate woodwork. The home was sandwiched in between two rotting houses of similar architecture that were in dire need of repair.

Rapp parked his car in front of the nice Victorian and looked at his dashboard clock: 9:16. Events at the White House would be under way. He reached for his digital phone, but decided against it. Irene would have enough going on. She didn't need a call from him, and besides, he wasn't in the mood for bad news. Rapp got out of the car, his holstered Beretta bulging underneath the right armpit of his suit coat. He pulled his sunglasses down a notch on his nose and started up the sidewalk.

Standing on the porch was Milt Adams, all five feet five inches of him. His head was shaved and his dark black skin glistened in the sunlight. Despite his slight stature, he gave one the impression of a much larger individual.

As Rapp reached the steps, a rather large German shepherd was coming down from the porch straight for him. Rapp tensed at his natural urge to pull out his gun and shoot the dog. He hated dogs—strike that—he didn't hate dogs per se, just the guard-dog variety. They were an occupational hazard that he was none too fond of. Knowing that to show fear was suicidal, Rapp stood as stiff as a board with his hands at his side. Sure enough, the dog came right up and stuck its snout in his crotch. Rapp's immediate reaction was to take a step back, but it did no good, the dog simply followed, sniffing loudly.

From the porch, Milt Adams shouted in a deep drill-instructor voice, "Rufus, heel!" The dog immediately wheeled and headed up the steps, heeding the command and taking up a post at his owner's side. Adams reached down and scratched the dog under the neck. "Good boy, Rufus. Good boy."

Rapp stared up at Adams, awed that such a deep, booming voice had just come from such a little body. Adams could not have weighed more than one hundred fifty pounds, and the voice Rapp had just heard could have given James Earl Jones, Isaac Hayes, and Barry White all a run for their money.

"Are you Mr. Kruse?" asked Adams.

"Yes." Rapp walked up the first two steps and stuck out his hand. "You must be Milt Adams."

"That's correct. It's nice to meet you."

"Likewise."

Adams motioned for Rapp. "Follow me, I've got everything set up inside."

The two men walked into the house, the dog following at Rapp's side. Adams continued straight ahead, down a long hallway to the rear of the house and the kitchen. The hardwood floors had been recently redone with a shiny coat of polyurethane, and the kitchen floor was tiled in a classic black-and-white checkerboard pattern. The trim was all restored to its natural wood finish with a light stain.

Adams opened a glass-paned cupboard and grabbed two mugs. "You look like the black type."

"That'd be great." The German shepherd parked his butt right next to Rapp and leaned his head against Rapp's thigh. The proximity of the canine made Rapp increasingly uncomfortable.

Adams finished pouring the coffee and turned around. He took one look at Rapp's stiff posture and said, "You don't like dogs." It was more a statement than a question.

"Ah . . . not really."

Adams handed him a cup. "What's the problem? You been bit before?"

"Several times." Rapp winced as he thought of one time in particular.

Adams surveyed his guest; the longer hair and facial scar made him begin to wonder if this man really worked for the Secret Service.

"Don't worry," Adams offered. "As long as you don't hurt me, Rufus won't hurt you." The owner of the house started across the room. "Let's go down to the basement. That's where I have everything."

Rapp watched Adams cross the kitchen and followed. The damn dog would not leave his side. Rapp was impressed with Adams, who hustled down the steep steps like a man half his age.

When Rapp reached the basement, he stopped and looked around the large room. It was a retired man's wet dream. The floor was painted a spotless gray and looked clean enough to eat off. Tools of every kind hung from brown pegboard along one wall, and each spot was labeled to ensure optimal organization. Along the far wall, six metal storage cabinets were lined up, each of them again labeled with a laminated catalog of the items within. Two drafting tables and a computer dominated the wall to the right. In the center of the room several white sheets covered something roughly the size of a pool table. Cocking his head sideways, Rapp tried to sneak a peek under the sheets, but couldn't see anything.

The wiry Adams stopped at the drafting table on the left and turned on a bright overhead lamp. He motioned down at the three-by-four-foot blueprint on the table. "This is an overview of the White House and its grounds. Director Tracy tells me you're interested in finding a way to get into the mansion unnoticed." Rapp nodded. Adams looked up questioningly, as if studying Rapp. After a moment, he said, "Something tells me you're not Secret Service, Mr. Kruse."

"Please call me Mitch, and no, I don't work for the Secret Service."

"Okay, Mitch, who do you work for?"

"I'm an analyst for the CIA."

A wry smile creased Adams lips. In his deep voice he replied, "Analyst my ass." Rolling up his left sleeve, Adams revealed a thick wormlike scar that sliced from his elbow almost down to his wrist. Holding it up for Rapp to see, he said, "Got this on Iwo Jima . . . bayoneted by some crazy Jap." Adams pointed to Rapp's face. "You've got a nice thin scar there. Can't even see it unless you're looking at you from the side. You've had some nice plastic surgery done on it, but my guess is it used to be a big ugly thing like this one here on my arm." Adams studied him again. "You didn't get it from analyzing satellite imagery, did you?"

Rapp played it cool, asking, "How'd you know I had plastic surgery?"

"My oldest daughter is a doctor over at GW. I can see the work of a talented surgeon, so let's cut the shit. What do you really do for Langley?"

Rapp looked at Adams deliberately. He liked his *cut-to-the-heart-of-the-matter* style and decided the old man was a little too wily to play games with. So Rapp decided to give it to him as straight as he could.

"I can't get into the details, but I'm more than a paper pusher."

"Is Kruse your real name?"

Rapp shook his head.

Adams eyed him suspiciously and then shrugged his shoulders. "Well, I'll have to trust Director Tracy. If he says I should give you the information, I'll give it to you." Adams turned his attention back to the blueprint and ran his finger over it, tracing a line.

"There is one way to get into the White House belowground." Adams flipped up the first blueprint and revealed another one. "It's the most well-known . . . the tunnel that comes over from the Treasury Building." Adams stabbed his finger on the right side of the blueprint and drew a line showing Rapp where the tunnel was. "This is the tunnel that the terrorists used."

"That's it?" asked Rapp surprised. "There's only one tunnel?"

Adams nodded. "There's only one tunnel. All the BS Hollywood puts out has most people thinking there's a dozen secret tunnels heading in every different direction." Adams shook his head. "Not true."

Disappointed, Rapp said, "So there's no other way in belowground."

"I didn't say that." Adams held up a finger and smiled. He then stepped over to the other drafting table. "During the Reagan administration the Army Corps of Engineers installed a new heating, ventilation, and cooling system. This HVAC they installed was really impressive stuff . . . very high tech. Besides providing all of the basic heating and cooling requirements, the system is designed to keep the air pressure inside the White House higher than the air pressure outside."

"Why?" asked Rapp.

"Maintaining a higher internal pressure ensures that all air flow, either through open doors, windows, or cracks, will always flow out instead of in. This way if anyone tries to introduce a biological or chemical weapon into the building's environment, they couldn't do it by simply releasing the toxin upwind from the building. They would have to get inside the building and release it, and even if they did, the system is equipped with alarms and filters."

Rapp thought he saw where Adams was going and asked, "Where does the system get its air?"

"The system has two sets of intake and exhaust ducts. The first is located on the roof of the White House, and the second is located here." Adams pointed to an area on the South Lawn. "The duct is hidden under a clump of fake bushes not more than fifteen yards from the fence on the east side, just south of Jackie Kennedy's rose garden. The duct drops thirty feet straight down and then runs for a little over two hundred feet, where it connects with the main system in the engineering room of the third basement."

Rapp looked at the drawing. "What kind of cover is there around this duct? Could you get to it without someone from the roof seeing you?"

"There's plenty of cover. Come over here, and I'll show you on the model." Adams walked over to the middle of the room and proudly pulled two white sheets off the large table. Lying before them on the table was a detailed model of the White House and its grounds. "This is what retirement does to you, Mitch. I started this project almost twenty years ago with one of my nephews. It took me almost all of that time to get half of it finished, and then I retired and finished the rest of it in six months."

Rapp stared at the model and searched for the duct in question. Reading his mind, Adams reached down and moved a small bush. "Here's your way in." Adams's skinny black hand pointed at a green metal shaft that came out of the ground and then looped back down in an inverted U with the open end pointing at the ground.

Rapp studied the trees and bushes between the vent and the White House. "You're sure someone on the roof wouldn't see me approaching the duct?"

"I don't think so. Your problem, as I see it, is whether or not they are in control of the Secret Service's surveillance and alarm system. This entire area"—Adams pointed at the fence—"is loaded with sensors. If they have our system, they'll know you're there the second you step over the fence."

Rapp folded his arms and grabbed his chin. Looking down at the model, he studied the large horseshoe-shaped fence that ringed the South Lawn and nodded.

"We can overcome that, though." Adams dismissed the problem with a wave of his hand. "Through a diversion or something. . . . Your real problem is going to be finding your way around once you get inside the building. There are secret doors, elevators, stairs, passageways—you name it . . . and you won't find any of them on a blueprint or a model. Hell, half the agents on the presidential detail don't know where all of the stuff is. You are going to need someone with you who knows their way around that place. . . ." Adams paused for a second. "Or you're going to have to tell me what you have in mind, so I can help you plan it."

Rapp looked up from the model and studied Milt Adams. A decision had to be made. Adams had to be either brought onboard or kept in the dark, and Rapp didn't have the patience to debate the pros and cons with Kennedy and Stansfield.

DALLAS KING WAS standing in a small office across the hall from the FBI's command post. He had been there for five frustrating minutes while a paramedic worked on Tutwiler. King looked down at the attorney general and shook his head.

The paramedic that was checking her out finished taking her blood pressure and said, "I think she's in shock."

"Shit." King paced back and forth. "So what are you telling me? Can she speak to the press or not?"

"No." The female paramedic, who was still on one knee, frowned. "She needs to get to a hospital." Tutwiler was sitting frozen on a brown leather couch, her eyes staring blankly into space.

King placed his hands over his mouth and swore three times in rapid succession. Next, he grabbed at his hair and said, "I fucking knew it."

Turning back toward the paramedic, he said, "Take her to Bethesda, and I don't want anyone talking to her." King yanked the door open and began marching down the hallway, his arms swinging wildly. When he reached the other side of the building, he ignored the gaggle of Secret Service agents standing outside the conference room and entered without knocking.

King slammed the door behind him and screamed an explative.

Vice President Baxter, startled by the unexpected intrusion, spun around in his chair with a look of thorough irritation on his face. "Dallas, I said I wanted to be alone."

"The stupid bitch is in shock."

"What?" asked a confused Baxter.

"Tutwiler . . . the bitch is in shock . . . she cracked." An angry expression contorted King's face. "She can't talk . . . She's on her way to the hospital."

Baxter closed his eyes and moaned, "Oh, great."

King began pacing up and down next to the conference table, while Baxter buried his face in his cupped hands.

"It's nothing we can't handle," insisted King, trying to find an angle, a way to spin the story. "It's just a temporary setback." King walked the length of the room twice and then said, "I'll leak it through the right sources that the whole thing was Marge's idea, and when it blew up in her face, she cracked . . . and then we'll have Director Roach handle the press briefing. We'll be fine."

With his face still in his hands, Baxter added, "For now." Then lifting his head up, he said, "This thing is only going to get worse. We are going to have to storm that place eventually, and from what everyone is telling me, we are going to lose a lot of hostages. It's just like I told you yesterday, Dallas; we are *screwed.*" Baxter growled the last word. "Any way you slice it, I'm going to have the blood of a lot of people on my hands, and my name will forever be associated with this damn mess."

King shook his head. "Nothing's over. If there's a way out of this, I'll find it." Rubbing his hands together as if he were trying to warm them up, he said, "For now, we continue to walk this thin line. Marge is out of commission, so we'll move Director Roach and the FBI to the forefront. If this sick bastard releases one-third the hostages, we should probably have a photo op with you consoling them. It won't hurt for you to take credit for that, but once it's over and he starts making his next demands, you should keep a low profile. This isn't over yet, Sherman. Stay with me."

17

SLEEP HAD BEEN out of the question. After Warch had discovered someone was trying to breach the bunker door, everyone was up for the night. Tensions were running high as the grinding noise grew a little louder with each passing hour. Another foreboding sign was that the door was no longer cool to the touch. Areas of heat could be felt as one placed one's hand in different spots

In an effort to lower the tension and keep his people focused, Jack Warch had drawn up a duty schedule with Special Agent Ellen Morton, the day shift's whip. The first order of business was to collect all of the radios and phones. With nine Secret Service agents in the bunker, that amounted to nine encrypted Motorola radios and nine digital phones. One of each would be kept on and monitored around the clock. Since the batteries on the phones were interchangeable, Warch's phone was to be used and the batteries from the other phones were to be rotated through.

While one agent monitored the communications, another agent was to stand post by the bunker door and report any strange noises or occurrences. Two more agents were assigned to remain at all times between the president and the bunker door. While these four agents were manning their posts, the other four were to sleep or eat. The two teams, as they were now referred to, were on four-hour rotations. Warch was the only one not included in the rotation.

After checking on the battery supply, Warch walked over to the thick vault door and placed his hand flat on the surface. He ran his other hand through his thinning hair and tried to remember the details that had been passed on to him about the construction of the bunker. If he remembered correctly, it could withstand any conventional bomb and most nuclear bombs as long as it wasn't a direct hit. If the White House was ground zero, they were toast like everyone else. As for how it would hold up against a bunch of bloodthirsty terrorists using drills and God only knew what else, Warch had no idea.

The commanding agent turned away from the door and glanced over at the president, who was sitting on one of the couches with his chief of staff. The president looked at Warch and gestured for him to join them.

President Hayes was one of those men who shaved twice a day. Having already missed two shaves his face was covered with a solid growth of gray and brown whiskers. His tie and suit jacket were lying on the bunk he had slept in. Looking over at Special Agent Warch, the president said, "Jack, please take your tie off, and tell the men to do the same."

After the raid Warch had torn his tie off in frustration. His feelings toward his president were at an all-time low. Hayes and his chief of staff had circumvented Secret Service security procedure, and people were dead because of it. Now, over twenty-four hours later, he had put his personal feelings aside and put his tie back on. He had a job to do, and part of that job was to show respect to the presidency, regardless of the individual.

Warch nodded his thanks to the president and began to tug at the silk knot around his neck.

"Anything new to report?"

"I'm afraid not, sir." Warch kept his expression neutral.

"Are you sure," started Valerie Jones, "that those aren't our people trying to drill through the door?"

Warch paused and checked his desire to snap at the president's chief of staff. He had already been over this with them twice. "It's not our people."

"Are you sure?" Jones's tone was more pleading than asking.

Warch exhaled a tired sigh and said, "I don't like it any more than you do, but it would make no sense for our own people to drill through the door. They have the code. All they have to do is punch it in like we did, and the door opens."

Jones moved forward on the couch, tugging the hem of her black skirt as she did so. "What if the terrorists damaged the door control?"

Warch called on his patience. They had already been down this road before. He decided he would go over it with her one last time. "Outside this door"—Warch pointed over his shoulder—"is a second room. That room has two reinforced steel doors. One leads into the tunnel, and the second one leads into the third basement of the White House. Again, my people have the codes to get through either of those doors. So there would be no reason for them to be drilling now."

"No." Jones shook her head. "You're not listening. I said what if the terrorists blew apart one of the other doors and that damaged the control panel for this door?" She pointed at the door with her bright red fingernail.

"Ms. Jones, you are the one who is not listening." Warch kept his voice low but firm. "If our people were the ones drilling out there, they would have called us and told us so." Warch drew her attention to the nearby table filled with radios and digital phones. "They would not be jamming our communications and drilling at the same time." Warch didn't see it as his job to like or dislike people at the White House, but this Valerie Jones was really getting on his nerves.

Jones started to speak again, but President Hayes reached out and placed his hand on her knee. "I think Jack has made his point, and I agree with him. It's the only thing that makes sense."

"Who says it has to make sense?"

Hayes eyeballed her and said, "Valerie."

Jones sat back and folded her arms. "Sorry, I'm just trying to think of a way out of this mess."

Hayes ignored her and looked to Warch. "What do we do now?"

Warch was tempted, really tempted to let fly, to explain very forcefully to Ms. Jones that they wouldn't be in this mess if she had followed Secret Service procedure, but now was neither the time nor the place. That would all be discussed later, if they ever got out of this mess alive.

Warch thought about the president's question for a moment. He looked over at the seemingly impervious bunker door and wondered how long it would take for the terrorists to breach it.

Looking back to the president, Warch knew he had to stay positive. "The FBI's Hostage Rescue Team is the best. I'm sure they're making plans to retake the building as we speak."

RAFIQUE AZIZ GRINNED as he watched the money flow into the Swiss bank account. His people in Iran would start transferring the money into different accounts within the hour. He was winning, but his elation was tempered by the news about his mentor Fara Harut. Aziz wondered what his captors could get out of him—if he was still alive. Harut was a tough old man, but no one was tough enough to withstand torture.

As Aziz tried to assess the potential damage, he wondered if it was wise to deviate from his plan slightly—to demand the return of Harut. As he drummed his fingers on the table, he decided no. The Americans might not have him; it could have been the Israelis or the British. If he went back on his word, it might provoke them into a premature attack, and Aziz was not ready for that. He needed his hands around the president's neck, or his chance for survival would be close to zero.

For now he would stick to his plan. It was time to talk to the FBI. Aziz had been ready to kill another hostage at ten A.M., but the money had started to flow and kept flowing. It was nearing noon and almost all of the money had been transferred. Aziz picked up the phone and dialed the number that the FBI had given him. After two rings the now familiar deep voice of McMahon answered.

"You have kept your word," said Aziz, "and I will keep mine. At half past noon, I will release one-third of the hostages. Keep your people back. I don't want to see any of them on the street, or I'll open fire. Do I make myself clear?"

"Yes. Which door will you bring them out of?"

"That is not your concern," snapped Aziz. "I will release my next set of demands at seven A.M. tomorrow. Until then I do not want hear from you." The terrorist hung up the phone and looked at his watch. It was exactly 11:53. Aziz decided he would release the hostages immediately instead of waiting until twelve-thirty. This would keep the FBI off balance. Aziz doubted they would try anything this early, but after his execution of their national security adviser, it was best to be safe.

ANNA RIELLY FELT weak. Her captors had allowed them to go to the bathroom around eleven, and Rielly had been able to grab several handfuls of water from the sink while she was in the bathroom. The water hitting her empty stomach had made her realize just how hungry she really was. The terrorist with the slicked-back hair had again followed her into the stall and watched her.

Back in the White House mess, Rielly looked up from her uncomfortable position on the floor and noticed him gloating over her still. She wondered when he would strike, and if he would do it alone or with the others. Her vision started to blur. Lowering her head, she brought both fists up to her eyes, fighting the tears before they started flowing uncontrollably.

She could handle anything but this. *Would it be better to die?* she honestly asked herself.

RAFIQUE AZIZ CAME marching into the White House mess and glared at the huddled mass of frightened hostages. No one dared look at him after seeing what he was capable of.

With his hands on his hips, Aziz said, "Everybody, listen to me and you will not be hurt." Aziz began to walk around the circle. "If I tap you on the shoulder, I want you to go stand against the wall by the door. A third of you are being set free. If your government cooperates tomorrow, another third of you will be set free."

Aziz knew the second part of the statement to be a lie, but honesty was hardly his strong suit. "If any of you talk or do not cooperate in any way, you will be forced to sit back down." Aziz began tapping the shoulders of those hostages closest to the door. Those farthest from the door quickly realized they would not be released. Several of them started to cry, and Aziz shouted, "Silence, or I will come over there and shoot you!"

Anna Rielly couldn't believe it; her prayers were about to be answered. As the leader worked his way closer, her sprits soared. She was going to be set free. Rielly grabbed Stone Alexander and told him to sit up. The pretty male reporter's hair was pasted to one side of his head, with a large clump sticking straight up in the air, and he gave no sign that he knew what was going on. Aziz tapped Rielly on the shoulder and then Alexander. Anna stood and pulled Alexander to his feet. As she walked toward the door, she felt as though it were all a dream. Rielly looked at the other hostages that were standing by the door and smiled. It was really going to happen.

Her smile vanished instantly when she felt a hand on her shoulder. Trying to ignore it, Rielly took another step, but the fingers dug in deep and yanked her to a stop. Alexander kept walking in his trancelike state toward the others that were being set free.

The terrorist with the slicked-back hair, the one who had driven the delivery truck into the underground parking garage of the Treasury Building, yanked Anna Rielly to a stop and yelled to Rafique Aziz in Arabic. Aziz stopped his count for a second, looked at the woman his man was talking about, and nodded his consent. Then, pointing to another hostage that was still seated, he said, "You take her place." Aziz could not have cared less what his men wanted to do with these women. They were the spoils of war.

With a quick yank, Rielly pulled herself from the terrorist's grip. "Take your filthy hands off me."

Abu Hasan, somewhat surprised at the strength of the slender woman, paused for a brief second and then raised his hand. In a wide arcing motion he swung at her head with an open hand.

Rielly, at her father's suggestion, had enrolled in self-defense classes after the rape. She had taken them very seriously, and the instincts were still there. She saw the blow coming and raised her forearm. The blow knocked her slightly off balance, but she remained defiantly on her feet.

What Rielly didn't know was that she would have been better off if she had kept her instincts in check. Like most Arab men, Abu Hasan was used to submissive women and was not about to tolerate this type of behavior, especially in front of the other men. This time he swung with a closed fist and hit a cowering Rielly in the temple.

The blow sent Rielly to the floor, where she curled up in a ball. Kicking her in the back viciously, the terrorist then grabbed her by the hair and dragged her back to the main group of hostages. He released her hair and dropped her to the floor like a sack. Rielly lay there, her hands covering her face as the tears flowed from her eyes, her back and head screaming in pain. She wasn't crying as much from the pain as from mental anguish. Anna Rielly knew what was going to happen to her, and the vision of what lay ahead only made her cry harder.

18

THE JOINT CHIEFS briefing room was once again crowded with people. Gone were the politicians from yesterday, replaced by members of the military's Joint Special Operations Command and the FBI's Hostage Rescue Team. At the far end of the table, FBI Director Roach was accompanied by several of his deputy directors, his international and domestic terrorism chiefs, and the commander of the Hostage Rescue Team, Sid Slater.

Skip McMahon had been left back at the command post to keep an eye on things and to get the debriefing of the recently released group of hostages started. Secret Service Director Tracy was also present with several of his deputies, and CIA Director Stansfield and Irene Kennedy were seated next to Flood at the head of the table, opposite the FBI contingent. The rest of the table was dominated with Pentagon brass and Special Forces types.

General Flood was far more comfortable with this audience than he had been with the one the day before. He would not have to mince words with this group; they all spoke his language. Flood's confidence was also bolstered by the briefing he had received from Stansfield and Kennedy an hour earlier. Now that he had a clearer picture of what Aziz had in mind, he could prepare his battle plan, and as far as the general was concerned, it was exactly that, a battle plan. Flood and Stansfield had come to the conclusion, after the early morning debacle at the White House, that Vice President Baxter did not have the fortitude and vision to lead them through this crisis. Those were Stansfield's words; the general had actually used the words "nuts" and "guts."

It came down to the issue of history, Flood had explained. Not in the sense of *making it* as much as *setting a precedent*. As a military historian Flood knew all too well the pitfalls of taking the easy road in times of crisis, of negotiating for today without an eye to the future. In the not-so-recent past Neville Chamberlain had shown all the world, and future generations, how appeasement and negotiations worked when dealing with a madman. More recently, George Bush had given a valuable lesson in how to deal with a megalomaniac. Simply cutting off an arm does not suffice; pulling up short of a complete victory is not enough; the only way to solve the problem is to lop off the head of the man behind the aggression.

The general had decided he would do everything in his significant power to end the crisis at the White House in a quick and decisive manner. Negotiating, delaying, handing over concessions, were all a distraction from the big picture—the future of international terrorism and how it affected the national security of America. The money they had released this morning had instantly saved the lives of twenty-five people, but how many lives would it cost down the road? How much of that money would be used to train and fund terrorists, how much of it would be used to strike against America and her citizens both abroad and at home?

Flood and Stansfield had made a pact to do everything possible to persuade the vice president to take action—to make sure Rafique Aziz did not walk out of the White House alive. Their options were plentiful, as the United States was fortunate to have not one but three highly skilled, world-class counterterrorist strike teams: the FBI's Hostage Rescue Team, the Army's Delta Force, and the Navy's SEAL Team Six. These three groups fired more ammunition in one year than an entire division of marines, and it paid off. Each of the three units always had teams on standby, referred to as go-teams. When on the go-team rotation, one was expected to stay close to home, carry a pager twenty-four-seven, and be ready to drop everything and hightail it to HQ in two hours or less. For the FBI, they scrambled out of the HRT's headquarters in Quantico, Virginia; for SEAL Team Six, it was Little Creek, Virginia; and for Delta Force, it was Fort Bragg, North Carolina.

Yesterday morning, when the White House was hit, the pagers started going off, and within hours all three teams were converging on the White House, vying for intelligence and position. There was a competitive edge between the three that was fostered more than anything by shooting competitions and mock takedowns. They all shared information on training and lessons learned in the field and were respectful of each other, but in the end they each thought their team was the best.

This was where the problems started. Like three quarterbacks fighting for the starting spot, they clashed, invariably, because of egos. And make no mistake about it, the men who ran these teams had huge egos. This was the issue General Flood was going to try to handle.

The general looked down at the assemblage and started calmly, "We have been given full authority by the vice president to prepare plans for the rescue of the hostages and the retaking of the White House. It goes without saying that none of what we are about to discuss is for public consumption." Pausing, the general held up a finger. "First issue. There is a certain myth that has been promulgated over the last several decades that we are forbidden by law to use the American military in domestic policing operations. In my mind, and the minds of many others, including Director Roach, this very narrow interpretation of the law does not apply to our current crisis. This is not Waco or Ruby Ridge; this is a paramilitary assault on a federal building by foreign soldiers, and we are going to use every resource at our disposal to resolve this conflict." The general paused to make his point clear. "We have three top-notch counterterrorist strike teams at our disposal, and we plan on using all of you in one way or another." Flood looked at the leaders of each unit to make sure he was understood. "I am a firm believer in interservice rivalries. It's a great training tool that helps instill unit cohesion and a sense of fighting pride. But," cautioned the general, "there is no place for that rivalry in war, and this is war. Over twenty people have died already, and we are sure to lose more. Now, I have been receiving reports about little turf wars flaring up around the White House between your people." Flood looked individually at the leaders of Delta, HRT, and SEAL Team Six. "As of this moment, this bickering is over," growled Flood. The general let his words sink in. "We know what your strengths are. Delta is best at taking down airliners and has a slight edge on airborne assaults, HRT is best at negotiating and has the most practical experience in standoffs, and SEAL Team Six has a clear edge in jumping, diving and explosives."

Flood pointed to the director of the FBI. "I have already consulted with Directors Roach, Tracy, and Stansfield and General Campbell, and we are in agreement on the following deployment of assets. First"—the general stressed the word and held up his forefinger—"the FBI's Hostage Rescue Team will deploy across the street from the West Wing in the Executive Office Building and make plans for a ground assault. If we need to go in on short notice, HRT will probably be our first option." Flood shifted his attention to Colonel Bill Gray, the man in charge of Delta Force. Gray was a former ranger and had been with Delta since its inception in 1977. "Billy, you and your people still know your way around Andrews, National, Dulles, and Baltimore?"

"Yes, General." One of Delta Force's specialties was handling hijackings, and they had developed the good habit of gathering advance site intelligence at potential airports. With the cooperation of airport officials, Delta would send operators to various installations to learn the ropes as mechanics, flight attendants, baggage handlers, and a variety of other skills that might come in handy in the event of a hijacking. Delta also liked to conduct security checks on the airports to see how their systems, procedures, and people would stand up. Delta's operators would ferret around the facilities, sometimes announced and sometimes unannounced, and check out underground runway tunnels, rooftop sniping positions, and other areas of interest. The simple logic being, the more advance work they did the easier it would be to handle a real crisis.

Flood continued. "Good. We've decided to use Delta Force to handle anything that goes down at the airports, and also, as an airborne strike force if needed." Flood looked at Colonel Gray. "General Campbell will brief you on the deployment of your assets later." The general pulled back and looked around the room. "This is no Waco, ladies and gentlemen. Once we go in, we go in and we keep going in until we take the building. If we send HRT through the door, we need Delta Force up in the air and ready to come in hot." Flood looked to SEAL Team Six's commanding officer, Dan Harris, the same man who had helped Rapp kidnap Fara Harut. "SEAL Team Six is going to play two roles. First and foremost they are to advise both Delta and HRT on explosives, and secondly they will be used as the primary chase team. If Aziz leaves the country, Six will pursue." Flood had other plans for SEAL Team Six, but he was not about to discuss them in front of the group.

"Director Roach and I have decided that General Campbell, of the Joint Special Operations Command"—Flood pointed across the table at the bristly haired ranger—"will coordinate the activities of all three units. Dr. Irene Kennedy"—Flood gestured to his left—"from the CIA, will commence an intelligence briefing in this room as soon as I'm finished. Each unit will also be augmented with Secret Service agents who will act as liaison officers in regards to questions about the floor plans of the White House and the West Wing, where we currently believe the majority of the hostages are being held."

Flood paused for a moment and looked at his watch. "I want fully briefed strike teams in place and ready to move by twenty-one hundred this evening. That gives us eight hours." Looking at the other members of the Joint Chiefs sitting around him, Flood said, "These men and their units are our number one priority. If they ask for something, they get it." Then addressing the entire group, the general said, "Dr. Kennedy will now brief you on the intelligence situation. Director Roach"—Flood nodded to the head of the FBI—"the show is yours. Director Stansfield and I have some business to attend to." With that, the chairman of the Joint Chiefs started for the door as Stansfield slowly rose out of his chair. When the two men reached the door, Flood grabbed one of his aides and said, "Wait five minutes and then bring Admiral DeVoe and Lieutenant Commander Harris to my office."

THE BLUEPRINTS were spread out on the large table in General Flood's office. Mitch Rapp was nodding his head in understanding as Milt Adams showed him the whereabouts of a secret passageway not noted on the drawing. Adams had changed into more appropriate attire and was wearing a blue suit, with a white shirt and solid maroon tie. The tie was held in place by a shiny brass USMC tie bar.

Rapp looked down at a marking on the blueprint and asked, "That door is fake?"

"Well, it's not fake exactly. It works, but it's always locked."

"How are we going to get through it? . . . Do we have to pick it?"

"No." Adams grinned dubiously, and then reaching into his pocket, he extracted a large key ring. "This right here"—Adams found the right key—"this is an S-key." He held up the key proudly for Rapp to see.

"What in the hell is an S-key?" Rapp asked.

"An S-key," Adams said in a dramatic tone, "gets you into all of the sensitive areas. All of the agents on the presidential detail have one and only a select few others. This little key opens stuff like the weapons lockers and"—Adams tapped the blueprint—"doors that lead to places that don't exist."

Rapp took the key from Adams and studied it. He had taken a liking to the old man. He knew his stuff, and if Rapp's gut was right, he could trust him in a pinch. "If this thing is so important, how did you just walk off the job with one?"

Adams snatched the key back, acting more offended than he really was. "How many times do I have to tell you? I ran the place. Those goofy White House ushers like to think they run things . . . the way they always strut around; well, let me tell you, it was my place. When something needed to get done, I was the one they called."

"Take it easy, Milt. I believe you. I'm just ribbing you a little bit."

"You're a funny guy, Mr. Secret Agent Man." Adams reached out with surprising quickness and poked Rapp in the stomach.

At that exact moment, the door to General Flood's office opened and in walked Director Stansfield and the chairman of the Joint Chiefs himself. Flood wasn't more than a step into the room before he was tugging at the buttons of his uniform blouse; he always seemed to be in a hurry to get out of the constricting tunic. By the time he reached the conference table, the jacket was off. "This must be Milt Adams," he said. The capacious general walked over to the considerably smaller Adams and extended his hand. "It's nice to meet you, Milt." Flood then gestured to Stansfield. "Have you met Thomas Stansfield?"

Adams shook his head and extended his hand. "Nope."

Stansfield smiled ever so slightly. "It's nice to meet you. I've heard a lot about you." Stansfield pumped his hand. "General Flood tells me you fought with the Marines on Iwo Jima."

"Yep. The Sixth Ammunition Company."

There was an awkward moment of silence, and then the general said, "Mitch here tells us you think you may have found a way into the White House." Flood glanced down at his conference table.

"Yep." Adams waved them over to his blueprints and proceeded to show Stansfield and Flood the way in.

Adams was about sixty seconds into his song and dance, and everything seemed to be going pretty well with one exception. He kept using the plural *we* instead of the singular *I.* Stansfield picked up on this and began glancing at Rapp for clarification. Milt Adams had offered his guide services to Rapp, and Rapp had instantly seen the value in bringing Adams along. What he hadn't yet figured out was how to pitch the idea to his boss.

General Flood made the question moot when he interrupted Adams by asking, "What's this 'we' stuff?"

Looking up from the blueprints, Adams waggled his thumb back and forth between himself and Rapp. "Mitch and me . . . that's who the 'we' is."

"Hmm," snorted Flood with a frown thrown in for good measure. "Aren't you a little old for this kind of stuff, Milt?"

"I might be old, but I'm fit as a fiddle." Adams turned to Rapp. "Should I show 'em?"

Slightly embarrassed, Rapp nodded and said, "Sure." Milt had already given Rapp proof of his fitness.

Adams hit the deck and ripped off twenty push-ups in quick order; then he sprang back to his feet, barely out of breath. "I do a hundred push-ups and two hundred sit-ups every morning, and I walk five miles a day." Adams licked his lips. "Except Sundays . . . Sundays are my day off."

General Flood eyeballed the little spark plug before him, unsure of what to make of the unorthodox display and slightly envious, since he had let his own fitness slide so far.

"I don't think his fitness will be an issue," Rapp added hastily. "If there's any heavy work to be done, I can handle it. The key is his knowledge of the interior. It'll be invaluable to me."

Stansfield was skeptical. "Why not grab someone from the Secret Service?"

"They don't know where everything is." Adams shook his head. "They know where some of the stuff is, but not all of it. I know every inch of that building."

Flood studied Adams for a moment and said, "You know things could get hairy in there."

Milt Adams looked up at the general with a no-nonsense grin on his face. "You know, General, I spent almost two months on Iwo. We lost over six thousand marines, and the Japs lost over twenty thousand soldiers. I saw buddies get their heads literally blown clear off; I saw men burned to death; I saw people die in the worst ways you could imagine." Adams shook his head, "No offense, gentlemen, but it's all child's play compared to the hell I went through on that island."

Flood had been in battle himself, but nothing that even came close to the hell that had occurred in the battle for Iwo Jima. "I would imagine you're right." The general was beginning to admire the old man's spunk. After another moment of consideration, Flood said, "Mitch, if you think it's a good idea, I'm behind you." Then turning to the director of the CIA, he asked, "Thomas?"

Stansfield, with his typical calm demeanor answered, "If Mitch thinks it wise . . . I'm behind him as well."

Just then there was a knock on the door, and everyone turned. General Flood bellowed across the room, "Enter."

Lt. Commander Harris and Admiral DeVoe stepped into the room and saluted. The admiral said, "You wanted to see us, General."

Flood returned the salute and said, "Yes. Come over here, gentlemen. I don't want you to think your talents are being squandered while Delta Force and the FBI get all of the action. I have plans for you, but I didn't want to discuss them in front of the group."

The two naval officers approached the group. Admiral DeVoe was the commander of the Naval Special Warfare Group and in charge of all SEAL teams. Harris, looking quite a bit more like an officer than the last time he and Rapp had met, walked at his boss's side. His ponytail and beard had been removed at the direction of Admiral DeVoe. The unruly hygiene of a terrorist was fine when Harris was holed up down at HQ in Little Creek or out in the field, but a meeting with the Joint Chiefs was cause for a more by-the-book appearance.

"I think you know these two gentlemen." Flood pointed to Rapp and Stansfield.

Harris nodded professionally. "Director Stansfield, Mr. Kruse." The admiral did the same.

Rapp stuck out his hand. "It's good to see you again, Harry."

Harris locked on to Rapp's hand and shook it firmly. "Good to see you, Mitch."

Flood grabbed the two naval officers by the shoulders and showed them the blueprints strewn out across the conference table. "Gentlemen, I've asked you to join us because I'd like your opinion on something."

19

Washington, D.C.

AS THE SUN set on the capital, two hulking C-130s descended from the darkening sky on their final approach to Andrews Air Force Base. The base, located a short hop to the southeast of the White House, had been chosen by the Joint Special Operations Command as the forward staging area for what was now known as Operation Rat Catcher. Security at the base had been doubled for the arrival of its newest contingent, and all nonessential personnel had been removed from the staging area. The Army took its secrecy surrounding Delta Force very seriously.

The large matte green cargo planes moved in perfect synchronicity, both banking for the runway at the same time and dropping their landing gear, their powerful turboprop engines rumbling in the stagnant humid air of the Potomac River Valley. The first plane touched down smoothly, followed just a dozen seconds later by the second. The control tower directed the two planes to a group of large hangars, where they were met by Air Force ground crews, who had been told in advance not to turn on the bright floodlights. The people who had traveled from Pope Air Force Base in North Carolina were used to working in the dark and rather preferred it.

As the planes taxied to a stop, they spun ninety degrees on a dime and left their tails facing the open doors of a sprawling hangar. Bright yellow chocks were thrown under the wheels by the ground crew, and the loud engines were cut. A hydraulic whir announced the lowering of the rear cargo ramps, revealing a mass of black-clad men standing in two rows, almost seventy in each plane. They represented the bulk of the A and B assault squadrons of Delta Force, the U.S. Army's supersecret counterterrorist assault and commando force.

The men filed down the ramps. They came in all shapes and sizes, but all were at the apex of physical condition and walked with the grace and confidence of world-class athletes. Each man carried a large black backpack loaded with equipment. Most of them had H&K MP-10 submachine guns with integral suppressors strapped to the top of the packs, but there were others who carried assault shotguns, sniping rifles, and even several who had 7.62-mm heavy-caliber machine guns.

Colonel Bill Gray, Delta Force's commander, stood by the door of the darkened hangar and looked proudly at his men as they filed past. Gray was also dressed in the standard black ninja jumpsuit, although it was highly unlikely that he would be going into the fray, unlike his cowboy counterpart at SEAL Team Six. Gray got along well with Lt. Commander Harris, but thought it irresponsible for him to lead individual strikes, a point that he had just recently brought up with the general staff of the Joint Special Operations Command.

Colonel Gray had stayed in Washington after his afternoon meeting at the Pentagon rather than flying down to Bragg and coming right back. The colonel, who stood just above six feet, had a full head of close-cropped black hair and bushy eyebrows to match. The native Texan had the unanimous respect of his men due to the fact that he never asked them to do anything he hadn't already done or wasn't willing to do.

At the end of both columns, Gray spotted the two men he was looking for and moved out to meet them. As he approached, the two men saluted. Gray returned the salute and asked, "How was the flight up?"

The two men standing before Gray were the commanders of his A and B squadrons, Lt. Colonel Hank Kleis and Lt. Colonel Pat Miller. Kleis answered, "No sweat. We've been locked and loaded since two; we just had to wait around for it to get dark."

Colonel Gray nodded. "How are the men?"

"Good," answered Kleis. "If they can't get up for this one, I should be drummed out of the service."

Gray looked to Miller, the quieter of the two.

Miller answered, "They're ready."

Nodding, Gray looked over his officers' shoulders and watched the load masters taking equipment off the planes. "Here's how we stand. Pat, you and B squadron are in charge of the airports. Hank, you've got the airborne assault on the White House. Get your communications secured ASAP, and pass the word that I want a staff meeting in thirty minutes." Gray pointed over his shoulder. "There's a briefing room at the rear of the hangar; we'll meet in there. Also tell your troop leaders to bring their sergeant majors. We're gonna get a big intel dump from Langley and the Secret Service, and I want them in on it." Gray turned, and without his having to say anything, the two junior officers fell in astride their senior. "Training is going to be tricky for this. We don't have time to build any mock-ups." The colonel was referring to Hollywood-type sets that Delta used to train for real-life takedowns. The full-scale mock-ups were usually built on a remote area of the massive Eglin Air Force Base, in northern

Florida, and done with blueprints provided by the CIA and satellite imagery provided by the NSA.

"General Flood tells me there is no way this thing will last for more than a week and that we could conceivably be ordered in tonight, so we need to be ready to go, *pronto*. Hank"—Gray pointed to the commander of his A squadron—"I want you to divide the White House into sections immediately and get your troops assigned to handle specific sectors of the building. If we get the phone call in two hours, I want to have, at the very least, a basic plan . . . . As time goes on and we get more intel, we can fine-tune it."

Gray turned to his B squadron commander. "Pat, I want advance teams in place at Reagan, Dulles, and Baltimore. Prewire at least two planes at each airport for video and sound, and do it quietly . . . . We don't want the press covering any of this. Put your people in the airline-mechanic uniforms while they're doing it. The less attention we raise the better. Langley tells us that Aziz is using the Situation Room, so we have to assume he's getting real-time coverage from the media. The FBI is sending us some agents to help with subpoenas." Gray stopped abruptly and slapped both men on the back. "Now get moving. I want updates at the staff meeting in"—Gray looked at his watch—"twenty-eight minutes."

The two squadron commanders hustled off in earnest to form up their groups, and Gray turned back toward the open hangar door. Grabbing his secure digital phone from his tactical assault vest, Gray hit the speed dial for the operations center at the Pentagon. As the colonel waited for the encryption to kick in, he noticed a string of navigation lights descending on the runway. They would be his MD-530 Little Birds, flown by the Army's 160th Special Operations Regiment. These were the stealthy, almost silent, helicopters that would be crucial in any assault on the White House. Farther down the valley, Gray could see another string of red and green lights. Unlike the Little Birds, Gray could already hear this second flight of helicopters. Those would be his MH-60 Black Hawks. Faster, larger, and louder than the Little Birds, the Black Hawks would be used to chase Aziz if he headed for an airport.

Gray watched as the first of the Little Birds came in and touched down softly. Seven more of the small black helicopters quickly followed. Gray shook his head. Everything was happening too fast. If they went in tonight, it wouldn't be a calculated raid; it would be a bloodbath. They would lose hostages, and he would lose men. He needed more time to get things set up.

*   *   *

TWO MILES NORTHWEST of the White House sat the Naval Observatory, the official residence of the vice president of the United States. The large circular estate was located off Massachusetts Avenue on Embassy Row, atop a hill. Its many gardens and rolling wooded lawn provided a serenity and seclusion that was quite absent at the Executive Mansion.

Irene Kennedy drove north in her maroon Toyota Camry on Massachusetts Avenue. Every time Kennedy drove through this area of Washington, she couldn't help but think that this one-mile strip of asphalt had to have the single largest concentration of electronic surveillance equipment in the world. With all of the embassies spying on each other and their host country, and the FBI, the CIA, the National Security Agency, the Defense Intelligence Agency, and the National Reconnaissance Office all spying on the embassies, it was unlikely that any conversation went unrecorded.

As Kennedy continued north, the large plantation-style home of the vice president came into view on her left, its fresh white paint bathed in floodlights. Kennedy drove past the main gate and the slew of reporters and camera crews that had besieged the compound. Not far past the main gate, she took a left onto Observatory Circle and worked her way around the north side of the estate. A small unmarked gate appeared on her left, and Kennedy turned off the city street and onto the private drive.

Four uniformed Secret Service officers and a German shepherd approached her car. The men all wore flak jackets over their white shirts. Kennedy rolled down her window and presented her credentials.

The officer looked at her ID and said, "Could you please pop your trunk, Dr. Kennedy?"

After the dog had taken two laps around the small sedan and the trunk had been thoroughly checked, Kennedy was granted admission. Two white steel retractable bollards standing three feet tall and one foot wide dropped down beneath pavement, and then the heavy black gate opened inward. Kennedy maneuvered her car up the winding driveway and passed several of the outlying buildings that were used for offices. Near the main house she saw her boss's limousine and parked next to it. She was several minutes late for the nine-thirty P.M. meeting.

The normal complement of uniformed officers was bolstered by the black-clad, machine-gun-toting men of the Service's Emergency Response Team. These heavily armed men could be seen patrolling the elevated tree line just beyond the fence. They moved ominously from shadow to shadow, determined not to allow another debacle to take place. A second line of ERT officers ringed the actual residence, and the vice presidential detail was inside the home, never more than one room away from their charge.

One of the vice president's staffers appeared in the entrance doorway, and Kennedy was ushered into the large foyer. Director Stansfield was sitting on a couch to the right with his legs crossed. He was, as always, wearing a dark conservative suit, white shirt, and striped tie. Stansfield peered over the top of his spectacles when Kennedy entered, a questioning expression on his face.

Kennedy plopped down next to him and said, "It looks good. Mitch went over to the White House and checked out the fence line. He thinks they can get to the shaft without any problems."

Stansfield nodded thoughtfully. "What do you think?"

Kennedy glanced up at the ceiling for a second. "We need someone in there, and he's the best we have."

"What about bringing Adams along?"

"I'm not crazy about the idea, but again, I have to defer to Mitch. He's the one with the field experience." Kennedy looked at her boss. "You seem to have some reservations."

Stansfield pondered the comment for a second and shook his head. "No. I trust Mitch. How are you holding up?"

Kennedy rolled her eyes. "I could use a little sleep, but besides that, I'm fine."

The sound of dress shoes clicking on the hardwood floor caught their attention, and both looked to see Dallas King coming down the hallway. The vice president's chief of staff was dressed in a pressed French blue dress shirt and a pair of black slacks, looking dapper as always. King stopped about ten feet away and said, "The vice president is ready to see you."

Stansfield and Kennedy followed the swaggering young chief of staff down the hallway.

Without knocking, King opened the door to Baxter's private study, and Stansfield and Kennedy followed. Vice President Baxter sat in a large leather chair in front of the fireplace reading over the speech he was to give to the nation in a little over an hour. Upon seeing his guests, he set the speech and his pen down.

Stansfield and Kennedy sat on the couch, and King stood in front of the fireplace next to his boss. Baxter leaned forward and folded his hands. "What would you like to talk to me about?"

"We think," Stansfield started, "that we may have found a way to get someone into the White House undetected by the terrorists."

"Really," Baxter said, showing his interest by moving forward to the edge of the chair. "How?"

Stansfield looked to Kennedy, and she said, "There is a ventilation system that circulates all of the air in the White House. The main intake and exhaust ducts are located on the roof, but there is a backup duct that leads from the basement of the White House to an area on the South Lawn."

Baxter looked at Stansfield and said, "I've never noticed any ventilation ducts on the South Lawn."

"Neither have I," replied the director of the CIA. "They're concealed with trees and bushes. We've done a reconnaissance of the area and feel we can get to it without the terrorists being alerted."

"So what do you want to do?" asked King.

Kennedy remained focused on the vice president. "Before we can consider staging a rescue of the hostages, we must know what's going on inside. Unless we get someone on the inside to coordinate an attack, our chances for success will be almost nothing."

"So, we're not talking about sending in a team of commandos." Vice President Baxter squeezed his hands together. "I want to be very clear about that. Until we're sure what he wants, I'm not going to rush into anything."

"We only want to send in one person." Kennedy spoke in a reassuring voice. She thought it would be best to leave Milt Adams out of the picture for now. "Once that person has given us a clear picture of what we're up against, we will present you with a plan to retake the building by force."

"If needed," added King.

"If needed." Kennedy glanced up at King and then back to the vice president.

King placed one hand on the mantel of the fireplace and the other on his hip. He had a feeling he knew whom the CIA would use to check out the building. "This person," King started to ask, "would he by any chance be that Mr. Kruse fellow?"

Kennedy and Stansfield shared a look, and Kennedy replied, "Yes."

"Well, that's funny," said King in an off voice, "because I did some checking on your Mr. Kruse, and I don't think his dossier matches up with the man I met yesterday."

"'Mr. Kruse' is an alias for the man you met," Stansfield answered flatly.

"What's his real name?" King asked.

"That's classified."

"Come now." King smirked. "If we're going to risk the lives of all of these hostages by sending your man in, I think at the bare minimum we should know who he is."

Stansfield looked at King for a moment and then turned to the vice president. "There is no rational reason that I can think of for telling you his name."

"I can," answered King with confidence. "If we are going to stick our necks out, I want to know who this guy is and where he's from."

Secrecy was an issue Stansfield never budged on. Being a former field operative himself, he understood firsthand the perils of sharing information too freely. That, combined with the fact that King needed to be reminded of his station in life, caused the director to reply, "Mr. Kruse has been sent on highly delicate missions by three presidents, and not one of them ever knew his real identity. I am not about to tell the chief of staff for the vice president—who, I might remind everyone, has a penchant for talking to the press—the real identity of one of my top operatives." Stansfield turned to Baxter and in the same even tone asked, "Mr. Vice President, maybe you and I should talk about this alone?"

Baxter looked at King sideways. The message was clear—get back in your cage and stay quiet. Turning his focus back to Stansfield, Baxter said, "I don't need to know his real identity, Director Stansfield. I trust you. One thing, however, does concern me . . . this Mr. Kruse fellow seems to be a bit volatile. Possibly uncontrollable."

"What are you basing that assumption on?"

"From what I saw firsthand at the Pentagon, yesterday."

"What you've seen, sir," answered Kennedy, "might lead you to believe he is uncontrollable, but in reality he is extremely reliable. He follows orders to a T, and, most important, he gets results." Kennedy knew her words were slightly skewed, but she also knew there was no one better suited for the job than Mitch Rapp. "His only fault, which some would argue is why he is so good, is that he doesn't tolerate mistakes or stupidity." Kennedy stopped momentarily and then added, "In Attorney General Tutwiler's case I think he proved to be correct."

Vice President Baxter nodded soberly. "Yes, he did."

"Mr. Vice President," Stansfield interjected with finality. "Mr. Kruse is one of the best operatives I've ever seen . . . and you know how long I've been doing this."

Baxter leaned back in his chair and folded his hands in front of his mouth. "Are there any legal issues to be concerned about?"

"Such as?"

"Using an employee of the CIA for something like this. The American people are very squeamish about your agency operating within our borders."

"Technically, I think we're fine, and given the circumstances, I don't think anyone is going to make an issue out of it."

"As long as he's successful," added King. "Does the FBI know anything about your plan?"

"No."

The vice president stood and walked over to a window away from the group. Baxter thought about the potential pitfalls. If this Kruse didn't perform as advertised, there could be some serious repercussions. Why wasn't someone from the FBI sent in? Why didn't they wait to see if they could get more hostages released? The questions would go on and on. Baxter saw a risk hell, the whole thing was a risk, and his political instincts told him to protect himself. After another minute of thought, Baxter decided to walk that thin line again.

The vice president came back over and sat. "Director Stansfield, I have given you . . . " Baxter paused, searching for the most innocuous word, *"permission* to collect intelligence in this matter. What you choose to do specifically is up to you. I don't need to be kept in the loop for every decision along the way."

Stansfield, an expert at interpreting politicalspeak, understood the vice president clearly. It was another Iran-Contra. Baxter wanted Stansfield and the CIA to stick their necks out, and if things fell apart, he would have his plausible denial.

Stansfield looked at Baxter and nodded his understanding. There would be time to handle these details at a later point. For now they needed to get the ball rolling.

Baxter continued, "I'm reluctant to do anything until Aziz releases his next set of demands, which, of course, will be tomorrow morning. If we can exchange more hostages for money, I'm inclined to do it."

"Sir," said Kennedy, "if I may be frank, I don't think he's going to keep asking for money."

"What do you think he will ask for?"

Stansfield leaned forward and fielded the question. "That is anyone's guess." The director of the CIA wasn't about to divulge his ace in the hole, their custody of Fara Harut—especially to someone like Baxter. "But, I would agree with Irene."

Baxter pondered what the next demand might be and then turned his attention back to the matter at hand. "Who knows about your plans for Mr. Kruse?"

"General Flood, a select few others at the Pentagon, and us."

"No one at the FBI?" Baxter repeated.

"No."

"For now I think you should go about collecting your intelligence independent of the FBI. . . . They have enough to worry about."

Stansfield again read between the lines and nodded. The FBI was to be kept in the dark about Rapp. More proof that the vice president wanted to insulate himself from any potential disaster.

Baxter looked at Stansfield and asked, "Is that all?"

"Yes, I think so."

"Good. Thank you for keeping us informed." Baxter motioned for the door. "Now, if you'll excuse us, I need to get ready to address the nation."

Stansfield and Kennedy stood and started for the door. As they neared it, Vice President Baxter called out, "If you decide to send your man in, please keep him on a short leash."

Stansfield gave his silent answer with a nod, then followed Kennedy into the hallway.

20

THEY HIT THE first checkpoint three blocks away from the White House. A quarter of a moon shone in the night sky, and not a cloud was in sight. Rapp was riding in the backseat of the long, black Suburban with Milt Adams. Lt. Commander Harris of SEAL Team Six was in the passenger seat, and Chief Petty Officer Mick Reavers was driving. Following the Suburban through the checkpoints were a plain blue van and a larger black box van. Lt. Commander Harris handled the D.C. Metro Police at the first two checkpoints and then the Secret Service agents at the last checkpoint. Word had been sent down from on high that the CIA was moving in some sensitive equipment to conduct surveillance.

Approaching the White House from the east, they pulled through the last checkpoint at Pennsylvania Avenue and Fifteenth Street. Reavers, the large linebacker type that had been along on the mission to grab Harut, drove the Suburban onto Hamilton Place and continued past the southern edge of the Treasury Building. The White House was now in sight, ahead and to the right, the top floor of the mansion visible above the trees. On the right was the entrance to the underground parking garage that the terrorists had used just yesterday to assault and take the White House. A white Suburban was now parked at the top of the ramp, blocking its use. Straight ahead was a closed gate the led onto the south grounds of the White House.

Reavers extinguished the headlights and turned left onto East Executive Avenue. Continuing south for another fifty feet, Reavers took a hard right at the direction of Milt Adams and pulled up on the curb, the front grill of the truck stopping inches from the heavy black fence. As had already been decided, the blue van backed up onto the curb about twenty feet to the north of the Suburban and stopped with its rear bumper almost touching the fence. The large, black box van parked on the street, right in between the two vehicles, creating a space in the middle that would shield the men from prying eyes.

Doors began to open, and bodies piled out of all three vehicles. Everyone, even Milt Adams, was dressed in the standard black Nomex jumpsuits worn by Navy SEALs. Three of Harris's SEALs set up a security perimeter on the outside of the vehicles, while four more unfurled a massive black tarp. In a little over a minute they had the tarp stretched over the top of all three vehicles and secured. With the tarp in place, two of the men went to work on the fence. With a small handheld hydraulic jack, they began prying apart the vertical bars so Rapp and Adams could pass through.

Harris and Rapp approached the fence and tried to spy a look at the roof of the White House. The trees and undergrowth between them and the residence were dense, hopefully dense enough to conceal their movements.

Harris raised his small secure Motorola radio to his mouth and asked, "Slick, whada'ya got for me?"

Lying on his belly less than a block away, Charlie Wicker peered through a pair of night-vision binoculars. Wicker was set up on the backside of the pitched roof of the Treasury Building. Arriving thirty minutes in advance of the others, he had been watching the terrorist sitting atop the roof of the White House, trying to discern any patterns. Wicker lowered the lip mike on his headset and said, "He has no idea you're there. He spends most of his time looking west, over at that ugly building on the other side of the White House."

"Good," replied Harris. "Anything else to report?"

Wicker squinted as he looked at the hooded man no more than one hundred fifty feet away—the only thing separating them was a half inch of bulletproof Plexiglas. "Yeah . . . I think I can take this guy out with a pair of fifties." Wicker was referring to a .50 caliber sniping rifle. The heavy-caliber weapon was used by Special Forces snipers to take out targets at distances exceeding a mile.

"I'll keep that in mind. Let me know if he starts looking our way. Over." Harris turned to Rapp. "So far so good."

"Good." Rapp led the way and he, Harris, and Adams walked over to the blue van. The side cargo doors were open, revealing an array of equipment stacked in electronic racks, or, as the man sitting behind the main console called them, "pizza racks." Marcus Dumond was a twenty-six-year-old computer genius and almost convicted felon. Rapp had brought Dumond into the fold at Langley three years earlier. The young cyber genius had run into some trouble with the Feds while he was earning his master's degree in computer science at MIT. He was alleged to have hacked into one of New York's largest banks and then transferred funds into several overseas accounts. The part that interested the CIA was that

Dumond wasn't caught because he left a trail; he was caught because he got drunk one night and bragged about his financial plunders to the wrong person.

At the time, Dumond was living with Steven Rapp, Mitch's younger brother. When the older Rapp heard about Dumond's problems with the FBI, he called Irene Kennedy and told her the hacker was worth a look.

Langley doesn't like to admit that they employ some of the world's best computer pirates, but these young cyber geeks are encouraged to hack into any and every computer system they can. Most of these hacking raids are directed at foreign companies, banks, governments, and military computer systems. But just getting into a system isn't enough. The challenge is to hack in, get the information, and get out without leaving a trace that the system was ever compromised.

The wiry Marcus Dumond poked his head out the open door, a cigarette hanging from his mouth and a pair of thick glasses perched on his nose. "Commander Harris, can you tell your men to cut a hole in the tarp? I have to raise my communications boom."

Harris turned to one of his nearby men and told him to cut the hole. Dumond then stepped out of the van with a large fanny pack. Over by the box van, a long folding table had been set up and a series of blueprints and schematics were being taped to the side of the van. Portable red-filter lights provided limited lighting and gave everyone's face an eerie, sallow look. Setting the pack atop the table, Dumond opened it and extracted a small black object. Holding it in front of Rapp, Harris, and finally Adams, he said, "Micro video-and-audio surveillance unit. You guys have both used these, right?" Rapp and Harris nodded. The objects were about an inch and a half thick, about four inches long, and about three inches across. At the top of the unit was a small, thin bump about the size of a pen tip. The tiny, highly sensitive microphone was encased in black foam. Next to it was a thin three-inch fiber-optic cord, at the end of which was a tiny lens.

Dumond turned to Adams. "These little babies have two settings, regular and pulse. The regular will last about three days, and the pulse will give you almost twelve. The pulse still supplies full audio but only gives a snapshot every five seconds." Dumond shrugged his shoulders. "It's up to you guys how you want to use them, but I would suggest a little of both . . . just in case." Flipping the small unit over, Dumond said, "I've attached Velcro to the back of every unit. Here"—Dumond picked up a plastic bag—"are the corresponding Velcro patches. I've also thrown in these little alcohol wipes to clean the surface before you attach the Velcro patch, especially if you're in a place where there's a lot of dust, like a ventilation duct. I've packed twelve black and twelve white units." Dumond turned to Rapp. "You know the routine. Install them at choke points and areas of high traffic. I can maneuver the cameras a little bit from remote, but I advise against it. It burns a lot of juice, so try to give us a good angle when you set them up. Any questions?" Dumond paused, giving them a chance, and then said, "Good, let's check your communications and get you on your way."

Dumond led the three men over to the blue van and retrieved two secure radios and headsets. Dumond had already checked out the units on the way over from Langley. Turning Adams around, Dumond placed the radio in a specially designed pocket that sat just above his left shoulder blade. Dumond then placed the headset on Adams and showed him how to adjust the lip mike. In the meantime, Rapp placed his radio in his vest and turned his black baseball cap backward. Over the top of the cap he secured the headset and checked the mike with Harris.

After they were positive the units worked properly, Dumond cautioned, "I'm probably going to lose you guys as you go through the tunnel. The jammer they are using to black out the president's bunker is creating a dead zone. All our sensors tell us that the interference dissipates as you reach the upper levels of the mansion, so I want you to come up to the second floor as quickly as you can and reestablish radio contact." Dumond reached back into the van and grabbed another pack. "I'm also going to give you this secure field radio. It has more range and power. And I put some extra radio batteries in here just in case." Dumond held up a small black nylon pack.

Rapp looked at the radio pack and started to wonder if he'd be able to carry all of the equipment through the shaft. Then responding to Dumond's statement, Rapp replied, "We'll try to get to the second floor, but I can't promise anything until I get in there and see what they have. If everything is booby-trapped, we might not even get out of the basement."

"I'll get us out of the basement," Adams said confidently.

Rapp took the second pack from Dumond and asked, "Anything else for us?"

"Nope." Dumond stuck out his fist, and Rapp did the same. Banging Rapp's once on top and once on the bottom, Dumond said, "Good luck, Mitch." Then looking to Adams, he said, "Try and keep this guy out of trouble, will you?"

"I will." Adams smiled.

Rapp thanked Dumond and grabbed Adams. As they walked back over to the Suburban, Rapp's thoughts turned to something he'd been debating for most of the day. The question was whether to arm Adams with a weapon. Rapp's concern was not whether Adams could shoot straight enough to hit anything, but whether he would accidentally shoot Rapp in the back. It was no small concern considering the fact that the Special Forces community rarely went a year without someone accidentally getting shot, and those people were cream of the crop.

With reservation, Rapp asked, "Milt, what do you think about bringing a gun with you, just in case?"

Adams reached into his pocket and pulled out a .357 revolver. "I already have one."

Surprised, Rapp extended his hand. "May I?" Adams handed him the gun, and Rapp immediately recognized it as a Ruger Speed-Six. Before automatics became all the rage with cops, the Speed-Six was a popular, dependable gun for a lot of police departments. The barrel was short, making it easy to draw, and since it was a revolver, jamming was not an issue. Rapp considered for a moment if he should give Adams one of his own silenced weapons and then decided against it. He would just as soon have Adams use a gun he was comfortable with. Besides, if it ever got to the point where Adams had to start shooting, they'd already be well past the point of stealth.

Rapp handed him the gun back and asked, "Do you want a holster?"

Adams shook his head. "Naw . . . I'm used to carrying it in my pocket."

"All right." Rapp stood awkwardly for a second looking down at the tiny Adams, wondering if he really knew what he was getting himself into.

Adams sensed Rapp's mood. "Don't worry about me, Mitch. I wouldn't be doing this if I didn't think it was the right thing."

Rapp smiled and nodded with more respect than Adams could have guessed. The right thing, he thought to himself. What a difference between his generation and Milt's.

Rapp took the next five minutes to get his gear together. With all of his weapons, communications equipment, surveillance equipment, and some limited rations, his gear weighed more than seventy-five pounds. Because of the tight space of the shaft, he and Harris had decided it would be best if he towed it behind him with a rope.

Finally, with all of their equipment assembled, Rapp, Adams, and Harris waited at the fence line for the green light.

IN A WINDOWLESS room on the seventh floor of the main building at Langley, a select few had gathered to monitor the progress of Mitch Rapp and Milt Adams. The room was strikingly similar to a television network control booth. On the main wall was a bank of nineteen-inch monitors, four rows of them, running ten across. In front of the monitors, at a slightly elevated table, sat four technicians. At their disposal was the latest in video-production equipment. Behind them, and elevated still further, sat Dr. Irene Kennedy, General Campbell, and several of their assistants. The work surface at this level was cluttered with phones and computers. At the third level sat Director Stansfield, General Flood, Colonel Bill Gray, and Admiral DeVoe. The fourth, and last row, was occupied by a half dozen other high-ranking pentagon and CIA officials. Conveniently absent from the group was any representative from the FBI, something that Irene Kennedy did not like.

The four monitors in the bottom left corner were showing the networks and CNN preparing for the vice president's national address. Ten of the monitors, just above the bottom four, showed different shots of the White House's exterior. One was zoomed in on the terrorist sitting in the rooftop guard booth, and the others were either trained on specific doors and windows or general areas.

The remaining twenty-six monitors were pale blue with the exception of one near the middle. It glowed with a reddish hue, showing Rapp and the others at work in the strange red light.

Irene Kennedy's hair was pulled back, and she was wearing a light weight operator's headset, as were all of the others in the first two rows. Kennedy nodded slowly as she listened to Marcus Dumond. After a moment she raised the arm of her headset and turned to look up at the two men sitting directly behind her. "Everything is ready. They're waiting for authorization."

Stansfield and Flood looked at each other briefly, Flood nodding first and Stansfield following suit. Stansfield then looked down at Kennedy and gave his okay.

The director of the CIA watched Kennedy relay the orders and wondered again if he should pick up the phone and tell FBI Director Roach what they were up to. He had in part covered himself by passing the word that they were conducting electronic surveillance, but this was much more than that. If things went bad, it could jeopardize the safety of the hostages.

21

THE WORD WAS passed, and the red-filter light was extinguished. The relatively cool night had turned thick and muggy under the canvas tarp. It had been decided that Rapp would go first, followed by Adams, and then Harris. Rapp felt for the slit in the tarp and pulled it to the side. Taking the main pack, Rapp wedged it through the bars, and then with the smaller packs that Dumond had given him, he turned sideways and squeezed through the bent bars. Adams and Harris followed, and the three of them walked softly through the underbrush, ducking under branches and bending limbs out of their way.

They were careful to stay off the paths that the Secret Service had laid out through the underbrush. The paths were designed to funnel fence jumpers into areas loaded with sensors, and although they didn't think the terrorists were using the perimeter security system, there was no sense in pushing their luck.

When they reached the immediate area of the vent, Lt. Commander Harris whispered into his headset, "Slick, do you have any movement on the roof?"

The reply came back instantly. "Nope. He's still looking to the west."

There was just enough light from the streetlamps for the three of them to see each other. Rapp nodded to Adams; they had both heard the same report over their headsets. Taking his signal, Adams plucked several of the fake bushes from the ground. The bushes were designed to conceal the ventilation hood during all four seasons. Adams moved the shrubs out of the way while Rapp and Harris unfolded a smaller black tarp. With the tarp in place over the top of the hood the three men crawled under it and went to work. Rapp held a small tool pack while Harris aimed a red-filter flashlight for Adams. The old man of the group started by spraying lubricant along the seam in the sheet metal. Then, with a small cordless drill, he zipped out eight screws. Slowly, they began to wiggle the hood back and forth, trying their best to prevent the screeching of metal on metal. The lubricant diminished most of the noise, and inside of sixty seconds they had the hood off and out of the way.

Harris set up a lightweight aluminum tripod while Rapp lowered his gear to the bottom with a climbing rope. The black tarp was thrown over the top. Harris clipped a pulley to the tripod and fed a rope through, taking one end to the fence and tying it to the winch on the front of the Suburban.

Rapp stuck a small flashlight into the open shaft and looked down at the bottom. Harris returned a second later and tied the rope around Rapp's ankles, then put on a pair of gloves. Then after grabbing the rope, he nodded to Rapp and leaned back, ready to take up the slack. Rapp gave Harris the thumbs-up, and then bending at the waist, he stuck his head in the open shaft and began to ease himself inside.

Over his headset Rapp said, "Lower me."

Lt. Commander Harris slowly began to play out the rope until all of the slack was gone, about eight more feet total. Harris then whispered into his headset telling his men back at the Suburban to let the winch out. In the shaft, Rapp started his descent and turned on his small miner's lamp that was strapped over his baseball cap.

As he neared the bottom, he whispered over his headset, "Stop." Dangling like a landed catch, Rapp turned himself so he could bend at the waist and make the ninety-degree turn into the shaft without breaking his back.

"Okay, real slow. Let me out four more feet." He started to move again, and Rapp grabbed on to the sides of the horizontal vent, pulling himself inside. A bit of static crackled through his earpiece, and he said, "Stop. That's good." Rapp pulled his legs toward him, and in a sit-up-like position, he trained the miner's lamp on his feet and untied the rope around his ankles. When he was finished, he said, "Take it back up."

The rope disappeared from sight, and Rapp flipped over onto his stomach. Wasting no time, he grabbed the long rope that he'd used to lower his gear into the shaft and untied it. Then taking a short rope that he'd brought along, he tied one end to the top of his gear and the other end to his left ankle. Rolling back onto his stomach, he trained the small light down the long narrow shaft. It looked as if it went on forever. Rapp could barely make out the turn some two hundred feet away. The shaft seemed to get tighter. Rapp grimaced. He had what he liked to refer to as a healthy phobia of being trapped in places the size of a coffin.

Reluctantly, Rapp started forward down the cramped space, his forearms doing most of the work. Into his lip mike, he whispered, "Milt, I'm moving out." With his gear in tow, Rapp plodded forward like an alligator. The reception on his radio was becoming increasingly cluttered.

*   *   *

NOT LONG AFTER they had lost contact with Rapp, Milt Adams was also lost. The only thing Kennedy and the others could do was wait. Kennedy found herself thinking that this was how the NASA mission controllers must have felt during the Apollo lunar missions. When the astronauts went around the back side of the moon, they would enter a period when communication was impossible. The roomful of scientists would sit nervously at mission control and hope the spacecraft and its men would make it back around without any problems. That was the position they were in now. There was nothing they could do but wait.

Kennedy took off her headset, looked up at a row of clocks on the wall to her right, and remembered there was one thing she could do. Dead in the middle of the wall was the clock noting the local time in Washington, D.C. It was almost eleven in the evening. Several clocks to the right, Kennedy found the time she was looking for. Picking up the secure phone in front of her, she dialed a number by memory. It was an important phone number. It was just before seven in the morning in Tel Aviv, and if her counterpart wasn't in, he would be shortly. After several clicks and whirs someone picked up on the other end.

"Fine."

The word was not an answer to a question, but rather the last name of the man answering the phone, Colonel Ben Fine of the Israeli foreign intelligence service, Mossad. Colonel Fine was Kennedy's direct counterpart, the man in charge of Mossad's counterterrorism section.

"Ben, it's Irene Kennedy."

"Irene," said Fine excitedly. "I'm sorry I haven't called, but I figured you'd be busy."

"Have you been following the crisis?" asked Kennedy in a tired voice.

"Very closely. Is there anything I can do to help?"

"Yes, as a matter of fact, there is." Kennedy looked down at the sheet of paper in front of her. "I'd like you to look at a list of names for me."

"How many?"

"Ten. We have good intel on seven of them, but the last three we've come up blank on." Kennedy again looked at the list of names that had been provided by Dr. Hornig.

"You can count on me putting all of my resources into it. Send me the list, and I will personally make sure it gets taken care of immediately."

"Thank you, Ben. I appreciate it."

There was a pause, and then colonel said, "I have a question for you, as long as I've got you on the line. There have been several reports, all unconfirmed of course, that a certain high-ranking member of Hezbollah is missing." The Israeli colonel stopped talking for a moment and then added, "You wouldn't know anything about this, would you?"

Kennedy lifted her eyes and looked up at the bank of television sets. "I might have some insight into the subject."

Fine didn't reply right away. Instead his silence conveyed an implicit tit-for-tat request. "I assume when the time is right, you will enlighten me."

"I had planned on it," answered Kennedy honestly.

"Good," stated a satisfied Fine. "Do you need anything else from me?"

Kennedy thought about it for a moment and said, "No, not that I can think of, but anything you can do with the names would be greatly appreciated."

"I will get started right away, and do not hesitate to call if you need anything else."

"I won't. Thank you, Ben." After setting the phone back in its cradle, Kennedy placed the list of names in a file folder and walked to the end of her row. Looking up toward the back of the room, she waved the file and caught the attention of one of her people. A man in his early thirties came down the stairs, and Kennedy handed him the file. "Fax this to Colonel Fine immediately." The man nodded dutifully and started back up the stairs, headed for the secure fax machine.

WHITE NOISE hissed through the earpiece. *I have to be near the end,* Rapp thought to himself. The tunnel seemed to be getting smaller and smaller. Rapp was sweating profusely, and his heart rate was much faster than it should have been. Irritated by the noise of his radio, he reached up and took the headset off, letting it fall around his neck. He knew Milt Adams wasn't far behind, because he had heard him sneezing. It must have been the thin layer of dust that lined the metal walls of the duct. There wasn't a lot of it, but Rapp himself had fought back the impulse several times.

Rapp paused for a second and took in a deep breath. He lowered his sweaty head onto his arm and told himself to relax. He was expending far more energy than necessary due to his slightly panicked state. Rapp lay still for almost a minute as he got his breathing under control. His watch told him that he had been in the shaft for almost fifteen minutes. Longer than he had expected. It couldn't be that much farther. After making the left turn that would take him parallel to the southern end of the mansion's foundation, he had turned the miner's light off. Rapp thought it was doubtful that anyone would be in the third basement—Aziz did not have enough men to patrol every area of the White House—but it was not worth the gamble of having the light spill through a crack or a seam in the ductwork.

After several more minutes of confined crawling, Rapp reached the end. He was drenched in sweat, almost all of it from nervous energy. Gently, he let his head fall down on his arm, and he listened to make sure no one was in the boiler room. For the next two minutes that was all he did. Outside the shaft he could hear the heating, ventilation, and cooling system going through the labors of regulating the climate within the old house, but other than that, the only thing he heard was the approaching Milt Adams and his not-so-quiet sneezing.

Rapp decided it was better to open the access panel before Adams and his involuntary reports arrived. He turned on his miner's lamp and ran his hand over the smooth surface of the duct until he felt a groove. Zeroing in with the light, he spotted what he was looking for. Just as Milt had said, there was an access panel right before the duct connected to the filtration system. A not-so-small wave of relief washed over him. The thought of it not being there, and having to crawl all the way back, had occurred to him several times. Before twisting the metal catches up, Rapp drew his silenced Beretta and turned off the miner's light. With the gun in his left hand, he felt for the catches with his right and turned the first one from its horizontal position to vertical. Adams had explained that the panel was attached with hinges on the bottom and two catches at the top.

After twisting the second catch, he slowly allowed the panel to swing downward and looked out into the dimly lit boiler room of the White House. The ventilation duct was hung from the ceiling and ran halfway across the room, where it connected to the hulking HVAC unit that occupied the majority of the room.

Poking only his head out, Rapp methodically searched the room for any signs of motion sensors or trip wires. After making sure it was safe, he pulled back into the duct and rolled over onto his back. He untied the rope around his ankle and noticed Adams crawling toward him roughly forty feet away. Neither man spoke. Rapp had been extremely clear about that aspect of the operation. There was to be no talking unless absolutely needed.

Rapp fed the loose end of the rope out of the opening, leaving several feet dangling toward the ground and the other end tied to his gear. Quickly, he scooted forward to the end of the duct, pushed himself out of the vent, and hung from his fingers, his feet dangling a little more than a foot from the ground. Gently, he let himself drop to the ground, immediately grabbed the rope, and pulled the rest of his gear down. With the pack on the ground, Rapp retrieved his silenced MP-10 submachine gun and turned on the small flashlight affixed to the underside of the barrel.

If Aziz had planted any security devices, Rapp saw no sign of them. Several moments later Milt Adams poked his sweaty, bald head out of the vent and stifled a sneeze with both hands. Rapp looked up in irritation. He set his MP-10 down and held his hands out for Adams. Adams squirmed his way out of the opening. Rapp grabbed him under the armpits and helped him down with ease.

As soon as Adams's feet hit the ground, he grabbed a handkerchief from his pocket and wiped his dripping nose. Rapp grabbed his submachine gun and whispered, "What's wrong?"

Adams blew his nose as quietly as possible and said, "All that dust in there . . . it makes my allergies act up."

Rapp frowned. "Are you going be all right?"

"Yeah." Adams finished wiping his nose. "I'll be fine."

Getting to work, Rapp opened the top of his backpack and retrieved a micro video monitor with a directional fiber-optic cable attached to the end. They would use this to see around corners and under doors. The black-and-white monitor, which was six inches across by five inches high, was zipped into a black nylon harness. Rapp helped Adams strap it firmly between his chest and stomach allowing the semirigid fiber-optic cable to hang at Adams's side.

Rapp took the barrel of his silencer and stuck it under the access panel. Standing on his toes, he closed the metal panel, and with the very tip of the silencer he pushed up one of the latches and secured it.

As Rapp looked toward the door, he whispered, "Any questions?"

"Nope."

"All right. Let's move out." Rapp walked quietly across the concrete floor to the doorway with his silenced weapon up and ready. Adams followed a step behind, and when they reached the door, he stuck the tip of the cable under the door to check to see what was on the other side. Rapp looked over his shoulder while Adams maneuvered the tip of the cable from side to side with a small dial. The coast appeared to be clear.

22

VICE PRESIDENT BAXTER'S national address had lasted less than five minutes. It was delivered at eleven P.M. eastern time, an hour later than most presidential addresses, due to the deep dissension between Baxter and King over what should be said. In the end, the speech consisted mainly of the standard condemnation of terrorism, the assurance that President Hayes was safe in his bunker, two minutes of nationalistic rhetoric, and of course, a solemn plea for prayers.

The early ratings were predictably high. The networks and the all-news channels were playing the crisis for everything it was worth. The newest angle they had started to play up was the theme of a government in exile. For the first time in the history of the republic such an address had been from the vice president's official residence at the Naval Observatory.

Dallas King stood nervously in the vice president's study, leaning against a bookcase while he listened to a Democratic pollster explain the early results from the national address. Several other staffers were ringed around their new commander in chief and offered their opinions on a variety of issues. All of the camera equipment and lights had been left in place on the assumption that they would probably be needed again before the crisis was resolved. The polling numbers were awesome, but expected. Dallas King listened with feigned interest. His mind was elsewhere.

King looked down at his chrome Tag Heuer watch and anxiously ran his right hand through his sun-bleached hair. He was late for a meeting, a meeting he hoped would encompass both business and pleasure. The handsome chief of staff didn't like the idea of leaving Baxter alone with the other staffers, but it was unavoidable. He shifted his weight away from the bookcase and started for the other side of the study, his black cap-toed shoes marking his steps on the spotless hardwood floor. When King reached a well-worn Persian rug, he reached out and snatched his sport coat from the back of an old wooden chair.

Vice President Baxter folded his arm across his small belly and smoothed an errant strand of his slicked-back hair. "Where are you headed?"

"I have some business I need to take care of." King winked at his boss as he casually draped the coat over his left shoulder. The wink was a signal that they could discuss his activities when they were alone. Baxter nodded, and Dallas moved for the door, saying, "I'll see you in the morning. If anything comes up, you can reach me on my cell."

With that King opened the door, nodded to the two Secret Service agents posted in the hallway, and walked out across the large porch with a lively spring in his step. His metallic blue BMW convertible was parked backed into its space next to a large black Secret Service Suburban. King threw his coat onto the passenger seat and jumped in behind the wheel. He started the car and reached for the button to lower the top, and then decided he should wait until he made it through the gauntlet of reporters at the front gate. He nosed the little sports car out of the spot and gunned it down the hill for the main gate. King flashed his brights twice to make sure the Secret Service officers knew he was coming. By the time he reached the gate, it had already begun to open. Instead of using his brakes, King shifted the car back into first gear and deftly released the clutch. The low-slung car growled as it slowed, and then, when there was just enough room to make it through the opening, he shifted into second and hit the accelerator.

The large tract of land, almost twice the area of the White House grounds, was besieged by the media. The main gate off Massachusetts Avenue was crowded with news trucks pulled haphazardly onto the curb, and the reporters and cameramen tried frantically to get a photo of King's car as it sped past. King kept his foot on the gas as the car shot onto Massachusetts Avenue, the Secret Service stopping traffic in both directions. He raced northward up the avenue. King checked his rearview mirror and cranked the stereo. Four blocks north of the observatory, and out of sight of main gate, he yanked the car back into second gear and turned hard to the right, the wide tires of the BMW squealing into a one-hundred-degree turn onto Garfield. King floored it through the residential neighborhood at speeds approaching seventy miles per hour. At Twenty-ninth Street he took a hard right turn, and one block later at Calvert, he slowed to about ten miles per hour, paid no heed to the stop sign before him, and shot out in front of an approaching cab. The wild maneuver solicited both the horn and the finger from the cabbie. King ignored both as he raced through the light at Connecticut and crossed over into the Adams-Morgan neighborhood.

He was late, and the woman he was meeting would not be happy. King took another hard turn at Eighteenth Street and slowed his speed as he entered one of the most congested areas in town. Two blocks later he pulled up in front of Stone's, a posh, hot new bar. King stopped the car and yanked up the emergency break just as a valet appeared at his door. Grabbing his black sport coat, he handed the man a ten-dollar bill and said, "Keep it close."

Standing just inside the door was an Asian woman in a body-hugging red dress with a slit that seemed to run from the floor to her left hip. She looked up at the dashing Dallas King and offered her cheek. When she stepped forward, the slit in her dress revealed a long, toned thigh.

The young hostess had no idea what King did for a living, nor did she care. All she knew was he was handsome, well-dressed, and graced the trendy bistro with his presence at least once a week—and usually with a different woman. The stunning jewel had been asked out by approximately every other man who entered the establishment, and she was beginning to wonder when this one would get around to the task.

As King kissed her cheek, the woman slipped her hands inside his suit coat and placed them gently just above his belt line. King felt the gentle touch of her hands on his waist, and a sexual jolt hit him straight in the groin. Letting his nose linger by her smooth skin for a second, he took in a deep breath of clean, fresh perfume. With a furtive grin he said, "Kim, you look gorgeous, as always."

The young Asian woman took the compliment with a smile and slowly removed her hands from King's hips. "Thank you."

King stared at her for a moment, allowing her the chance to ask him the obvious question about what was going on at the White House. The moment came and went, and it dawned on King that the beauty before him was either severely hampered in the brain department or she honestly had no idea what he did for a living. In either case she wasn't about to run out and join the local Mensa chapter.

King winked and then made his way toward the rear of the restaurant.

The bar area was crowded. The hostage crisis had given the city something to talk about. For Washington bar owners a scandal or crisis was like a big sporting event. Several of the more astute bar patrons recognized the young Californian as Vice President Baxter's chief of staff and began to whisper as King worked his way through the crowd.

As King walked past the trendy rag-rolled walls and secluded booths, he scanned the dining area for his newest infatuation. In the last booth before reaching the pay phone and the bathrooms, King saw her. Sheila Dunn had her laptop open, a cell phone in one hand and a glass of wine in the other. Upon seeing King, she said into her cell phone, "He's here. I'll call you back." The thirty-four-year-old reporter set the phone down but kept the glass of wine securely in her grip.

"Dallas, where in the hell have you been?"

"I'm sorry." King bent down to kiss the blond-haired woman sitting in the booth.

Dunn offered her cheek and said, "I have fifteen minutes to get my story in, and my editor is about to pull my hair out." With an angry look, she added, "You'd better talk fast."

King sat in the booth, and as he did so, a waiter approached. Dunn held up her nearly finished glass and said, "Two more of these," without bothering to say please, then turned her glare back in the direction of King. "You're an hour late. That's a hell of a way to try and endear yourself to me."

"Excuse me," King uttered, a touch irked by her comment. "I don't know if you've noticed, but we have a bit of crisis going on, and I'm just a touch busy right now."

"Don't patronize me, Dallas. I'm very aware of what's going on, and I have a deadline to meet, so when you say you're going to be here at a certain time and you show up an hour late, without calling, don't expect me to act like one of your congenial little empty-headed bimbos." Dunn took a deep breath and folded her arms across her chest. She had intentionally worked herself into this frenzy, figuring the more upset she was the more likely Dallas would be to hand over some good info.

This was the exact reason why King liked her. She was feisty. Most of the women he dated were great arm pieces, but they lacked something up top. Sheila Dunn was different. She wasn't knock-down gorgeous, as many of his women were, but her brains and drive made her every bit as attractive. Dunn was fairly plain looking. She had slender features, was not curvaceous in any sense of the word, but while many women her age had already seen their best days, Dunn was just moving into hers. She had the mature confidence of a woman who would hold her beauty for years to come. And most important, she was married, something that King had seen as an obstacle for years, but now embraced as a bonus. With the married ones it was all about sex. He didn't have to spend large amounts of money or play tiresome games.

Dunn had rebuked all of King's romantic advances, but the young Dallas could tell he was wearing her down. She was one of the *Post's* political correspondents, and King had gotten to know her since his recent arrival in the nation's capital. As Baxter's chief of staff, King had, as one of his first priorities, to cultivate sources in the media that could be used to leak information when needed.

He reached across the table and grabbed her hand. "How are things with your husband?"

"Shitty," was Dunn's terse one-word reply.

Rubbing her hand, he asked, "When was the last time you two slept together?"

She pulled back quickly. "Dallas, that's none of your business."

"Fine . . . you don't have to answer it, but you're far too beautiful a woman to be so lonely."

"Dallas, let's change the subject."

King had taken her down this road before, and he was gaining ground. Dunn was having serious doubts about her marriage. She knew that King wanted her, and she thought this might be the time to give up the jewel. This was the biggest story in three decades, and no one had any idea what was going on inside the White House or the FBI's command post. No one was talking. The crisis had people tight-lipped. If sleeping with King meant she could get some info out of him, it might be worth it.

The drinks arrived, and King took a big sip. He let the dry merlot run down his throat and then said, "You wouldn't believe the shit that's going on down there."

Dunn leaned forward and placed her forearms on the table. "Like what?"

Rolling his eyes, King said, "Tutwiler, that stupid bitch. She's the damn reason Schwartz and his secretary are dead. It was her stupid idea to jerk this nut-bag's chain and only send him part of the money." King stopped briefly and took a sip, thinking of the warning the man from the CIA had given all of them—that Aziz would react exactly the way he did.

"I tried to advise against it, but she won out. You know how she is. She took charge of the entire briefing at the Pentagon yesterday. The damn woman has the worst case of penis envy I've ever seen. She just couldn't pass up the chance to put all of those military types in their place." King stopped and shook his head. "And to make things worse, she's not around to take the heat. She had a fucking nervous breakdown after Schwartz got shot. They had to cart her off to Bethesda."

Dunn's jaw hung loosely. "You're kidding?"

"No." King shook his head for emphasis. "I wish I was. I wish she was here to take the heat." King pointed to himself. "Now I'm the one who's getting squeezed."

Dunn set her wine down and started tapping at the keys of her laptop. "So Tutwiler is out . . . What in the hell is the FBI up to?" Dunn watched King shrug his shoulders and take another drink. She was going to have to work for this one. "Come on, Dallas. Just give me some good background. I'm not asking you to give away any national secrets." Dunn paused to give him a second to think about it, and then in a soft voice she asked, "What's the FBI up to?"

King looked over the top of his wineglass. "They're planning for every possible contingency. Collecting information and trying to find a way out of this. Sherman has told them that unless they can guarantee getting the rest of the hostages out safely, we sit tight."

"What about the president? Is all that crap your boss spun in his address the truth?"

"He's fine." King nodded emphatically. "Just like Sherman said." Then waving his hand in the air as if the president was a nonfactor, he added, "The people at the Pentagon say he can last for weeks in that bunker." King took another drink and then leaned forward. With his nose perched above the screen of Dunn's laptop, King breathed in her perfume and said, "You smell great."

"Thank you." Dunn smiled halfheartedly and then got back to business. "What else is going on? Do you know what their next demand is going to be?"

"Nope. We're not supposed to hear anything until the morning." King's attention was drawn downward. Dunn's blouse was open one more button than normal, and a scintillating amount of soft skin was drawing his mind into a completely different area again. He looked down her shirt and said, "I want to get naked with you so bad."

Dunn grabbed him by the jaw and made him look her in the eye. "This stuff you gave me about Tutwiler is good, Dallas, but there's more going on than you're telling me, and if you want to get me into bed, you're going to have to do a lot better . . . and fast."

King felt the blood rushing to his groin. His mind scrambled for any piece of information that might seal the deal, but he'd told her everything that was going on. The truth was, nothing was going on. Everybody was sitting around and waiting to react . . . except . . . except one person. King pulled away and sat back. He couldn't talk about that, but there was something related that he could talk about—something that would play great in the press. "There is one thing." Pausing, he tried to gauge how much information he could hand over.

Dunn saw his hesitancy and drew closer. "What . . . what is it?"

King looked around the immediate area and then leaned forward. "Listen, no one can find out I told you this."

Dunn feigned insult. "Dallas, I've never revealed one of my sources."

Unimpressed, King rolled his eyes. "All I'm saying is that this is serious shit, all right?"

Dunn nodded eagerly. "You have my word. Your name will never be revealed."

The vice president's chief of staff looked around once again to make sure no one was eavesdropping, and then, in a whisper, he said, "The CIA knew about this attack before it happened."

Dunn's eyes almost popped out of her head. "What? And they didn't do anything about it?"

"No." King shook his head. "They only found out just before it happened. As soon as they found out, they alerted the Secret Service. That's why Hayes made it to his bunker."

"So the CIA saved the day."

King shrugged. "It was hardly a banner day, but I suppose you could say that."

Dunn smiled broadly. "This could be good." Frantically, she began typing. King watched her for about half a minute, and then Dunn closed her laptop. She packed it and her phone in her bag and said, "I've got to get this in before we go to press." Dunn stood. She was wearing a tight blue skirt that hugged her thin frame. Leaning over the table, she grabbed King by the jaw with one hand and said, "You and I aren't done. If you keep this up, you just might wear me down." Dunn pulled King's lips to hers and gently ran the tip of her tongue along his upper lip. She let her tongue hang there just long enough to leave him wanting more and then turned and left.

23

JACK WARCH STOOD by the bunker door and touched the smooth surface with the palm of his hand. It had been several hours since he had done so, and as far as he could tell the door was getting warmer. He took that as a bad sign. Warch had been beating his brains out all day over what to do if the terrorists got the door open before the Hostage Rescue Team intervened. He assumed from the explosions he had heard during the initial assaults that they had grenades. That would make it a short fight. He could put the president in the small bathroom on the other side of the bunker and buy maybe another five minutes. That would result in more dead agents and ultimately a dead or captured president.

Warch plopped down on his bunk. As he exhaled a deep sigh, he saw the president coming over. Warch straightened up a bit and started to stand.

Hayes gestured to him with a patting motion of his hand and said, "Don't get up. Do you mind if I sit?"

"Please," said Warch as he scooted over.

"You're from Wisconsin, right?"

"Yes, sir."

"I thought so. I saw your two boys running around on the South Lawn one Saturday morning in their Packer jerseys. I figured either you or your wife was from Wisconsin."

Warch half laughed. "No. My wife's from Minnesota. She hates it when I dress them up in the Packer gear."

"She should have thought of that before she married you."

"That's what I tell her." Warch smiled.

"What part of Wisconsin are you from?"

"Appleton."

"Ah, the home of Rocky Blier."

"Yep."

"I met him once," pronounced Hayes with satisfaction. "What a great man . . ." With a nod of his chin he added, "What a great story."

"Yeah, he overcame a lot. The best part about him, though, is he never let any of the success go to his head. He does a ton for the local community."

"That's nice to hear."

Hayes looked down at the floor for a while. The idle conversation seemed to be over. Sitting on the edge of the bunk, he rested his elbows on his knees and continued to study the ugly brown carpeting. After a moment he leaned back and glanced over at Warch.

"Jack, I'm sorry about all of this. I appreciate everything you and your people have done for me and my family." Hayes stopped and looked away.

Warch waited and then said, "Thank you, sir."

After several awkward moments of silence Hayes looked at his watch. It was almost midnight. "Well, another six hours, or so, and we'll know if they're coming to save us."

Warch nodded. "So, you think they'll come tonight?"

Hayes leaned back. "Well, if I know General Flood and Director Stansfield, they'll be pushing hard for it." Hayes's mind seemed to drift, and slowly he started to shake his head.

"What is it, sir?"

"I'm not so sure about the vice president."

"How do you mean, sir?"

The president eyeballed Warch. "Jack, I trust that whatever I say to you will go no further."

"That goes without saying, sir."

"I thought so." Hayes looked out across the bunker. Out of the side of his mouth he said, "I don't exactly trust Baxter." Hayes continued, "He wasn't my first choice . . . hell, he wasn't even in my top ten. The truth is the party stuck me with him. They said he could deliver California and the big Hollywood money. You need both to win the race, so he was the man. Experience and character were never factored in." Frowning, Hayes said, "I knew a week after the convention that he was the wrong man, but by then there was no turning back."

"Is that why you've isolated him?"

The comment surprised Hayes a bit. "You've noticed?"

"This is my fourth administration, sir. We're taught to keep our mouths shut, but that doesn't mean we don't see and hear everything that goes on."

All Hayes could do was nod. "Well, Baxter's the big wild card. He and Tutwiler." Hayes shook his head again. "I didn't want to have anything to do with her either, but it was all part of the deal."

"What about Director Roach? He's a good man."

"Yes, he is." Hayes nodded. "He's one of the best, but unfortunately he answers to Tutwiler."

Warch looked over at the door and then back to his boss. "Sir, if HRT doesn't get here in time, we need to take some precautions."

"Such as?"

Warch was short on details as he related what he thought would happen. He felt there was no sense in alarming the president over something that was out of their control. Hayes listened intently as Warch laid out his limited plan.

ANNA RIELLY WAS sleeping fitfully when she was stirred by something. Just as she opened her eyes, she felt a pair of hands grab her by the shoulders. A second later she was on her feet, face-to-face with the terrorist who had pulled her out of line. Rielly immediately began to lash out with her arms.

The terrorist grabbed her by the throat with his right hand and squeezed tightly. The young journalist continued to flail as her eyes bulged wider as the air was squeezed from her. White spots began to dot her vision, and in one last, violent attempt to break free Rielly rammed her knee up into her assailant's groin. The blow would have sent most men to their knees, but Abu Hasan was no normal man. Instead of buckling over, he grunted and took a half step back. Then his right hand shot forward and caught Rielly square on the jaw. She spun like a top and went straight to the floor.

The room was completely silent for the next five seconds. None of the hostages made a noise, and the other terrorists looked on to see what would happen next. Finally, Hasan bent over and let out a deep groan. This elicited a chorus of laughs and chuckles from the other three Arabs standing guard. Several of the women crawled from their spots to help Rielly, but before they could reach her, the terrorist stood partially upright and shouted a warning to them.

Still smarting from the knee to his groin, Abu Hasan lumbered forward, bent at the waist like an ape. Reaching down, he grabbed the unconscious Rielly and threw her over his shoulder. As he moved toward the door, he scowled at his friends, who were still laughing at him. When he reached the exit, he paused long enough to tell one of the other men, "I'm going to take this whore upstairs. Whoever wants her next can come and get her when I'm done."

IN 1948 PRESIDENT Harry Truman had grown concerned over the structural integrity of the 148-year-old White House. Engineers were brought in to investigate, and they found that the mansion was in danger

of collapsing. The less-than-sound renovation of 1902 and the enlarge-
ment of the third story in 1927 had weakened the structure severely. It was
recommended that the president and his wife vacate the house immediately, and they moved across the street to Blair House to allow a massive
four-year renovation to ensue. The first step was the meticulous disassem-
bly of everything within the White House. All of the furniture, artwork,
and fixtures were removed, and with painstaking effort, the floors, ceil-
ings, and walls were dismantled section by section. The mansion became
an empty shell while construction crews moved in to excavate two new
levels beneath the original basement. After the third and second basements
had been completed, a modern steel framework was erected to support
the mansion's aging walls.

The new third basement that had been added in the renovation was
designed to house the new boiler room and was only about a quarter the
size of the floors above it. Over the last several decades, much of the massive boiler had been replaced by the newer, more efficient systems designed to protect the building from chemical and biological attacks.

As Rapp and Adams stood at the boiler room's door, Adams pointed
out the most recent change to the White House. "Straight down the hall
and to the left is the president's bunker. As you turn the corner, you go
down a hall that's about fifty feet long, and then there's a reinforced steel
door. Once you're through that door, you're in the room just outside the
bunker."

Rapp nodded. "We're going up the stairs to the left . . . away from the
bunker . . . correct?"

"Correct."

"All right. Let's take one last look at this thing, and then we'll move
out." Adams manipulated the lens until Rapp was satisfied that door had
not been booby-trapped, and the cable was withdrawn. With his gun
ready, Rapp slowly opened the door and stepped out into the hallway.
They moved to the left and into the concrete stairwell, then ascended one
flight to the second basement. Adams stuck the tiny lens under the next
metal door and found nothing. With Rapp and his MP-10 in the lead,
they continued to the first basement landing and stopped. Adams checked
under this door as well, and Rapp became increasingly suspicious that they
had come this far and found nothing. He thought that Aziz would have set
up some type of an early warning system.

Whispering in Rapp's ear, Adams said, "No booby traps."

Rapp looked at the screen while Adams moved the tiny lens back and
forth, and asked, "What about the hallway?"

After moving the snake around a little, Adams gave Rapp a clear shot of the hall. "Midway down, right-hand side. That's our door."

"Good," Rapp whispered back. "Secure that thing, and when I give you the signal, open the door and follow me. Stay on my right and one step back no matter what happens."

Adams closed the screen against his chest, zipped it up, and then coiled the snake into a loose loop and strapped it to his hip. Rapp gripped his MP-10 tightly in both hands, the collapsible stock wedged between his cheek and shoulder. With the thick black silencer leveled at the closed door, Rapp nodded.

Adams jerked the door open, and Rapp took one step forward, sweeping the gun from left to right. He walked quickly forward, and Adams followed closely behind. The metal fire door closed automatically behind them. Both men walked softly, making almost no noise. Rapp spun several times, nervously checking their six, looking for any sign of a motion sensor or trip wire. A third of the way down the hall, Adams stopped at another gray metal door, extracted his S-key, and opened the door to reveal a hidden elevator.

Rapp swore under his breath while they waited for the elevator to arrive, exposed in the middle of the hallway. When the doors finally opened, Adams silently shooed Rapp into the tiny compartment and pressed the proper button. The elevator was big enough to handle four people at the most.

As the elevator started to move, Rapp handed his gun to Adams, and with both hands, he took his headset from around his neck and secured it over his baseball cap. Static crackled loudly from his earpiece, but as they rose it lessened. The elevator ascended quickly and noiselessly. By the time they reached the second floor, the static was greatly decreased, and Rapp had his weapon back in his hands.

When the elevator stopped, Adams gave Rapp an uneasy look. Rapp nodded and said, "Don't worry." And with a grin to help ease the tension, he added, "I'll go first." Then pulling his lip mike down, he whispered, "Iron Man to command. Over." Rapp waited several seconds for a reply and then repeated his words. After the third check, he thought he heard something, but it was too broken up to discern. They would have to move to the stash room and set up a more powerful secure field radio.

Rapp looked up at the small light above his head. It would have to be extinguished before they opened the door. After popping the frosted glass cover off the fixture, he reached up and gave the hot bulb several quick turns with his bare hand. The bulb flickered and then went dark. Rapp then pulled a circular red plastic filter from one of his pockets and attached it to the flashlight that was affixed to the barrel of his submachine gun. When he turned on the flashlight, a faint red light illuminated the floor of the elevator.

Adams pressed a button, and the elevator doors opened to reveal a wall. There was no crack to wedge the snake under, so they would have to chance it and go forward without looking. Slowly, Adams ran his hand along the wall until he found what he was looking for. As Adams pressed the catch, the wall popped outward several inches, revealing the tile floor of the president's bathroom. The lights were off, and the room was dark, with the exception of the faint red light coming from under the barrel of Rapp's gun.

Rapp checked the way and slid through the narrow entrance, taking three cautious steps toward the bedroom. Milt followed close behind. The door was open. Rapp checked for trip wires and then looked into the actual bedroom. The door that led to the hallway was slightly open, and a sliver of light spilled into the dark room from the hallway. Before entering the bedroom, Rapp looked back over his shoulder and whispered, "Close that."

Placing both hands on the wall, Adams pushed it back into place. The wall shut with a slight click, and all traces of the hidden elevator disappeared.

Rapp stepped cautiously into the room. He moved across the president's bedroom to the door that led to the Truman Balcony, the semicircular porch that overlooked the South Lawn. When Rapp reached the door, he froze in his tracks. He had missed it on the first sweep, but caught the slightest glimpse of it on the second. A thin clear wire ran across the base of the door about twelve inches off the ground. Rapp's right hand snapped up next to his head in a tight closed fist. Milt Adams, a combat veteran, knew the hand signal all too well and froze in his tracks.

At first, only Rapp's eyes moved, and then his head swiveled from side to side. Adams was good enough to not say anything. It was apparent from Rapp's body language that he had found something.

What Rapp had founded was a filament trip wire, and he knew it was attached to something that petrified him. Rapp hated bombs. One of the qualities that had made him so successful during his almost decade of service with the CIA was knowing his own limitations. He didn't have the patience or the skill to deal with explosives, so he tended to avoid them like the plague. The problem with bombs was there were a hundred different ways to set them off, and a dozen of them could happen before you ever got within a foot of the actual device. There could be a pressure pad under the carpet, a magnetic plate, infrared beams, microwave beams, motion sensors, tremble or mercury switches—the list went on and on. And with Rafique Aziz involved, Rapp had no doubt these devices would be really hairy. One thing was certain, however: the trip wire was attached to something, and Rapp had to find out exactly what it was.

The door leading to the balcony was bordered on both sides with drapes. Rapp stepped carefully to his right and looked behind a chair situated between the door and a window to the right. Sticking the black silencer of his gun behind the curtain, he pointed it down and found nothing on this side of the door, but on the left side, he could discern the rectangular shape of a box. The trip wire was tied to a switch on the side of the bomb and a nail on the other side of the door. Rapp crossed over to the other side of the door and examined the box from a closer angle. It appeared that the trip wire was the only exterior trigger device.

Rapp wiped a bead of sweat from his brow, and then reluctantly, he drew back the curtain. The box was simple, about eight inches high and six wide. In the upper right corner was a small red digital readout and a green light that blinked every three seconds. Gingerly, he let the drape fall back into its natural hanging position and took a step back.

If the box was loaded with Semtex, the Czechoslovakian version of C-4 plastique, there was probably enough to blow the entire wall halfway across the South Lawn.

Milt Adams leaned over and whispered, "What did you find?"

"A bomb." Rapp wiped some more sweat from his face. "If we set one of these things off, they'll be picking us up with a vacuum cleaner, Milt. Let's leave this alone and get ourselves set up."

Adams led the way across the bedroom to a large walk-in closet. Rapp followed him in and left the door open, as they had found it. On the left was a substantial closet organizer. The smaller compartments near the bottom were filled with pairs of shoes, but as the organizer rose, the cubicles grew larger and were occupied by shirts and sweaters. Near the far corner Adams stopped and reached up along the edge. After feeling around for a second, he found what he was looking for and pressed the obscured button. The organizer popped outward several inches at the one end, and then Adams swung it open three more feet.

They entered the hidden room and pulled the organizer shut behind them. Adams turned on the wall light and slid a heavy steel bolt across the doorway. The small room, referred to as the "stash room" by the Secret Service, was eight feet long by six feet wide, and the ceiling was almost ten feet high. The walls were lined with bulletproof Kevlar and a fire-retardant cloth on both the exterior and interior walls. The room also contained four biohazard suits complete with oxygen tanks and gas masks. These were packed in storage lockers that were bolted to the walls above their heads, along with some weapons and a first aid kit. The room was built in response to a small plane crashing into the South Portico in the fall of 1994.

THE TECHNICIANS IN the first row of the control room at Langley had faintly heard Rapp's original signal. They had been working diligently for five minutes to clear up the link as Irene Kennedy and General Campbell watched from one row back. The two knew enough to let their people work and stay out of their way.

With the help of Marcus Dumond, who was manning the control panel of the CIA's communications van parked outside the White House fence, they were making progress. The telescoping boom on the back of the van was helping penetrate the electronic interference the terrorists were using.

When Rapp began to transmit on the powerful secure field radio, there was a collective sigh of relief in the control room as forty-plus minutes of tense radio silence came to an end. General Campbell was the first to speak. "Give me a sit rep, Iron Man."

Rapp's reply came back slightly garbled but audible. He recounted how the insertion had progressed and the device he had discovered in the president's bedroom. After Rapp had given as much detail as possible about the explosive device, he asked Campbell and Kennedy what they wanted him to do.

Campbell thought about it for only a second and replied, "Continue your reconnaissance, and we'll figure out what to do about the bombs."

"Roger that," replied Rapp. "I'll get to work."

Back in the control room at Langley one of the technicians in the front row raised his hand up and snapped his fingers. Kennedy leaned forward and listened to what the technician had to say, then spoke into her headset. "Iron Man, we need you to conduct a radio check on your portable. Over."

Rapp was holding the handset to the secure field radio to his ear and replied, "Roger." He put his headset back on and adjusted the lip mike. "Testing, one, two, three, four. Do you read? Over."

They could hear Rapp well enough to understand what he was saying but not as clearly as when he used the field radio. The larger problem was that Rapp was having a hard time receiving signals. After several tries Rapp lifted the lip mike of his headset and picked up the handset to the field radio.

"My radio isn't working. Over."

"We can hear you on our end, Iron Man," replied Kennedy. "Are you saying you can't receive us?"

"That's correct."

Kennedy looked to one of the technicians to see if there were any answers. All she got was an unknowing shrug. Into her headset, she said, "Iron Man, we'll work on that. For now, why don't you check out the rest of the second floor and then check in on the field radio in thirty minutes?"

"Roger that. I'll start to set up the surveillance cameras. Over and out." Rapp placed the handset back in its cradle and started to organize his gear. Taking the fanny pack of miniature surveillance units, Rapp extracted five of the devices and placed them in his web vest.

"Staircases first?" asked Adams.

"Yep." Rapp grabbed his gun. "Just like before, Milt. Keep your eyes peeled, and don't walk anywhere where I haven't walked first. All right?" Adams nodded. "Any questions before we get going?"

"Yeah." Adams looked slightly embarrassed. "I *gotta* take a piss."

Rapp grinned, appreciating the much needed levity. "We can take care of that. In fact we'll make it our first stop. All right, let's move out."

Adams pulled the bolt back, and he and Rapp quietly walked out into the large closet. Adams pushed the bookcaselike organizer back into place, and it stopped with a soft click. With his gun at the ready Rapp stood outside the bathroom while Adams went in and took care of business. Rapp took the time to look around the room and noticed something he had missed earlier. Something odd. The president's bed was in disarray. Rapp walked over to the bed, and on closer examination he saw something startling, something that made his blood boil. There was a substantial splotch of blood on the white sheets and dangling off the side of the bed was a woman's bra.

Rapp shook his head in disgust at the scene. When Adams came out of the bathroom a moment later, Rapp pointed at the disturbing evidence. Neither man said a word. After a long moment Rapp walked across the room to a small end table situated near the door that led to the Truman Balcony. Taking one of the small surveillance units from his pocket, he attached one of the Velcro patches to the underside of the table and secured the tiny device.

Rapp motioned to Adams. "Let's go." He moved for the main door and stopped when he reached it. Adams stuck the tiny black snake under the door and checked the hallway. The lights were on, and the picture was very clear.

The cross hall on the second floor of the family residence was wide, about fifteen feet. It was brightly lit and the walls were adorned with built-in bookcases and several oil portraits of past presidents. Various groupings of couches, chairs, tables, and lamps gave the space the dual role of informal living room and hallway.

Adams manipulated the snake back and forth and whispered, "It looks clear."

Rapp nodded and said, "Let me take a look first, and then I'll wave you out." Rapp looked at the camera one more time and checked the hallway. Slowly, Rapp turned the knob and opened the door, taking the first step into the brightly lit hallway.

24

HER EYES BLINKED several times before they could stay open. Anna Rielly let out a weak groan. It took her a second to regain her senses, and even then she had no idea where she was. All she knew was her head ached and she was having a hard time breathing. As her eyes came into focus, she saw stairs and then a pair of legs and boots. For a second she thought she was dreaming, and then everything fell into place. The terrorist was carrying her over his shoulder.

She tried to lift her head, but a searing pain shot through her neck. She knew she had to fight no matter how much it hurt. Rielly commanded herself to ignore the pain, and with as much strength as she could muster, the young journalist bolted upright and grabbed onto the slicked-back hair of the man who was carrying her. Rielly kicked her feet violently and began to scream at the top of her lungs.

MITCH RAPP ALMOST jumped out of his skin. The female voice was so loud and so sudden that it caught him completely off guard. He was standing exposed in the middle of the hallway, bathed in light. The violent scream had shattered the stillness and sent his nerves right to the edge. Rapp paused just long enough to ascertain which direction the scream was coming from and then immediately began to move, while Milt Adams stood frozen two steps behind. Like a big cat, Rapp began a rapid retreat. Instinctively, his right hand reached back in search of Adams. His left hand kept the lethal barrel of his MP-10 aimed in the direction of the scream, and he pushed Adams back into the open doorway of the president's bedroom.

With Adams now in the lead, they hurried into the closet, and Rapp closed the door behind them. Adams had the door to the stash room open and paused for a second to see what Rapp wanted to do. Rapp pushed him into the small room and pulled the organizer closed behind them.

Adams turned on the light and grabbed his heart. "Jesus, how you do this shit for a living?"

Rapp, his own adrenaline pumping, grabbed the monitor around

Milt's neck and tuned the picture to the tiny surveillance device they had just planted less than twenty feet away.

ANNA RIELLY CLUTCHED her stomach with one hand and the wrist of the terrorist with the other. Her shoes had fallen off, and she could see them halfway down the hallway as the thug dragged her across the carpet. Tears streamed down her cheeks, and the pain from the kick to her stomach was so intense she thought she might vomit.

Abu Hasan liked the fight. He considered it part of the thrill, part of the domination. This one, the dark one, was much better than the one he had taken care of last night. The blond had turned out to be boring. There was no fight in her, only tears. Hasan smiled widely as he rounded the corner and saw the door to the president's bedroom. It was the perfect place to rape this American whore. Hasan thrust open the door with one hand while he held on to Rielly's ponytail with the other. After dragging her another ten feet, he violently lifted her off the ground and threw her onto the king-size bed. Drawing his knife, he yelled at her, "Take your clothes off, you bitch."

Rielly started to get back up. There was no way she was going to give in. She would rather die than be raped again.

The terrorist blocked her arms and sent the butt end of the knife crashing down and into Rielly's temple. The blow knocked her unconscious, and Rielly went limp, leaving her completely motionless and vulnerable on the bed.

Abu Hasan wasted no time. Taking his knife, he began cutting off her clothes. The more skin he revealed the faster he cut. Once he had her pants off, he ripped at her blouse, and then stopped for a second. Lustfully, he looked down at the young woman before him and admired her tanned, firm body. Slowly, he reached down and ran his hand over her leg. He stopped at her black lace panties, and then with a violent yank, he tore them from her body.

MILT ADAMS WAS disturbed by what was happening in the other room, but it wasn't as scary as the transformation taking place right in front of him. Mitch Rapp's face had taken on a very different look. His eyes had twisted into a menacing stare, his jaw sat clenched, and a sheen of sweat now coated his forehead.

Rapp shook his head several times and muttered something through his clenched teeth. Inside his mind a battle was being waged. The logical side was telling him that the mission was more important than what was going on in the other room. All of his professional training had taught him that he should stay put and continue to collect information without announcing his presence, that the lives of the other hostages were more important, that killing Rafique Aziz was more important. Despite knowing what he should do, there was another voice in his head that was saying something entirely diffcrent.

BACK IN THE control room at Langley, all eyes were on the big board. A surveillance device had been activated by Rapp, and its grainy transmission was being received on one of the monitors. The technicians at Langley worked with Marcus Dumond, who, with the aid of the communications boom on the back of the van, was homing in on the frequency and trying to filter out the disturbances. Over the course of several minutes the picture bcgan to clear, eventually revealing a lone man in a lit doorway.

Without taking his eyes off the screen, General Campbell asked Kennedy, "Is that the president's bedroom?"

"It must be," replied Kennedy as she squinted at the monitor. She watched as the man in the doorway turned and walked quickly back into the room. A second man's profile appeared in the doorway, and Kennedy immediately recognized it as Rapp's.

"Why are they going back into the closet?" asked Campbell.

Kennedy frowned. "I don't know."

One of the technicians turned around and said, "We've got audio on the unit."

"Put it on the speaker system," stated Kennedy, without taking her eyes off the monitor. A sccond later a scratchy audio came over the room's overhead speaker system.

There was a loud noise, and General Flood, who was sitting one row behind Kennedy and Campbell, asked, "What in the hell was that?"

Kennedy stared at the monitor showing the open doorway of the president's bedroom with the lit hallway beyond and said, "It sounded like a scream."

Just then a man appeared in the doorway dragging a woman behind him. As if on cue everyone in the control room moved closer to the screen in an attempt to discern what was happening. Within seconds it was brutally apparent what was unfolding before them.

Kennedy, in an unusually tense voice, snapped, "Get me Iron Man on the radio right now!" Kennedy knew Rapp better than anyone in the room and possibly better than anyone in the world. Kennedy knew she had to assert some control over him and assert it quickly, if she had even the slightest chance of stopping him from doing what she knew he was contemplating.

THE MP-10 WAS on the ground in the corner and had been replaced by the silenced 9-mm Beretta. Rapp stared at the gun. Angry beyond comprehension, he felt like punching a hole in the wall. He told himself to bring it back a notch. Too much anger led to poor judgment. But Rapp hated thugs, people that took from others, animals that did what they wanted to do with little or no thought of what their actions did to fellow human beings.

Mentally, Rapp was gone. The decision had been made. There was no turning back. The woman in the other room was somebody's daughter, probably somebody's wife, and maybe some poor kid's mother, and there was no way he could allow himself to sit in the safety of the bulletproof room and let it happen.

The secure field radio spurted a quiet beeping noise, and a green light on the panel began to flash. Adams reached for the handset, and Rapp stopped him.

"Don't answer that."

Adams slowly withdrew his hand. He no longer recognized the man sitting next to him. Rapp reached out, turned the power switch on the radio to the off position, and pulled his headset down around his neck. Standing, he retrieved his matte-black combat knife and kept it in his left hand. He looked at the pistol in one hand and the knife in the other and paused.

Standing, Milt Adams licked his dry lips, and with a worried expression on his face, he asked, "What are you going to do?"

Rapp looked sideways at him and after short pause said, "I'm going to go out there and kill that piece of shit. It's not what I should do, but it's what I'm gonna do."

Adams swallowed hard and with a nod said, "Good." Then after a second, he added, "Do you want me to help?"

Rapp shook his head and closed his eyes. "No . . . Turn off the lights, and open the door. Then stay here, and be quiet."

Adams did as he was told. He couldn't see Rapp, but could feel him as Rapp slid through the passageway and into the closet.

ANNA RIELLY OPENED her eyes and tried to focus. Above her was darkness, but to her right there was light. Slowly, she turned her head and saw her attacker. The man had already taken off his shirt and was working on his pants. Rielly tried to move, but her arms wouldn't respond. Looking down, she saw her bare chest through tear-filled eyes. She was living the nightmare.

MITCH RAPP STOOD at the closet doorway for several seconds and listened. His eyes were closed. He wanted them to adjust to the darkness as much as possible. There was a noise from the bedroom. It sounded as if the woman was crying, and then he heard a male laugh. Rapp opened his eyes and looked at his two weapons. He could shoot equally well with either hand, but he was better with the knife in his left hand. Rapp decided that if he could get close enough, he would use the knife, and he had few doubts he could. Before leaving, he started the timer on his watch and then reached for the door. Slowly, cautiously, he turned the handle and began to open it.

RIELLY SOBBED AS she looked at the man looming over her. He was laughing, his disgusting cigarette breath enveloping her face. He held his erection with one hand and reached out with his other hand, pawing at Rielly's groin. The young journalist clamped down with her legs and screamed. The terrorist yanked her legs apart and slapped her across the face. Rielly tried to fight, but her strength was gone. All she could do was cry as he lowered his body on top of her.

THE DOOR OPENED slowly. Rapp peered through the crack and saw the light from the hallway spilling into the room. From his angle he could see a man with his back to him taking off his clothes and standing at the foot the large bed. The man began to climb onto the bed. Now was the time to move. With his knife in his left hand and the gun in his right, Rapp proceeded slowly. He took his first step and then quickly looked to the left and the right to make sure no one else was in the room. He stepped silently, without vibration or noise, carefully placing his heel and then the rest of his foot on the floor.

Halfway across the room, Rapp slid his gun back into his holster. The terrorist was holding the woman's hands above her head and was trying to enter her, the woman's sobs muffled by the man's body.

Rapp moved quickly to the bed, his right hand open and stretched outward, the left tightly clutching his knife. With fluid precision, he grabbed the hair of the terrorist with his right hand and yanked the man's head back. With his left hand, Rapp stuck the tip of the knife directly into the man's neck and thrust it upward. The sharp knife sliced through muscle and penetrated deep into the base of the brain. With a forceful twist of the knife, Rapp shredded the fragile brain stem. Abu Hasan never knew what happened in his final second on earth.

Still holding the man's hair, Rapp pulled him off the woman and dropped his lifeless body on the floor with as little noise as possible. He placed the bloody knife back in its scabbard, and Rapp held out his hands to the naked woman on the bed.

"Don't scream. We need to move quickly." The woman looked up with shocked eyes and tried to cover her exposed breasts with her arms. Rapp reached down, untucked the sheet that she was lying on top of, and gently folded it over her body.

He knew he had to move fast. There was no telling when someone else might come along. Looking the woman in the eye, he said, "Listen, I have to move you. I'm going to pick you up and bring you someplace where you'll be safe."

Rapp placed one knee on the bed, and Rielly flinched like a scared and beaten dog. Moving slowly, he said, "More of them could come at any minute. I need to get you out of here." After giving her several seconds to think about the alternative, Rapp placed one hand under her legs and the other under her upper back. Cradling her to his chest he stood and whispered, "Everything's gonna be all right." Rapp walked quickly across the room and into the closet. In a voice just above a whisper he said, "Milt, turn the light on." Almost instantly the light inside the stash room came on, and the hidden door opened wider.

Rapp moved the woman inside and placed her on the floor. Then grabbing his backpack, he opened it and extracted a small kit. Handing it to Adams, he said, "Give her some water and a couple of these." Rapp pulled out a packet of Tylenol 3. "I have to get back out there and try to figure out what to do with that body."

RAGIB QUASAR LOOKED out across the mass of huddled hostages and checked his watch. It was nearing midnight, and his turn was approaching. There were two other terrorists in the room, and Ragib looked at the one closest to him. The man nodded, signaling for Ragib to go ahead. They were all eagerly awaiting their turn, and the sooner Ragib was done with the woman the sooner the other two would have their chance.

Ragib grinned and flashed his open hand to his compatriot three times, telling him to give him fifteen minutes. With excitement, he strode from the room, his pace picking up as soon as the door behind him closed.

*   *   *

RAPP CLOSED THE main door to the bedroom and studied the body
for a second. It was no good trying to hide it. Aziz would know his man
was missing and would immediately deduce that he had been killed. There
had to be another way. Rapp grew impatient as he stood over the dead terrorist, racking his brain for a way out of the mess. After searching the dead
man's discarded clothes for information, it came to him. Rapp grabbed the
terrorist's knife from the pile of clothes, and he hoisted the body back on
to the bed, laying the dead man on his stomach.

With the terrorist's own knife, Rapp stabbed him three times in the
upper back. Rapp was careful not to use all of his strength, only sending
an inch or two of the knife into the flesh. After pausing for a second,
Rapp flipped the dead man over and stabbed him three times in the chest
and twice in the neck. Blood was beginning to flow freely over the white
sheets. For the finishing touch, he sliced the man's forearms and hands to
make it look as if he had tried to block the blows.

Rapp took several steps back and looked at the body. He checked the
area in front of him and around his feet to make sure none of the blood
had gotten on his boots, and then he pulled the body off the bed and onto
the floor again. With the bedspread already disheveled and blood all over
the sheets, it just might work.

RAGIB BOUNDED UP the last step and looked down the long hallway.
He knew the president's bedroom was on the left. He had visited it last
night. Ragib smiled to himself while he thought of the fun he'd had with
the blond. She wasn't much of a fighter, but this one would be different.
She had already shown some tenacity. Ragib just hoped that she wouldn't
be beaten to a bloody pulp by the time he got there. He was a little early,
and with any luck he would be able to hear Abu Hasan's moans of ecstasy.
The bearded terrorist walked down the hallway, his AK-74 at his side and
a look of anticipation on his face.

RAPP GRABBED THE pile of clothes and began to go through them
again. In the combat vest he found a radio and held it up to his ear. There
was no traffic at the moment. He was tempted to take it, but that would
tip Aziz off. If the radio was gone, they would change frequencies and
they would also begin to wonder if the woman had acted alone.

Rapp studied the device. It was made by a French company he knew
little about. He placed the radio back where he'd found it and checked his
watch. Four minutes and twenty-three seconds had passed. Rapp was
standing over the body when he felt an almost indiscernible tremor.
Someone was coming down the hall. He drew his gun and bounded across

the room to the closet. Just as he closed the closet door, he saw the main door to the bedroom begin to open. Rapp stood at the door for only a second and then cautiously retreated into the stash room, closing and bolting the door behind him.

BACK IN THE control room at Langley, Irene Kennedy had given up trying to raise Rapp on the radio. Instead she sat with everyone else in total silence and watched the events unfold. No one spoke. They all watched, riveted by the real-life drama unfolding on the one small monitor. At first no one knew what Rapp was doing when he began to stab the man who already lay dead on the floor. Then people began to catch on.

General Flood turned to Stansfield and said, "Damn, that kid thinks on his feet."

Before Stansfield could reply, Rapp had bolted across the room and into the closet. Almost simultaneously, the bedroom door was opened and a man in green combat fatigues stood silhouetted by the hallway light.

Everyone watched as the man walked across the room and suddenly snapped up his gun from his side, spinning three hundred sixty degrees. Next, the lights came on, and then a series of excited calls over the radio.

25

WASHINGTON, D.C., WAS a city, a federal district, and most notably, the capital of the United States of America. The originally square geographic area was located at the confluence of the Potomac and Anacostia Rivers and was bordered by Maryland on three sides and Virginia to the southwest. Founded in 1790 and originally called the Federal City and District of Columbia, after Christopher Columbus, the city was later renamed by Congress for the nation's first president. Because the city's four corners pointed in the four directions of the compass, it was conveniently split up into quadrants.

The southeast quadrant was by far the most economically deprived. The heart of the area was the neighborhood of Anacostia. This violent portion of Washington accounted for more than half of the city's annual murders and was literally a war zone in the shadow of the nation's Capitol.

On the top floor of a rat-infested tenement building in the heart of Anacostia, a man with bleached white hair and a fresh set of tattoos worked diligently as the clock approached midnight. The building was largely deserted, except for some drug addicts who used the lower floors to trade sex, stolen property, and sometimes even cash for their mood-altering chemical of choice. The building had been chosen by the group because the police rarely patrolled the area, out of fear for their own safety.

In the grungy apartment on the fifth floor the windows had been covered with three-quarter-inch plywood—the sturdy boards bolted into the window frames making them impossible to kick in. The door had also been reinforced with two-by-fours and plywood, and a series of new locks had been installed. Inside the room two motion sensors, mounted in opposite corners, had ensured the room's integrity for almost two weeks.

Rafique Aziz had ordered the white-haired man sitting on the folding chair to find the safe house almost five months ago, but Aziz had been adamant about waiting until the last possible moment to set it up. They did not want to attract too much attention. The man sitting in the dirty apartment was Salim Rusan, the same man who, for the last six months, had been an inconspicuous bellman at the Washington Hotel, the same man who had taken aim with his SVD sniper rifle at the Secret Service just yesterday.

Rusan was no longer an inconspicuous individual. Thanks to the FBI, his employee photo from the hotel had been splashed all over television and every newspaper in the country. That was why Rusan had not seen daylight since walking into this apartment the morning before last. It had all been predicted by Aziz. The group's leader had been explicit about every detail before the raid on the White House, and that is why he had given Rusan only two ten-round magazines. Aziz had other plans for Rusan, and he wanted him far away from the White House when the police and the FBI showed up.

After Rusan had fired all twenty of his rounds, he had left the Soviet-made sniping rifle right there on the balcony overlooking the White House and fled the building by a staircase. When he made it to the street, he proceeded two blocks to the Metro Center stop at Twelfth and F Street and caught the first southbound train. Ten minutes later he was walking through the slums of Anacostia, his hotel uniform replaced with a Chicago Bulls hat and a leather jacket.

Everything had been waiting for Rusan when he arrived. The copious amount of rat droppings and cobwebs had been cleaned up, and the apartment was stocked with everything he needed. Most of the supplies had been bought at the REI store in Bailey's Crossroads, Virginia. It was paid for in cash. The recreational equipment included a cot, a sleeping bag, several folding chairs, two tables, and some cooking equipment, all of it designed for campers. A battery-powered generator purred in the corner and provided juice for a small TV, a radio, a police scanner, and several lights. Two red Coleman coolers contained enough food and water to last him at least five days, but he doubted he would use all of it. Tomorrow morning he would venture back out into public and sow the seeds for a special surprise.

Rusan looked at his watch and then the cot. He had done everything Aziz had told him to do. He had shaved off his entire beard, with the exception of his mustache and goatee. With a pair of clippers, he had buzzed his hair to within a half inch of his scalp and then bleached it until it was white. Next came the bleaching of the facial hair and eyebrows and then the pierced right ear. That was the difficult part, working backward in the mirror and then trying to stop the blood after he had shoved the needle through the earlobe. The finishing touch was a series of fake tattoos, the most conspicuous, an upside-down pink triangle on his right biceps with the words "Queer Nation" emblazoned underneath. Rusan was not completely comfortable with the disguise. He hated homosexuals, but it had not been his idea; it was Aziz's. And when Aziz gave an order, it was best to follow it.

Rusan had one task to perform before he left the apartment in the morning. Looking at his watch, he debated whether he should take care of it now or get some sleep first. As he fingered the blocks of explosive Semtex and the box of detonators sitting on the other side of the table, he decided to wait until morning. He would sleep better knowing the bombs were unarmed.

RAFIQUE AZIZ AND Muammar Bengazi walked up the main staircase of the mansion. Aziz was furious. They had been lucky enough to take the White House without losing a single man, and now, when he was within twenty-four hours of achieving his ultimate goal, he had lost a valuable man due to outright stupidity. Momentum was something that Aziz was acutely aware of. The battlefields of history are littered with the corpses of soldiers whose commanders failed to notice the crucial role it plays in every conflict. Bengazi walked a half a step behind, ashamed that one of his men had been foolish enough to get killed by a woman.

When they reached the second floor of the mansion, Aziz and Bengazi proceeded directly across the hall and into the president's bedroom. Every light in the room was on. Aziz walked to the other side of the bed and looked down at the bloody naked body. Ragib, the man who had found his slain comrade, was standing on the other side of the body, his radio in one hand and his assault rifle in the other. He started to speak, but Aziz raised his hand and silenced him. The leader of the group said nothing for a long while as his eyes took inventory of the scene.

After several minutes, Aziz looked up. The expression on his face was one of controlled anger. In a curt tone, he asked, "What in the hell happened?"

Ragib nervously began to recount the events, content that for now Aziz hadn't executed him. Ragib told him how Abu Hasan had knocked the woman out and dragged her from the room. He gave his leader the details of what he had found and what little he knew about the woman.

When Ragib was done, Aziz looked at the body for a second and then at the nervous man standing before him. No bad deed was to go unpunished. Examples had to be made; fear had to be maintained. With no warning whatsoever, Aziz brought his hand up and slapped Ragib across the face.

Ragib held his ground, offering his chin for another blow. Although he was stronger and bigger than Aziz, he feared his leader deeply. Fighting back or blocking the blow was not a consideration.

Taking the muzzle of his MP-5, Aziz shoved it under Ragib's chin and backed him up until he was pinned against the wall. "Give me one good reason why I shouldn't kill you for your stupidity."

"I have no excuse." Ragib kept his voice calm, knowing that any sign of fear or disrespect could end his life instantly. "I deserve to die. I was stupid."

MITCH HAD MADE it into the room with seconds to spare. Milt Adams knelt in the corner next to the woman Rapp had just saved and tried to keep her calm. The battered woman had been shaking for the better part of five minutes, and Adams was beginning to worry that she might be slipping into some type of shock.

Rapp tried his best to ignore Adams and the woman and stay focused on what the people back at Langley were saying. He had already received his reprimand for not seeking the approval of the high command before saving the woman. Rapp liked to use the phrase "high command" to describe anyone who sat comfortably in a dark room that was dimly lit with computer and TV screens and gave orders to operators in the field. On this particular mission, he respected the people who were giving orders. Kennedy was someone whom he trusted implicitly, and Campbell, Flood, and Stansfield had all been in the field before—something that went a long way.

Rapp, however, had a new axiom in life. The stubborn half German had just recently figured out that instead of fighting the system, it was often better to say yes and then go off and do whatever you thought was best. Washington was a bureaucratic monolith that more often than not moved with the speed and agility of a five-hundred-pound man. Like most clandestine operators, Rapp saw Washington's role as a secondary one, and because of this he had developed the habit of being very cautious about what information he passed on while in the field. Rapp had discovered that the less they thought he was doing the more support they seemed to give him, while inversely the more he told them, especially bad news, the less support he seemed to get. Kennedy almost always went to bat for him, but there were others in Washington who had built their entire careers on doing nothing.

Rapp sat on his heels, his eyes trained on the monitor, his left ear receiving the audio from the president's bedroom and his right ear receiving the audio from Langley. The only voices coming from Langley were those of Kennedy, Campbell, Stansfield, and Flood. None of them had bothered to criticize him for saving the woman. They all knew or hoped they would have done the same thing. General Flood had, however, stressed that from this point forward there was a chain of command firmly in place, and it was to be used.

Using his new axiom, Rapp replied with a simple, "Yes, sir."

For the next several, tense minutes the group discussed how to proceed, but before long, there was no need to speculate. The entrance of two men into the bedroom silenced all radio chatter.

Rapp squinted at the small monitor and instantly recognized the body language of the smaller man. The hair on Rapp's neck stood on end, and his palms became moist. When Rapp heard the voice of this man, his heart began to race almost out of control. Instinctively, Rapp found himself reaching for his MP-10. The desire to kill seemed to possess him. Rafique Aziz was on the other side of the wall, probably no more than ten feet away, and his back was to the door.

As Rapp rose to one knee, the voice of Irene Kennedy came over the handset. "Iron Man, I know what you're thinking, and it's not going to happen. The odds aren't right. There are three of them and one of you."

Rapp paused, tempted not to reply. Unfortunately, he had already tried that one, and it wasn't going to work twice. Rapp exhaled and said, "I can take them down and end this right now," his voice a little edgy.

Kennedy's even voice came right back, "Or you could get killed and ruin our only chance for finding out what's going on in there."

"I won't get killed," answered Rapp in a tense voice. "At least not before I take all three of them down first."

Back at Langley, Kennedy spun around in her chair and looked up at Director Stansfield. She shook her head vigorously at her boss. Stansfield, for his part, sat calmly in his chair with one arm folded across his chest and the hand of the other one under his chin. Touching the arm of his headset, he said, "Iron Man, hold for a second while we discuss our options." Stansfield pressed a button on his console and leaned forward. General Flood scooted his chair over several feet, and Kennedy and General Campbell placed their hands on the long table that ran in front of the elevated row.

Kennedy was the first to speak. "I don't like the odds."

Stansfield looked from Kennedy to Campbell, and the general replied, "I don't know . . . I'm tempted. We've had a bull's eye on this guy's head for a long time, and Mitch is awfully good."

Stansfield turned to the chairman of the Joint Chiefs. Flood rubbed the knob of his chin with his hand. Frowning, he answered, "We're not even an hour into this operation, and we have sixty-plus hostages on the line. I think we wait." With a shake of the head, Flood added, "If he doesn't get all three of them, we're in deep shit."

All of them turned and looked at the monitor showing the three terrorists. One of them turned and walked closer to the door.

Stansfield shook his head and punched the button on his console. Adjusting the lip mike of his headset, he said, "Iron Man, you are to hold your position. I repeat, you are to hold your position."

Back in the stash room, Rapp squeezed the tough plastic handset so tightly his knuckles turned white. In his mind he was swearing the same four-letter word over and over while kicking himself for answering Kennedy's call. He should have put a bullet in the field radio and gone out and ended it.

Thinking he still had a chance, Rapp stated, "I respectfully disagree. I have three targets, all standing within fifteen feet of each other." Rapp looked at the monitor. "They have their backs to my position, and I have the element of surprise on my side. This is not a difficult takedown."

This time it was General Flood's voice that came back over the radio. "Iron Man, you are not to move, and that is an order. We need your eyes and ears in there, and we have time on our side." Flood's voice boomed with authority. In a slightly softer tone he added, "You'll get your chance, son. Just be patient."

Reluctantly, Rapp replied, "Roger that." Then, taking the handset, he tapped the ear portion against his forehead repeatedly. *Next time,* he told himself, *just do it. Don't bother asking.*

RAFIQUE AZIZ STILL had the muzzle of his MP-5 stuck firmly under the chin of Ragib. If he'd had more men at his disposal, Ragib would be dead, but he needed every last body. That was why Aziz had brought so many explosives. It was the only way he could neutralize the advantage the Americans would have in manpower.

Ragib, his head contorted in a painful, twisted position, spoke cautiously. "I will find her. I promise you, Rafique."

Slowly, Aziz backed away, letting his rifle fall to his side, considering whether it was worth looking for the woman. He grabbed the pile of clothes on the floor. Hasan's pistol was still in its holster, and his rifle was on top of the dresser on the other side of the room. The bloody knife was on the floor near the clothes, so the woman was unarmed. Sideways, Aziz looked at Ragib and asked, "Was this the same woman Abu Hasan had me pull out of line this morning?"

Ragib nodded his head vigorously. "Yes. It is the same woman."

Aziz scoffed and looked at Bengazi, who was standing closer to the door. "I know this woman. I met her when I arrived for my meeting with that fat pig Russ Piper."

In typical mute form, Bengazi said nothing. Aziz nodded as things started to make a little more sense. He remembered Russ Piper telling him abut the woman's family. "The woman's father is a Chicago police officer." Aziz looked down at the dead body before him. "That helps explain this."

When Aziz was done looking at the body, he bent down and grabbed the pile of clothes. From them, he took the pistol and the radio, then walked over to the dresser and grabbed the extra assault riffle. Aziz turned and tossed the rifle across the room at Ragib.

With his own rifle in one hand, Ragib caught the other rifle with his free hand. "Do you want me to find the girl?"

Aziz thought about it for a second and then said, "No. She can do us no harm. All of the exits are wired. Chances are she'll set off one of the bombs and kill herself."

Bengazi cleared his throat and got Aziz's attention.

Aziz looked at his second and said, "Yes."

"I think at the very least we should do a sweep of this floor and the third." Bengazi paused. "It shouldn't take more than twenty minutes."

Aziz thought about it for moment and replied, "All right, but let's do it quickly."

As they prepared to leave, Ragib pointed to their dead comrade on the floor and asked, "What do you want me to do with Hasan?"

Without looking back, Aziz said, "Leave him there, and let the stupid fool rot."

26

BACK AT LANGLEY a lively discussion was under way. General Campbell wanted to broaden their vague mandate by sending two more people through the ventilation shaft. His reason was sound. They knew Aziz had brought a large amount of explosives into the White House, and they now had evidence that Aziz had strategically deployed the devices. Before any type of an assault could take place, those devices would have to be defeated, or, at the very least circumvented. To do that, they needed more information, and that meant getting someone with technical expertise into the White House.

General Campbell and Irene Kennedy had again resumed their huddle with their respective bosses. Campbell stated confidently, "Six has the people and the equipment in place, and no one knows explosives better than they do. One call to Lieutenant Commander Harris and we can have them in the shaft in under five minutes."

"I'd prefer to have Iron Man look around a little more," Stansfield said.

Campbell sighed. "I'm not so sure we shouldn't have let Iron Man take them out a couple of minutes ago."

Stansfield raised an eyebrow. "It was a very risky play for so early in the game."

"Yeah, but one that might have been worth it. . . . And if we get it again, I'd like to be in a position to increase the odds."

"So"—Flood leaned forward, placing an arm on the table—"you want to move these people in immediately."

"Yes." Campbell looked at his watch. "It's almost oh-one-hundred. The sun's gonna be up in five hours. The sooner we get a clearer picture of what we're up against the sooner we can end this thing. Plus, like all of our Special Forces personnel, these demo experts are cross-trained. You put two SEALs on Iron Man's flanks and"—Campbell nodded confidently—"the next time we get a chance to take out Aziz, we're not gonna miss."

Stansfield cautioned, "Right now we have three armed terrorists moving about the mansion in a very surly mood. It might be wise to let them cool down before we start."

"I agree," replied Campbell. "We just heard them say they're gonna check the second and third floors, which should take about twenty minutes. Even if we get our people moving in under ten, it'll be close to a half hour before they make it in. And besides, they're coming into the third basement, not the second floor."

"What about Mitch?" asked Kennedy.

"He can sit tight until Aziz is done checking the second and third floors, and then he can head back down using the elevator."

Kennedy thought about it for a moment and then said, "It sounds reasonable to me."

Both Kennedy and Campbell looked up at Flood and Stansfield. General Flood looked at Stansfield first and then Campbell. "Tell Commander Harris to get his men ready to move, but they are to wait for my order before they cross the fence line." Campbell and Kennedy went back to their spots, leaving the two older men alone. Flood moved close to Stansfield and asked, "How does this change things with the vice president?"

Stansfield pondered the question momentarily and then replied, "I'm not sure; he was awfully vague in his direction. He seemed to leave the door open for everything up to the point of an actual raid."

Flood shook his head and muttered, "Vice President Baxter is severely hampered in the leadership department. . . . He is not the person we need for this crisis."

Stansfield slowly nodded. "He's trying to cover all of his bets."

"So what do we do?"

The director of the CIA thought about it for a moment. "He was vague for a reason. . . . I almost got the feeling he wanted to be kept out of the loop."

"He wants his deniability." The general was not happy. "Well, screw him and the horse he rode in on. We can tell him in the morning when he gets his lazy ass out of bed."

ON THE EAST side of the White House, Lt. Commander Harris and his men were busy getting ready. The air under the tarp was soupy. Condensation had formed on the sides of the three vehicles, and rivulets of water were dripping to the ground. Every man was sweating profusely, but they all ignored it. They were used to working in conditions far worse than this.

Harris had already chosen his two men. The first was Nick Shultz, a thirty-eight-year-old chief petty officer. Shultz was an EOD—explosive-ordinance disposal specialist—who had been on the teams since he was twenty. Due to his natural knack for explosives, he had spent a fair amount of time as a basic underwater demolition/SEAL instructor—for the grueling twenty-six-week course that all candidates must complete before they can become a SEAL. However, what made Shultz one of the very best experts was his steady, unflappable demeanor.

The second man Harris had picked was Danny Craft. The choice was actually a foregone conclusion, since Craft was Shultz's swim buddy. Craft was Shultz's junior by ten years. Where Shultz was calm and introspective, Craft was active and outgoing. And where Shultz was plain-looking, Craft was boyishly handsome. Looking quite a bit younger than his twenty-eight years of age, Craft had used his blue-gray eyes to woo college coeds on both coasts. There was rarely a free night that the young SEAL spent alone.

The two men were polar opposites, and as the older Shultz had expected, this worked to their advantage. Craft saw things that Shultz didn't and vice versa. Over the last two years they had honed their skills and become a very effective duo.

As they prepared for their insertion, the two men stood side by side in front of a long folding table and checked their equipment one last time. Besides their weapons and specialized tool kits, they were bringing one exceptional piece of equipment. Laid out on the table before them was a mobile X-ray imager made by Safety and Security Instruments out of San Diego. The first two pieces of the unit were the RTR-4 X-ray Imager and the XR-200 X-ray Source. The two units worked in conjunction with a third piece of equipment, the RTR-4 control unit. This portable Pentium computer was mounted in a supersturdy gasket-sealed aluminum case with shock-mounted components. The active-matrix color flat-panel display on the control unit would provide Shultz and Craft with a real-time sneak and peek into the guts of Aziz's bombs. Without the RTR-4, any attempt to open the outer casing of the bombs would be a game of Russian roulette.

Standing fifteen feet away, in the open doorway of the CIA communications van, Lt. Commander Harris was busy listening to General Campbell and Irene Kennedy back at Langley. Harris was waiting for an opportunity to make his pitch, but hadn't found it. General Campbell was asking a lot of questions, as was Kennedy. When there was finally a pause, Harris made his move.

"General Campbell, I'd like to request permission to go in with my demo boys. I think—"

Campbell cut him off. "Request denied. I want you with your team." Harris held the handset of the secure field radio to his ear. He was not to be deterred so easily. "I respectfully disagree, sir. I think I would be more valuable helping conduct the recon of the building."

"You are to stay put, Commander."

The voice was not Campbell's. It was General Flood's. Harris, slightly caught off guard, had not expected Flood to be listening in on the conversation.

The highest-ranking officer in the entire U.S. military continued by saying, "If things proceed well, there's a good chance we'll be sending you and your team in."

"Yes, sir," was the only reply Harris could muster.

"Now get your boys moving. Iron Man will be waiting for them on the other side."

BACK IN THE stash room, Mitch Rapp was reorganizing his gear for his incursion back into the bowels of the two-hundred-year-old mansion. Things were happening fast, but he was more than happy to receive the professional services of a couple of SEAL demolition experts, especially since it would mean he would not have to deal with the bombs.

One thing he did want to do before he headed out, though, was talk to the woman he had grabbed from the president's bed. Rapp had been so busy talking to Kennedy and the others that he hadn't had the chance to find out who the woman was and, more important, if she had any information that might help them.

Moving his gear to the side, Rapp took off his baseball cap and scratched his head. Watching Adams give the woman some water, he noticed for the first time that she was very attractive, stunning actually. Rapp scooted forward on his knees to get a little closer and asked, "How are you feeling?"

Rielly had wrapped herself tightly in the sheet and had one arm out. Looking up at the man kneeling in front of her, she replied timidly, "I'm fine." But, before the last syllable left her mouth, the tears started again. Rielly brushed some of them from her cheek and added, "I'm not fine . . . I'm a mess."

Rapp laughed at her blunt observation. Reaching out, he grabbed her shoulder and said, "You're fine. Everything's gonna be fine."

Rielly looked up again, her bottom lip quivering slightly. "I'll never be able to thank you enough for what you did." Grabbing his hand, she squeezed it and said, "I owe you my life."

Rapp blushed slightly. "Now . . . now . . . there's no need to be melo-dramatic." He didn't know how to deal with the unusually personal gratitude of the woman, having grown used to his deeds going unnoticed by all but a select few.

"I'm serious." Rielly squeezed his hand tighter. "I'm not being melodramatic. You saved my life."

"Well," Rapp started uncomfortably, "he might not have killed you."

"Oh," scoffed Rielly in between sniffles. "That's a hell of a consolation." She started to cry even harder.

Milt Adams was still sitting next to Rielly. He looked at Rapp and shook his head. "You need to learn how to accept someone's gratitude, you big oaf. 'You're welcome'—that's what you say to the pretty little woman."

With his hand still on the woman's shoulder, Rapp scowled at Adams. Etiquette was hardly a concern of his at the moment. Rapp turned back to the woman, whose moist cheek was now resting on his hand. After squeezing her shoulder lightly, Rapp reached out with his other hand and brushed some of the tears from her cheek.

"You're welcome," he started tentatively. "I'm glad I was there to help." Rapp held her cheek for a moment and then lifted her head, so he could look her in the eye. That was when he noticed them, the greenest eyes he had ever seen. So beautiful were they that Rapp lost his concentration for a second and forgot what he was about to ask.

He blinked several times and then remembered where he was headed. "I need to ask you some questions. Are you up to it?"

Rielly nodded and wiped the remaining tears from her cheeks. Taking part of her sheet, she blew her nose quietly and said, "God, I haven't cried this much in years."

"Well, you've been through a lot." Rapp was making a concerted effort to say the right things.

"What a shitty couple of days." Rielly shook her head and managed a laugh.

"Yeah . . . I'd imagine they don't get much worse." Rapp looked at his watch and said, "Listen, I have some things I have to do, but I want to ask you some questions first."

Rielly nodded.

"Good. Let's start with your name."

"Anna . . . Anna Rielly."

"I'm Mitch and this is Milt."

Rielly wiped her hand on the sheet and extended it. "Nice to meet you, Mitch." Rielly gave a warm smile, showing off her dimples. "Very nice to meet you." Rapp grinned and shook her hand. Rielly then turned to Adams and shook his hand.

"What do you do here at the White House?" asked Rapp.

"I'm a reporter."

From the look on Rapp's face, one would think they were on their first date and she had just told him she had a husband. *Oh, shit,* Rapp thought to himself. *This could be a problem.* "Who do you work for?"

"NBC. It was my first day on the job."

"Nice timing," Rapp said with a raised eyebrow.

"No shit." Rielly shook her head.

"Where have you been held for the last several days?"

"In the White House mess."

Rapp looked to Adams, who nodded and said, "That's where I thought he would hold them. No exterior windows and the room is big enough."

Rapp was worried about whether Aziz had kept all of the hostages together or split them up. As a general rule that decision depended on assets and the layout of the building. With this in mind, Rapp was inclined to believe that with Aziz's limited manpower, he would be forced to keep all of the hostages in one place.

"Were all of the hostages kept in the mess?"

"Yes." Rielly shrugged her shoulders. "At least I think so."

"How many of you?"

Biting her bottom lip, Rielly thought about it for a moment and said, "I don't know. Eighty . . . one hundred . . . a hundred and twenty . . . ? I don't know."

"I really need you to think about this one. You don't have to answer it right now, but I need you to try and remember how many people were in the mess."

Rielly nodded. "I'll try."

"What about Secret Service agents? Were they held in the same room as you?" Rapp knew Aziz well enough to bet that he would at the very least separate the Secret Service agents from the hostages.

"I don't know. When all this started, I'd only been on the job for about fifteen minutes. I don't know what any of the agents look like."

"You don't have to know them personally to be able to pick them out. They all have short haircuts, athletic builds . . . They stand out." Rapp looked at her proddingly. "Come on, you're a reporter." With a grin he added, "You're supposed to notice stuff like that."

Rielly thought about it. "I don't remember seeing anyone like that."

"What about any marines or other military types?" asked Milt Adams.

Rielly shook her head immediately. "I know for a fact I didn't see anyone in a uniform."

Rapp nodded to Adams, approving of the timely question. That settled it for him. Aziz was either holding the Secret Service and military personnel in a different location, or he had killed all of them. Knowing Aziz, the latter was a distinct possibility.

"How many different terrorists did you see?"

Rielly closed her eyes for a second. "I think I saw six of them, and I'm pretty sure I saw the leader. Some Prince something or other. I actually met him on the street on my way in the morning all of this started. He got out of a limo with Russ Piper, the chairman of the DNC. Russ is an old friend of my family." Rielly paused. "I haven't seen him since this whole thing started. . . . I hope he's all right."

"The leader is not a prince," said Rapp. "His name is Rafique Aziz."

Rielly had a spasm of shivers and said, "Well, whoever he is, he's evil, and I don't mean just crazy or goofy, I mean evil. He shot someone in cold blood just because they asked for blankets and food. He just lifted his gun without any warning and shot the man in the head."

"That would be Rafique Aziz," said Rapp somberly. Then looking down at his watch, he decided he had better get moving. "Well, Ms. Rielly, we'll have to continue this later. I have to go take care of something."

"Please call me Anna." Rielly smiled.

"All right, Anna. I don't know how long this will take, but I should be back in an hour or less. Milt here will take care of you, so don't worry. I know he doesn't look like much, but don't let that fool you."

Adams looked at Rapp deadpan. Rapp grabbed the small fanny pack for his short excursion and strapped it around his waist. He turned his baseball cap around backward and placed his headset over the top, but after hearing only static interference, he turned off the small radio.

Rielly watched him intently as he moved about the room on his knees. When he grabbed his submachine gun and stood, Rielly asked, "Who do you work for, Mitch?"

"The post office." Rapp nodded for Adams to get up and then looked back at Rielly. "Anna, we'll have to finish this interview later." With a wink, he added reassuringly, "Keep an eye on Milt for me."

27

THE SEARCH OF the second and third floors of the White House had taken almost twenty-five minutes. The three men worked in unison, one always covering the other two, as they went from room to room checking the closets and under the beds. Aziz had been sure they would find her cowering in one of the closets, but they had not.

They descended from the third floor. Aziz, walking in the lead, was thinking. He was thinking about the building and how old it was, how much it bothered him that he couldn't just walk from one building to the other without going outside. If he could just have gotten his hands around the president in his office, he would not have had to spread his people so thin. But Aziz knew if he wanted to get the Americans to meet all of his demands, he would have to extract the cowardly president from the safety of his bunker. And the only way he could do that was if his little thief, his gift from Saddam, was successful in his task.

Aziz stopped suddenly and did an about-face. Bengazi and Ragib stopped just short of running into their leader. They were tired and their reaction time dulled. Aziz pointed back down the hall and said, "Follow me. I have decided there is something else we need to check while we are here."

The two men stood aside, and Aziz marched off in the direction from which they had come. As they continued down the staircase to the first basement, Aziz opened the fire door and stepped into the hallway. He stood there for several seconds, looking in both directions, and then he walked back into the staircase and continued down to the second basement. He repeated his actions on this floor, pausing just long enough to look down the hallway.

When they reached the third basement, Aziz pointed to the stairwell door and said to Ragib, "You wait here." Aziz then marched down the hall with Bengazi.

When the corridor ended, the two men turned to the left and continued for another thirty feet. Aziz was immediately surprised by the lack of noise. When he had checked on his little thief some four hours earlier, the sound had been pronounced. Slightly alarmed by the change, Aziz

211

brought his assault rifle up to a leveled position. Bengazi, sensing his boss's tension, did the same. The outer door that Mustafa had broken through on the first night was only half open. As Aziz approached, he could see only a portion of the outer room to the president's bunker, and his little thief was not in sight. Aziz walked to the left so he could see the right side of the room. There was still nothing: no sound, no Mustafa.

Without stopping, Aziz slid through the partially opened door and snapped the muzzle of his MP-5 to the left. What he saw upset him instantly. Against the far wall, Mustafa was sitting on the floor, asleep in an upright position—his short arms wrapped around his potbelly and his mouth open with a stream of drool running down his chin. Aziz took three steps and forcefully kicked the man's feet.

Mustafa's eyes opened instantly, and Aziz shoved the muzzle of his rifle to within an inch of his face. "What in the hell are you doing?"

Nervously, he replied, "I was taking a nap."

"I can see that. Why aren't the drills running?"

"They needed a rest." The safecracker tried to move farther away from the weapon, but there was nowhere to go. "If I run them nonstop, they will burn out."

Aziz moved the rifle away from the man's face. The answer had satisfied him for the moment. "Are you still on schedule?"

"Yes." Mustafa rolled his plump body onto one knee and stood. "I am actually several hours ahead of schedule."

Aziz raised an interested eyebrow. "Really. When do you expect to have the door opened?"

Mustafa looked at his watch. "If the drills continue to work well, I think I can have the door opened around seven this evening."

Aziz smiled. "That would make me very happy." Slapping the shorter man on the back, Aziz said, "You have done good work, Mustafa."

"Thank you." Mustafa bowed his head slightly, accepting the rare compliment.

Aziz looked over at the shiny vault door. In less than twenty-four hours he would have his hands on the president. Mustafa's news of being ahead of schedule helped assuage Aziz's anger over the loss of Hasan. Once he had the president, he could breathe a sigh of relief.

LEAVING THE STASH room was a tense process. The only eyes Rapp had outside the room were the sole surveillance unit he had placed in the president's bedroom. This assured him that it was safe to exit the stash room, but Milt cautioned him that the large closet also had a door at the opposite end that led into the First Lady's bedroom.

"All right," Rapp whispered, and Adams opened the wall several inches. Not moving, not breathing, Rapp peeked through the crack and listened. Stepping into the closet, he immediately noticed that its door to the First Lady's bedroom was open. Rapp checked to his left and his right twice and then walked toward the First Lady's bedroom. He stood at the doorframe for a moment and listened. The room was empty.

Directly across the room was another door, which was closed. Rapp figured it was either a closet or a bathroom. Whichever the case, it made no difference. The fact that the door he was standing in had been left open and the one across the room had been closed, however, was significant. It meant that Aziz and his men had done a sloppy job on the search. Each door should have been opened, checked, and then closed.

Because of this inconsistency, Rapp felt confident enough to close the door to the closet. He quickly rummaged through the closet, grabbing a sweatshirt, a pair of sweatpants, and a pair of white sweat socks. Rapp went back to the stash room door and handed the clothes to Adams.

"Give these to Anna." Rapp looked at the shelf to his right and saw a blanket and two pillows. "Here, take these too. Try to get her to sleep." Rapp began to close the door and said, "And make sure you don't bolt this thing. If I'm in a hurry to get back in, I don't want to have to stand out here and knock."

Adams nodded and said, "Good luck."

Rapp closed the organizer tight and silently moved across the president's bedroom. Three steps and he was across the entrance hall and into the bathroom. Reaching behind a light to the left of the medicine cabinet, he found the button and pressed it. The wall sprang open an inch, and with his gloved hand, Rapp pulled it open several more feet. With the push of another button, the elevator's doors opened, and Rapp began his near silent descent. Seconds later the elevator stopped and the doors opened. Rapp retraced his earlier steps, down the hallway and into the stairs leading to the third basement.

When he arrived at the landing door, he reached for the handle and stopped just inches short. The stairwell was darker than the hallway on the other side, and a half inch of bright light bordered the bottom of the door. Rapp had seen something. His eyes had caught some type of motion, a variance in light. Cautiously, Rapp backed up, wondering if the SEALs could already have arrived.

With his gun leveled, he kept his eyes trained on the patch of light. After only seconds he saw the shadow again. Frowning, he opened up the monitor, this time not daring to holster his weapon. With the monitor opened, his gun in his left hand and the snake in his right, he moved to the far side of the door handle and slowly inched the tiny lens forward along the concrete floor. Rapp's eyes went back and forth between watching the screen and watching the progress of the snake. An inch at a time, he nudged it forward. The first thing Rapp saw on the screen was a pair of boots. As he pushed the lens forward, combat fatigues came into view and then the distinctive barrel, handgrip, and curved magazine of an AK-74. Rapp pulled the snake back deliberately and swore to himself.

Why was a bad guy all of the sudden down here in the basement? They had come across no one on the way in. Why now? As Rapp leaned flat against the wall, he tried to make some sense of it. After a while he decided it must have been the girl. He had to make a decision, and the sooner he made it the better. Waiting in the stairwell was not an option. There was no cover, and someone could come along at any minute. It was too big a risk. Opening the door and shooting the terrorist was an option, but one that would have to be a last resort. Rapp was left with only one real course—go back and tell Kennedy and Campbell to put the SEALs in a holding pattern until he could make sure the basement was clear.

Rapp looked down at the corner where the white concrete wall met the hinges of the door. He reached inside the cargo pocket of his pants and extracted one of the micro video and audio surveillance units. Dropping to a knee, he attached a Velcro patch to the wall and then carefully positioned the unit so the tiny fiber-optic lens would have a view under the doorway.

Rapp ascended to the second floor of the mansion quickly, taking less than two minutes to cover the distance from the third basement. When the small elevator reached the second level, Rapp turned on his monitor and checked the view of the president's bedroom. All was clear on the video and the audio, so he closed the screen and stepped out onto the tile floor of the bathroom. From there, it was across the way and into the large closet once again. With the doors closed, he found the hidden latch for the wall organizer and opened the way to the stash room.

Adams and Rielly were sitting wide-eyed on the floor when Rapp entered and Adams said, "You're back kind'a quick, aren't you?"

Rapp shook his head while he dropped to his knees in front of the secure field radio. "Yeah, we've got a problem downstairs."

"Like what?"

"We've got a Tango running around down in the third basement."

"A what?"

Rapp pressed several buttons on the control panel of the radio. "A Tango . . . a bad guy . . . a terrorist." Rapp brought the handset up to his ear.

With a worried expression, Adams asked, "Did he see you?"

"If he saw me, Milt, he wouldn't still be walking around." Rapp turned his focus to the radio and said, "Iron Man to control. Over." Rapp had to repeat himself before he got a reply.

Kennedy's voice came back clearly, "Iron Man, this is control. We read you. Over."

"We have a problem. There is at least one Tango in the third basement. I repeat, one Tango in the third basement."

"Where in the third basement?" was General Campbell's question.

"Two minutes ago he was standing just outside the stairwell, by the door to the boiler room."

"Any others in sight?"

"Not that I could see, but my only shot was with the snake under the door." Rapp added earnestly, "My immediate suggestion is to put the brakes on the next two through the chute. It's not worth the risk at this time to bring them into an unsecured area."

"Hold for a second, Iron Man," was Campbell's reply.

While Rapp waited for the brass on the other end to finish their little powwow, he opened up his monitor and attempted to get a feed from the second surveillance unit he had placed in the basement. He was still playing with the unit when Kennedy came back on the line.

"Iron Man, any thoughts on what the Tango is doing in the basement?"

"Probably looking for the girl, which means Aziz and Bengazi might also be down there."

There was another period of silence over the line while the brass conferred. Kennedy came back ten seconds later and said, "Iron Man, we concur. Stay put while we see if we can slow things down."

"Roger." Rapp pressed the speaker button and placed the handset back in its cradle. From the tiny speaker on the control panel of the radio, an electronic hum told Rapp the line was still open. Turning his attention back to the monitor strapped to his chest, he went to work trying to get something from the surveillance unit in the basement.

AZIZ'S SPIRITS HAD rebounded. The news that he would have his hands around the neck of the president by dusk today had helped temper the loss of the idiot Hasan. If he could just hold out until then, the chances for complete success would double, if not triple. The next fifteen or so hours would be the tensest of the siege. Aziz corrected himself on that point: it would be the next five hours. Once the sun was up he would be safe again. But come nightfall the chances of a strike would increase once again. Aziz had gone to great pains to study the techniques used by the world's elite counterterrorist strike teams, such as Germany's GSG-9, France's GIGN, Britain's SAS, and of course, America's three premier teams. The groups all shared information on training, strategy, intelligence, and tactics, and competed in annual competitions to help hone each other's skills.

All of the groups followed a fairly standard procedure when confronted with a hostage crisis: initial deployment of assets; intelligence collection; planning, development, and practice of the takedown; mission approval; and finally, execution of takedown. All of the groups were good, and the three U.S. teams were always ranked at or near the top in every category except one. When it came to mission approval, the U.S. teams were consistently ranked at the bottom. The common critique from the international counterterrorism community was that the U.S. had too many people in the chain of command. Too many people throwing their opinions into the arena and thus slowing down a process that depended on speed and efficiency.

This was one of the things Aziz was planning to exploit. This, as well as the American media and ultimately public opinion. The morning would bring a new day in the media cycle, and Aziz would begin to implement another crucial part of his plan. If he succeeded, it would keep the dogs at bay for another day. The politicians were his allies, and he needed to keep them believing there was a way out of the situation. Aziz needed to keep them and their opinions directly involved in the chain of command, because as long as they stayed involved, the generals would be unable to strike.

As Aziz walked down the hall with Bengazi, he started to see one fundamental flaw in his plan. He had succeeded in negating the Americans' manpower advantage through the use of explosives and the exterior surveillance cameras he had seized from the Secret Service. With the amount of explosives he had deployed, any attack would result in the deaths of all the rescuers and, if need be, the hostages too. The flaw, Aziz was now sure, was created once again by the separation of the West Wing and the Executive Mansion. The West Wing was one hundred percent secured, but the mansion was not. If the Americans found out that he was in the process of extracting the president from his bunker, there was no telling what they might do. It was entirely likely that they would risk everything to prevent the president from falling into his hands.

As Aziz and Bengazi neared the end of the hall, Aziz stopped and said, "Muammar, I want you to stay here for the rest of the night. I will send you a replacement at"—Aziz looked at his watch—"seven. I want you to make sure that nothing happens to my little ferret." Aziz pointed in the direction of the bunker. "If you fail me this time, you will be begging for a quick death." The subordinate nodded while maintaining his ramrod posture.

Aziz turned to go back upstairs and was confronted with two doors. One of them he had not noticed before. Turning to Bengazi, he asked, "Where does this lead?"

"To the boiler room," the heavily bearded Bengazi answered.

"Boiler room," Aziz repeated while he mulled over the words. "Was it secured after we took over?"

"Yes," stated Bengazi. "I checked it personally."

Aziz stood looking at the doorway, thinking for a long moment. "Do you remember," he asked Bengazi, "the incident at the Indonesian consulate in Amsterdam . . . back in the seventies?"

Bengazi's face twisted as he tried to jog his memory. After a while, he replied, "Yes, I remember what happened. The terrorists surrendered after a long standoff with the police."

"Two weeks," answered Aziz, referring to how long the siege had lasted. "Did you know that during the standoff the CIA assisted the Dutch government by getting one of their people into the building via the sewer pipe?"

"No."

"Neither did the terrorists. The man came in through the basement and bugged the building. Everything the terrorists said and did was heard by the Dutch authorities." Aziz looked back at the door. "When was the last time you checked this room?"

"I checked it yesterday afternoon."

"A lot has happened since then. I think we should check it again." Without waiting for Bengazi's opinion, Aziz started for the door.

THE TWO SEALS trudged forward through the ventilation duct in complete darkness, Craft in the lead and Shultz close behind. This is what they had trained their whole lives to do. There wasn't a Special Forces operator in the service worth his salt who wouldn't have given his left nut to be in their position. All the push-ups, early morning runs, icy swims, hour upon hour of target practice, live fire drills, parachute jumps that ran into the triple digits—it all came down to this.

"Apprehension" was a word that didn't belong in their vocabulary. Maybe "caution" from time-to-time, but not "apprehension." These men relished the task before them and knew all too well what the stakes were. Death was a distinct possibility. They had seen team members die in both training and covert operations. That was the life they had decided to live, and there wasn't a day they regretted the decision.

The younger Craft was in the lead because he had asked to be. The two SEALs were now experiencing the same problem that Rapp and Adams had. The closer they got to the White House the worse their radio reception became. Like the two that had gone before them, they had removed their earpieces after a while because the static became so bad.

It had not occurred to anyone, either at Langley or at SEAL Team Six's mobile command post, to have Shultz and Craft string along a phone line—a military practice that had been commonplace for almost a century, but had gone by the wayside with the recent onslaught of high-tech radios and billion-dollar satellites. Events had progressed too quickly, and a low-tech solution to a critical battlefield problem had been missed.

Craft was glad he had remembered to put on his elbow and knee pads before being lowered into the ventilation duct. He had about thirty pounds of gear on his body and was pulling another thirty behind him via a rope. Wiggling like a reptile, he could move only four to six inches at a time, and his elbows were doing most of the work.

The two men moved quietly for the most part, the only real noise coming from the equipment they dragged behind them. The noise wasn't much, no more than that of a shirt sliding down a clothes chute. It was hard to tell how far they had gone, but to Craft it seemed as if they were nearing the end. He stopped momentarily and looked behind him. All he found was more blackness and the sounds of his swim buddy squirming his way forward. Craft decided to shed some light on the situation. Turning onto one side, he extracted his pistol, a Heckler & Koch USP .45 ACP. Attached to the pistol was both a cylindrical suppressor and a laser-aiming module. Craft turned on the laser, and the red dot bounced off the walls of the duct. Aiming the pistol straight ahead, Craft found the end of the shaft not more than thirty feet away.

AZIZ PLACED HIS hand on the doorknob and nodded to Bengazi. Bengazi took up position opposite Aziz and signaled that he was ready. When Aziz opened the door, Bengazi swung his rifle and half of his body into the now open space. Bengazi looked down at the expansive room from a slightly elevated position. A small grated metal landing was just on the other side of the door, and three steps led from the landing down to the stark concrete floor of the boiler room. One dim light off to the left provided minimal lighting. After Bengazi looked from one side of the room to the other, he checked on both sides of the doorframe for more light switches. After coming up empty, he spotted a group of four switches at the bottom of the grated steps. Bengazi moved down the steps and slapped all four switches up with the palm of his hand. The room lit up with powerful overhead lamps.

Aziz stepped onto the landing and surveyed the room, his MP-5 gripped in both hands. He nodded for Bengazi to move out ahead while he slowly came down the steps. Neither man spoke. Bengazi had known Aziz long enough to recognize when he was spooked.

Aziz did not know exactly what he was looking for. As he peered around the room, he wondered if he wasn't being overly paranoid. There had been very little time for sleep over the last week, and his nerves were getting raw. The truth, however, was that it is impossible to be too paranoid when dealing with the CIA. He should have thought of this possibility earlier, but so much had changed from the original plan. It was a grave oversight on his part. He had been thinking of too many things and spreading himself too thin, but he was focused now. Nothing mattered more than getting his hands on the president, and if that meant sacrificing some of his assets to secure this area of the basement, it was a gamble that was well worth it.

As Aziz moved across the room, a good ten paces behind Bengazi, his eyes searched the floor for any type of drain, grate, or pipe. While he looked, he wondered how big the sewer pipe must have been in Amsterdam. Not any pipe would do; it would have to be big, and he doubted that anything big enough to support a human would be running into the White House.

Aziz was looking under one of the large boilers when he heard a soft whistle from Bengazi. Standing up straight, he looked over to his man, who was standing with one finger over his lips and the barrel of his rifle pointing up.

Aziz stood with his neck craned upward, watching the metal duct that ran from the wall diagonally across the room to some large piece of equipment. Listening intently, he focused everything on the duct. After a short while he thought he saw something, a glimmer off the lights, a buckle in the metal. Aziz's brow furrowed. Again he saw something, some type of movement. Aziz stepped from his cover to get a closer look.

Some twenty feet away Bengazi shook his head at him and tried to wave him back. Aziz ignored him and continued to approach the duct. Finally, when he was directly under the structure, he heard the noise. It sounded like a rat moving behind the walls of an old building. Something was definitely in the duct.

Aziz looked behind him and took several steps back, putting himself in direct line with the length of the duct. Then, raising his MP-5, he sighted in on part of the duct that protruded from the wall. With the wooden butt of the rifle squeezed tightly between his right shoulder and cheek, he depressed the trigger and unleashed a volley of automatic fire, the heavy rounds slicing through the thin metal with ease.

Nine rounds were fired in total, the noise from the shots careening off the concrete floors and walls, leaving the ears of Aziz and Bengazi ringing. The smell of spent rounds filled the air, and a cluster of shell casings rolled aimlessly about the floor near Aziz's feet.

Aziz did not move. He stood his ground with his rifle still pointed at the duct, his eyes fixed on the straight line of bullet holes he had just laced into the thin metal. At first there was nothing, no movement and no noise other than the ringing of the shots that had been fired, and then, out of one of the holes, something dark beaded into a droplet and after an eternity it broke free. Both Aziz and Bengazi watched it fall to the ground. The drop hit the gray concrete floor and splashed into a spidered crimson pattern. Without hesitation, both Aziz and Bengazi stepped back and opened up on the duct with a relentless hail of bullets.

28

THE APARTMENT WAS nice. It had been decorated by his mother. She had insisted on flying to D.C. to help her son get settled in. Now that Dallas was an important figure in Washington, he'd have to entertain. Mrs. King had loaded up her son with the best that Williams-Sonoma, Pottery Barn, and Restoration Hardware could provide. The two-bedroom apartment in Adams-Morgan cost him nineteen hundred dollars a month, but it was worth it. It was only a couple of blocks away from some of Washington's best nightspots, there were plenty of women around, and it was close to work.

Dallas King sat at the breakfast bar in the kitchen with a cup of coffee in one hand and the remote control to his TV in the other. He was waiting for the seven A.M. top-of-the-hour CNN news update. Dallas took a sip of coffee and looked down the hall to his bedroom. Through the cracked door he glimpsed the lean leg of his lovely little Asian hostess, Kim. She had been everything he had hoped and then some. After King finished his meeting with Sheila Dunn, he had moved to the bar for one more glass of wine. Someone must have explained to the hostess who he was because she began asking him questions about the crisis. King worked it for everything it was worth, stressing his role as Vice President Baxter's closest adviser, complaining about the pressure, and finally telling her how much he wanted to be with her. By the time one A.M. rolled around, he had her punched out and on the way to his apartment.

As he sipped his coffee, CNN came back from a commercial break. King turned up the volume and listened to the anchor start off with the lead story of the morning. Footage of a candlelight vigil that had taken place the night before flashed across the screen. The anchor announced that an estimated fifty thousand people had taken part in the silent march from the Lincoln Memorial to the Capitol. Next came more footage of massive crowds pressing against police barricades in an effort to glimpse the White House. This relatively calm footage was replaced by images of protestors burning American flags in Gaza, the West Bank, Baghdad, and Damascus.

King shook his head and muttered, "If they keep that shit up, we'll have no choice but to storm the place."

The anchor and the correspondent talked for almost a minute about the official reactions of governments around the Middle East and then broke away for a live briefing being delivered by Director Roach of the FBI.

Roach stood in front of a Justice Department podium and started out reading from prepared text. The director gestured to an easel on his left, saying, "This is the photo we released yesterday of Mohammed Battikhi—the man we believe to have fired shots from the roof of the Washington Hotel during the opening moments of the attack on the White House. We now know his real name to be Salim Rusan. He is at large and considered to be extremely dangerous. Right now we are offering a one-million-dollar reward for any information leading to the arrest of Rusan and a second individual." One of Roach's aides removed the first photo and replaced it with a second of a man wearing a green uniform. His hair was slicked back, and he had a gold chain with a cross hanging from his open collar.

"This man worked for the White Knight Linen Service Company," Roach continued, "and went by the name of Vinney Vitelli. His real name is Abu Hasan. We are not sure if he is at large, but we are very interested in talking to anyone who has dealt with him in the last year."

Roach continued to talk, giving a number to call, but King wasn't listening. His eyes were open wide in disbelief. It couldn't be. King stood, almost dropping his coffee cup. Tugging at the collar of his white bathrobe, he raced for the TV. "Oh, my God, it's him!"

NO ONE IN the bunker had slept for more than a half hour at a time, and some of the agents had not slept at all. The noise of steel assaulting steel grew louder as morning approached. President Hayes remained confident that the FBI would come. He'd been through the briefings, he had listened to the experts state that the best time to attack was right before dawn. It was when people were most sluggish and hence easiest to surprise.

It started to brighten, this time of the year, around five-thirty, and the sun was up by a quarter past six. Each of the eleven felt a fevered anticipation as morning drew near, but as the hours passed by, there was collective letdown, followed by depression, as the nerve-racking sound of the door being breached gnawed at their ears. Each individual, including the president, asked himself or herself the same question over and over again. Can we hold out for another day?

Valerie Jones was coming back from the small bathroom, where she had finally, after two days, decided to remove the makeup from her face. Considering the situation, she felt that any hang-ups about her wrinkles and the dark circles under her eyes were foolish.

Jones had spent all night thinking about the president's rebuke the day before. She had worked far too hard to get where she was, and she wouldn't allow anyone to pin the blame on her for admitting a terrorist into the Oval Office. In Jones's mind the truth was never that simple. There were always eight sides to every story.

There was no way she was going to roll over now and watch her career go up in flames. Jones had been concentrating on angles all night. Who could influence Hayes to help put the story in the proper light? Whom could she use to focus Hayes's anger on? The first question was easy to answer. Jones knew enough senators and big donors. She could get them to whisper in the president's ear or, if needed, lean on him. The way she would spin it would be to hold up Russ Piper and the DNC as sacrificial lambs. All Jones did was put him and his guest down in the appointment book. That menial task was hardly worth ending someone's career over.

As far as getting her boss to focus his anger on something or someone else, Jones was working on that. She proceeded back to the couches and sat next to him. If she could get him thinking in another direction, she just might hold on to her job and her career.

President Hayes didn't bother to look up when his chief of staff sat. Jones studied him for a second and then asked, "Why wouldn't they have come?"

Hayes shook his head. "I don't know. They must have a good reason."

"Like what? Isn't it our policy not to negotiate with terrorists?"

Hayes glanced over at her. "We don't always stick to policy."

"Well, who's making the decisions?"

The president looked at her with his tired eyes. "As I told you yesterday, if they're following the Constitution, which I'm sure they are, the powers of the presidency will have been transferred to Vice President Baxter."

Jones rolled her eyes. "That isn't good news."

The president did nothing at first and then nodded slowly in agreement.

"Why wouldn't he send in the FBI?"

"I don't know, Valerie." Hayes sounded very impatient. The tension and lack of sleep were working on his nerves.

"Well, it makes no sense." Jones moved forward cautiously. "Everything you said about the FBI striking before sunrise made sense. I don't understand why they wouldn't have come."

"There's a lot we don't know about. They could have plenty of good reasons why they're waiting to attack."

Jones was keenly aware of the problems between President Hayes and Vice President Baxter. She and the president had discussed them on many occasions. If she could get the president to focus his anger on Baxter, her minor role in this debacle would be forgotten.

In a voice just barely above a mumble Jones planted the seed that she hoped would shift the president's righteous ire in a different direction. "Or Baxter likes being president."

IRENE KENNEDY STOOD in her office and watched the sun rise over the trees of the Potomac River Valley. Any attempt to count her hours of sleep over the last week would be a wasted exercise. They were too few and too far between. She had more pressing things on her mind, and besides, thinking of sleep only caused her to worry more about Rapp. Kennedy had been hoping to steal a couple hours on the couch in her office after the two SEALs had made it into the White House and reported back on the bombs, but that never happened. Things had fallen apart, and they had done so miserably.

At 2:23 A.M. Kennedy had been sitting in the control room at Langley when an irate Skip McMahon called. McMahon had been rousted from his cot in the Executive Office Building just minutes earlier by Rafique Aziz. He had stumbled down the hall and into the FBI's command post in his boxers and T-shirt. Once on the phone, McMahon was further confused by the wild accusations Aziz had flung at him. Everything Aziz said came up empty with McMahon. McMahon tried in vain to deny the accusations, but Aziz only grew more irritated. As Aziz began to threaten to kill hostages, McMahon began to link the recent events with a phone call he had received from FBI Director Roach, the previous evening. Roach had explained to McMahon that the CIA would be moving some sensitive surveillance equipment into position by the east fence of the White House. In less than a minute, one of McMahon's agents had a set of blueprints rolled out on the table before him and was stabbing his finger at the location of a ventilation duct on the South Lawn. As things fell into place, McMahon assured Aziz that he would get to the bottom of the thing within five minutes. McMahon's next phone call was to his colleague and good friend, Irene Kennedy.

That was when the control room at Langley started to piece together what had happened. Upon receiving McMahon's call, General Campbell ordered Harris to send one of his men into the shaft to find out what was going on. Not long after that, the two SEALs were pulled out of the shaft by an electric winch. Nick Shultz had fulfilled the SEAL code of honor of never leaving a man behind in battle, dead or alive.

When the shooting started, Shultz was trailing just far enough behind to be safe from the shots, but within reach of the gear that Craft was pulling behind him by rope. Struggling, he pulled his swim buddy back through the narrow confines of the duct, inch by inch, praying his friend would be alive when they reached the other end. It was all for naught. Craft was dead.

Now, standing at the window of her seventh-floor office at Langley and watching the sun climb into the morning sky, Kennedy wished she could turn back the clock and do it all over again. Do it right, do it the way she had wanted to from the start. Kennedy had promised herself when she got into this business of ordering men into harm's way that she would do everything possible not to become a detached bureaucrat. Seventeen men had died under her watch at Langley, the majority of them in one seriously botched operation. Craft would bring the total up to eighteen, and as with those before him, Kennedy would visit his grave.

A knock on the door pulled Kennedy from her trance, and without turning, she said, "Come in."

The door opened and closed, but whoever had just entered had chosen to stay silent until recognized. Kennedy finally turned and saw a far from jovial Skip McMahon standing across from her.

"Skip, I couldn't say anything to you last night. There were far too many people around."

McMahon, dressed in a suit and tie, stared her down—his hands on his hips and deep dark circles under his eyes. "I can't believe you didn't tell me."

"I'm sorry."

McMahon shook his head slowly from side to side. "You and I have never played these games. We've always been straight up with each other."

"I know; I apologize. It's just that things happened too fast last night. I wanted to tell you . . . I asked if I could bring you in on it, and I was told to wait."

"By who, Thomas?"

"It goes higher than that."

McMahon frowned skeptically. "How much higher?"

Kennedy turned away, not entirely comfortable with telling McMahon.

McMahon reached out and grabbed Kennedy's chin, forcing her to look him in the eye. "No more games. I want the truth."

Kennedy reached up and pulled his hand down. "You have to keep it to yourself."

"The hell I do," snapped McMahon.

"Don't talk to me like that," chided Kennedy while taking a step back. "We're friends."

"Well, friends don't let friends get ambushed by hanging them out to dry."

"Skip, this came down from above. I wanted to tell you, but I couldn't . . . and I didn't have enough time to convince them otherwise."

"Who authorized those men to go in, and who decided to shut the FBI out of it?"

Kennedy sighed and said, "Vice President Baxter."

"That motherfucker!" McMahon wheeled away from Kennedy, his fists balled up in anger. "That arrogant motherfucker. Where in the hell does he get off . . ." McMahon stopped short of finishing the sentence and strained to regain some composure. Through clenched teeth, he said, "This is an FBI operation. Not the CIA and not the Pentagon. If I am not briefed fully and truthfully by you people, I will march right over to the . . ."

McMahon was cut off by the intercom on Kennedy's desk. "Dr. Kennedy?"

Kennedy walked over to her desk and pressed the button. "Yes."

"They are waiting for you in the director's conference room."

Kennedy looked at her watch. It was several minutes past seven. "We'll be right there." She looked up at McMahon and said, "We have to get going, but I want you to promise me you'll keep this to yourself until I have a chance to explain further."

Shaking his head, McMahon frowned and said, "Nope . . . I'm gonna go in there and chew some ass."

Kennedy reached out and grabbed his wrist firmly. "No you are not. There is a lot more, Skip. And if you want to know what is really going on, you keep quiet until the meeting is over."

THEY WERE THE last two to enter Director Stansfield's private conference room. As Kennedy and McMahon took their seats, an agitated Director Roach was already letting the others know how the FBI felt about the current situation. "Horseshit" was the phrase he used to describe the mess the others had created and the lack of professional courtesy they had displayed.

Seated at the head of the table was Director Stansfield. To his left were Vice President Baxter and Dallas King. To the director's right sat General Flood and Director Roach. McMahon and Kennedy took seats next to each other on Director Roach's side of the table. It was a small meeting and intended to be so.

FBI Director Roach had paused for a brief moment when Kennedy and McMahon entered and then continued, saying, "I can see no valid reason for not informing us that you were sending those men into the building. It absolutely mystifies me." Roach shook his head. "Skip and I have already talked about it . . . we would have agreed with sending them in. I just don't get it."

Vice President Baxter leaned forward and stabbed his index finger into the tabletop. Staring at General Flood, he started angrily, "I did not authorize sending any SEALs through that air duct."

Flood looked back at Baxter with barely masked contempt and then turned to Roach. "It's my fault. I was given the authority to conduct surveillance, and we were presented with a unique opportunity."

"I still don't see why you couldn't pick up the phone and call us," said Roach.

Flood sat up a little straighter. He wanted to tell the director of the FBI that he was left out of the loop because the vice president had suggested it, but that was not the way things were done in Washington.

"In the flurry of events that took place early this morning, I made a critical mistake of not informing both of you." General Flood looked to Baxter and then Roach. "I will make sure that it does not happen again."

Both Roach and Baxter grudgingly accepted the general's apology with a nod, but Skip McMahon was less cordial. With his gruff demeanor, which was in many ways similar to the general's, McMahon placed a big fist on the table and asked bluntly, "What else haven't you told us?"

Flood and Stansfield kept their poker faces fixed, while Baxter and King shared a look that caused McMahon to ask the question again. "What else? You can't send me out there to get blindsided again. I need every advantage I can get over Aziz."

Director Stansfield liked Skip McMahon. In many ways he admired him. This was an unusual situation, however. McMahon was under an immense amount of pressure, and he was the person dealing with Aziz—the only person. Aziz had been adamant about that. Stansfield, always thinking a dozen moves ahead, did not like the idea of telling McMahon everything. The older spymaster saw a potential problem. He envisioned Aziz with a gun to a hostage's head making a demand that McMahon could not meet. He saw the dangers of telling McMahon too much, of putting

McMahon in a position where he might be tempted to give Aziz some of that information in exchange for the life of a hostage. Stansfield couldn't do that. Rapp was far too valuable a card in this game to start waving around for the other players to see.

Stansfield observed McMahon as he stared down Baxter and King, sensing that they knew something. Knowing he had to act fast, before one of them opened his mouth, Stansfield decided to kill two birds with one stone.

"There is something I should tell you." Stansfield reached down next to his chair and grabbed the morning's copy of *The Washington Post*. Standing, to further draw McMahon's attention away from King and Baxter, Stansfield walked around the table and set the paper in front of McMahon. Stansfield pointed to a front-page headline that read *"CIA Saves Day by Warning Secret Service."*

"How this story ever got to the *Post* is something that I will deal with later." Stansfield looked across the table and gave Dallas King a knowing look. "But, in the meantime, I will bring you up to speed on a highly classified subject. We have in our possession certain intelligence that we deem to be highly accurate. That source did in fact provide us with the information that enabled us to alert the Secret Service to a potential attack just minutes before the actual attack took place. That source has also provided us with information pertaining to the demands Mr. Aziz will put forth and the men and equipment he brought with him."

McMahon looked up at Stansfield, who had worked his way back to his seat. "That's how you knew about all of the plastique explosives?"

"Yes."

"What about the demands?"

"That I am willing to share with you, but"—Stansfield again glanced over at Dallas King—"it is extremely confidential information that is not to be passed on to anyone." Looking back to McMahon and Roach, he added, "I trust both of you, so I assume you will keep this confidential."

Both of the FBI men nodded, and Stansfield said, "Aziz's next demand will be to ask that the UN vote to lift all economic sanctions against Iraq. He is going to make a slight concession, in an effort to sound reasonable, and state that all sanctions regarding weapons of mass destruction may remain in place."

"The UN," started McMahon, "can they move that fast?"

"If we want them to, they will," answered General Flood.

"There is one last demand." Stansfield stopped and looked around the room, wanting to hedge his bet just a touch. "But unfortunately we are still trying to find out what it is."

McMahon looked at Stansfield. In all the years that he had been working for the FBI, he had never come across an individual as cool and analytical as Thomas Stansfield—on either his side of the law or the other. The man was impossible to read. McMahon turned away from Stansfield and looked immediately to his right to see if he could get anything from Kennedy. He studied her face for even the slightest clue to whether Stansfield was being forthright about the family jewels or if he was still holding out. She stared back at him blankly, just like her boss, giving nothing away.

After several seconds of silence, McMahon looked across the table at Vice President Baxter and Dallas King. Before entering this meeting, Kennedy had told him that Baxter had authorized the insertion of the SEALs, but just minutes ago, General Flood had taken the blame for the whole mess. Either Kennedy was lying or General Flood was covering for the vice president. McMahon decided to play along until he could get Kennedy alone, and then, he would get to the bottom of the whole thing.

Dallas King took his forefinger and as nonchalantly as possible wiped the bead of sweat that had formed on his upper lip. He felt as if he were standing in downtown Phoenix at high noon in the middle of July. Every time someone looked at him, he wondered if they knew. Since seeing the photo of his beer-drinking buddy on CNN this morning, King had been an absolute basket case. At first he tried to convince himself that it wasn't the same man. The guy that he drank beers with was named Mike, and he was a student. Mike didn't wear his hair slicked back like the man on the news. King tried to convince himself that it wasn't the same person, but it was futile. As he recollected his relationship with the mysterious Mike, there were too many strange coincidences. For several weeks straight he had run into Mike everywhere he went. Mike had conveniently known all about the Stanford basketball team, King's alma mater.

King closed his eyes and pinched the bridge of his nose as he remembered the evening they took the late-night tour of the White House. King remembered how Mike had claimed he had an uncle who used to work for the Secret Service under Kennedy. He convinced King to show him the Treasury tunnel, saying that it was originally designed as a bunker during World War II. Mike told King that during the Kennedy administration, the staffers used to sneak women down into bunk rooms off the tunnel and have sex.

And that's exactly what they had done that night. President Hayes was out of town, and King had no problem gaining access for his newfound friend and a couple of hot young ladies. King couldn't believe how unlucky he was. Of the hundreds of people who worked at the White House, this crazy terrorist had to pick him. Squeezing his nose even tighter, he said to himself, *How could you have fucked up so bad?* The pressure was unbelievable. He needed time to think, time to maneuver.

MITCH RAPP WOKE up to the sound of Milt Adams snoring and a brown ponytail in his face. His left arm was pinned under Rielly's neck, and his right arm was draped across her chest. Rapp lifted his head up and tried to retrieve his right arm. This only spurred Rielly to clutch his arm tighter.

How they had ended up sleeping in this embrace might have seemed a little strange, but the stash room was not particularly spacious. After the debacle earlier in the evening, Rapp had stayed on the radio with Langley until almost four A.M. At that time the FBI was screaming to find out what was going on, and the entire operation was put in a holding pattern. Kennedy had ordered Rapp to get some sleep, and they would call him with orders in the morning.

Rapp, in turn, had let Langley know how he felt, telling them that if they had allowed him to act when he wanted to, Aziz and the other two terrorists would be dead and one Navy SEAL would still be alive. It was no surprise to Rapp that Langley signed off without responding to his statement. Rapp then forced himself to bring it back down. He had done enough clandestine insertions to know that when you are given the opportunity to grab a couple of hours of sleep, you should take it. Rapp found comfort knowing that the next time he came across Aziz, he would shoot first and ask questions later. There would be no more checking in with Langley for the green light.

Rielly had surprised Rapp by taking his arms and wrapping them around her as they lay down to go to sleep. As he drifted off, Rielly had kissed Rapp's hand and whispered something he didn't quite catch. He was more than a little surprised by the warm feeling the little kiss had given him.

Now, craning his neck away from Rielly, Rapp looked at the secure field radio that was sitting between him and Adams. The overhead light was still on, and he could see just enough of the control panel to know that the radio was still on. Rapp had absolutely no idea how long he had been sleeping. He didn't want to wake Rielly but saw no other choice. Taking his left hand he reached up from under Rielly's neck and pried her hands loose. His digital watch told him it was 7:41 A.M. He'd had at least two hours, maybe two and a half. Rapp figured that was more than enough for now. This was hardly the time or the place to be sleeping in. If Langley wasn't going to call him, he would have to call them and get things moving.

29

RAFIQUE AZIZ WAS showered, shaved, and back in the expensive suit he had worn for his historic visit to the White House. All of his men were still at their posts except one. That man was standing behind a television camera in the White House pressroom. The morning sun spilled in from the windows running along the side of the narrow room. Aziz stood behind the familiar podium at the front of the room and checked his watch. It was nearing eight. Behind him, mounted on a blue curtain, was the White House logo.

Aziz watched his man move from the camera to a control panel at the rear of the room. The man looked up from his position and yelled, "I started the two-minute countdown. All of the networks should be receiving the feed."

Aziz grinned, taking satisfaction that he was about to put into play another part of his ingenious plan. He was going to go over the heads of the military and the FBI once again. Like everything else, this had been planned. He was about to appeal to the American people and thus the politicians. The only new touch was that he would be able to incorporate the repelling of the early morning raid into his speech. That had got him excited. It had been very close. The hostages and the building were wired to blow, and Aziz had no doubt that any attempt by the Americans to free the hostages would result in a bloodbath. That was a price he was willing to pay. He did not want it to come to that, in the interest of self-preservation, but if it did, he wouldn't hesitate for a second to annihilate everybody, including himself.

The speech that he was about to give would serve to make sure that a raid by the FBI would never happen. Aziz had followed American politics closely and watched how the leaders handled conflicts, especially those with his new benefactor. Aziz had admiringly watched Saddam Hussein mimic the actions and rhetoric of Adolf Hitler. Just like Hitler in the days prior to World War II, Saddam knew how to push, pound, cajole, lie, cheat, and basically do whatever he wanted, right up to the point where his adversaries were prepared to put their foot down. Saddam had turned it into an art form, playing the weak United Nations and the political left in America and Europe for everything they were worth. Continually ignoring everything he had already agreed to, Saddam would flaunt his insolence in the face of the Western powers, and then, just as they were preparing to engage in military action, he would send his envoys to the UN. As the might of American warships and allied air power massed at his borders, he would act defiant until the very end, and then, and only when real action was imminent, he would back down.

Six months later the whole process would start over again, and each time the resolve of the arrogant Western powers would be weakened. Saddam had proven that the American politicians had no stomach for war. They loved their surgical strikes and cruise missiles, but were they really that effective? In Aziz's opinion the answer was no. If one bothered to look beyond the TV clips and sound bites, the damage the surgical strikes caused was minimal.

Aziz was prepared to take a cue from Saddam. In less than a minute he would offer the American people that olive branch, and in turn the stage would be set for his last demand, and his triumphant return to his country.

Aziz looked toward the camera and straightened his tie. He had originally considered giving this speech from the Oval Office, but had decided it would only serve to undermine the entire intent of his plan. The American people would be livid over him sitting in the president's chair. It had been hard for him to resist the temptation to give the speech from the same place that so many other presidents had addressed the nation, especially since he would have loved nothing more than to rub the faces of the arrogant American public in the fact that he was in control of the White House. But now was not the time to prod and poke. Now was the time to pull back from the brink and get the politicians working for him.

Aziz's man at the back of the room held up his hands and started the countdown. Aziz placed both hands on the podium, and when the signal was given, he cleared his throat and began to recite his speech from memory.

"It is with a heavy heart that I come to you this morning." Looking somber and passive, Aziz stared into the camera with his dark eyes and said in perfect English, "I wish the American people no harm and wish for this conflict to come to a speedy conclusion. I apologize to the families of the men and women who have died in this conflict. I know that this will seem empty and hollow to many of you, but you must please understand that this is a war . . . a war that your military and political leaders have started. I beg you, as a nation, to ask yourselves in front of your God, who has harmed whom in this conflict?" Aziz stopped and looked into the camera, his face utterly devoid of aggression.

"Since the end of World War Two, the West . . . mostly you . . . the Americans and your Israeli allies, has killed over a half million of my Arab brothers. Over five hundred thousand human beings." Aziz again stopped and stared into the camera, wanting to stress this number. "You sit here in this great nation, with all of your wealth and comfort and technology, and you are numb to the pain and suffering that my people have gone through and continue to go through. I ask you for a moment to put yourself in my shoes, in the shoes of the Arab people. Who is the bigger barbarian, the terrorist who kills thirty people with a car bomb, or the president who gives the order to kill thousands by sending his air force to do his dirty work?

"This is a question that we will probably never come to agreement on, but it is one that, at the very least, we should understand is a universal tragedy. I have not come to you today to try and place blame, but rather to make the first step in putting all of this behind us. I have come to you seeking peace.

"When this conflict started, I warned your FBI that any attempt to re-take this building would be futile. I further warned them that such an at-tempt would result in the execution of hostages. Despite these warnings, your arrogant FBI tried to sneak a group of their commandos into the building last night. Their attack was repelled, just as I told them it would be, and resulted in the death of an unknown number of their people. I had intended to kill one of your fellow countrymen this morning to punish the FBI and your leaders for their reckless actions . . . but I have decided to spare that person's life as an example of my good faith. I do not think it is right for an innocent person to pay with his life for the stupidity and ar-rogance of the small group of warmongers that runs your country.

"It is my sincere hope that we can resolve this conflict peacefully, and it is you, the peace-loving American people, that I am appealing to. Enough blood has been shed. It is time for us to stop living as enemies." Pausing for a second, Aziz looked down and then back up. "But before we can do that, America must come to the Middle East peace table as a truly independent advocate, not the big brother of Israel. I have two demands left, and if those demands are met, I will give you back this great house, and the people in it, without further harm. The first of my demands is simple. By six o'clock today, the U.S. must convince the United Nations to lift all economic sanctions against Iraq. I fully understand the need to keep the blockade in place against materials that would enable Iraq to develop weapons of mass destruction, and I think those provisions should stay in place. My concern is that my Arab brothers and sisters are starving and dying because of a feud between the leaders of the West and the leaders of Iraq. This is wrong, and it should be ended.

"If this demand is not met by this evening"—Aziz's expression turned more stern—"I will be forced to kill one hostage every hour until it is met. Let me state again that any further attempt to free the hostages by force will be met with harsh punishment. With the push of one button, this whole building will crumble to the ground, killing everyone in it." Aziz continued his glare. "If my demand is met by this evening, I will release half of the remaining hostages, and then I will give you my last demand. If that demand is met"—Aziz shook his finger—"we can spare the innocent people that have been caught in the middle of this conflict, and we can begin mending fences among our two peoples."

Aziz glanced down for a second as if searching for something special. When he looked back up, he said, "I ask you, as citizens of this great nation, the greatest nation the earth has ever known, to help me make these first steps toward a lasting peace. I wish you all the best and will pray for you. Thank you, and may your God bless you."

Aziz nodded his head once, and his man at the back of the room cut the live feed. Walking quickly to his right Aziz grabbed his MP-5 and yanked at his tie. He started for the Situation Room, where he could gloat over his performance and watch the pundits dissect his every word.

VICE PRESIDENT BAXTER sat with his mouth agape, watching for the second time Aziz's nationally televised address. The heavy armor-plated presidential limousine rocked ever so slightly as it raced across the Chain Bridge on its way from Langley back to the Naval Observatory. A stream of motorcycles, police cruisers, sedans, vans, Suburbans, and two other limousines both preceded and followed the black Cadillac. Dallas King sat next to Baxter on the spacious backseat, his digital phone held firmly to the left side of his face. King was already on his second call in as many minutes. He was in classic political-crisis mode and happy to be doing something other than obsessing over the imminent demise of his short-lived career. Before Aziz's original address had concluded, King had been punching numbers into his tiny phone and barking out orders.

With one eye on the small color TV in the back of the limo, he nodded his head and then said, "No. Don't waste your time asking any of the regular questions. I couldn't care less who they voted for last time or if they plan on voting this time. I don't want to have to say it again. This is an issue that transcends party lines. I want the nuts and bolts, and I want them within the hour. We can go back and get specifics later." King stopped talking for a second and listened to the Democratic pollster on the other end. He started shaking his head in frustration.

"You're not listening to me. I don't want you to skew the results . . . at least not yet. I want to get an honest feel." King listened and nodded. "That's right. After we take a stance, we can go back and push for the numbers that will back us up, but for now I want to know what they think of this guy." King paused again and looked at the small TV. It had not been lost on King that Aziz came off very well on TV, a hell of a lot better than most of the politicians in this town. He was very well spoken, looked sincere, and was movie star handsome to boot.

"Don't forget to get me the splits on the women versus the men. The soccer moms are going to eat this guy up." King paused once again and then said, "Yep, put together a dozen questions and call me back in five minutes."

Pulling the phone away from his face, King pushed the end button and looked to see his boss's reaction to the speech. Baxter's expression had turned from one of surprise to a mysterious frown. King asked, "What do you think?"

"We're fucked," mumbled Baxter without taking his eyes off the TV. "The press is going to go berserk over this failed raid."

Looking at his boss, King thought, *You think they're mad about this? Just wait until they find out I gave one of them a tour of the building last month.* King gathered himself. "The press will be fine. This story is so big and it's moving so fast this little speech will be old news by tomorrow morning."

"I don't think so," said Baxter, not yet prepared to look at any upside. "This little incident has 'congressional investigation' written all over it."

King looked at his boss, who was still staring at the TV with a look of defeat on his face. "This whole thing, from start to finish, has 'congressional investigation' written all over it, and this one incident will be a footnote. . . . Besides, we insulated ourselves from it. General Flood has already taken the blame, and he did it right in front of Director Roach . . . the man who will eventually investigate the whole thing."

"I don't know . . . It still stinks."

"The whole thing stinks. You just have to remember, when this is all over, it's gonna be the guy who stinks the least who comes out smelling like a rose." King pointed at his boss. "And I'm going to make sure that guy is you."

"Dallas"—Baxter grimaced—"I don't think you're being realistic about this. All of this stuff is not just going to be swept under the rug. The press is going to want answers, and they are going to want to know if I authorized sending those men in last night."

King shifted sideways in his seat. He wanted to choke his boss and scream, "If only you had my problems!" Instead in a calming voice, he said, "For the last time, don't worry about the press. I can handle them. You need to get your spirits back up and start acting like the president. We're going to have to react to this new development, and if the polls come back the way I think they will, we really might have a chance to squeeze our way out of this mess."

Baxter turned his head toward his aide and asked, "How?"

"I haven't figured it out yet, but I will."

Baxter looked away from King and checked his watch. Then with a sigh, he said, "I suppose I'd better call a meeting with the National Security Council."

King nodded. "That would seem to be the next logical step."

Baxter waved his right hand as if shooing away a fly. "Take care of it."

"When and where?"

Twisting his lips, Baxter gazed out the window and said, "Ten o'clock at the Pentagon."

30

"YOU KNOW WHAT he's doing, don't you?" Rapp sat with the handset of the secure field radio gripped tightly in his left hand. He stared blankly at the wall in front of him while he listened to General Campbell give his take on Aziz's national address. They had played the speech for Rapp over the radio and had asked if he would like to hear it again. Rapp had declined. He knew exactly what Aziz was up to and didn't need to waste a second more analyzing it.

Rapp nodded in response to what General Campbell was saying and said, "That's right. He's trying to play you guys for patsies."

"Excuse me," replied the stern ranger on the other end.

"Patsies," repeated Rapp, never one to choose his words too carefully. "He wants Vice President Baxter and all of the other politicians up on the Hill to roll over and meet him at the bargaining table. Then, once he gets what he wants, he'll go back to the Middle East, disappear, and a year from now he'll be building more bombs and killing more people."

"What if he seriously wants to make peace?" chimed in Irene Kennedy.

"It's out of the question," Rapp replied emphatically.

"How can you be so sure?"

"Irene, don't play this game with me. I don't have the time or the patience to sit here and listen to you play devil's advocate. You know as well as I do that Rafique Aziz could give a rat's ass about the American people, or his Arab brothers and sisters, for that matter. Hell . . . the only Arabs he cares about are the ones that want to wipe Israel off the map. As far as the rest of us are concerned, he'd slit our throats in a second if we got in his way."

"Then what's he up to?" asked Kennedy.

Rapp sat back, swinging one of his legs out from underneath him as he thought about it. He looked over at Rielly, propped up in the corner with the blanket wrapped around her. She was watching him intently.

Looking away from her, Rapp said, "He's trying to find a way out of this without getting his head blown off. We know he's a meticulous planner. He thinks everything through from start to finish and prepares multiple contingencies in case things go wrong. As I look at his plan, the one big problem I see is how he gets out of there . . . how he gets home. We can bank on the fact that he's thought it through every step of the way in terms of how we'd react. And from that, we can assume he knows there would be a strong contingency in the government that would push hard for an all-out raid. Now, if he had gotten his hands on the president, everything would be a little different. My guess is that he was planning to use Hayes as his bargaining chip to get home, but he blew it, and now he's been forced to fall back and use a different plan."

"And what would that be?" asked General Campbell.

Rapp looked up at Rielly while he thought about it. She was still staring at him with those emerald green eyes. He knew she was listening to everything he said, but there wasn't much he could do about it.

Rapp looked away and said, "He's trying to manipulate the media and sway public opinion. He knows without the president he's not getting home. Let's face it—" Rapp paused, feeling somewhat awkward about saying the next part in front of Rielly, but there was really no other way. After clearing his throat, he said, "If you look at the big picture, we all know every one of those hostages is expendable, and if we know it, so does Aziz. If he was to continue an aggressive, hostile position, he would eventually force us to storm the place. There is no way we could just sit by while he killed hostages on national TV. So by going in front of the public this morning and putting on this bullshit peace-loving attitude, he's taken the wind out of our sails. Baxter won't let us take action until an effort is made at peace."

"I agree," said Kennedy. "In the end, he knows every single one of those hostages is expendable. The president was his trump card, and he didn't get it."

General Campbell added, "He's trying to give the politicians a way out of this mess without firing a shot."

"Well, that's not gonna happen as long as I have a say in the matter."

"Iron Man," stated Campbell in a firm voice. "I don't want you doing anything unless you are authorized. The last thing we need right now is you running around half-cocked. Now, Irene and I have to get over to the Pentagon for a meeting, and in the meantime, we want you to stay put. When we get back, we'll have a better idea of how we shall proceed. Am I understood?"

Rapp looked down at the floor and held his temper in check. He'd already learned his lesson. Don't ask a question if you're not going to like the answer.

"Yes, sir," was Rapp's simple two-word reply as he placed the handset back in its cradle. Pausing for a second, he looked at the power switch and debated his next move. After about fifteen seconds of indecision he turned off the radio and looked up at Rielly.

Anna Rielly sat passively in the corner with the blanket wrapped tightly around her body. Milt Adams sat in the opposite corner, behind Rapp, and chewed on a granola bar. Rielly continued to stare at Rapp and finally asked, "What was that all about?"

Rapp glanced sideways at her as he began rifling through one of his packs. "Nothing."

"It sure sounded like something to me," Rielly said.

"Listen, Anna, you're a reporter. I can't exactly let you in on what's going on."

Rielly smiled. "Who am I going to tell? What do you think, I'm going to call the station with your radio and give them a live update?"

Rapp grabbed several more granola bars from his pack and held one up for Rielly. "Here, chew on this." And with a grin, he added, "And stop asking questions."

Rielly took the bar and while she tore the wrapper off asked, "Who do you work for, Mitch Kruse, the FBI?"

"Ah . . . no. Not exactly."

"What are you, then—military?"

Rapp ignored the question and continued looking for something in his pack.

Rielly smiled and said, "Hey, listen, you saved my life. I don't care who you work for." Rielly continued to watch him.

Rapp stared back for a long moment thinking about what he should say. Finally, he replied, "Anna, if I tell you something off the record, will you promise that you'll never report it? That is, since I saved your life and all." Rapp said the last part with a smile.

Rielly took the question seriously. "I'm a reporter. Whatever you tell me in confidence will be kept a secret."

Chuckling, he said, "My dad always said, 'Don't bullshit a bullshitter.'" Rapp studied an abrasion on Rielly's cheek and a spot of dried blood on her lip.

Changing the subject once again, Rapp pulled a penlight from his assault vest and said, "Now, let's see how you're doing this morning." Holding the light up in front of her face, he said, "I want to check your eyes and see how your pupils dilate." Rapp held Rielly by her chin and checked the left eye first and then the right. Both dilated properly, and then he asked her to follow the light as he moved it from one side of her face to the other. Again she checked out fine.

Turning the light off, Rapp gently touched the abrasion on her cheek and asked, "How does this feel?"

Rielly frowned and said, "I don't know. How does it look?"

After studying her face for a second, Rapp nodded. "I'd say considering what you've been through, you look pretty good. Darn good actually." He meant it.

Rielly smiled slightly. "Well, in that case I feel fine."

Looking back toward Adams, who was on his second breakfast bar, Rapp asked, "I'd say we have a regular tough girl on our hands."

"I'd say so," replied Adams with a nod for emphasis.

Rapp turned his attention back to Rielly's cheek, and when he got closer to inspect the mark, she said to him, "You know women have a higher tolerance for pain than men."

"So I've been told." Rapp fished a sterile alcohol pad from his first aid kit and tore the small package open. Gently, he started to wipe the dried blood from the corner of Rielly's mouth, and then the light scrape on her cheek.

When Rapp was done, he turned her head from side to side to check for any other cuts. He had not missed the obvious beauty of the reporter. He felt slightly guilty, under the current circumstances, for letting his mind wander, but it couldn't be helped. Her skin was soft and smooth with just the right touch of color. Rapp nudged her chin to the side and noticed a trail of dried blood that ran down the back of her neck. He wiped away the blood and then placed both hands on her scalp. Rielly flinched slightly and pulled away.

"Does that hurt?" asked Rapp.

Rielly nodded, and Rapp said with a smile, "What happened to that high tolerance for pain you were bragging about a moment ago?"

"I don't know, but whatever you just touched hurt like hell."

"Try to hold still for a second. I want to find out how bad the cut is." Rapp lifted and separated her thick brown hair. The cut ran only about an inch but looked to have broken the first several layers of skin. Holding one hand on her scalp, he reached behind him and grabbed another sterile alcohol pad. Without looking, he said, "Milt, would you do me a favor? Take those blueprints that you brought, and spread them out on the floor."

Rapp wiped the cut several times and then waved his hand over the area to dry the alcohol. Rielly's face twisted in pain. After a moment, Rapp let her hair fall back down onto her shoulders and sat back on one heel. "How's that?"

Rielly brought her hand up and gently touched her head. "I'm fine if

I don't move too much." But Rapp noticed the flicker of pain moving across her face when she raised her arm.

"What was that?" asked Rapp.

Gently, Rielly touched her side. "Something hurts in my side."

"Can you stand up for me?"

"I think so."

Rapp helped her up. "Does it hurt on the back, the front, or the side?"

She gestured with her hand. "The back and the side."

"I need to take a look at it. Are you all right with that?"

Rielly looked at Rapp's concerned face, and the corners of her mouth turned up ever so slightly. Reaching out, she placed her hand on his cheek and said, "If I can't trust you, I don't know who I could."

Rapp blushed slightly and said, "Good, then turn around so I can take a look." Rielly did as she was asked, and Rapp lifted up her sweatshirt.

Her skin was a golden olive from her narrow waist up and then the discoloration began to appear. Halfway up her back, on her left side, a red mark about four inches long and three inches wide had started to form. He checked for bright red streaks and found none. Rapp touched the area softly at first, and Rielly showed no sign of pain. Then he pressed a little harder, and she winced sharply.

"Can you take several deep breaths for me?" Rielly did so without pain, and Rapp let her shirt fall. "It's probably just a bruise, which can still hurt like a bitch, but it's ten times better than having a broken or cracked rib." With a smile, he added, "You must be one tough chick."

Rielly smiled slightly. "I have a lot of brothers."

Rapp nodded. "I think you're going to be all right, but then again, I'm no doctor."

"What are you, Mr. Kruse?" asked the persistent Rielly.

Squeezing her shoulder, Rapp said, "I've got some work to do." Turning toward the seated Adams, Rapp said, "Milt, I need you to show me every stairwell and elevator that leads from this floor to the third, and from this floor to the first."

DALLAS KING WAS already on his second battery. His digital phone had left his ear only momentarily over the last hour and a half. He walked at a hurried pace next to Vice President Baxter as their entourage moved down the wide hallway of the E Ring at the Pentagon. A slew of serious-looking Secret Service agents surrounded them. King thought the large contingent a bit much; they were, after all, in the Pentagon; but he had other things to worry about. As the group continued forward, the sea of people before them parted as Pentagon employees moved out of the way and clung to the walls while the current commander in chief passed by.

The buzz level was high. Everyone had either seen Aziz's national address or heard about it. Now the natural question was, what would the U.S. government do in response? The answer was actually tied to a lone individual in Omaha, Nebraska. Reginald Boulay was his name, and at this exact moment he was giving Dallas King the results of his Husker Poll. Boulay had built up his poll over the years and made it into one of the most accurate in the political-consulting business. And he only supplied it to a few well-paying clients. The numbers from the Husker Poll were never found in the newspapers or on TV. Boulay wasn't in the business to skew results by push polling and a variety of other techniques; he was in it to get the most accurate results possible. And he did it by asking brutally honest questions in plain English. King had decided after talking to two of his regular pollsters, and being irritated at their inability to understand what he wanted, that if there was ever a time to spend money on Boulay and his Husker Poll, now was it.

King nodded as he listened to Boulay relay the results. Although King had honestly expected them, he was, nonetheless, surprised. They reflected the new trend in America, almost a refusal to judge and condemn. King had sensed it while listening to Aziz's speech and wondered if he was smart enough to know what he was tapping into, or if he was just one lucky bastard.

The handsome King liked what he was hearing from Boulay. According to the Husker Poll, a little over sixty percent of those surveyed felt that Vice President Baxter should exhaust almost all options in an effort to resolve the crisis in a peaceful way. When it came to lifting economic sanctions against Iraq except those involving weapons of mass destruction, the numbers jumped to almost eighty percent. As Boulay had explained it to King, "There's about twenty percent of the population that would just as soon level the White House before giving these terrorists a thing, and nothing you do or say will change that."

King had also expected that. The zealots at either end of the spectrum would always be around. They were not the people you had to worry about. The rest of the populace was whom he had to keep his eye on— the sixty to eighty percent of the people who were not too far from the middle on any given issue. As a political adviser, King saw it as his job to try and get those people leaning in his direction or, more precisely, to position his boss in the middle of them. That would be his next course of action. After asking Boulay to fax him the results, King ended the call and brought the vice presidential armada to a screeching halt. Grabbing his boss by the arm, King stopped at the next door on the right and pulled Vice President Baxter over with him. The Secret Service agents were used to this type of semiprivate consultation between their charges and their aides, and without having to say a word, they turned their backs to the vice president and deployed in a protective shell.

King placed a hand on Baxter's shoulder and said in a whisper, "It's just like I thought. Over sixty percent of the people want to see a peaceful resolution to this mess, and almost eighty percent think we should lift the economic embargo against Iraq, just so long as the military embargo is kept in place."

Baxter nodded and said, "So we're safe if we push for the UN to raise the sanctions?"

"I think so," said King with confidence. "Besides, if we can get him to release another third of the hostages, we'll be in a really good position to get some mileage out of this."

Baxter pointed down the hall toward the direction of the room they'd be meeting in. "They aren't going to like this."

King shrugged. "They're not going to like anything short of storming the place with a battalion of commandos. You have to prevent that from happening. You have to take the higher moral ground. You have to protect the lives of those innocent hostages."

"What about policy? What about precedence?" Baxter shook his head. "We think the American people are behind it, but what about the Hill? There're going to be some hard-liners up there who are going to scream bloody murder over this. Hell, some of them are already pissed that we gave them the Iranian money."

"Fuck 'em," snarled King. "They're gonna hate you no matter what you do, and if you do what they want and send in the troops, you're gonna have a group of hard-liners from the left trying to crucify you." King shook his head. "You can't please both groups. You have to stay with the majority of public opinion and stick with your base. That's where your protection is."

It was Baxter's turn to shake his head. "That's comforting. Public opinion, which you are so infatuated with, is about as predictable as the weather." Baxter continued shaking his head. "Public opinion is like a mob. It's fine just so long as you can predict where it's going, but the second you screw up and they turn on you . . . you're screwed."

King looked at his boss, his eyes sagging. He had been working non-stop for the last three days, he was tired, he was sick of hearing his boss whine, and he had bigger problems of his own. "Sherman"—King's face twisted into an expression of contempt—"maybe you should just quit. If you can't see that we have a golden opportunity here to build you up as a great statesman, as the man who saved the day, as the politician who stepped in and brokered the peace during the biggest crisis this nation has faced in possibly"—King paused while shaking his head—"its entire history? Then maybe you really should just let General Flood and Director Stansfield and the rest of the warmongers storm the place, destroy that great building, and kill all of the people in it, and then you can go down in the history books as the butcher who sent fifty Americans to their death because he was afraid to step up to the plate."

Baxter stood silently and looked at his chief of staff. He was not used to being spoken to in such a manner by anyone, not even a peer. This was probably the principal reason why King's words sank in. It was true, Baxter thought to himself. If he wanted to be president someday, which he did badly, more than anything in the world, he would have to stand up and be a leader. Slowly, he started to nod in an affirmation of King's words.

31

GENERAL FLOOD, GENERAL Campbell, Director Stansfield, and Irene Kennedy were all sitting next to each other at one end of the long table of the Joint Chiefs briefing room. Across from them sat the secretary of defense and the secretary of state, both with one aide. When Vice President Baxter entered, he and Dallas King sat at the head of the table with the other members to their immediate left and right, leaving over two-thirds of the massive table's seats unoccupied. The crisis was wearing on everyone. Eyes were bloodshot, and hands were a little shaky from either a lack of sleep or too much coffee or both.

Vice President Baxter folded his unsteady hands and placed them on the table. His kick in the pants from King had given him a newfound sense of focus and determination. Instead of asking for opinions, Baxter looked to the secretary of state and said, "Charles, I want you to light a fire under the UN's ass and get this vote taken care of before the end of the day."

Secretary of State Charles Midleton bowed his head and asked, "How much pressure may I use?"

"As much as you want. Threaten to veto every resolution midway into the next century, threaten to pull all funding—just do whatever it takes to get the vote passed by the end of the day. Once we get the hostages released, we can always go back later and pass a reversing resolution."

"It might not be that easy," warned Midleton as he adjusted his glasses.

"I don't care. Get it done, and we'll worry about the rest of it later."

Director Stansfield cleared his throat. "Excuse me. Aren't we getting a bit ahead of ourselves?"

Baxter's head snapped to his left. He wasn't in the mood to debate anything. He was only in the mood to give orders and have them followed. But now, as he looked across the table at the cool and grandfatherly Thomas Stansfield, his newfound confidence wavered just a touch. Stansfield was quite possibly the most harmless-looking individual that Baxter had ever met, but the rumors about the old spymaster caused one to think twice before locking horns with him.

Baxter eased back several inches and asked, "How do you mean, Thomas?"

"I think it would be prudent if we analyzed what was said and then decided on a course of action."

"I feel that I have all the information I need to make this decision. Aziz is willing to deal . . . deal for American lives, and in return we will have to give in and do something that, as humanitarians, we should probably do anyway."

"And what would that be?" asked General Flood in an uneasy tone.

"Stop starving the Iraqi people."

"We," started an irritated General Flood, "are not starving the Iraqi people. Saddam Hussein is starving his own people by refusing to comply with the terms of surrender for a war that, I'd like to remind everybody, he started." Flood stabbed his thick forefinger at the surface of the table. "We have confirmed intelligence reports that Saddam has funded Aziz with the express purpose of carrying out a terrorist attack on U.S. soil. With that information how can we even consider asking the UN to lift the sanctions?"

"We don't know for sure if those reports are accurate," retorted the vice president.

Thomas Stansfield looked the vice president squarely in the eye and said, "I would stake my entire career and reputation on the validity of that information."

Baxter felt himself losing ground. Leaning all the way back in his chair, he brought his hands up and said, "I'm not going to sit here and defend Saddam Hussein. I hate the man. I find him despicable, but what I want to do is free as many hostages as we can, and then we can go back later and fix things."

"'Fix things.'" Flood was getting angrier. "What if we can't go back nd 'fix things'?"

"I think almost everybody will recognize that we were forced to make some decisions under duress. Hell, basically with a gun to our head."

Flood moved his glare from the vice president to the secretary of state, who was sitting directly across the table. "Charlie, how badly do the French want to get back into Iraq?"

The secretary of state replied without enthusiasm but bluntly, "Badly."

"How about the South Africans?"

"Badly."

"How about Russia?"

"Badly."

"Do you have any reason to believe that after we've opened the gate, they would turn around a week or a month from now and pull back out?"

"I doubt it. They've been itching to get the embargo lifted for years, and they're already doing a fair amount of business with them on the sly."

Flood turned back to Baxter. "It won't be that easy to just reverse course when, and if, this whole mess is resolved."

"I know that there is nothing easy about this, General." Baxter knew he had to reassert his authority. "You don't need to explain the obvious to me. My number one concern is the lives of the American citizens that are being held hostage. If I have to change a foreign policy, that isn't even working, to gain their freedom, I will gladly do so." Baxter tilted his head back indignantly.

"You would jeopardize the entire foreign policy and national security of this country for the lives of forty to fifty-some people?"

"I think you're being a little melodramatic, General Flood."

"Melodramatic," Flood repeated the word while his face reddened. "This is a war, Vice President Baxter, and in war there are casualties. Saddam Hussein has attacked us. He has paid this terrorist, this mercenary"— Flood flipped his hand in disgust—"call him what you want, to come and attack us. Men like Saddam and this Aziz only understand one thing, and that is force. Overwhelming force!"

Baxter looked at the general with scorn for challenging him. Disagreement was one thing, but this was a show of disrespect. "General Flood, your opinion has been noted. Now, if we could move on to some other issues . . ."

"Sir," stated the general loudly. "If or, more accurately, when it becomes known that Saddam had a hand in this whole mess, the American people are going to want action, and there will be some uncomfortable questions asked of those who were making the decisions."

Baxter's temper began to unravel. "Are you threatening me, General Flood?"

"No." Flood stared him right in the eye. "I am merely, once again, stating the obvious. We are not the only country in possession of this information. Some of our most faithful allies know what is going on, and they will not sit idly by while we jeopardize their security."

"General Flood," bellowed Baxter, his temper finally getting the best of him. "Do I need to remind you how the chain of command works? I am in charge here." Baxter pointed to himself. "And I am going to put the interests of those hostages above everyone else's, especially those of another country. Whether they be an ally or not."

Flood did not flinch, he did not twitch, he did not move a muscle; he simply returned the vice president's stare and said, "First of all, I am very

aware of the chain of command, and secondly, I would be derelict in my
duty if I didn't inform you that you couldn't be more wrong in ignoring
the national security of our allies. Israel has been one of our staunchest. In
your effort to find a short-term solution, you are, in my opinion, moving
one of our closest allies and possibly this entire nation toward war."

Before Baxter had a chance to come completely unglued and Flood
had a chance to elaborate, the door opened and a female naval officer entered. She apologized to the group and approached Irene Kennedy. The
officer handed Kennedy a piece of paper and left.

Dr. Kennedy opened the paper and studied the note. It concerned a
little issue completely forgotten about. Desperately wanting to find out
what her counterpart had to say, she stood and said, "If you'll excuse me,
I need to check on this." Kennedy waved the note in the air and left the
room.

MITCH RAPP HAD everything ready to go. Bringing Adams along had
proven to be a big help. Not only because of his knowledge of the building, but also because it gave Rapp an extra set of very capable hands.
Adams had just finished showing Rapp the exact spots for a third time.
Rapp looked at the layout of the second floor one last time and double-
checked the number. When he was done, he had come up with five different locations.

Turning to Adams, he said, "Do you think you can handle the monitor and the devices at the same time?"

Adams nodded. "Yep."

"Good. That'll free me up to keep an eye out for any surprises." Rapp
then grabbed the small fanny pack and took out all of the micro surveillance units except five. Handing the pack to Adams, he pointed at the
blueprints and said, "We'll place them in the five locations you suggested.
After we put each one in place, we'll check it on the monitor and make
sure it's working." Rapp then grabbed the monitor and helped Adams get
strapped into it. When he was done helping Adams, he began checking
out the rest of his gear.

As Rapp slid the bolt on his submachine gun back, Rielly asked, "Is
that an MP-Five?"

Rapp looked up, frowning, more than a little surprised that she could
even make a guess let alone get the manufacturer correct. "Close. It's the
new MP-Ten. How do you know what an MP-Five looks like?"

"My dad's a police officer in Chicago."

"Oh, that's right."

"What are you going to do?"

"A little reconnaissance."

"Where?"

Rapp placed the submachine gun on the ground. "You sure do ask a lot of questions."

"I'm a reporter. It's my job."

Rapp frowned and nodded as if he had just been reminded of a particularly bad thing.

Rielly picked up on the expression and asked, "Is there something wrong with that?"

"Normally"—Rapp shrugged his shoulders—"probably not. But under the current circumstances, I can see where we might have a problem."

"And why would that be?"

"Why?" Rapp tilted his head. "Because when this whole thing is over, you will probably have one hell of a story to tell."

"I owe you a lot. I wouldn't report anything that you didn't agree to."

Rapp slid his pistol out of his thigh holster and pulled back on the slide. The cylindrical brass round was where it should have been, and Rapp let the slide go forward. "What if I don't want you to report a single word of this mess? What if I want you to act like we never met, and none of this ever happened?"

"That's not realistic."

"Well, then we have a problem."

Looking at him, she wondered why he would have to be so secretive. "Who do you work for?"

"I can't tell you that." Rapp shoved his pistol back in its holster.

"Seriously, I'd like know."

"And seriously"—Rapp shook his head and opened his eyes wide— "I can't tell you."

"It must be the CIA." Rielly kept her eyes on him, trying to get the slightest hint of a reaction. She got nothing. "It has to be the CIA, otherwise you could tell me."

"Wrong. Are you a woman of your word?"

"Yes."

"Good. Then someday, if we both make it out of here alive, I'll tell you my life story." Rapp smiled, showing a set of long dimples on both cheeks.

Rielly smiled back and nodded. "So you work for the CIA."

"I never said that," replied Rapp.

IRENE KENNEDY STOOD over the secure phone in General Flood's office and felt a sinking feeling in the pit of her stomach. On the other end

was Colonel Fine of the Israeli foreign intelligence service, Mossad. Fine
had just given Kennedy a brief overview on the three names she had given
him the night before. There was no surprising information on the first
two terrorists, but the third was an entirely different matter. Mustafa Yassin
was the man in question, and Kennedy was curious. The colonel had
come up with three matches on the name Mustafa Yassin. The first was a
fifty-seven-year-old officer in the Jordanian army, and the second was an
eighteen-year-old suspected Palestinian dissident.

When Colonel Fine finished giving the background on the individuals, Kennedy asked, "Could you repeat the info on the last Yassin, please?"

"Sure, but let me caution you, Yassin is a fairly common name over
here, so this might not be the same guy. The last Mustafa Yassin is an Iraqi.
We don't have a lot of information on him, but what we do have all re-
volves around the invasion of Kuwait. Since then there has only been one
update added to his file. According to our intelligence, his alias is the Thief
of Baghdad. When the Iraqis rolled into Kuwait and started looting, it was
this Yassin fellow who they put in charge of breaking into all of the bank
vaults."

"What else do you have on him?" asked Kennedy.

"Not a lot, but this isn't the guy I would worry about. My bet is Aziz
recruited this eighteen-year-old fellow from Gaza as cannon fodder."

Kennedy looked down at Flood's desk and thought about the possibilities. "Can you locate him?"

"I already have my people checking on all three. So far I've only been
able to confirm the whereabouts of the Jordanian officer."

"I thought you kept close tabs on these dissidents."

"We do," started Fine, "but things are a little stressed over here right
now. What is the phrase you like to use? . . . The natives are restless. We
have another intifada on our hands. Aziz seems to have motivated every
Palestinian between the age of two and seventy to pick up a rock and
protest."

Kennedy had been so focused on the immediate concerns of the crisis that she hadn't thought of the repercussions it might be having abroad.
What Fine said made sense, and if they didn't step in and handle things
more firmly, it would only get worse.

"Ben, it would be a big help if you could track down this kid as soon
as possible."

"I have my best people on it, Irene. I can assure you of that."

"Thank you, Ben. Is there anything else?"

"Well . . ." There was a four-second pause. "The word on the street is
that you grabbed Sheik Harut, the night before last."

"Where are you hearing that?"

"Several sources, actually. The Huns are all guessing it was either you or me, and since I know it wasn't me, then it must be you."

"I'm not in a position to discuss that matter right now, but I can assure you when I know anything about it, you will be briefed fully."

Fine didn't say anything for a long while and then said, "Irene, this is uncomfortable for me, but there are those in my government who are very unhappy with the way this crisis is being handled."

Kennedy turned around and sat on the edge of General Flood's desk. There were many that, put in her shoes, would simply have told the colonel that the U.S. was doing just fine managing the crisis, and that it would appreciate it if its allies would keep their opinions to themselves.

Fine continued. "It is our fear that you may make a short-term decision that could be catastrophic to Israel's interests."

Kennedy thought about Fine's words honestly and refused to let nationalism seep into her thought process. There was no doubt that Israel had a lot on the line, and it didn't take a Rhodes scholar to figure out how they would like the crisis resolved. Kennedy usually stayed out of this type of discussion, but in the current situation, and considering her own frustration with Vice President Baxter, she felt it prudent to try to assuage some of Fine's fears. She also knew that whatever she said would be relayed up to the highest levels of the Israeli government.

"Ben, people like us don't make policy; we only advise. Having said that, however, I can assure you that at every juncture of this crisis, there have been those of us who have forcefully stated our concerns over our relationship with your country—our concern that we don't lose focus on our long-term commitment to Israel's security and stability in the Middle East."

Fine again digested the comments in silence and then added tensely, "There are those in my government who are very nervous." Pausing, again Kennedy could hear the stress in his breathing. "There are many who don't like the fact that you are dealing with Aziz . . . that you have done an about-face on your position of not negotiating with terrorists."

Kennedy chose her words carefully. "There are many in my own government who do not like this change in policy, but this is an extremely difficult situation."

"Who has made these decisions to negotiate?"

"Ben, you are moving into an area that I am not comfortable discussing."

"Well, then let me say this last thing. We have a good idea where this is headed, and we will do whatever it takes to protect our own security." Fine stopped and then repeated himself. "Whatever it takes."

"I understand," replied Kennedy. The colonel couldn't have been clearer, and Kennedy knew that he had been told what to say by someone above his pay grade. Quite possibly the prime minister himself. "Is this something that I should pass on as an official or unofficial position of your country?"

"It has always been our position that we will do whatever it takes to protect ourselves."

"Then why the need to remind me?"

"Because," started Fine, "this is an unusual situation, and we would not want anyone to question where Israel stands on this issue."

"Fair enough, Ben. I will make sure that your position is well known." Running a hand through her hair, she added, "I need to check on some things. Could you do me a favor and let me know just as soon as you track down your eighteen-year-old dissident?"

"Of course. When can I expect to hear more about Sheik Harut?"

Kennedy knew she had to give him something or at least the promise of something. "You can expect me to brief you fully when I have a chance to take a breath." Kennedy intentionally let loose a tired sigh.

"I understand. Please keep me informed, and I will do the same."

"Thank you, Ben." Kennedy kept the phone in her hand and disconnected the call by pressing the button in the cradle. Quickly, she punched in seven numbers, and when the person on the other end answered, she asked to be connected to a certain location via code word. Approximately twenty seconds after that Dr. Hornig was on the phone.

"Jane," started Kennedy, "I need you to ask Harut what he knows about one of the terrorists named Mustafa Yassin. Specifically, ask him if Yassin is a teenage Palestinian or an Iraqi."

"May I ask what this is all about?"

"I can't really get into it right now; I just need some verification."

"All right. I'll see what I can do."

The door to General Flood's office opened, and the general himself entered with General Campbell and Director Stansfield. Kennedy turned away from them and said, "I have to go. How long do you think it will take to get the info?"

"I don't know . . . We seem to be losing him a bit."

"How do you mean?" asked Kennedy as her face twisted into an expression of concern.

"The techniques we use are not exactly beneficial to the long-term health of the human brain."

"You mean you're losing him as in, he's turning into a vegetable?"

"Crudely put, yes . . . but we have extracted an extraordinary amount of information. I have found out some very interesting things that will give us terrific insight into the minds of—"

"That's fine, Jane," Kennedy cut Hornig off, "but I really need you to ask him those questions about Yassin. And the sooner I get the answers the better. I have to go now. Call me as soon as you get anything." With that Kennedy hung up the phone, just as General Flood made his way around the backside of his desk.

Flood looked at Kennedy and asked, "What's wrong now?"

Kennedy exhaled and said, "We might have a problem."

"What kind of problem?" asked Flood.

Looking across the room, Kennedy placed her hands on her hips and said, "I'm not sure, but I hope to know more within the hour." Then looking to her boss, she said, "Colonel Fine passed on a little message for us."

Stansfield nodded knowingly and said, "I was beginning to wonder when they would weigh in."

Kennedy walked over to where Stansfield and Campbell were standing. "He said that they will do whatever it takes to protect themselves."

Approaching the group several steps behind Kennedy, Flood pronounced, "Good for them. At least someone is sticking by their guns in this mess."

"What happened after I left?"

The group settled into their seats, and General Flood began to recount for Kennedy the strategy laid forth by Vice President Baxter. Judging from the facial expressions around the room, even Thomas Stansfield's, it was clear what was thought of the vice president's plans. It seemed as if things were only going to get worse.

32

THE DOOR WAS so hot in one spot that Warch could only touch it for a second or two at a time. He took this as a terrible sign. That, and the fact that nightfall had come and gone and there had been no abatement in the drilling. Things were getting bleaker by the moment, and you could see it on the faces of the tired agents.

To make matters worse for the Secret Service agents, President Hayes had done the unthinkable. He had ordered all of them to place their weapons on the small table near the kitchenette. The president made it clear that there were to be no acts of bravado. That they would surrender without a shot. In Hayes's opinion, if the terrorists got the door open, there was no sense in further bloodshed. At that point the battle would be over.

Warch had tried only once to change President Hayes's mind, but it was to no avail. Hayes was steadfast in his decision that there would be no more bloodshed. As Warch stood by the vault door, Hayes came over. The president placed his hand on the door.

"It's getting warmer."

"Yep," answered Warch.

"Any bright ideas?"

"Nope."

Hayes gestured for Warch to follow him. They walked over to the couches and sat, Warch on the love seat, and Hayes on the couch.

Hayes looked at Warch and said, "Jack, stop beating yourself up. There's nothing else we can do."

"It's not in my personality to give up, sir."

"Well, that's admirable, but I just want you to know that I appreciate everything you and your men have done."

"Thank you."

A question had been burning in Warch's mind since the attack. With the president in such a complimentary mood, Warch decided to ask it. "Sir, who was that prince, and how did he get in to see you?"

Hayes had thought long and hard about this over the last two days, and he kept going back to his meeting in the Situation Room three nights ago.

The meeting where he had authorized the abduction of Fara Harut. In that meeting he had seen a black and white photograph of Rafique Aziz. It was an old one, but the eyes had left an impression on him. The face was different, but there was something about the eyes that made him think it was Aziz.

"I can't be sure, but I think it might have been Rafique Aziz. Or if it wasn't, it was one of his people."

Warch nodded. "I told you about the call I got from Irene Kennedy, right before the attack." Hayes nodded. "Well, I've never seen a photo of Aziz, but whoever that man was standing in the Oval Office, I didn't like the look in his eye."

"I've seen a photo of him, but it was old."

"Sir, I'll understand if you don't want to answer this question." Warch looked at the president to see if he was open. Hayes nodded for Warch to go ahead. "I have my suspicions, but I'd like to know for sure. . . . What did these terrorists hang in front of the DNC to entice them into getting a face-to-face meeting with you?"

Hayes thought for a moment. It was ingrained in his political instincts to avoid answering this question. He had worked on the Hill for twenty-plus years, and the only thing that was as certain as hot summers in Washington was congressional investigations. And when this whole thing was over, they would see an endless stream of investigations, reviews, and reports. If recent history had taught Hayes anything, it was that the cover-up usually created more problems than it solved. If national security wasn't on the line, it was best to get everything out in the open. For this mess, that would damage the party—how much was anyone's guess—but it was better than dragging the whole thing out for years.

The politics of greed had shown its ugly head in the worst of ways, and because of it they were now in this fix. Hayes knew what was the right thing to do, and it was probably better to do it now, while he felt a sense of honor, because, God only knew, if he waited until he was out of this, he'd have a room full of lawyers and consultants telling him to keep his mouth shut and say nothing. Feeling indebted and unusually forthright, Hayes began to tell Warch what had happened.

AZIZ GRINNED FROM ear to ear as he watched the pundits, experts, and analysts go over every word of his speech to the American people. He had changed back into his fatigues and was sitting in the Situation Room. He now sat, remote control in hand, simultaneously watching six TVs, with his feet up on the long conference table. He was spending more and more of his time with MSNBC on the main screen, but whenever he saw someone on one of the other stations with a title such as former FBI agent, or counterterrorism expert, he couldn't resist switching to that station.

The analysis was almost exactly as he thought it would be. For every law-enforcement type, there was a former State Department official, politician, journalist, or religious leader that would talk of a peaceful solution to a horrible situation. His favorite comment so far had come from some Baptist minister who had noted an incredible amount of religious tolerance on the part of Mr. Aziz in his acknowledgment of "our Christian God."

They were literally falling all over themselves in an attempt to make it sound as if a nonviolent end to the crisis was within sight. They were saying things like, "The ball is now in Vice President Baxter's court. If he wants to find a way out of this horrible siege, this will probably be his best chance."

Aziz loved it. The pressure was a reality. It was no longer something he hoped he could elicit. If things went as planned, he would be in a perfect position for his final demand and his triumphant return to the Middle East. The U.S. would meet his most recent demand. Most of its allies would just as soon begin trading with Iraq again. As long as military hardware and technology were off the table, the deal was palatable to all but Britain and Israel.

Aziz confidently rubbed his chin as he thought of the moment when the vault door would be opened, the moment he looked into the eyes of a defeated president of the United States—the sheer joy of being able to gloat over President Hayes, hold a gun to his head, and watch him cry. After he had broken Hayes and made him think his life was about to end, he would show him the slightest ray of hope, and slowly, he would reveal to him how there was a peaceful way to resolve the entire crisis. Then he would change back into his suit and shock the world by going on national TV with President Hayes.

The endless parade of military personnel and Secret Service agents who had sworn on their reputations that the president was safe in his bunker would be embarrassed and shamed. They would be shunned in favor of the politicians who could broker the safe release of the president and the hostages.

Aziz was relishing his exceedingly favorable luck when an image on one of the TVs caught his attention. His feet were off the table in a second, and the remote control was pointed toward the main TV like a gun. As the channel changed, the unmistakable image of Sheik Fara Harut took center stage. Aziz's eyes widened as he listened to the anchor on NBC talk about reports out of the UN that Iran was protesting the abduction of an Islamic cleric. A moment later a woman appeared on the TV.

Aziz listened to the anchor say, "We're fortunate to have with us Sheila Dunn from *The Washington Post*. Sheila, you wrote an article that appeared on the front page of the *Post* this morning. Can you explain how that article might tie in with this most recent development between Iran and the UN?"

"Yes." Dunn looked seriously into the camera. "I have it from the highest sources that CIA alerted the Secret Service that the White House was targeted for a terrorist attack. It appears that this warning was given with just minutes to spare."

The anchor leaned forward, placing his elbow on the desk. "How do Sheik Harut and Iran figure in this?"

"Well, Iran has filed a grievance with the UN stating that a group of commandos from a foreign country carried out a mission in the Iranian town of Bandar Abbas three nights ago that left dozens dead and Sheik Fara Harut missing. Sheik Harut is the spiritual leader of the group Hezbollah, and he and Rafique Aziz are very close. So it stands to reason that the CIA obtained the advance information of the attack from Sheik Harut."

"Do we know what role, if any, the CIA played in this raid?"

"No." Dunn shook her head, acting as if she was really disappointed. "Both the Pentagon and Central Intelligence Agency have refused comment on the subject."

Aziz turned the television off. He would make them pay. The connection had been made, and there was no way they could lie their way out of it. Someone would die for this. Abruptly, Aziz turned and started for the door.

A SPECIALLY OUTFITTED U.S. Army Black Hawk helicopter ferried Kennedy, Stansfield, General Flood, and General Campbell from the Pentagon to Langley. When they arrived in the control room on the seventh floor, they all stood in silence while they looked up at the wall of monitors. One of the watch officers had called Kennedy and warned her what was happening. In truth, it didn't surprise her. If she hadn't had so many other things on her mind, she probably would have predicted it.

Thomas Stansfield stood, impassive, looking at the large wall, taking in the tiny images. General Flood and General Campbell were a different matter, however. They were men who were used to giving an order and having it followed to the letter—and almost always without question. In this particular situation General Campbell couldn't have been more specific. He had told Rapp in very clear English that he was to stay put until further notice.

In addition to the monitor that showed the inside of the president's bedroom and the one that showed Lt. Commander Harris's makeshift command post, four more monitors now showed images. They said it all. Those screens didn't come to life all on their own, and since Mitch Rapp was the only person capable of installing them, it was obvious that he had directly disobeyed General Campbell.

Kennedy looked at one of the watch officers sitting in the back row. "Have you tried to raise him?"

"Repeatedly."

"Any luck?" Kennedy knew the answer before the man started to shake his head.

Director Stansfield walked toward the front of the room so he could more closely examine the monitors. He tried looking at the monitors both with and without his bifocals. Two of them covered staircases. The old director knew from memory which ones they were. The other two monitors covered the wide main hallways that cut east-west across the second and third floors. As Stansfield was watching, a fifth monitor came on-line. This one showed a staircase that he was not familiar with. The row of technicians and analysts to his left began talking in earnest as several of them hurriedly flipped through books about the White House. After about twenty seconds one of them pronounced that the staircase in question was the one that led from the third floor to the roof.

Stansfield looked from the monitor back to the rear of the room to find General Flood and General Campbell engaged in a heated and animated discussion. Watching the two generals talk, Stansfield's face maintained its always neutral expression. His discerning mind was, however, busily extrapolating the problems, complaints, and solutions that this most current bump in the road would create. In a matter of seconds Stansfield had the solutions formed, filed, and ready to be stated in his always unambiguous fashion. Slowly, he started back up the stairs.

When he reached the two generals, he placed a hand on General Flood's shoulder and said, "Let's go to my office where we can talk."

Stansfield started for the door and gave Kennedy a look that told her to join them. The group proceeded through a locked and guarded door, down a ramp, and then onward to the director's corner office. As soon as Stansfield heard his soundproof office door close, he knew what was about to happen—and it did.

"This is absolutely unacceptable," stated a barely restrained General Campbell. "I gave him a direct order! I don't care how good his reasons may or may not be; this is bigger than him, and we cannot have him running around doing whatever he wants, when he wants!"

Stansfield turned around to face Campbell. Kennedy, the last one to enter the room, stopped midway between her boss and the generals. Stansfield nodded slowly, acknowledging Campbell's complaint.

With his jaw clenched, Campbell continued, "I ordered him to stand down because I knew we would be out of the loop for at least an hour. What happens if he gets caught . . . if he kills one of Aziz's men? We need to be here." Campbell pointed at the ground. "We need to be monitoring every little move, so if the shit hits the fan, we can give the order to move." Campbell was so upset it seemed that his bristly flattop was standing even more upright than usual. "Your boy needs to start following orders, or I swear to God—" The stocky ranger stammered for a second, his neck veins bulging. Campbell didn't finish the thought, but it was obvious to all that he was thinking of physical confrontation.

Stansfield nodded slowly in an effort to validate Campbell's anger. Somewhere in the back of his mind he wondered who would actually win that fight. Campbell, although twenty years Rapp's senior, was not a man to be trifled with. Shifting his gaze from the Campbell to Flood, Stansfield asked, "Would you like to add anything?"

Flood shook his sizable head. "There's nothing left to say. It's a no-brainer. Rapp is wrong, and he needs to be reeled in."

Stansfield digested Flood's comments. They were every bit as warranted as Campbell's. The director of central intelligence walked around his desk and looked out the window for a brief moment. The day was as it had been for the last two, sunny and bright. Turning back to the generals, Stansfield said, "We have a difference of opinion, gentlemen. I'll tell you what I see. I see a man who is trained to act on his own. A man who is used to spending days if not weeks in the field without the aid or *interference* of his country. Mitch Rapp is not a soldier, and he most definitely is not a politician. His ability to know when to take risks, when to push ahead, when to pull back, is uncanny. It's, quite honestly, the best I've ever seen. He thrives in this environment where every decision could mean life or death."

Stansfield paused for a moment and then in an almost academic tone continued, "He has a much clearer picture of the tactical situation, not only because he is on-site, but because he is not distracted by all of the things that we are." For clarity, he added, "Most notably, he doesn't have to deal with Vice President Baxter."

Clutching his hands in front of him and then letting them fall to his side, Stansfield continued, "Now, with all due respect, gentlemen, you know I think very highly of both of you, but you must understand, Mitch is not a soldier. He has been trained from day one to think independently. If you want to get mad about this, which you have every right to, then get mad at me. He is my responsibility."

Stansfield stopped just long enough to make it seem as though he was giving them a chance to reply and then said, "We've made a mistake with you two." He pointed to Campbell and Kennedy. "I don't want you attending any more meetings. I want you right here monitoring Rapp and his progress. There are too many meddlesome issues that General Flood and I can handle. I want you two focused on Mitch and how best to aid him. He is our eyes." The elderly spymaster looked from Campbell to Kennedy and back. "The way I see it . . . he's doing exactly what we sent him in there to do. Now, General Campbell, if you want to go in there, and get Mitch on the radio, and read him the riot act, that's fine. That is undoubtedly your prerogative, and I'm not going to stand in your way. But, it won't do us a bit of good, because he won't listen."

Stansfield could see that his words were getting to Campbell. The ranger's demeanor had calmed ever so slightly. "What I would propose is that I have a talk with him and explain how important it is that he communicate his every action so we can deal with something if it comes up."

Before Stansfield could start his next sentence, the large phone on his desk started to ring. Stansfield looked down to see where the call was coming from. On the small screen were a string of letters that caused his brow to knot into a frown. The light on the secure phone continued to blink and Stansfield debated whether he should answer it. After two more rings his frail hand moved slowly toward the receiver.

THE AMBULANCE FOUGHT its way through the late morning traffic. Downtown D.C. was a quagmire. The security perimeter around the White House had been expanded from two to three blocks to the north, east, and west. To the south, Constitution Avenue had been blocked off, and the section of the National Mall between Seventeenth and Fourteenth was also closed. The normally congested downtown was unbearable.

The driver of the ambulance inched forward on Pennsylvania Avenue. In his side mirror he could see the large dome of the Capitol, and in front of him, a sea of cars locked in gridlock trying to make their way into the heart of the business district and around the White House. Salim Rusan was surprisingly calm. Part of this was due to his faith in Aziz's plan, and part of it was due to the fact that he would much rather be stuck in traffic than stuck in the White House.

The ambulance was the last car to make it through the stoplight at Ninth Street. The monolithic Hoover Building appeared on his right— the famed FBI headquarters. Rusan did not smile. It was not in his personality. He was more like Bengazi than Aziz. He was a worrier, and that was why Aziz had chosen him for this crucial mission. Rusan was both the backup plan and the surprise. Depending on how things went, he was to do one of three things. The first was easy and harmless, and despite what Aziz had told the men, Rusan seriously doubted that option would ever present itself. It would be either the second or the third plan that would have to be executed, and both of those would lead to death. Rusan was sure of it. Not just the death of his comrades, but the hostages, the American FBI agents, and hopefully hundreds of others. Rusan's only hope was that in the chaos that would erupt when the Americans tried to retake their White House, he could further add to the confusion and buy some of his friends the time to get away. Rusan thought he had a chance to survive. The plan for his escape was good, well thought out, and just might work.

It was unnerving, nonetheless, to be heading back into the center of the crisis, to the spot where, just three days earlier, he had fired from the roof of the Washington Hotel and killed a dozen-plus Americans. The boldness of the plan was what gave success a chance. Practically every law-enforcement officer in the world was looking for him. The old him, he corrected himself. They would never make the connection between Salim Rusan, the dark-haired Islamic militant terrorist, and Steve Hernandez, the openly gay paramedic from Miami. No, he would continue to inch his way toward the White House, taking his time. When he reached the first roadblock, he would hit the lights on the roof, roll down the window, and tell the D.C. police that he had been told to come down in case they needed him. Aziz had told him it was standard procedure for this type of crisis. He would be one of dozens of ambulances waiting to rush people to the hospital if the need arose.

Rusan had time. The American assassins did not show their faces when the sun was out. They would wait until it was dark, and if Aziz's timetable was right, they would come either tonight or tomorrow. As long as he had everything in position within an hour or two after the sunset, he would be fine.

33

DEEP IN THOUGHT, Anna Rielly sat, feet pulled close, arms wrapped around her shins, and her chin resting in the valley between her knees. Her shoulder-length brown hair was pulled back in its ponytail again. The long sleeves of President Hayes's black sweatshirt were rolled up several times. She was comfortable, warm, and had a little bit of food in her stomach along with two Tylenol 3s, which helped dull her aching jaw and ribs. All things considered, she was doing pretty darn well.

How strange life could be, she thought to herself. One week ago she was in Chicago working at the station, living in her apartment in Lincoln Park. She was ready for a change, in both her career and her personal life. Since the rape, things had been jumbled. There had been the boyfriend who couldn't handle what she had been through. He was a pharmaceutical rep, and when offered a promotion and transfer to Phoenix, he jumped at the chance and told Anna he couldn't love someone who couldn't love him back. She'd blamed herself for that one until she was healthy enough to realize that if he had really loved her, he would have given her more than seven months to recover.

It had actually turned out to be a blessing. Spending the last several years alone had allowed her to grow in strength. Independence and self-reliance were great things. The best part about them was that the only person who could let you down was yourself. The downside, which she was now experiencing, was that you woke up one day and realized you had either pushed everybody away or not allowed anyone to get close enough. Either way, you were left with a lonely existence.

Rielly thought fate had to figure into the equation somewhere. It always did for those large and defining moments in life. What kind of twisted fate had led her to this strange moment, this crossroad? If she hadn't gotten the job as the new White House correspondent, if she had missed her flight to D.C., if her alarm had failed to wake her up three days ago, if she had been released with that first group of hostages, if that pig hadn't dragged her up to the president's bedroom? Rielly's eyes got big. If Mitch Kruse, or whatever his real name was, hadn't stepped in when he did? *Wow,* Rielly thought as a shiver ran up her spine. The thought of Kruse not showing up when he did was horrifying. She owed him a lot. More than she could probably ever express.

Rielly stared blankly at the wall opposite her. Her thoughts settled in on the man named Kruse, and on the odds of him appearing exactly when he did and all of the possible outcomes in between. It was staggering. Call it fate, call it a guardian angel, call it what you like, but someone or something had stepped in and put him there at that exact moment in time. A smile fell across Rielly's face, and she looked upward to say a little prayer of thanks.

BEFORE PICKING UP the phone, Stansfield told Kennedy to listen in on a second phone located on the other side of the room. He then asked Generals Flood and Campbell to stay silent. Stansfield's hand reached down and picked up the handset. At the same time, he sank into his chair and brought the phone to his ear.

"This is Director Stansfield."

At first there was only breathing, heavy breathing, and then the words hissed forth. "I know all about you. Who you are, what you've done, and all of the people you've sent your minions to kill."

Stansfield looked down again at the readout on his phone. The black letters said, "WH Sit Room." The hostile voice he recognized as that of Rafique Aziz, and it didn't even come close to riling the director of the Central Intelligence Agency. Instead, Stansfield leaned back and asked, "What can I do for you, Mr. Aziz?"

"Do for me," spat an obviously agitated Aziz. "You can tell me what you have done with Fara Harut!"

It was a statement made with confidence; Stansfield was sure of that. The director stayed cool and replied, "I have no idea what you are talking about."

"Don't insult me," screamed Aziz. "I know what you have done, and I want to know where Fara Harut is immediately, or you are going to have more dead hostages on your hands!"

Aziz was screaming so loud that Flood and Campbell could hear him from where they were standing. The two men stepped forward while Stansfield replied, "It is not my intention to insult you. I sincerely have no idea what you're talking about."

"You are a snake," screamed Aziz. "I should have known better than to have thought for a second that you would give me the truth! I swear I will make you pay for what you have done!"

Aziz was now yelling so loud Stansfield pulled the phone away from his ear and listened to Aziz ramble from a more comfortable distance of six inches.

The voice squawked from the earpiece. "You give me the truth right now, or I will walk down the hall and put a bullet in the head of one of the hostages, and when I come back, if you do not have an answer for me, I will go back and kill another, and I will keep doing it until you tell me what you have done with Fara Harut!"

"Mr. Aziz," replied an unflinching Stansfield, "I have no idea what you are talking about. If you would tell me what has got you so angry, I will do my best to find out where Fara Harut is."

"Don't toy with me! I know who you are, and what you do! You are a liar and a murderer of innocent women and children!"

Stansfield sat calmly in the chair, the phone still held several inches away from his ear. He had to think quickly, and he had to get Aziz to back down.

"Well, Mr. Aziz, if that's the way you feel about me, we must have a lot in common." Without giving Aziz a chance to reply to the shot, Stansfield continued, "By the way, I must commend you for your speech this morning. It really played well with the politicians. I tried to advise them that you were not serious. That you were performing. To and for what, I have not yet figured out, but I have my ideas."

"Silence!" screamed Aziz. "I want to know where Fara Harut is immediately, or someone dies!"

"Mr. Aziz, you don't want to do that, and this is why." Stansfield glanced up at the two generals for a second and then said, "Right now you've done a very good job making certain people in my government think that you have turned over a new leaf and that you are a man who will actually keep his word. Myself and several others know this is all a sham. If you kill another hostage, I will take a tape of this conversation to the vice president and I will leak it to the media so everyone can hear that you are truly not the man you tried to portray yourself as this morning. And then . . . well . . . you know our rules of engagement. You were lucky we didn't storm the place after you killed National Security Adviser Schwartz and his secretary. If you start killing hostages again, we will be left no alternative other than to retake the building . . . and that of course means you will die."

"Your men will die!" screamed Aziz. "You are a bigger fool than I thought. I will blow this whole building sky high and all of the hostages with it."

"And you will die also, which just happens to suit my needs perfectly. Things will be much easier if you cease to exist." Stansfield leaned back in his chair. "You are threatening the wrong man, Mr. Aziz, and you know it." Now came the time to lie, to really make Aziz think that he was everything Aziz thought he was and then some. "I could not care less what happens to the hostages. I just want to make sure that you and your wretched comrades are dead when this whole thing is over. If we have to lose forty or fifty hostages to mount your head on the wall . . . it's a small price to pay."

"I am not afraid to die! Even if I die, I will have won!"

"I don't think so," replied Stansfield in his calm analytical voice. "You see, after you have killed yourself, we will pluck President Hayes, and quite a few others, out of the rubble, and you will have ceased to be a problem. We will rebuild the White House in six months, and everything will return to normal."

Aziz was enraged, but he knew that Stansfield had him boxed in. For now at least, but, oh, the surprise they would be in for when their president wasn't so safe. Now was not the time to push things; no matter how much Fara Harut meant, Aziz could not do anything to precipitate an attack by the Americans until he had the president in his hands. Aziz would have to swallow his pride and make a tactical retreat. His ego, however, was far too large to do so without taking a parting shot.

"You are too sure of yourself, Mr. Stansfield." Aziz spoke in a low ominous tone. "Things are not always as they appear. We will talk again this evening, and by then you had better know where Fara Harut is."

With that the line went dead. Stansfield set the phone back in its cradle and looked up at the two generals. General Flood asked, "What in the hell was that all about?"

Stansfield glanced up at Kennedy as she walked across the large office. "He knows Harut is gone and thinks we have him."

"I got that part of it. What was the rest of it about?"

"He said if I didn't tell him right away where Harut was, he would kill a hostage."

"And that's when you decided to play chicken with him?" asked Campbell.

Stansfield shrugged his shoulders. It was hardly the phrase he would have used to describe his method. "I took a risk. I obviously don't want to see any of those hostages killed. All I did was give him the answer that fits his belief of who I really am." Stansfield rubbed his forefinger under his chin. "And he blinked."

Kennedy placed both hands on her hips and frowned. "There was more to it than that, Thomas. He didn't just blink, he rolled over and showed you his belly, and did it way too fast. It was out of character."

"Maybe he's getting tired?"

Kennedy shook her head. "No, there's something else going on. Something I haven't told you about yet because I wanted to check on a few things before I got everybody worried." Kennedy moved her hands from her hips and folded them across her chest. "I picked up something in Aziz's voice. When you"—Kennedy pointed to Stansfield—"told him that he would be doing us a favor by killing himself, because when it was all over we would pull President Hayes from his bunker and so forth . . ." Kennedy made a rotating motion with her finger. "When you were finished, the first thing he said in response was, 'You are too sure of yourself, Mr. Stansfield. Things are not always as they appear.' Did you notice the tone in his voice?" Kennedy looked at her boss hard and gave him a second to recall what Aziz's words had sounded like.

She continued, "He sounded like he knew something that we didn't." Stansfield looked at her as if she was reading a little too far into things, and she responded, "Let me fill you in on some other information first, and then it might make more sense." Stepping toward her boss, Kennedy looked up at the generals and said, "That phone call I received from Colonel Fine this morning was in regard to three names he was checking for me. Three names we got from Harut. One of the names had three matches. The first was an officer in the Jordanian Army, and he's already been ruled out. The second, and we thought the most likely, was an eighteen-year-old Palestinian kid with suspected ties to Hamas. And the third was a man known as the Thief of Baghdad. It turns out the third of the three Mustafa Yassins is the Iraqi who was in charge of looting all of the banks and vaults after they invaded Kuwait."

General Flood shook his head. "It's obviously the second one, Irene."

"It could be," conceded Kennedy with a nod, "but what if it's the third one? What if Aziz brought along this Thief of Baghdad, knowing there was a good chance the president would get to his bunker? What if, at this very moment, this man is working on getting the president out of his bunker?" Kennedy stopped and looked each man in the eye, one at a time, while she gave them a chance to think about it. "What if Aziz said to Thomas, 'You are too sure of yourself. Things are not always as they appear,' because he knows President Hayes is not as safe as we thought?"

Everyone's eyes got a little bigger as Kennedy finished stating her case. General Flood looked down at Stansfield and said, "I think this is something we need to bring to the attention of the vice president."

Stansfield stared back at him blankly for a while and then said, "Not quite yet. We need a little more proof before we go to him."

"Well, how do we get that proof?"

"I have a pretty good idea," Stansfield replied with a nod.

34

RAPP BACKED DOWN the long cross hall of the second floor. Each step was placed carefully. Heel first and then toe. The cross hall, which was more a long room than a hallway, was brightly bathed in the late morning sunlight. Rapp and Adams, dressed in their black Nomex jumpsuits, stood out against the light-colored walls and carpet. They felt secure, though. Having been out of the stash room for over an hour, they had placed all five of the surveillance units and checked each one to make sure it was working. At no time during their sweep did they see or hear a sign of the terrorists. Even when they checked out the back staircase that led to the rooftop guard booth, there had been nothing. With the units in place, Rapp felt infinitely more comfortable, now that he had a secure base from which to operate.

How they felt back at Langley would be a different matter, entirely. Rapp had known this before he stepped out of the stash room with Adams some seventy minutes ago, but that was just tough shit. There were too many people sticking their fingers in the pie. This thing needed to be streamlined, and someone needed to take action. Sitting around and playing cautious was not in Rapp's nature, especially where Aziz was concerned. Rapp knew whom he was dealing with, he knew what Aziz was up to, and if nobody else could figure it out, to hell with them. This was not one of those moments in life where disagreement was acceptable. This wasn't a policy decision where it was difficult to quantify the benefits of one course over the other. This was black and white. Rapp knew what had to be done, and everyone else could kiss his ass if they weren't on board.

As they made it back to the president's bedroom, Adams entered first and then Rapp. Rapp stood in the doorway for a moment and took one last look to his left, straight ahead, and to his right. Behind him, on the other side of the bedroom, a stench was beginning to drift from the body of the dead terrorist. Rapp noticed it and cringed at the thought of how bad the smell would get in another day.

Adams tapped him on the shoulder and said, "I've gotta piss like a racehorse."

Rapp stepped back into the room and nodded to the bathroom.

Adams went in and closed the door behind him. A couple minutes later he reappeared, a look of relief on his face.

"You just wait." Adams looked at Rapp. "You're too young to understand, but someday you'll know what it's like."

"Yeah, if I only live that long." Rapp took the thick barrel of his silencer and pointed to the closet. "Let's check on Anna."

Adams went in first and pressed the hidden button. As the closet organizer swung out, Adams stepped into the stash room. Rapp poked his head in and said to Rielly, "Do you need to use the restroom?"

Rielly nodded enthusiastically.

"Follow me, and don't make any noise." Then looking to Adams, Rapp said, "Monitor the stairwells until we're back, and let me know if you have any movement."

Rielly stood and followed Rapp quietly, which was easy to do in her stocking feet. Walking into the bathroom, Rielly closed the door behind her and for the first time saw herself in the mirror. She had one hell of a shiner on her cheek, and her skin looked a little pasty. Without wasting too much time in front of the mirror, she got down to business and took care of her more immediate needs. In the middle of that task, she was struck by the bizarre thought that she was sitting on President Hayes's toilet. The same toilet that quite a few presidents had used.

When she was done, she closed the lid. Hanging on a bar next to the sink were two sets of washcloths and hand towels. Rielly couldn't resist. She felt disgusting and dirty. Opening the faucets, she doused her face with water and began to rub a bar of soap vigorously in her hands. After cleaning and drying her face quickly, she had another idea. Rielly soaped up one of the washcloths and wetted another and one of the hand towels. Next, she checked the medicine cabinet and grabbed the president's shaving kit. Wrapping everything up in a larger bath towel, Rielly opened the door and found Rapp waiting for her.

Rapp looked at the towels and asked, "What's that all about?"

Clutching the bundle in her arms, she looked up and said, "A little sponge bath."

Rapp pointed to himself with a big smile on his face and said, "For me."

Rielly almost laughed, but instead shook her head. "No, for me."

Rapp kept the smile on his face as the two of them went back into the stash room. Once inside, the door was again closed and bolted. Rapp looked at the radio and knew that he had some explaining to do. Deciding it was better to get on with it, he knelt down and powered up the unit. Milt Adams had the monitor opened on his chest and was checking the reception on each surveillance unit again.

When the unit was ready, Rapp picked up the handset and said, "Iron Man to control. Do you read? Over." It didn't surprise Rapp that a voice came back right away—he had expected that—it was the particular voice that surprised him.

"Iron Man, you've been a little busy since we last spoke."

Rapp hesitated for a moment. "Yes, sir. I thought it was the right thing to do."

"I concur," said Thomas Stansfield, "but from now on, let us know what you're up to. We are receiving clearly on both the visual and the audio. They should be a big help. Now I've got something rather immediate that I need you to check on. We have reason to believe that the president might not be as safe as we thought."

Rapp's eyes darted from the console of the field radio to Milt Adams. "Please clarify."

"Aziz may have brought someone along who specializes in breaking into vaults." There was a pause. "Is that clear enough?"

"I think so. How quickly would you like me to verify this?"

"As quickly as you can without risking exposure."

Rapp sat on his heels. He thought about the location of the bunker. The third basement. The only way in or out was one staircase. The same one where an unexpected guard had been posted last night.

"Sir, let me discuss this with Milt and see what type of a plan we can put together. I'll get back to you in five or less." Rapp set the hard plastic handset down and looked to Adams. "Zip that thing up and get your blueprints out."

Adams could tell by both Rapp's expression and tone that something serious had just been discussed. After he finished zipping the monitor up, Adams pulled out his sheaf of blueprints.

Rapp scooted forward on his knees. "Excuse me, Anna." Rielly was sitting in the corner with her legs stretched out in front of her. As Rapp moved around her, he looked at the blueprints and said, "Show me the entire third level and all ways in or out."

Adams reached to the bottom of the stack and pulled out the last sheet. Then grabbing it with both hands, he laid it down on top. "This is it. There's only one stairwell in and out. The one that we used." Looking up from the blueprint, Adams asked, "Tell me what you're looking for, and I might be able to help a little more."

Rielly appeared on her knees at Rapp's side. She looked down at the blueprint and asked, "What's that?"

Rapp felt a tinge of anxiety. Another nuisance to deal with. Why couldn't things be simple for once? Rapp cocked his head to the side and looked at Rielly, who was studying the blueprint in earnest. It was time to take this obstacle off the table. There were going to be too many variables coming down the homestretch, and he needed to keep the process as simple as possible. The more he had to think about, the better the odds were that he'd screw up. And screwing up on this one meant that someone would die. Most probably himself. There was one thing that would free them up a bit. Rapp had thought about it earlier in the day and decided if Rielly would go along with the idea, it would make things easier from a logistical standpoint.

"Anna, we need to talk."

Rielly looked up at him from the blueprint. "What about?"

"I need to be able to speak freely with Milt, and I can't do that with you sitting here. So you have to promise me that you will do something when we get out of here."

"Sure."

"I am going to need you to sign a national security nondisclosure agreement."

Rielly moved back a little bit. She was familiar with the document, and the thought of signing such a thing was ludicrous. She was a reporter, for Christ's sake. She would be bound by law never to discuss the matters outlined in the document, and that most probably meant never being able to tell her story. Her head slowly started to move from side to side.

"I don't think so. I don't like the idea of the government holding something like that over my head. I'm a reporter. It wouldn't be right."

Rapp got a little angry. It showed in the way his eyes squinted just a millimeter or two. At that moment he looked at Rielly, and all he saw was a beautiful, selfish, self-centered woman. He didn't have the time or patience for this. "Fine," he pronounced in a tone that was anything but. "I'll have to remember that our careers are our number one priority. In fact, I probably should have kept that in mind last night." Rapp turned away from Rielly and grabbed the radio handset. "Iron Man to control. Over."

"What was that supposed to mean?" asked Rielly in a wounded voice.

Rapp put his hand up to quiet her and spoke into the handset. "We are going to go investigate right now. This will only be a light recon. I repeat, a light recon. If we meet any resistance, we will abort and try to find another way to verify. Over." Rapp nodded several times and said, "Correct."

After placing the handset back in its cradle, Rapp looked at Adams and said, "Come on, Milt. We'll finish the rest of this conversation in the elevator." Rapp grabbed his submachine gun and rose to one knee.

Rielly reached out for his arm. "Hold on a minute. What's with the attitude all of the sudden?"

"The attitude." Rapp pulled away and stood. "Last night when that piece of shit dragged you up here to rape you, I turned this radio off because I knew that the people running this show would have told me to stay put, that the mission was bigger than just one person." Rapp stared her straight in the eye and pointed at himself. "What I did last night was not a real big career enhancer, but all I saw out there was a woman who needed help and some piece of shit that deserved to die. Cut and dry, plain and simple." Rapp turned to Adams. "Let's go."

Rielly was shocked by the extreme change in his manner. She attempted to speak, but Rapp cut her off.

"Anna, I'm done talking." With his submachine gun up and ready, he placed his free hand on the bolt and said, "If I come across any paper and pens, I'll grab them so you can start working on your tell-all story." With that parting shot, Rapp slid back the bolt and slipped into the walk-in closet.

35

THEY STEPPED INTO the small elevator without talking. Adams shut the door and pressed the button. Rapp stood rigidly against the wall, his head slowly thumping backward into the wood paneling. He was more pissed than he ought to be, he thought. This was a childish romantic crush, a fleeting hope for something he hadn't felt in so long. It was stupid. With all of the shit that was going on around him, with all of the high stakes, it was a complete waste of time and energy to allow himself to be distracted for even a second by something so utterly juvenile.

Somewhere in Rapp's brain a red stamp crashed down on Anna Rielly's file, and she was banished to a part of his memory that was rarely accessed. It was as simple as that. Compartmentalize and move on.

With her out of his mind, Rapp looked at Adams. Adams looked back with a prying expression.

"What?" asked Rapp a touch too defensively.

Adams kept his basset-hound eyes locked on Rapp until his new partner repeated his question. Then Milt licked his upper lip once and said, "Don't you think you were a little hard on her?"

Moving away from the wall, Rapp began to fidget in frustration. "She's a nonissue, Milt. We have more important things to worry about."

"Are you gonna let me in on the secret?"

"Yep, and it's a doozy." Rapp took the MP-10 and cradled it across his chest as the small elevator reached the first basement. "It appears Aziz brought along some guy who specializes in breaking into vaults." Rapp stopped, to see if Adams could connect the dots.

It didn't take long. The expression on Adams's smooth face went from an inquisitive frown to one of surprise. "That's not good."

"Nope." Rapp shook his head. "Our job is to find out if Hayes is as safe as we thought."

Thinking several steps ahead, Adams plucked the folded blueprints from his vest. The series of sheets were like an unruly road map. Adams opened the documents and shuffled the right one to the top. Shooing Rapp out of the way, he held it up against the wall and said, "This is where it's located."

Rapp looked at the layout of the third basement. "Only one way in?"

"Well, not really. Hold that side for me."

Rapp grabbed one side of the blueprint while Adams held the other with his hand. "There's another way down to the third basement." Adams touched a spot on the blueprint. "This is the anteroom to the vault. This little rectangle area here. It doesn't make a lot of sense from a strict design and engineering standpoint, but it's one of those things you need to implement into a design when you're trying to add things to a two-hundred-plus-year-old building."

Adams touched another spot on the blueprint. "This is the boiler room, where we came in, and this is the hall that I told you led to the bunker." Adams traced his skinny black finger down the hall, took the left-hand turn, and tapped it on a door. "This is one of two ways into the anteroom. It's a three inch thick steel door. Over here on this wall of the anteroom is the second door. This is probably the one the president used to enter the bunker."

"Why do you say that?" asked Rapp.

"Because this door leads up a short staircase to a tunnel that runs all the way under the West Wing to where there's a much longer set of stairs that lead all the way up to a hidden door just off of the Oval Office." Adams pulled another sheet from the back and showed Rapp the location of the tunnel and where it went. "This tunnel used to be the bunker until this new one was completed just this last year. As this tunnel comes over from the West Wing, it stops here. At that point you can either go down this little flight, which empties you into the anteroom, or you can go up a flight of stairs that leads to one of those doors that don't exist."

Rapp liked where this was headed. "Where is this fictitious door located?"

Adams changed pages again and tapped a spot. "Right here. Just down the hall from where we are right now, in the china storage room."

"That's perfect."

"Not quite." Adams shook his head. "These doors that lead to the anteroom are hermetically sealed with rubber gaskets. If we go down through the tunnel, we wouldn't be able to hear or see anything in the anteroom unless we open the door to it, and I doubt you want to do that."

"No." Rapp thought about the options for a second. "Yeah, you're probably right. That means they would have had to get through one of these outer doors first to get to the bunker door."

"Yep, and this is the door they would have gone through." Adams changed back to the drawing that showed the layout of the third basement. "This way they only go through one door. If they tried to come in through the tunnel door, that's assuming they could find it to begin with, they would have had to go through an extra door."

"That makes sense." Rapp looked at the drawing. "So we have to go down the stairs we used when we came in and hope that a guard isn't posted like he was last night."

"I'm afraid so."

"Okay." Rapp took his hand off the blueprints. "Put those things away, and let's get ready to move out. You know the routine."

After he was done putting the blueprints back in order, Adams folded them up and stuffed them inside his black vest. Then, unzipping and turning on the monitor, he pressed the button to open the elevator door. Rapp stood over his shoulder while Adams stuck the tip of the snake under the outer metal door leading to the first basement. The tiny lens gave them a slightly warped view of the hallway looking up from the stark concrete floor. Adams maneuvered the lens all the way to the right and then back to the left.

"Looks good," proclaimed Rapp as he stepped back and readied his gun.

Adams pulled the snake back with his right hand and coiled it against his hip.

Rapp took the doorknob in his right hand, pulled, and scooted quickly into the hallway. He brought his MP-10 up and swept to the right and left. Adams was just two steps behind, having had to pause for just a second to shut the outer door to the elevator. In less than three seconds Rapp was at the door that led to the two lower floors. A twist of the metal knob with his gloved right hand and he was through the door, his thick black silencer moving everywhere his eyes went. Whether he had one hand on the weapon or two, it made no difference. At these close distances, one-handed, he could hit a head-size target with about ninety-five percent accuracy on the first shot. With both hands on the efficient and compact Heckler & Koch, it was a guaranteed one hundred percent.

After checking the stairwell above, Rapp began his controlled descent, keeping his body pressed against the wall, always looking down and checking each new stair as it came into view. Adams followed quietly, several steps behind. Rapp was gaining confidence in him.

When they hit the landing in between the second and third basements, Rapp stopped. The tiny surveillance unit he had placed next to the door was barely discernible. If he hadn't known it was there, he doubted he would have seen it. Stopping for even five seconds, out in the open like this, seemed like an eternity, but Rapp was trying to get a feel as to whether someone was on the other side of the door.

He went down the last four steps and stopped, his eyes fixed on the half-inch sliver of light that framed the base of the metal fire door. For another long five seconds, Rapp crouched and stared. Still nothing.

Rapp waved Adams down. The older man descended the last flight cautiously, holding on to the monitor as if it were the head of a baby. Stepping back and holding his submachine gun ready, Rapp directed Adams to slide the tip of the snake under the door.

As Adams moved the device to the left, a pair of boots came into view. They were walking toward the door. Rapp reached out and pulled Adams's hand back, keeping his gun trained on the door. After waiting several seconds for the boots to pass, Adams and Rapp retreated in silence.

"BROODING" MIGHT HAVE been the right word, at least at first. But that smug emotion was gone now, replaced by one of self-loathing and personal disgust. Disgust, she told herself. Not disappointment or disrespect, it was disgust. Mr. Secret Agent Man's parting slam had stung, and Anna Rielly's first response had been to fold her arms tightly across her chest and ask herself just who that gun-toting ass thought he was. Where in the hell did he get off judging her so quickly? He didn't know who she was. He was just another one of those arrogant white males, like so many of her dad's cop friends, who thought they were the only ones that knew what life was all about. They had no idea how important it was to have a truly free press. Just who in the hell did he think he was? The voice in the back of her head responded, *He's the man who risked his life to save yours.*

At that point, Rielly's mood turned from brooding to self-loathing, and now she sat feeling not so hot about herself.

THE ELEVATOR STOPPED at the second floor, and without having to be told, Adams was already working the monitor to check the different surveillance units. For his part, Rapp was trying to figure out their next step beyond calling Langley. There had to be a way to check on the president. When they got back in the stash room, he would get Adams to spread out his blueprints and see if there were any other options. But that meant Rielly, and that wouldn't work. She already knew too much as it was, and things were only going to get worse.

Adams finished checking the surveillance units and told Rapp the coast was clear. Rapp nodded, and after a couple seconds, he said, "When we get back to the stash room, I'm going to need you to step outside with Anna for a couple of minutes while I talk to Langley."

The twisted expression on Adams's face gave Rapp the impression he wasn't too fond of the idea.

"What's wrong?"

"I don't like the idea of sitting outside of the room with her and my little six-shooter." The horizontal lines on Adams's shiny black forehead deepened. "I think you're overreacting." Adams saw an instantaneous change in Rapp's demeanor. The lid on the kettle started to wobble. In earnest, Adams added, "Just a bit . . . I mean, I understand your need for secrecy and everything, but—"

Rapp cut him off. "She's a reporter, end of discussion, let's go." Rapp jerked his thumb toward the door.

It was obvious Rapp wasn't going to budge, so Adams zipped up the monitor and opened the door. Rapp stepped onto the white tile floor first, and Adams closed the door behind them. Another quick trip across the hall and they were back in the large walk-in closet.

Rapp pointed at the ground. "You stay here. Use the monitor to make sure no one is coming. I'll leave the door unlocked. At the first sign of trouble, come back in the room."

Rapp didn't give Adams a chance to ask any questions. Turning immediately, he opened the organizer and stepped into the stash room. Rielly was sitting in the corner right where they had left her. Rapp looked down at Anna Rielly and wished she weren't there. Wished he could just erase her from his mind.

"You're back awfully quick," was the only thing Rielly could think of.

Ignoring her words, he stuck his hand out. Rielly grabbed it, and Rapp pulled her to her feet. He maneuvered her toward the open door and ignored her question. Pushing her out into the closet, Rapp pulled the organizer shut with a slight click.

He dropped to one knee, grabbed the handset to the field radio, and said, "Iron Man to control. Over."

A female voice answered and told Rapp to hold. Less than ten seconds later Thomas Stansfield's smooth voice came over the thin plastic receiver. "What did you find out?"

"I came up dry on the first run, sir. There was a Tango in the hallway. We couldn't proceed past the stairwell."

"What level was the Tango on?" This time it was General Campbell's voice.

"Third basement." Rapp rubbed his brow with his right hand. "He was positioned just outside the doors for the stairwell and the boiler room." There was a pause, and Rapp imagined a gaggle of military aides shuffling blueprints around and showing the general the exact location.

"Any thoughts on why he would be there?" It was Stansfield again.

Rapp finished kneading the skin on his brow. "Off the top of my head, I can think of two. First, the guy is down there to make sure no one comes through the shaft again, or second, he's down there to make sure no one interrupts the progress of this Yassin, or whatever his name is."

There was the exhaling sigh of thought and then the words, "I would concur. Do you or Milt have any ideas on how we might circumvent this guard?"

"Maybe." Rapp began rubbing his forehead again. "Give me about ten minutes, and I'll call you back."

Rapp set the handset back in the cradle. Now it was time to grab Milt and figure out a way to verify whether or not the president was safe. What to do with the reporter?

Standing, he popped open the door and pushed it outward. Adams and Rielly were standing in the dimly lit closet talking quietly. Rapp motioned for Adams to join him and then said to Rielly, "You're going to have to stay out here while we talk."

Adams stepped forward, grabbing Rielly's arm and bringing her with him. "She's got something to say to you."

Rapp stood in the opening, reluctant to move, looking at Adams and wondering what in the hell he had said. Looking to Rielly, he saw that her feisty attitude was gone. After a long moment, Rapp retreated a step and allowed the two of them to enter the stash room.

36

SEALS DON'T LIKE to sit around, especially when there's action to be had, and even more so when one of their own has been killed. Lt. Commander Harris wanted a piece of that action, and although he would never admit it to the brass, he wanted to put a bullet in the head of every terrorist in the White House. No prisoners.

Now Harris was in the process of exactly that as he strode up the steps of the Old Post Office on the corner of Twelfth and Pennsylvania. He had walked the four and a half blocks from his makeshift command post on the east fence of the White House with the bullish Mick Reavers. They were still there manning the CP, despite the debacle of last night. Rapp and Adams were, after all, still in the building, and the powers that be at the Pentagon had yet to decide on a redeployment, if any. Harris knew that was a distinct possibility. At any minute he could get the order to pack himself and his men up. The press was asking a lot of questions concerning Aziz's statement that he had turned away an assault. If they pushed hard enough and the politicians started chirping, Six's plug would be pulled. JSOC didn't like operating in the light, and if the current trend continued, they would most certainly pull Harris and his men away from the White House and back under cover.

There was one other alternative, but Harris didn't want to think about it. He wanted to believe that the Navy and ultimately the Pentagon would do the right thing. But he knew from past experience that that didn't always turn out to be the case. In a crisis, SOP for the Pentagon often was to circle the wagons and offer up a sacrificial lamb. The beast served to the press was usually the unit commander, and that of course was yours truly, Lt. Commander Dan Harris.

Harris was dressed in his fire-retardant black coveralls. Surprisingly, he and Mick Reavers didn't attract too much attention. By the third day of the crisis, the spectators had grown used to seeing heavily armed men going to and fro in black ninja jumpsuits. The two SEALs had left their submachine guns back at the command post, but both still carried their H&K USP .45 caliber handguns in their thigh holsters.

As Harris and Reavers bounded up the steps two at a time, they were met at the top by Charlie Wicker. Wicker turned and opened one of the heavy old doors. Harris and Reavers fell into step behind Wicker, all three men swiveling their heads as they walked into the large old building. Their discerning eyes took an almost instantaneous inventory of all that was around them. Exit signs, windows, strange-looking people—you name it. They did it out of habit. Always know your surroundings.

Wicker approached a bank of elevators. The one on the far left was held for them by a security guard. As they stepped into the elevator, Wicker looked at the security guard and said, "Al, this is Lieutenant Commander Harris."

The balding man stuck out his hand. "Al Turly, Commander. Nice to meet you."

"Same here." Harris grabbed Turly's hand and gave him the requisite bone-crushing handshake. Then, pointing to the mound of flesh next to him, he said, "This big fella is Chief Reavers."

His hand still stinging from Harris's handshake, Turly decided to skip the nicety with the even larger Reavers. When the elevator reached the top floor, Turly led the way down the hall. At the end of the hallway they came upon a door labeled Bell Tower. Extracting a key, Turly opened the door, and they stepped into a stairwell that appeared to have been built not too long after the Civil War. The narrow staircase was flush against the wall on one side and on the other was only a railing. They were inside the dingy bell tower of the grand Old Post Office.

Turly, not wanting to slow the others down, let them take the lead. He had already taken the wiry little one up to the top once, and he thought his heart might leap from his chest. As Turly expected, the three black-clad men marched up the steps two at a time. Within seconds they were out of his sight, only the echoes of their footsteps letting him know they were above him. Turly slowed his pace. Ten months from retirement. It wasn't worth it.

The three SEALs reached the top without so much as breaking a sweat. Wicker climbed up the ladder that was bolted to the wall, and with one hand he pushed open the hatch that led to the bell tower. Pulling himself up and through, he spun around on his butt and stood. Harris was next and then Reavers. All three men stood side by side, looking west out the large aperture. The bell tower atop the Old Post Office had the second most commanding view of all Washington after the one from the Washington Monument. From this eagle's nest they looked straight down Pennsylvania Avenue past Freedom Plaza and Pershing Park, over the southwest corner of the Treasury Building, and there, perfectly bathed in the bright afternoon light, was the White House.

Wicker retrieved a pair of binoculars with a laser range finder from his vest and handed it to his CO. After turning his black baseball cap around, so the brim was out of the way, Harris held the binoculars up to his eyes. The commander of SEAL Team Six zeroed in on the roof of the White House and sought out the tiny rooftop guard booth. After a slight adjustment, the blue hue of the bulletproof Plexiglas was in the crosshairs. Harris paused for a second and watched the hooded man sitting behind the protective glass. Harris's forefinger pressed a button, and a second later three red numbers appeared. Harris handed the binoculars to Reavers and turned to Wicker.

"Eight hundred and twenty meters?"

Wicker nodded confidently. "Yep."

"What's the forecast for tonight?"

"A lazy southeasterly breeze, between two and five knots."

Harris nodded. That was child's play for Wicker. He could hit this shot from almost double the distance at five knots. "What about the glass?"

"It's half an inch. I've shot through it before on the range." Wicker continued his confident stare, eyeballing the White House with his naked eye.

"That's the range; this is real life. We need to know how old that glass is, the manufacturer's testing data, everything we can get our hands on."

Wicker kept his eyes on the White House, supremely confident in his skills—knowing that there were only a handful of men in the whole world that matched him in skill, and none that could exceed.

"The glass was installed in ninety-two and is due to be replaced within the next year. I studied the manufacturer's testing data two years ago and have all the info I need right up here." Wicker tapped his temple with his forefinger. "If that glass was brand-new, I could still do it, but it's been baked by the sun now for seven years. Its strength has been reduced by at least sixty percent. With two fifties we'll be able to drill right through it." Wicker nodded confidently and added, "Hell, the first shot might even get him."

Harris was a little surprised that Wicker already had the stats. "How did you find out about the glass?"

"I called some of my fellow snipers at the Secret Service."

"When?" asked Harris.

"Two days ago." Wicker kept his gaze on the White House.

Harris smiled. He loved it when his men were proactive. "You've been thinking about this shot for that long?"

Wicker turned, a devilish grin spreading across his lips. "I've been thinking about this shot ever since we ran that exercise eight years ago."

Harris knew the exact exercise Wicker was referring to. It had been on his mind since the onset of this entire cluster fuck. Slowly, Harris began to nod. And then with a smile of his own, he looked to Wicker and said, "Don't ever tell anybody that. The boys at the Secret Service might not understand your professional curiosity."

"Oh, they understand." Wicker nodded. "We've talked about this shot a hundred times."

The "boys at the Secret Service" that they were referring to were the men of the countersniper unit, widely regarded as the best professional shooters, from top to bottom, in the world. There wasn't a single shot at the Secret Service that could match Wicker under combat conditions, but in a controlled urban environment, they were awesome.

Harris looked back at the White House. Snipers were a weird lot. Kind of like goaltenders in hockey or pitchers in baseball. They were loners, fiercely independent, and more than a little superstitious. "What do you need to make it happen?"

Wicker pulled several pieces of paper from his vest. Unfolding them, he held them up for his CO. "First thing we have to do is build a shooting platform. With the right men and equipment, I can have it ready by sundown."

Harris looked at the drawings. "What about the noise?"

Wicker reached over and flipped to the second page. "We place a top over the platform and line it with acoustic foam. We leave a nice narrow slit at the front, and we're set. Only about five percent of the report will make its way out of the slit, and that won't travel more than a block, tops."

Harris loved that Wicker was ahead of the game. Handing Wicker the drawing, he slapped him on the back and said, "Good job, Slick. I like it. Make it happen as fast and quiet as you can. Get out of your coveralls, and tell the rest of your boys to wear their civvies." Looking at his watch, he added, "I want you operational by eighteen hundred."

With that Harris started down the hatch, confident that Wicker would have everything in place by the appointed hour. Now came the hard part. He would have to convince the big boys that an exercise he had participated in eight years ago would work today. Harris already had the pitch formed. He would keep it as simple as possible and use SEAL Team Six as the tip of the spear. Delta and HRT would provide the overwhelming force when the time was right.

THE WORDS WEREN'T going to come easy. At least not at first. Anna Rielly was both a proud and a stubborn person, but she was not, as Rapp thought, an ingrate. Milt Adams had closed the door to the stash room, and Rielly was left facing the man who had saved her life.

As Rielly looked at him, she decided she liked him much better when he smiled. In his current serious mood, he looked dangerous. Not just his dark clothes and the various weapons strapped to his lean body, but his chiseled jawline and those dark eyes. The man had an intensity about him that Rielly hadn't noticed before. His tanned weathered face had the strong lines acquired by a man who does not spend his days in an office. It was the eyes, though, that both drew her in and made her want to shiver. Dark pools of brown. So dark they were almost black. Framed on top by two thick eyebrows. This was the man who was capable of killing. The man who had plunged his knife into her assailant.

Rielly's mouth must have been slightly open because it was suddenly void of moisture. She closed it and swallowed hard; then opening it slowly, she said, "I'm sorry for the way I handled that situation earlier. I don't want to seem like I'm"—she paused, struggling to get the next word out—"ungrateful."

Rielly had to look down. It was difficult to look into those dark eyes and make the apology. "I'm not crazy about signing anything. Especially something the government wants me to sign." Rielly looked up and made a halfhearted effort at a smile, but the dark orbs on Rapp's face turned her gaze back down.

"I realize this thing is a lot bigger than me, and if there is anything I can do to help save the rest of the hostages, I'm more than willing to do my part. As far as what happens when this is over . . . if you wish to remain anonymous, I will honor that. If you feel, or whoever you work for feels, that you need to edit my story before I tell it . . ." Rielly was forced to pause again, feeling very uncomfortable with this particular concession. Still looking at the ground, she said, "If you really feel the need to edit out material that you are absolutely sure is too sensitive to report . . . I'll go along. I'll probably do it kicking and screaming, but I'll do it."

Rapp was conflicted. His opinion of the young and attractive Ms. Rielly had already been etched into his mind and filed away. Now it appeared he might have been mistaken. She had been wrong, but now she was correcting that, taking a big step to humble herself and admit it. The ball was back in Rapp's court.

37

HER ELBOWS RESTED heavily on the table. The hum of computers, faxes, scanners, and monitors droned in the background. The control room at Langley was in the midst of a lull. Kennedy's hands cupped her chin, and her eyes were closed. Opening her eyes, she looked at the red digital clock on the wall. It was almost half past noon. She let out a yawn and stretched her arms above her head. Things were about to happen. She had felt it herself and seen it in the look Thomas Stansfield had given her.

The light on her phone blinked once and then began to ring. She grabbed the handset and answered, "Dr. Kennedy."

"Irene, it's Jane. I've been busy trying to get an answer to your question, but things have proved a little more difficult than I thought."

"How so?"

"Well, the subject is not entirely with us."

Kennedy frowned. "Will he be coming back?"

"No." There was a substantial pause and then, "At least, I don't think so." Then in a slightly defensive tone Dr. Hornig added, "You must remember, this is all new, very cutting-edge stuff."

"Did you get anything out if him?"

"From what little I could gather, Harut had no idea what this Yassin fellow's talents were. But please keep in mind, he's not all there."

Irene didn't want to hear excuses; she wanted answers. "Did you get anything out of him?"

"I'm afraid not."

"Okay. If you find anything out, please let me know." Kennedy disconnected the call and dialed an international number. While the secure satellite technology at Langley started the process, Kennedy turned around and checked to see what her boss was doing.

Thomas Stansfield sat comfortably in his chair while Jonathan Brown, the deputy director of central intelligence, relayed a slew of congressional complaints and inquiries. From what little Kennedy heard, she gathered that the congressman and senators on the Hill were demanding to know what in the hell happened last night.

The familiar voice of Colonel Fine answered on the other end, and

Kennedy turned around. "Ben, it's Irene. Have you found anything out on Yassin?"

"Nothing firm. Some rumblings and rumors here and there, but we haven't been able to nail him down."

"Which one are we talking about? The Iraqi or the Palestinian?"

"I have heard nothing back about the Iraqi, but I have several sources who are claiming they have seen the eighteen-year-old Palestinian within the last four days."

"Hmm," pondered Kennedy.

"Let me caution you, though. We have not been able to track him down."

"I know, but we are definitely leaning closer to one than the other."

"My contacts in Iraq are not as deep, Irene. The man could be there, but I need more time to track him down."

Kennedy looked back at Stansfield and let him know that she needed to talk to him. Into the phone, she said, "Ben, I have to run. Thank you for the info, and please let me know the second you find out anything else."

"Before you go," said Fine loudly, "I have something I wish to discuss." Fine paused and then continued. "There are people in my government who are threatening to tear apart the entire peace accord if your country persists with this position of negotiation. We have a very good idea what Aziz's last demand will be, and we are prepared to occupy the territories with troops if it comes to that."

Kennedy stopped everything she was doing. She dissected the colonel's words carefully. Israel was prepared to go to war. "Has your ambassador been informed of this?"

"I do not know."

"Has your prime minister informed our vice president?"

"I do not know."

Kennedy paused momentarily. "Ben, Director Stansfield has the interests of Israel very high on his list, but he is only one man. Now is not a time to play games through back channels. I would suggest that certain people in your government start banging the drum and bang it loudly. They know who to talk to." Kennedy stopped for a moment and added, "Don't worry about your support from Langley. We have never wavered on this issue, and are not about to."

There was a moment of silence and then, "Good. I will pass that along."

"And I appreciate the information, Ben. Please let me know the second you find anything more."

Kennedy hung up the phone and swiveled her chair around. Brown was still talking to Stansfield. Kennedy was not sure about the new deputy director. It wasn't due to a lack of confidence in his skills. He was intelligent and professional. Her issue with Brown lay more in where his bread was buttered. Brown was not an insider at Langley. He had been with the Agency for less than a year. In his early fifties, he was a former federal prosecutor and judge who, after leaving the bench, went to work for one of Washington's poshest law firms, making close to a million dollars a year. After pressing the flesh with all of the bigwigs in Congress for a half dozen years, he had obtained a nomination for the deputy director slot and was confirmed.

It was a safe bet that his allegiance was more with the senators who had confirmed him than with the man he was now talking to. It was that simple fact that kept Kennedy from speaking in front of the man. She waited for several minutes until Brown left, then rose and approached the elevated desk behind her.

Stansfield leaned forward and asked, "What is it?"

General Flood also leaned forward, sensing that Kennedy might have obtained a valuable piece of information.

"I just spoke to Colonel Fine. He's gotten nowhere in terms of the Yassin from Iraq, and with the young Palestinian, they have several contacts who have claimed to have seen him in the last four days."

Flood shook his head and said, "That's it, Thomas. We have to tell him."

Stansfield's face remained passive, and Flood persisted. "It's our duty. Iron Man hasn't come up with anything definitive, but it sure does look like something is going on down in that basement. Aziz doesn't have enough men to tie up one of them down there."

"What about the ventilation duct?" asked Kennedy. "Maybe he's afraid we'll try and use it again."

"Bullshit," grumbled Flood. "All he has to do is booby-trap the only stairwell that leads up from the basement, and he has us boxed in."

Kennedy agreed.

Flood leaned toward Stansfield and said, "We have to tell him, Thomas. We should have told him this morning."

Stansfield looked at the large general. He knew Flood was right but also knew how Vice President Baxter would react. He would wiggle. He would question the validity of their conclusion. He would put off making any decision until he absolutely had to. Despite all of that, Flood was right. They had to tell him.

DALLAS KING SAT across from his boss and watched him talk on the phone. The afternoon sun spilled through the windows of the vice president's study at the Naval Observatory. King was still obsessing over his roll in aiding the terrorists. He had decided only one thing thus far, that he would keep his mouth shut. There wasn't a snowball's chance in hell that he would volunteer what he had done to the FBI. It would do no good. They couldn't turn back the clocks. What he had to do right now was damage control. Who else knew about the late-night excursion? There were the two women of course, but they were bombed. There was Joe, the Secret Service officer who had let them in. King thought about checking up on Joe, but that might make things look worse if the story came out. No. For now, he would sit and do nothing and hope that no one would ever link him to the terrorist.

Aides shuffled in and out of the room on an almost continuous basis. The large dining room and living room of the mansion had been converted into offices for Baxter's support staff and the dozen or so essential personnel who had been displaced when the Old Executive Office Building had been shut down by the Secret Service.

It was one of those essential aides who quietly entered the room and approached King. In a voice low enough to not distract the vice president, she said, "Director Stansfield and General Flood are on the line, and they wish to speak to the vice president immediately."

King stood. "Which line?"

The young woman held up two fingers and began her retreat. King watched her leave. Out of habit he checked out her backside as she sauntered for the door. It was nice. He'd been eyeballing her for the better part of the new year, but knew it would be trouble. Office romances were a big no-no. Stick with the married women, King told himself.

King made his way over to a credenza on the other side of the large study. After running a hand through his hair and checking himself out in an ornate gilt-framed mirror, King grabbed the receiver from the phone and stabbed the blinking red button.

"Director Stansfield, General Flood, Dallas King here."

It was General Flood who spoke first. "Dallas, where is the vice president?"

"He's right here, but he's on the line with the secretary general of the UN."

"Well, tell him we need to speak with him." Flood's voice was even gruffer than normal.

King held the receiver to his left ear and with his right forefinger he smoothed out his eyebrows. Looking into the mirror to check on his grooming, he replied, "As I said, he's on the line with the secretary general, and it's rather important. Is there something I can help you with?"

Flood, the highest-ranking officer in the entire United States military, was used to people jumping to his requests. Add to this the tense situation and a lack of sleep, and the result was predictable.

"Goddamnit," bellowed Flood. "You've got some things to learn about the chain of command, son. When the chairman of the Joint Chiefs calls and says he wants to talk to the vice president, you put him on the phone!"

King pulled the receiver away from his face and looked at it with a frown. Under his breath, he said, "Give me a break." Then into the phone, he replied, "Let me see if he can take your call." Without waiting to see if that was okay, King pressed the hold button and set the phone down. Looking into the mirror one more time, he straightened his tie and checked his perfect white teeth.

Walking across the spacious study, he approached the vice president's desk and gave his boss the proper signal. Baxter looked up and when the moment was right, he said, "Excuse me, Mr. Secretary. Would you hold one moment please?" Baxter covered the phone. "What now?"

"General Flood and Director Stansfield are on line two and they want to talk to you *immediately.*"

"*Immediately.*" Baxter repeated the word in the same tone as King.

"Yep, General Flood has got his undies in a bind about something. He snapped at me when I told him you were busy."

Baxter took his hand off the receiver and said, "Mr. Secretary, I want to continue this conversation, but I must take an urgent call. May I call you back in a few minutes?" Baxter nodded several times while he listened to the secretary general of UN and then said, "Thank you."

King looked down at his boss and said, "I think I'd better listen in on this." Baxter nodded his consent, and King quickly crossed the room and stood poised above the phone on the credenza. When his boss reached down to punch the proper line, King did the same.

Baxter said, "Hello, General Flood."

"Mr. Vice President, I'm on the line with Director Stansfield. We've come across some troubling information that we must bring to your attention." In less than a minute Flood brought Baxter up to speed on what was going on in regard to Mustafa Yassin and the information provided by the Israelis and CIA.

Dallas King watched his boss silently from across the room. He listened to Flood, and in some twisted way the news excited him. King knew it shouldn't, but this was real high drama, and he was one of just a few who were privy to this jarring information. The president was not as safe as they had thought.

General Flood moved from stating the facts into stating his case, and he did so with two sentences. "Mr. Vice President, under no circumstances can we allow the president to fall into the hands of these terrorists. Delta Force and HRT are ready to retake the White House on your order."

Vice President Baxter let out the moan of a man who could take no more bad news. And then after a moment or so of fidgeting, he asked, "How can we be sure? Aziz has said nothing about the president in any of his demands."

"We can't be sure," answered Flood. "But we sure as hell can't take the risk of letting the president become a hostage."

"What if this information is wrong?" Baxter looked up at King. "We still have quite a few hostages in there, and from what you've told me, the odds of them surviving a takedown are not good."

"Sir, at this point I see no other alternative. We cannot, under any circumstance, allow Rafique Aziz to get his hands on President Hayes."

There was a long pause while Baxter looked up at King. Finally he sighed into the phone and asked, "What is it that you want from me, General Flood?"

"I want you to do what's right. I want you to give me the green light to retake the White House."

King was shaking his head vigorously at his boss. No one was going to commit to anything until he and the vice president had a chance to discuss it. Vice President Baxter looked up at King and nodded. Then into the phone, he said, "General, this information seems a little thin to me. As I've already said, you have full authority to move your people into position, and to collect intelligence, just so long as you don't endanger the lives of the hostages. But I want to make myself clear on this once again. I am the only person who will authorize the takedown of the White House." Baxter straightened up in his chair. "Am I clear on this?"

"Yes, you are, sir," answered a frustrated Flood. "That has never been in doubt . . . That's not what's at issue here. What is at issue is the safety of the president of the United States." In firm voice Flood added, "I am asking you for the authorization to take back the White House. I am asking you to prevent President Hayes from falling into the hands of Rafique Aziz."

In a soft voice, Baxter answered, "General, this is not an easy decision. I need some time to think about it."

"But, sir," snapped Flood. "We might not have the time."

Baxter shot back, "I am running the show here, General Flood, and I will decide how much time we may or may not have. Now, I would suggest that while I'm consulting with my aides, you try and find out if this threat to President Hayes is real or imagined. I mean, for Christ's sake, two days ago your own people stood up and told me he could last a month in that bunker." Baxter shook his head.

Barely able to restrain himself, Flood looked to Stansfield for some support. The director of the CIA simply shook his head. Into the phone the general asked, "What do you want me to do, sir?"

"I want you to keep me informed, and make sure you do nothing to precipitate any more violence from Aziz."

"Yes, sir."

With that, the conversation was over. General Flood had hung up without waiting to see if Baxter had anything to add. Dallas King put the handset back in its cradle and walked toward his sullen-faced boss.

"You handled that perfectly." When King reached the desk, he added, "Off the top of my head, we have several things working in our favor. First, this information they have sounds a little thin to me. I mean we can't trust the Israelis for shit right now. They'd just as soon see us nuke the place. And secondly"—King tapped his chin with his finger—"there's an angle here. Is the president's life more valuable than fifty of his fellow countrymen? There's an awfully strong argument to be made against the imperial presidency. No one American life is greater than any other single American life."

Baxter frowned and said, "Come on, Dallas. Who's going to buy that load of crap?"

"Your average Joe, that's who." King pointed his finger at his boss. "Even if what Flood says is true, which I doubt, since those guys can't seem to find their ass with both hands, that doesn't mean we need to storm the place. With the exception of Marge's big fuck-up, this Aziz guy has been pretty reasonable. So far he hasn't asked for anything that we can't go back and fix later, and the polls tell us that, with the exception of a bunch of right-wing extremists, the American people want to see this thing resolved peacefully. Our job here is to continue to walk this fine line, Sherman. If they can't give you solid proof that the president is in imminent danger, I wouldn't budge an inch. We'll get these UN resolutions passed by the end of the day, and in the morning Aziz will release the next group of hostages. That's two-thirds you will have saved."

King stopped and looked out the window. A thought had just occurred to him. Maybe he was cheering for the wrong results. If the terrorists were killed, most of his problem would be solved.

"Dallas, what are you thinking?" Baxter asked.

King shook his head and turned his attention back to his boss. "Nothing. I was just trying to figure something out."

JACK WARCH WAS on his fourth set of crunches, the modern-day version of the much hated sit-up. He had considered skipping his daily regimen, but decided he had nothing better to do. Warch did four hundred crunches every day of the week except Sunday, and on alternate days he threw in two hundred push-ups, a three-to-five-mile jog, and some stretching. He had it down to a science, which allowed him to stay in shape without spending hours at the gym.

As Warch finished his crunches, he eyed the pile of weapons sitting on the table across the room. The sight was irritating. All of that hardware and a room full of the best-trained bodyguards in the world and the president wanted them to surrender. It was ingrained in Warch's psyche to win, not to lose. Coming from the old Vince Lombardi school of "Show me a good loser, and I'll show you a loser," Warch couldn't stand the thought of them raising their hands in surrender. He had risen to the most coveted post in the Secret Service by sheer dogged determination, and he was sure now there had to be a better alternative than surrendering.

That's when it hit him, with three more crunches to go. Warch stopped, hands firmly clasped behind his neck, staring at the mound of black steel on the table. Some of the most accurate and lethal firepower made and nine highly trained individuals. Warch's mind started to scramble. He saw a crack, a slight opening, a way to pull off a Hail Mary. Jumping to his feet, he almost blurted out his idea, but forced himself to sit down on his bunk and think things through thoroughly. He had to have this planned. He had to be able to head off all objections and sell it to the president.

38

STANSFIELD ALLOWED GENERAL Flood to blow off some steam. As Flood paced back and forth in front of his desk, Stansfield nodded from time to time in an effort to let Flood know he agreed with him. The elderly director of central intelligence had expected Baxter's unwillingness to give them the green light, and in his usual analytical way, Stansfield was already looking three moves ahead. He could have forewarned the general how Baxter would respond but felt an angry General Flood would be better than a calm one. Things were coming to a head, and some decisions needed to be made.

Now would come the hard part. Stansfield knew Vice President Baxter would never pull the trigger. In his opinion, they should never have started down this road to begin with, but now they had to do something before it got worse. Baxter was maneuvering, trying to buy as much time as possible. The fact that he was doing it during a crisis with such far-reaching implications was almost unimaginable to Stansfield, and that was making his difficult decision much easier.

Thomas Stansfield was contemplating doing something that he had done only one other time in the fifty-plus years he had served his country. It was something that could end his career in public disgrace, but he was willing to take that chance. He still had his ace in the hole, and now was the time to use it.

General Flood looked like a football coach chewing out his team at halftime. Stansfield watched him walk back and forth, shaking his fist and letting a stream of expletives flow from his mouth. Stansfield stayed quiet, letting him take as much time as needed. Gradually the expletives became fewer and the pacing slowed.

The general approached, looking miffed. "You sure as hell are taking this well. It's not as if things weren't bad enough, and now we find out the president isn't safe. I mean, for Christ's sake, it doesn't take a genius to figure out that Aziz brought along this guy for this exact purpose. Now we know why he spaced the demands out the way he did. He needed time."

Stansfield nodded and moved in to test the water. "Yes, but what can we do about it? If Baxter doesn't give us the approval, we are left without recourse."

"There's nothing we can do about it. That idiot's calling the shots, and unless we can find a way to convince him to attack, this will only get worse."

Stansfield thought Flood to be a good soldier. The thought of ordering an attack without the approval of Baxter would not even enter his mind. With Stansfield, it was different. Spies were used to operating under a different set of rules; they were used to looking for creative ways to solve problems. Stansfield was not entirely free to do as he wished, but he had significantly more latitude than the general did. Although Stansfield's idea was clearly in violation of the orders Baxter had given him, he had already made up his mind, and he would go it alone. The others had too much to lose. Nearing eighty, Stansfield knew the end was not far off. If ever there was a time to stick his neck out, this was it.

Looking up at the general with an almost mystical expression, Stansfield said, "There is one other option."

Flood eyed him with skepticism. He had looked feverishly for a way out and had found none. "I don't see any way out of this other than hoping Baxter comes to his senses."

"There is one way, and it's right in front of us."

Flood was intrigued. "Enlighten me."

Stansfield shook his head ever so slightly and said, "I think it best if you remain in the dark on this one."

Flood's hands moved to his hips, and a strange look washed over his face. He paused, wondering for a moment if he was reading Stansfield correctly. "What do you have up your sleeve, Thomas?"

Stansfield looked out the large window behind his desk. Without turning back to Flood, the director of the CIA said, "We both know what needs to be done, General, and there's no sense in risking two when one will suffice." Slowly looking back over his shoulder, he said, "I think now would be a good time for you and General Campbell to go visit the front lines. Maybe have a talk with HRT and Delta. See how they're doing. Make sure they're ready to move when the authority is given."

Flood squinted, part of him wanting to know what Thomas Stansfield was up to, but another part of him wanting nothing to do with whatever the director was planning.

"Thomas, what are you up to?"

Stansfield gingerly walked around the desk and placed his thin hand on Flood's substantial biceps. Turning him toward the door, Stansfield started to walk with him.

"I have the best of intentions. Do not worry." Several steps closer to the door and he added, "Just make sure the boys are ready to go when the time comes."

LESS THAN a minute later they were standing in the control room. Flood had informed Campbell that they were going to visit the troops. HRT would be first and then Delta. The ranger assumed it had something to do with the call to Vice President Baxter and hoped they were about to get the green light. He quickly gathered his things and on the way out the door held his encrypted cell phone up to Kennedy and reminded her to keep him informed of any changes.

After the two generals and several of their aides were gone, Kennedy looked at her boss, who was standing one step above her. Stansfield looked back at her with his tired old eyes.

"Did Baxter give you the assault authority?"

"No, I'm afraid not."

Kennedy's lips pursed. "Why was General Flood in such a hurry to get out of here?"

"He had some things to take care of." Stansfield looked at his watch and then asked, "Is Mitch on the line?"

"Yes."

Stansfield thought it through one last time, making sure he had all of his bases covered. Then looking around the dark room, he said, "Irene, tell everyone to take a fifteen-minute break."

"Everyone?" questioned Kennedy. He surely didn't mean everyone.

"Everyone," stated Stansfield calmly and coolly. "I want the room cleared."

Kennedy, cut from the same cloth as her boss, knew the man did not mince or waste his words. She could only assume he had a very good reason for his rather unusual request and immediately went about the task of clearing the room. Rather than making a boisterous announcement to the entire group, she started with the front row and worked her way to the rear, telling everyone to finish up what they were working on and then head out. No one questioned her.

It took just under two minutes, and when everyone was gone, Kennedy and Stansfield were left standing alone in the dimly lit room. The wall of monitors at the front of the room cast a blue hue across everything.

Stansfield looked down at his protégé and said simply, "You too, Irene."

Kennedy was surprised. Her security clearance couldn't get any higher. There was nothing she couldn't hear or view unless it was compartmentalized. She studied her boss intently and wondered what could possibly be going on. Why would he need to be alone in this room? Stansfield stood in front of her like a statue, giving nothing away. Kennedy finally stepped for the door, her mind trying to retrace the steps that led up to this unusual situation.

RAPP HAD AWKWARDLY accepted Anna Rielly's apology. Somewhere in the back of his mind it registered that asking her to not tell this story was impossible. She would have to tell it to one degree or another— as long as she now accepted the conditions. From the corner the secure field radio beeped several times, announcing that an encrypted communication was received. Rapp reached over and snatched the handset.

"Yep."

"Mitchell, it's Thomas. Have you found a way to verify our most recent problem?"

Rapp was a little surprised that Stansfield had used his first name. "Maybe. Milt seems to think he might have a way, but it might be hard to pull it off from a logistical standpoint."

There was no immediate reply. After a moment Stansfield began to speak in a very slow and deliberate voice. "Mitchell, you've sacrificed a lot over the last ten or so years, and I'm very grateful for that." There was another pause. "I'm going to ask you to do something, and I don't want you to discuss it with anyone else." Stansfield stopped again, letting the gravity of his request sink in. "Am I understood?"

"Yes, sir."

"First, we must verify if President Hayes is safe in his bunker. Second, we need to reestablish radio contact with him. All radio and phone traffic from the bunker has been jammed, as you know. Find and disable that unit so I can speak directly to the president."

Rapp clutched the phone. "What are my rules of engagement?"

"I would prefer it if you did it as quietly as possible, but use whatever force you see fit. Just make sure you get the president back on line."

The magic words reverberated through Rapp's mind. He was free to do as he saw fit. Now he could really get things done. Almost as quickly as he had begun to celebrate, he saw that something didn't fit. "Does anyone else know about this?"

"Just you and me."

Rapp closed his eyes. This was unusual. "What about Irene?"

"No. Just the two of us."

"So I'll be operating without a net for a while."

"I'm afraid so." Stansfield wasn't pleased with this, but there was no other way.

Rapp nodded while he thought about his lack of backup. *Fuck it,* he said to himself. *You're used to working alone.*

Into the thin receiver Rapp said, "I'll take care of it, sir, but make sure the cavalry is ready. Things could get real ugly in here."

"I will, Mitchell, and please be careful."

"Always." Rapp replaced the receiver and looked up at Adams.

Some weird shit must be happening on the other side, he thought. Ticking through the possibilities of what might have precipitated Stansfield's unusual call, Rapp stopped a short while down the list. No sense in clouding the mind. He had enough to worry about right here.

Pointing at the blueprints, Rapp said, "We have to find a way to check this out."

39

BARELY A HALF hour had passed since Stansfield's edict. Rapp had to remind himself continually to be more cautious as he and Adams searched the blueprints for a way to accomplish the task. Rielly had edged her way over from her nest in the corner and now lay on her stomach, her hands under her chin. Every once in a while her white stockinged feet would kick up in the air behind her like a little teenager's. She was playing it smart for the moment, saying nothing and listening to everything. She had worked her way back into the group.

On at least three occasions Rapp had run through the different options, none of them all that appealing, and now resigned himself to take the direct route—the route that would most quickly accomplish his task but also endanger the lives of the remaining hostages. Feeling as if he'd been pent up in a cage since he'd landed at Andrews two days ago, it was difficult for him to resist the desire simply to go down to the basement, shoot the guard, shoot this Yassin fellow, and disable the scrambler. If he couldn't find another way, it might be the only solution, but there had to be another way, or the whole thing would end in a bloodbath.

Rapp was beginning to resign himself to what he had known when the whole mess had started. Take Aziz, enough Semtex to blow up the whole building twice, and you end up with a bunch of dead hostages. Why even risk the assault team? Just let the idiot blow himself up and end the thing.

Milt Adams flipped several sheets over and studied something. Rapp watched him, then asked, "What?"

Adams looked at the drawing and then up at the blank wall. He was trying to visualize something. Looking back down, he said, "This is the hallway on the third level. It runs down like this and takes a ninety-degree turn to the left." Adams tapped the spot with his thin finger. "There is a recessed vent here . . . at least, I think there is."

"What do you mean you 'think.' Isn't it marked?"

Adams shook his head. "No. That's why I'm saying I 'think' there is." Adams closed his eyes again, forcing himself to try to remember what the hallway looked like. "I really think there's a vent there." Adams tapped the spot again.

"Why isn't it marked?"

"These aren't the final blueprints. If I remember right, they were worried that there would be too much moisture in the hallway if they didn't have some ventilation. You see, this entire hall was added when they put the bunker in, and the bunker's environmental systems are buried underneath it so they can't be compromised." Adams brought his finger up and ran it along his bottom lip. "I'm pretty sure they spliced into the house's regular system through the floor right above." Adams pulled one of the sheets back over. It was the layout of the second basement.

He searched for the right spot and said, "This is where they would have done it. They would have just cut in a down chute and brought it in from the second basement." Adams grabbed the next sheet, showing the first basement, and pulled it over. His eyes darted excitedly back and forth over the drawing. "This could be perfect."

"What?" asked an impatient Rapp, wishing Adams would explain what good a little vent could do.

Adams brought his hands up as if he were a quarterback signaling how far to go for a first down. He slid the two hands forward and placed them on the outside of Rapp's shoulders. Then with a frown he said, "You're too damn big."

Frustrated, Rapp asked, "Milt, what in the hell are you talking about?"

"I'm almost sure this vent is there, but it's only eighteen inches wide. Your shoulders are all that plus a couple."

"Back up." With a confused look, Rapp asked, "Where will this vent get us?"

Adams flipped back to the drawings of the third basement. "This vent drops right down at the corner. If you could get to it, you would have a clear shot into the anteroom of the bunker . . . that's assuming the first door is open."

"But you're saying I won't fit."

"No. You could lower me down, but—" Adams stopped and rolled his eyes.

"You'd sneeze, and they'd hear it."

"Afraid so." Adams nodded.

Rapp swore under his breath. He would have done almost anything to get a look at what was going on in that anteroom. Rapp glanced up from the blueprint and looked at Rielly. She looked like a teenybopper at a slumber party with her ponytail and sweats. He looked at the rest of her body and was willing to bet that Rielly weighed a buck five tops. It took Rapp only a second to decide it was worth it. If she was going to write a story, she might as well earn it.

RETURNING TO THE *scene of the crime* couldn't have been a more accurate description. Salim Rusan had found a spot for his ambulance at the end of a line that ran almost a block long. Immediately to his right was the Willard Hotel, the Washington, D.C., landmark that boasted it had served cocktails to the likes of Abraham Lincoln, Mark Twain, Buffalo Bill, and countless others. In the middle of the block was the Willard Office Building, and next to that, on the corner, was Rusan's former place of employment, the Washington Hotel.

Across the street to his left was Pershing Park, named after General "Black Jack" Pershing, the commander of the American Expeditionary Force in Europe during World War I. The park was lined on two of its four sides with fire trucks. The firemen that were assigned to the trucks lounged about on the green grass of the park, some of them playing catch with a football, others with a bright orange Frisbee. A sandwich truck kept the firemen and ambulance drivers filled with coffee, soda pop, and a variety of sandwiches, soups, and microwavable dishes. Four D.C. police squads blocked the intersection barely thirty feet behind Rusan's ambulance at the corner of Pennsylvania and Fourteenth Street.

Salim Rusan had returned to within two blocks of the White House. He slouched behind the wheel of the ambulance, a book perched on the bottom half of the steering wheel, and pair of headphones covering his ears. He was hoping to avoid conversation. A very thin cover story had been crafted, one that would not stand up well after two or three well-pointed questions, especially in an industry where, Rusan assumed, many of the drivers knew each other. Fraternizing with the other paramedics could get hairy, so he would keep to himself.

Rusan twisted his wrist and looked at his cheap digital watch. It was approaching two in the afternoon. He had been sitting in his spot for almost three hours. So far so good. The other drivers congregated from time to time on the sidewalk or across the street at the sandwich truck. Several of them even played catch with the firemen. As he had thought, they seemed to know each other. The ploy of being immersed in a novel was working thus far, but he couldn't sit in the ambulance forever. There were several things he had to take care of, and that meant taking a walk among the enemy.

Rusan checked his side mirror again. The reporters and curious onlookers were milling about like cattle behind a police barricade one block back to the east at the corner of Thirteenth Street and Pennsylvania. Rusan could make out a cop sitting atop his mount eyeing the crowd. If he had time, he would have to try to plant one of the devices near the crowd. The key was to get people running in every direction—toward the White House and away from it. Looking across Pennsylvania Avenue, Rusan admired the shiny red fire trucks, lined up one after another. What a wealthy country. Wealthy and selfish. Selfish and greedy. It would be nice to sneak a bomb under one of the trucks and watch the whole row explode one after another. That would cause some serious confusion. But that was out of the question. Too many firemen. Too many of them milling about. Someone would see him.

Rusan checked his watch again. A nervous habit. The black digital letters hadn't change since the last time he'd checked, just forty seconds earlier. It was time to put the book away and get to work. Keeping the headphones on, Rusan stepped through the small passageway into the back of the ambulance. The gurney sat latched to the middle of the floor and the side compartments were all secured and locked. Using a small key, Rusan unlocked one of the cabinets and pulled out a plastic toolbox. Typically, it would have been filled with medical supplies to treat accident victims, but instead it was filled with small bombs that had been designed by Aziz. They were ingenious yet simple. Each bomb consisted of Semtex, a blasting cap, and a pager that acted as both the receiver and the power source. The bombs could be activated either by Rusan or Aziz from within the White House or, Allah forbid, someone dialing a wrong number and then punching in the wrong code, which the odds were astronomically against.

Rusan reached down and with his hand scraped the freshly ground coffee beans to the side. The smell of the coffee would help confuse any canines that the FBI might use to check for bombs. As an extra precaution Rusan had also rubbed cayenne pepper on the tires and back tailgate before embarking. If one of the pooches got a sniff of the pepper, they would want nothing to do with the truck.

Packed in the coffee grounds were six bombs. Two were shaped to be placed under toilet bowl lids: thin sheets, one inch thick with the pager and blasting cap imbedded in the claylike explosive. These two sheets of Semtex were wrapped individually in wax paper. Underneath the two sheets were four cans of diet Coke. The top of each had been carefully removed, and the cans had been packed with the malleable explosive, pager, and blasting cap.

Rusan picked up a black fanny pack that was lying on top of the gurney and carefully slid the two sheets of Semtex into the pack. After zipping it closed, he climbed back into the front seat and sat there for a minute. When he had gathered the nerve, he opened his door and stepped out into the sunlight. He sauntered around the rear of the truck, like a man who did aerobics twice a day, seven days a week. His tight pants and shirt, white hair, pierced right ear, and tattoos announced to all his sexual orientation.

Skipping up the steps of the Willard Hotel, Rusan pushed through the revolving door. When he stepped into the opulent lobby, he noticed two D.C. cops. Rusan smiled at them as he walked across the tile floor. He had scouted everything out. He knew exactly where he was going and where he would place the first four bombs. He continued across the lobby and up a short flight of stairs. The hotel was closed to the public because it was within the three-block perimeter that had been set up around the White House. When he entered the men's room, he quickly checked to make sure he was alone, which he was.

Once in the stall he had prechosen, Rusan pulled off the ceramic tank cover and laid it upside down on the toilet seat. He wiped the condensation off the lid and then carefully extracted the first bomb from his fanny pack. It fit inside the lid precisely. Rusan had taken photos of the lid to make sure there were no mistakes. Pressing the Semtex into place, Rusan made sure the bomb was affixed to as much of the surface as possible, and then he extracted a roll of duct tape. At each end of the bomb there were two inches of uncovered ceramic. Rusan cut three pieces, laying each one across the Semtex and making sure it was firmly attached to the underside of the cover. When he was done, he put the duct tape back and replaced the lid. Satisfied, Rusan unzipped his pants and began to relieve himself. One down, three to go.

40

IT HAD TAKEN almost no effort to convince Rielly. Adams actually made several attempts to douse her enthusiasm, but she would have none of it. She was in. Rapp wasn't sure if she wanted to do it out of patriotism, sympathy for the remaining hostages, or professional greed. He hoped it was one of the first two and not the latter.

The plan came together in short order. Adams was a natural problem solver with the tedious mind of an engineer. Rapp, with his practical experience, tried to simplify every aspect of the operation, knowing that the more complicated it became the stronger the chance that it would fail. For her part, Rielly listened well and asked pointed questions when needed.

Rapp had told them, "This is simple recon. Nothing fancy, just take a look and then get out." He then went on to brief Rielly on how they would proceed, and then before leaving the stash room, he gave her one more chance to back out. She didn't waver for a second. With everything covered and the clock ticking, Rapp grabbed the proper gear and gave Adams the go-ahead signal.

Adams slid back the bolt, and Rapp was the first one into the closet. Having already checked the surveillance units, they knew no one else was currently on the second or third floors. They moved quickly and quietly across the hall and into the small elevator. Rielly was in sweat socks and made no noise. When they arrived in the first basement, the doors slid open and Adams went to work with the snake. Rapp and Adams were working well as a team, but now with Rielly as the third wheel, it was another variable to worry about.

Adams retracted the snake, and over his shoulder he whispered, "All clear."

Rapp asked, "We go to the right, halfway down the hall?"

"Yep."

"Good," whispered Rapp. "Here's the routine." Rapp looked to Rielly, who was no more than a foot away. "When we open this door, I step out first. I sweep to the left and then the right. When I give you two the signal to move out, you go. Milt in the lead; you with your right hand on his right shoulder." Rapp was happy to see that her eyes were open wide, a sign that she was paying attention. "You keep that hand on his shoulder and keep your eyes on the back of his head. If he speeds up, you speed up; if he slows down, you slow down; and if he crouches, you get down. If I have to start shooting, I don't want to worry about you jumping out in front of me."

Rielly nodded and then blinked for the first time in a while. All of a sudden she didn't think this was such a good idea. Either it was colder down here or she was getting the chills from fright. Rapp asked her something, and she stared back at him with a blank expression.

"Are you nervous?"

Rielly nodded, eyes wide open.

"Good." Rapp grinned. "You should be." He grabbed her right hand and placed it on Adams's shoulder. "Just follow Milt, and everything will be fine."

Rapp cracked the door just an inch at first and looked down the hallway. With nothing in sight, he opened the door another foot and peered in the other direction. With his MP-10 leveled in his left hand, he opened the door the rest of the way and stepped out into the hallway. After checking both directions again, his right hand shot up and pointed for Adams and Rielly to move out.

Adams started out on cue, his bald head scrunched down between his shoulders as if bullets might start whizzing over his cranium at any moment, the all important S-key in his right hand. Rielly mimicked his posture and scampered behind him on the balls of her stockinged feet. As soon as they were clear, Rapp closed the nondescript door that concealed the elevator and fell in behind them. Within seconds Adams had stopped at another door and was inserting his key. He fumbled with it for a second, his hands shaking slightly. After one misfire, he stuck the key all the way in and turned the knob. Adams yanked the door open and was immediately pushed inside the room by Rielly, who was being pushed by Rapp.

Rapp pulled the door shut and looked around the rectangular-shaped storage room. Rielly was doing the same and whispered, "I thought we were going to the China Room."

"No." Adams shook his head. "The china storage room." He approached one of the many wheeled gray plastic containers that stood about four feet tall. Adams pulled off the protective cloth cover and revealed a collection of plates, saucers, and cups. "These things are spring-loaded." Adams picked up a china dinner plate. "When they decide which china they want for an event, they just wheel this whole thing into the kitchen elevator and they take it upstairs."

Rielly looked around the room. "All of these contain sets of china?"

"Yep."

"That's great." Rapp was already moving several of containers out of his way so he could get to the wall where the vent was located. Adams joined in, and they passed the wheeled containers from one to the other. While they were doing so, Rapp looked at a second door, located on the wall to his right, and asked, "Is that what I think it is?"

"Yep." Adams nodded as he looked up for a second.

"Good. I think it's gonna come in real handy." Rapp moved the last container and saw the vent cover on the bottom of the wall. It looked to be about a foot and a half wide and maybe a foot tall. Rapp stepped out of the way, and Adams moved in. Dropping down to one knee, he pulled out a small cordless drill and quickly backed out both screws. With his fingers, he pulled the slatted cover off and dropped all the way down to his stomach. With a flashlight in hand, he stuck his arm in first and then half of his head. After bouncing the light off the duct work for a couple of seconds, he found what he was looking for. The down chute that led to the lower floors and eventually the HVAC unit in the basement.

Adams pulled his head out and looked at Rapp, who was kneeling next to him. "It's right where I thought it was. Ten feet down this way, go straight down two floors, and she has to crawl about a dozen feet, and there's the vent."

"Which way does she go when she hits the third level?"

Adams jerked his thumb. "She keeps going the same way."

Rapp looked at his watch and said, "All right." Then turning to Rielly, he said, "Last chance to back out."

Rielly grinned reluctantly and looked at the small opening that Adams was lying next to. "I'm ready."

Rapp looked at her and again wondered what her motivation was. Standing there in the president's oversized West Point sweats, she did not fit the image of the brave and bold. Rapp thought she looked scrawny. He had to hand it to her, though; whether it was professional motivation, sense of obligation to her fellow hostages, or just good old Catholic guilt, the woman was tough. She'd had the crap kicked out of her, was almost raped, and yet here she was, willing to go right back into the fray.

Rapp nodded at her with admiration and said, "Give me a couple of minutes, and we'll get you on your way."

Rapp took off his fanny pack and laid out the climbing rope and one of the surveillance units.

"Is she going to have enough light in there?"

Adams thought about it for a second. "Yeah. It spills through the vents about every ten to fifteen feet."

"Good." Holding the rope up, Rapp turned to Rielly and said, "Go lie down over there by the vent, and we'll tie this around your ankles." Rapp cut a four-foot section from the end of the rope and tied one end to Rielly's right ankle and the other to her left. When he was satisfied with the knots, he tied the rope to the middle of the four-foot section. This allowed Rielly to move her legs independently, which would have been impossible if her ankles were tied together.

After asking her how the knots felt, Rapp asked, "Any questions before we get started?"

Rielly looked up from her position on the floor. "Yeah, how in the hell do I signal for you guys to pull me back up?"

Rapp frowned. "That's a good question. How about if you tug three times on the rope?"

"How?" Rielly craned her neck backward and looked into the duct. "There isn't enough room for me to do that."

"Yeah, I suppose you're right." Looking to Adams, Rapp asked, "Any ideas?"

Adams thought about it for a second, his lips scrunched up. Finally he said, "Yeah. I got one." Adams then sat and began taking his boots off. He took out the left bootlace, then the right, then tied them together. He tied one end to the long rope and the other one he loosely knotted around Rielly's neck. "When you want us to take you back up, tug on this three times."

Rielly nodded and Rapp said, "Good thinking, Milt." Then looking down at Rielly, he said, "Down this way about ten feet and then straight down until you hit the bottom. Now, remember when you reach the third level, you're going to need to turn yourself around one hundred and eighty degrees so you can bend at the waist. Then once you get back into the lateral duct, you can spin back onto your stomach." Rapp mimicked the maneuver with his hand. "From there, you crawl down to the first grate, and that's where you should have a view into the room just outside the bunker. Don't hang around long. This should take no more than a minute. Note how many people you see, if any, and what type of equipment. Then tug on the shoestring, and we'll pull you right back up."

Rielly nodded, her face tense with nervousness.

"And don't forget to flip back over on your back so you can make the turn when we're pulling you back up."

"All right, let's get going before I change my mind." Rielly rolled over onto her stomach and started squeezing into the vent. "Three tugs." That was it, and then she wiggled her thin body into the air duct.

It was cramped and dusty. Rielly doubted that Rapp could have fit in the duct, and if he could have, there wouldn't have been any room left for him to maneuver. It didn't take long to reach the shaft. As Rapp had said, it was maybe ten feet. Rielly paused at the top, only her fingertips and chin hanging over the edge. There was just enough light for her to see the bottom. It wasn't as far as she had expected. Slowly she started down. Her arms first, her head, then her whole upper body. After that the rope became tight and Rapp and Adams began to lower her. Rielly remembered what Rapp had said, and when she neared the bottom, she spun herself around so she could bend at the waist and make the turn.

She pulled herself into the lateral duct and rested for a second. The knots felt a little tight on her ankles, but were bearable. After gathering herself, she spun back onto her stomach, and that was when she heard it. A whining noise. The sound of machinery working. The sound of a drill. Rielly's heart rate quickened. The first vent was just ahead on her right. From where she was positioned, she felt as though she could almost reach out and touch it.

With some reservation she inched forward several feet and stopped. The noise had not gone away. As slowly as she could, Rielly scooted forward an inch at a time, using all of her concentration to make sure no noise was made. The duct became brighter with the light from the hallway. As she neared the grate, she grew nervous at how well she could see her hands.

Approaching the vent, she could start to see the off-white wall of hallway. The cover had a series of vertical slats that were angled to force the air down. Rielly laid her head flat so she could try to get a look straight down the hallway and into the bunker. What she saw caused her to hold her breath. Straight ahead, just down the hall, was the shiny vault door to the president's bunker, and attached to it were the objects that were making the noise she had been hearing. Drills of some sort. Three of them. One big and two small. Rielly moved her head around and tried to get better angles of the anteroom but could find none. On the floor there appeared to be a variety of toolboxes and some tanks. She could see only part of the room because the first door was not swung all the way open.

Rielly was finishing her inventory of what little she could see and was preparing to reach for the string around her neck when a man appeared. He came into her view from a part of the room that she could not see. Rielly's first reaction was to move back a little out of fear that he might be able to see her. She quickly realized this was stupid and told herself to calm down. The man, who looked more like a plumber than a terrorist, approached the drills with a cup in his hand. He touched the casings of each one with his hand and then went about measuring their progress with a tape measure.

Oh, this was going to be one hell of a story, Rielly thought to herself. She watched the man for another couple seconds and then tugged on the shoestring three times. After a slight pause she began sliding back down the vent.

JACK WARCH HAD decided on a course of action. He wanted to build a consensus among his agents first and then bring his plan to the president. He didn't want any surprised faces if the president asked them for their opinion. Warch had taken a minute or two with each agent, and all of them had enthusiastically backed their boss's idea.

Now came the hard part. President Hayes was sitting next to Valerie Jones on one of the couches playing a game of gin. Before walking over, Warch checked the door one more time. All indications were that they were running out of time.

Walking across the carpeting, Warch stopped just on the other side of one of the longer couches and cleared his throat. When the president looked up, he said, "Excuse me, sir. Do you have a second?"

The president looked back at the discard pile and said, "Sure." Hayes closed his hand up and set it facedown on the table. "Excuse me, Val." After getting up, he walked around the couches and joined Warch, who had walked over to the corner by the bathroom.

"What is it, Jack?"

"Sir, I want you to hear me out before you say anything." Warch gave his boss a stern look that told him he was very serious. Hayes nodded, and Warch continued. "I have an idea. One that I think will work, but it's going to take some balls on our part and a little bit of risk."

"Okay, let's hear it."

"I want to start out by saying that just sitting here is not a good option. Every one of my agents is willing to sacrifice his life for you, so I want you to stop thinking about us. We volunteered for this duty and we all knew what the risks were when we signed."

Hayes started to shake his head. "I'm not going to change my mind, Jack. There's been enough bloodshed. When that door opens, we are going to surrender peacefully and take our chances."

Warch snapped at the president, "Let me finish!"

Hayes backed up a half a step in surprise and nodded his consent for the special agent to continue.

Warch composed himself and started again. "We," he said, pointing to himself, "are not what is at issue here. You are what is at issue, and not just you as a person but you as the president. In the big picture, all of our lives"—Warch pointed to the other agents in the room—"don't add up to one president. The president must be protected at all costs. That's my first point." Warch held up his forefinger. "My second point is that just laying our weapons down and surrendering doesn't guarantee us anything. Who's to say they won't line us up and shoot every single one of us, including you?"

The president thought about it for a moment and then said, "There are no guarantees, Jack, but I don't see any other alternative."

"I have one. It's a little daring, but it's a heck of a lot better than sitting around and waiting for them to open the door."

"What is it?"

"It's something they'll never expect. We have nine highly trained agents in this room. Three of them have served on the Counter Assault Team and have extensive training in hostage situations. My proposal is"—Warch paused and took a big breath—"that instead of waiting for them to get this door open, we open it ourselves and catch them off guard."

The president frowned.

"Hear me out, sir. We have the firepower to get you out of here, and we'll have the element of surprise on our side."

Hayes folded his arms across his chest and thought about it for a moment. Looking at Warch, he said, "Tell me more. If we're going to do this, we need a game plan."

WHEN THEY PULLED her out of the vent, her black sweat suit was covered in dust, as was a healthy portion of her ponytail. Rielly flipped over onto her back and sat up. Rapp and Adams were poised just above her, eagerly awaiting the report.

Remembering to keep her voice at a whisper, Rielly nodded her head vigorously. "They're doing it. They've made it through that outer door you told me about, and they're working on the big shiny door that leads to the bunker."

"With what?" asked Adams.

"I'm not sure." Rielly gestured with her hands. "I think they're drills. At least that's what they sounded like. The guy who's down there pulled out a tape measure and held it up to the door."

Adams tried to ask another question, but Rapp stuck his hand out and stopped him. "From the top," he said to Rielly. "What did you see?"

Rielly took a deep breath and let her hands fall to her lap. "I saw three objects attached to the door. Like I said, I think they were drills. On the floor there were two boxes . . . like toolboxes. One was red and the other one was gray." Rielly stopped and tried to remember every detail. "There was one man. He walked from the left side of the room, where I couldn't see him because that first door isn't swung all the way open." Rielly's eyes danced over her story as she pictured it. "The man had a cup in his hand—it was probably coffee—and he walked over to the drills." Rielly's left hand was cupped as if she were carrying a mug and the right was held flat. "He placed his hand on the drills . . . I think he was checking to see how warm they were."

Adams nodded knowingly. "He's afraid they're gonna burn out on him."

Rielly shrugged. "Well, after he was done doing that, he pulled out a tape measure and held it alongside each drill."

"What did he look like?" asked Rapp.

"Not like the others."

"You didn't see him when you were being held in the mess?"

"No."

"How did he look different?"

"He was"—Rielly searched for the right adjective—"pudgy and I guess a little older."

"How old?"

"I'd guess late forties to fifty."

"Was he armed?"

This one stumped Rielly. Her eyes looked to the ceiling while she tried to remember. After a moment she shook her head and said, "I'm not sure."

Rapp accepted the answer and tried to think if he was missing anything. "Did you see anyone else? Hear anything else? Anything you can think of?"

Rielly shook her head. "Nope. I wasn't down there very long."

Rapp reached down and started untying the rope. "Nice work, Anna. Now I want you to wait here while I go back upstairs and report in. I think we're gonna have some more work to do, but I have to let them know that their hunch was right."

Rapp finished untying the rope and stood. Reaching for his gun, he said, "Milt, let's go."

Adams struggled up from one knee and pointed at his feet. "What do I do about shoelaces?"

After looking at Rielly's white stockinged feet, Rapp said, "Take the boots off and go in your socks. We're just going up and right back down."

Adams took the boots off, and then moving toward the door with Rapp, he said sheepishly, "Mitch, I have to go pee again."

Rapp looked at him sideways. Something clicked in his head, and he stopped. Turning back to Rielly, he asked, "Anna, did you say the guy was drinking coffee?"

Rielly nodded. "I think so."

Rapp smiled and glanced at Adams. "Milt, you're a genius."

41

HARRIS AND REAVERS pulled up to the main gate at Andrews Air Force Base and presented their credentials. They were saluted and waved through quickly. Harris was on a mission to find General Campbell, and the fact that General Flood was reportedly with him was all the better. Might as well hit them both up at the same time. Flood, after all, would have to give his stamp of approval to anything they would want to execute.

Reavers maneuvered the heavy Suburban around several turns and gunned the gas-guzzling V-8 engine. Harris had told him to step on it. Right now Delta was getting face time with the generals, and every second counted. SEAL blood had been spilled, and Harris was going to do everything possible to make sure they had a piece of the action.

Less than a minute later, Reavers came to an abrupt stop near General Flood's limousine and its two security sedans. Several Pentagon pukes were standing around in their cleanly pressed green uniforms, keeping an eye on the cars. Inside, no doubt, were more of them waiting to wipe General Flood's nose in case he got a sniffle.

Harris and Reavers jumped out of the Suburban, Harris with a file folder, Reavers with a submachine gun. The file folder Harris carried contained a "briefback." The briefback was a Special Forces document that outlined a specific mission that was being proposed down to the last detail.

Harris and Reavers moved toward the rear of the hangar, where Harris spotted two of General Flood's staff pukes milling about. Approaching the door, one of the general's aides, a major, put up a hand and attempted to ask Harris his business. Harris, not wearing any rank or insignia, continued right past the officer and opened the door. Reavers followed his boss and closed the door behind him.

Inside, standing in front of a chalkboard, were Generals Flood and Campbell. They were both listening to Colonel Gray, Delta Force's commander. Several other Pentagon, JSOC, and Delta intelligence and administrative types were seated at a long table working among themselves. Harris and Reavers approached the front of the room and snapped off salutes to General Flood. After Flood returned the salute, Harris apologized for the interruption.

"That's all right. We wanted to talk to you anyway." Then, gesturing to the blackboard, Flood said, "We were just going over several takedown scenarios. I'd like to hear what you think."

Harris eyed the old blackboard for a second and said, "Billy and his people know their stuff. They don't need me looking over their shoulder." Harris looked to Colonel Gray and winked. Gray gave his counterpart at SEAL Team Six an approving nod.

"I do have an idea about something else, however. A solution to an obstacle that we need to overcome before we even consider launching something like this." Harris gestured to a large diagram of the White House compound taped to the right side of the long blackboard. "We know from Iron Man's recon of the mansion that there are explosive devices to be dealt with. He found a bomb in the president's bedroom. Why put a bomb there if you're Aziz?" Harris looked quizzically at the two generals and Colonel Gray. "All of the hostages are over here"—Harris pointed to the diagram—"in the West Wing. The only reason I can think of is to bring the whole building down and add to the chaos surrounding any attempt by us to retake the building."

Flood thought about and slowly nodded. "I would agree."

"Knowing this, we can infer that, like with rats, when we see one, we can assume there are many more." Pausing for emphasis, Harris let them think about the harsh reality of sending dozens of operators into the building only to see them engulfed in a ball of flames and flying debris. "Before we launch any type of a mission, we need to get someone in there, and they need to find a way to neutralize those bombs."

Colonel Gray nodded emphatically. "This hasn't been lost on us. Right now we're banking on the fact that we can get in and shoot fast enough to stop one of them from hitting the plunger." Gray didn't look too enthused about his odds.

"And if Aziz has the hostages booby-trapped?"

Gray shook his head, knowing that this was probably the case. "We're screwed."

"Exactly. That's why I think we have to get a small team of operators into the building just prior to the main assault. To assess the situation and find a way to defuse or temporarily disable the bombs, otherwise we can kiss our asses good-bye."

The other men thought about the ugly scene, and after a moment General Campbell spoke. "Let me guess, Dan. You know just the person to handle this delicate aspect of the operation."

Grinning, Harris replied, "As a matter of fact I do, sir."

"Let's hear it."

With his voice a touch lower Harris said, "Did any of you ever get wind of a training op we did with the Secret Service eight years ago?"

General Flood, at the time, had been in Korea, and General Campbell had been on a special detachment working with the SAS in Britain. Colonel Gray, however, had been with Delta. Gray searched his memory. They were constantly doing training ops, but off the top of his head, he couldn't remember doing anything with the Secret Service.

"You're gonna have to refresh my memory," said the CO of Delta Force.

Harris leaned in a little closer. "It was very hush-hush. They wanted the boys at Six to help them test certain security precautions . . . and for obvious reasons, they didn't want it publicized. Especially after the results."

Before Harris could continue, one of the general's aides approached the group and apologized for the intrusion. Extending a secure digital phone, the captain said, "Director Stansfield is on the line, General."

Flood took the phone in his hand and said, "Thomas?" The general's eyes tightened, and he said nothing. After about twenty seconds, he said simply, "Shit." After another ten seconds, he replied, "I agree. I'll catch a chopper back. Get everything set up." Flood ended the call and handed the phone back to his aide. Then, looking at the men around him, he said, "We just got some really bad news. Iron Man confirmed that they are drilling into the president's bunker." Shaking his head, he looked to Colonel Gray and said, "Bombs or not, you're going in." Then looking to Harris, he said, "I have to get back to Langley, immediately. Whatever this idea of yours is, I hope it's good and I hope you can put it together in a snap."

Harris nodded confidently. "My men have been on it since this morning."

RAFIQUE AZIZ LEANED back in the president's chair. The long shiny surface of the Situation Room's conference table was laid out before him. Aziz's eyes were closed and his arms folded across his chest. It was the middle of the afternoon, and he was trying to get some sleep in anticipation of a long night. In front of him on the table was his MP-5. The overhead lights were extinguished, the glow of the bank of muted TVs at the far end throwing a dim light.

There was a knock on the door. Aziz's alert eyes snapped open, and he said, "Enter."

The door opened slowly, and Muammar Bengazi stepped into the room. "You asked me to wake you at three."

"Thank you." A yawn crept up from his throat. "How are the men?"

"They are well."

"Are you making sure they get some sleep? This will be their last chance for a long time."

Bengazi approached the conference table and placed his hands on the back of one of the leather chairs. "As you ordered, they are sleeping in two-man rotations for two hours at a time."

"Good."

"May I sit?"

Aziz rubbed his eyes. "Yes."

Bengazi set his AK-74 on the table and sat. Looking guardedly toward his leader, he asked, "What are your thoughts on tomorrow?"

Aziz unfolded his arms and checked his watch. "By nightfall we should have the president in our hands, and then"—Aziz's lips parted and turned upward at the edges—"we will truly have the upper hand."

"Will you tell them that we have him tonight, or will you wait until the morning?"

"I will tell them in the morning." Aziz gestured to the TVs. "They have been reporting that the UN will meet our demands. Vice President Baxter will keep them at bay until he gets his next batch of hostages tomorrow."

Bengazi was persistently guarded. "You do not think they will come tonight?"

Aziz shook his head, feeling so confident in his prediction that he didn't need to give a verbal response.

"I wish I shared your optimism, but after what they tried to do this morning I can't help but think they are preparing to attack."

The comment caused Aziz to smile. "That is why you are so valuable, Muammar. You are so cautious. They will not do anything until they hear the next round of demands." Aziz tapped the side of his head with his forefinger. "You need to understand the American mind. Especially the mind of the politician. Being decisive is not in their character. They will put off making a decision until they are forced to do so. Right now they have gained the release of a third of the hostages and they are playing under the assumption that they can continue to negotiate for the release of more."

Bengazi frowned. "It makes no sense to me. Surely the military is advising to attack."

"They probably are, but it makes no difference. As long as the politicians think they can free more hostages without firing a shot, they will do so."

"Not when they find out what the next demands are." Bengazi shook his bald forehead. "There is no way."

"When we have our hands on the president, everything will change. Speaking of the president, how is our little thief proceeding?"

"He says he is still on schedule. Sometime around seven this evening."

Aziz smiled with anticipation. "It will be a great moment."

Bengazi nodded slowly, not sharing in his leader's complete confidence. After looking down at the table for a while, he said, "I think we should announce that we have the president as soon as we get him out of the bunker."

"Why?"

"It will deter the Americans from attacking."

Shrugging, Aziz placed his hands behind his neck. "My plan will not change. When I make my final demand tomorrow, I will need the surprise of having the president standing beside me to shock the world into doing what is right."

42

RIELLY STRETCHED OUT on the concrete floor, her legs before her forming a V. First the left leg, hold it for a twenty count, and then the right. The stretching felt good.

While she worked out the soreness in her legs and lower back, she thought about her career. Rielly was, after all, an insider. She had pulled back the curtain and had watched and participated in the Mighty and Powerful Oz's show. The public was not allowed to peer behind that curtain, to see how stories were shaped, how careers were made or broken around those one-week periods known as Sweeps Week. The public never saw how producers and executives juiced up stories. Exaggerating some details and downplaying or ignoring others. How they went after something or someone, not based on how strong or important the story was, but what their ratings books told them.

Anna knew her story would be hot. It would be more than hot. It would be incredible. She would have to be cautious. NBC would try to suck the story from her on every possible outlet: the *Today* show, *Dateline*, CNBC, and MSNBC. They owned her; there were no illusions about that. She was on the clock, and her contract left no loopholes for appearing on other network news shows. To keep her happy, they would repay her with exposure, probably allow her to do some stories for *Dateline*. That was the way the game was played.

There would be a book deal, for sure, but she would have to be careful about that. She wanted to write it herself, and take her time—no big-bucks, hire-a-ghostwriter, and have-it-on-the-shelves-in-two-months deal. The key would be to find the right agent. One who was willing to push for money and more time. The result would be a more authoritative story. She honestly felt that this was a story that needed to be told, but in the right way—dignified, worthy of the seriousness of the situation and of the people who had died.

She would work with Mitch Kruse. Rielly smiled pleasantly at the thought of the man who had saved her. He was all man and then some. Nothing pretty about him. Handsome and rugged. A real man. As to his real identity, the no-brainer answer was that he worked for the CIA, but one could never tell. He could be FBI. They weren't exactly forthright with information either—at least when dealing with journalists. Rielly could hardly blame them, though. She'd seen her father and his fellow law-enforcement brethren get burned countless times by dishonest journalists. Rielly had vivid memories of her father's scathing criticism of reporters, especially newspaper reporters. Barely a week passed when he wouldn't throw the paper down in disgust and explain to her mother how the reporter had his or her facts all screwed up. Seeing how lax reporting affected her father served as motivation for Rielly to get things right. That's what she would do with the book.

Rielly smiled as the ideas fell into place. The very thing that would make the story all the more appealing, and at the same time honor Kruse's request, would be to keep him as he was—a very lethal, dark, rugged, and anonymous individual. She would be protecting her source, just like a good reporter, and it would only add to the intrigue of the book.

Rielly heard something on the other side of the door. Her heart leapt into her throat, but before she could scurry for cover, the door opened. Rapp and Adams quickly entered the room. Rielly placed her right hand on her chest and felt her pounding heart.

From her spot on the floor, she said, "You guys scared the hell out of me."

Rapp's face was tense. Sticking his hand out to help her up, he said, "Next time we'll be sure to knock."

Rielly ignored the comment and took his hand. Standing, she asked, "What's next?"

Rapp didn't speak at first. Instead he looked over at the room's second door. He was thinking something through. After a short while he looked Rielly in the eye. "We're gonna try something that might be a little risky, but there's no other alternative."

Rielly looked at the door, not knowing what was behind it. Kruse's intensity sent a shiver up her spine. With a forced confidence, she asked, "What's behind that door?"

DALLAS KING STRUTTED back and forth in front of Baxter's desk. The two had been debating what to do with the new information, that there was a good chance Aziz was in the process of extricating President Hayes from his bunker.

In his typical defeatist tone, Baxter had whined that it was over. Everything they had done was for naught. Helicopters would be sent in, the men in black would rappel from ropes, and the bloodbath would ensue. He would forever be remembered as the man who presided over the destruction of the White House and the deaths of dozens of Americans. His presidential ambitions were gone. Snuffed out. This would be a disgrace the fragile American ego would want to forget. And Sherman Baxter the Third in the Oval Office would be a constant reminder of this entire ugly week and this gruesome assault on the American way.

King stopped his pacing and started snapping his fingers in front of Baxter. "You're not listening to me. Pay attention."

"Shut up, Dallas. I'm listening to you. I just don't believe you." The vice president leaned back in his chair and tossed a black pen onto his desk. It hit a leather-bound desk calendar and skidded to a stop in between a photo of Baxter's family vineyard and a photo of his parents.

King looked down at his boss, not really hurt by the harsh words, but acting as if he were. King was practicing patience. His boss needed to be both coddled and whipped, depending on the situation. Looking down, the chief of staff pulled back the white cuff of his blue dress shirt and looked at his watch.

"Maybe I'd better leave you alone for a while. You seem like you could use some rest." King pulled his cuff back over the watch with an aristocratic flair.

Baxter pointed to King. "Don't speak to me with that condescending tone of yours, Dallas."

"Well"—King looked down at his fingernails—"my opinion doesn't seem to matter much to you, so I thought it would be best if I left you alone."

Baxter rocked forward. "Don't give me this crap, Dallas."

King turned to face his boss. Now was the time to dig in and then hit him over the head with both the carrot and the stick. "Then why do I have to fight you at every turn?" King put his hands on his hips and looked to his boss for an answer. "Sherman, no one ever said this would be easy, but for Christ's sake, I'm getting sick of your loser attitude." To himself he added, *If you had my problems, you'd want to crawl under a rock and die.*

Baxter pulled away, leaning back in his chair. After eyeing his agitated chief of staff for a second, he said, "I don't see what in the hell I should be so positive about."

"How about the fact—" King stopped and looked over both of his shoulders, making sure no one was around. Then leaning over the desk he whispered, "—that maybe a certain person might not make it out of the White House alive." Nodding his head confidently, he added, "One heartbeat away. Don't ever forget it."

Baxter looked down at his desk for a moment, too embarrassed to let

King see the thirst in his eyes. The politician in him told him to say the right thing. "I don't want to become president that way."

"I know you don't, but, Sherman, it would be your duty."

Baxter chewed on the thought.

"We don't know where this thing is going to end up," King continued. "That's why we have to stay loose. That's why I need your head in the game." King studied Baxter to see if he was getting through. "Keep the pressure on the UN, and I'll worry about the rest of it. I have some ideas on how we can handle things if Flood and Stansfield keep leaning on you, but I have to think them through."

King looked out the window while he thought about his plans. It was getting late in the day. Maybe four more hours of sunlight, and then it would be dark again. If they could just make it until the morning and get another third of the hostages released, that would go a long way toward a victory. Then they could turn Flood and Stansfield loose, and hopefully his other problem would then be taken care of.

43

RAPP POINTED TO the second door, saying, "Behind that is a reinforced steel door that leads into a tunnel. The tunnel that was used to evacuate the president when the attack started. It runs from here, down a flight of stairs, under the Rose Garden, and up into the West Wing."

Rielly was leaning against one of the wheeled storage containers, and Rapp and Adams were standing. Rielly listened intently to Rapp's plan. Talk of hidden tunnels and the evacuation of the president had her curiosity piqued.

"At this end, the tunnel goes down a flight of stairs"—Rapp gestured with his hand—"a quick turn to the left, and then down another short flight, where there's another door. That door," said Rapp, talking very fast now, "leads to the room just outside the president's bunker. The room that you could see from your spot in the ventilation duct."

Looking up, Rielly asked, "So where does that get us?"

"We need to reestablish communication with the president. Aziz is using some type of a jammer to block communication with the bunker."

"How do you know that?" Out of habit, the reporter was ticking down her notepad of questions.

"When the raid started, we were in communication with the president via Secret Service radio and cell phone for a short period. That is how we knew he was safe in the bunker. When Milt and I came in through the air intake, our reception got worse the closer we got to the White House. Up on the second floor the reception is a little better. We're pretty sure that the jamming unit is located as close to the bunker as possible for maximum effect."

Rielly took in his words and asked, "So why do we have to risk this just to talk to the president?"

This is where it gets tricky, Rapp told himself. He didn't want to lie to her, but at the same time, he knew he couldn't tell her what he had figured out—that the reason they were doing this was that the vice president wouldn't order the takedown. "Anna, I can't get into that with you right now, maybe later. Just trust me that there's a good reason why we need to reestablish contact with the president."

Rielly eyed him suspiciously, wondering what he was hiding. "This is one of those things we'll talk about over dinner when you tell me your life story."

Rapp laughed. "Yeah, sure. I'll put it at the top of the list."

Nice laugh, Rielly thought. He used it as defense mechanism. Every time he wasn't comfortable with a question or a proposition, he laughed and moved on. Rielly gave him a knowing look as if she could see past the smoke screen.

"So I'm going to crawl back down there and wait for that guy to go to the bathroom. And then I'm going to tug on the rope twice"—Rielly held up two fingers to make sure—"twice, and then you're gonna run down there and do whatever it is that you do for whatever agency it is that you work for, but can't say you work for."

Rapp's quiet laugh and smile popped up right on schedule. "That's about it."

"What if this guy doesn't need to go to the bathroom?"

"Don't worry, he will. My guess is he's been up for almost three days straight, and he's probably had twenty cups of coffee." Rapp looked over at the door and then back. "Any questions before we get started?"

"What if I give the signal and two seconds later he turns around and starts coming back?"

Rapp nodded and pointed to her. "Now, that's a good question. If that happens, tug on the rope four times, nice and hard." Rapp watched her nod and then again asked, "Any more questions?"

"Yeah," said Rielly. "What if I have to go to the bathroom?"

"Hold it." Rapp reached into his pocket and pulled out a Velcro patch and one of the mini surveillance units. "I want you to install this while you're down there. Lay it flat like this." Rapp set the small device in the palm of his hand and held it horizontally. "This little wick at the end contains a fiber-optic camera. Make sure it has an unobstructed view of the bunker door."

Rielly took the device and nodded. "I'm ready when you guys are."

"Milt?" Rapp looked at his partner.

"I'm good to go."

"Good." Rapp brought his hands together and said, "Let's do it." Rubbing them, he shrugged his head toward the second door and said, "Let's get that thing open, and then we'll lower Anna down."

Adams walked over to the gray door and extracted his S-key. He opened the outer door, and there stood a sturdy steel door with rivets securing the hinges and a handle on the right-hand side. Adams brought his face to within inches of the control pad and then stopped. Stepping to the side, he looked at Rapp and said, "You'd better give this a try. You're gonna be on your own when you open the second door."

Rapp agreed and stepped up to the control pad. He entered the nine numbers from memory and pressed "enter." Immediately there was the hiss of air releasing and then a metallic click. Rapp stepped back and brought his submachine gun up.

Adams looked at him and pointed to the handle. "Just lean on that thing, and she's all yours."

Rapp pushed Adams completely out of the way and pressed down on the handle. He didn't expect any trouble, but now was not the time to be lax. Rapp pushed the door in. Before him was a small landing and a set of stairs. The floor and lower half of the walls were covered with a brown carpet. Rapp stood hugging the doorframe, with his silhouette minimized. The thick black barrel of his MP-10 searched every inch of the dimly lit staircase before him.

He turned to Adams and Rielly, "Everything checks out. Let's get Anna on the move and hope this guy has a little bladder."

A minute later Rielly was wiggling her way back into the vent and Rapp was playing out the rope. When she reached the vertical shaft, Rapp carefully eased her down it. From there Rielly inched her way through the narrow confines until she came upon her spot. Gingerly, she inched forward the last several inches and peered through the slats. The high-pitched whine of the drills filled the air. Clutching the surveillance unit Rapp had given her, she looked out intently at the large shiny door of the president's bunker. No one was in sight. The pudgy man that she had seen the time before was not visible. Rielly watched the three bulky drills working to breach the door. She wondered briefly if she should tug on the string and give the signal. After a moment she thought better of it. She could see only part of the room, and for all she knew, someone was in there, or he was gone and could be on his way back.

Taking the arm of her bulky sweatshirt, Rielly reached in front of herself and cleared out a spot for the Velcro patch. She secured the surveillance unit to the spot and made sure the fiber-optic camera had an unobstructed view between the bottom of the opening and the first slat. With that done, she stretched out and tried to get comfortable.

WICKER HAD A crew of eight motivated Navy SEALs working feverishly. Planning ahead, as always, Wicker had called a lumberyard in Forestville, Maryland, and placed an order for the supplies he would need to build the shooting platform. When his CO, Lt. Commander Harris, had given him the green light, Wicker was on the phone within seconds.

SEAL Team Six's strike element, which would be used to chase the terrorists if they left the country, was billeted at Andrews Air Force Base, where they were biding their time in hopes that they would be sent into action. Wicker explained his situation to the unit's executive officer and told him that Harris had given him the okay. Wicker requested six men specifically, and within twenty minutes they had borrowed a truck from the motor pool and were on the way to the lumberyard. The fact that they had not obtained authorization for the truck was something the paper pushers could sort out later.

By a little past two in the afternoon they were downtown in their jeans and T-shirts unloading their equipment. Everything was ferried by hand up the bell tower of the Old Post Office, and now the men, all of whom were experienced snipers, were putting the finishing touches on the platforms. Building one platform would not work. Two shots would be fired by two men using fifty-caliber rifles. Although the platforms' construction was sturdy, if only one were used, the slightest movement by one man could send the other man's shot dangerously awry.

The two platforms were actually rectangular boxes constructed of one-inch plywood and reinforced with four-by-sixes and glued and screwed together. Wicker grabbed a hard plastic rifle case by the handle and laid it down on one of the platforms. With the others watching, he popped the clasps on the case and opened it. Inside sat a massive .50 caliber Barrett rifle. Sixty-one inches from muzzle to shoulder butt and weighing thirty pounds, it was one of the largest rifles in the world. It used the powerful .50 caliber Browning cartridge and was capable of taking out targets at distances in excess of one mile.

Wicker, not a particularly large man, was only a half foot taller than the rifle. Scooping the heavy black weapon from its foam encasement, he pulled the fixed bipod into its extended position and set it down. He climbed onto the platform, slid in behind the rifle, and drew close to the scope. He peered through the circular eyepiece, and within seconds he was staring at the hooded terrorist sitting in the guard booth on the roof of the White House. At this short distance, the .50 caliber Barrett would normally be way too much firepower, but considering the security afforded the terrorists by the bulletproof Plexiglas, it was the right weapon for the job. Not just one Barrett, but two.

Wicker shifted his weight and moved subtly while he kept the crosshairs of the scope centered on the hooded man six hundred twenty feet away. There was no wobbling. The platform was sturdy. Satisfied, Wicker stood and placed his rifle back in its case. While he put the case back in the corner, his men went to work to complete the project. Wicker looked at the setting sun and noticed a change in the weather just over the horizon. A welcome change. Grabbing the digital phone from his hip, he punched in a number and waited for the person on the other end to answer.

44

RIELLY DIDN'T HAVE her watch and had forgotten to ask what time it was before she was lowered into the vent. From the stiffness in her hip, she was guessing that she had been in the tiny space for at least thirty minutes, maybe even an hour. For the better part of that she had seen no movement from the room. With nothing else to do, her mind wandered and fatigue set in. Several times she caught herself dozing off only to have her head bob back up and bump the top of the vent. The cramped confines and the drone of the drills reminded her of lying in a tanning bed.

That she was not seeing any sign of the terrorists began to make her nervous. She started to wonder if the room was vacant, if now was the right time to give the signal. The problem was that she couldn't see all of the room. If they did this again, she reminded herself, ask for a watch and a better set of instructions.

As the minutes passed by, Rielly grew more stiff and tired. Finally, when she was really beginning to doubt that there was anyone in the room, she heard a sound that was different from the steady drone of the drills. She squinted so she could get a clear shot through the slats, and Rielly saw something move. It was a shadow. There was someone in the room. A moment later the pudgy man she had seen on her previous trip stepped into the full view of the open door and stretched his arms above his head, his potbelly bulging outward.

She watched as the man moved out of sight and then approached the drills to measure their progress as she had seen him do on her first trip. When he was done taking his measurements, he tossed the tape measure onto something that was not in Rielly's view, and then, with his hands stretched over his head once again, he started down the hall toward her, his mouth agape, a yawn squirreling its way out of his rodentlike face.

Rielly's face grimaced in disgust at the man's slovenly appearance and harsh features. At first she drew closer to the vent and then quickly moved back for fear of being discovered. As he neared her position, the fingers of her right hand reached up and fumbled for the black loop around her neck. Rielly found what she was looking for, and as the man turned the corner beneath her, she pulled hard on the shoelace twice.

*   *   *

RAPP AND ADAMS had stood alert for the first ten minutes, Adams standing by the open vent with the rope in his hands and Rapp poised at the top of the stairs, his MP-10 strapped across his chest and his silenced pistol in his left hand. Rapp had decided that the submachine gun was too much to handle for this little foray. After ten minutes of standing awkwardly across the room from each other, Rapp saw that there was a better way to utilize their time.

Crossing over to Adams, Rapp had taken the rope and asked Adams to pull out his blueprints. After Adams spread the documents out on top of one of the containers, Rapp gave him the rope back. He then proceeded to pick Milt's brain on the layout of the West Wing. Exactly where the tunnel came out on the other end and what he could expect to find when he opened that door. Rapp and Adams had already gone over most of this before, but Rapp wanted to make sure he had a good grasp of the floor plan. He knew if he could pull off this phase of the operation, his next task would be to get into the West Wing and get a firsthand look at how the hostages were being held.

From everything they could guess and from what Rielly had told them, they knew the bulk of the hostages were being held in the mess. The problem that Rapp faced was finding out if any of the Secret Service agents and officers were still alive and if so, where they were being held. As Rapp prodded Adams about the best way to check out the other areas of the West Wing, Adams lurched suddenly.

Looking at Rapp, he spat, "That was it. Two tugs."

Rapp was instantly moving across the floor. Looking over his shoulder, he whispered, "If you get the recall sign, start calling my name, and bust your ass down these steps so I can hear you." Rapp was gone, into the tunnel, racing down the steps like a running back going through a set of tires. Out of habit he had his pistol out in front of him, leading the way. When he hit the bottom step, he looked briefly down the length of the tunnel and then turned immediately to his left. Leaping down the next flight, he came to a crashing halt at the reinforced door and switched his gun from his right hand to his left.

Breathing a little heavier, he paused for a second to listen for Adams. Nothing, no warning from above. Pulling the numbers up from memory, he punched in the first eight and once again stopped to listen. Not more than two seconds later he punched the last number and stood back. The 9-mm Beretta went back into his right hand as the rubber gasket surrounding the door hissed. There was the metallic click of the locking stems retracting, and Rapp's left hand shoved down on the door handle. It was no time to be timid.

Shoving the door open three feet, Rapp led with the pistol. The first thing his senses picked up was the sound of the drills and then a strange smell. His eyes picked up the back of the open door that led out into the hallway, and as he continued to open the steel door and step into the anteroom, the door hit something and there was the sound of metal hitting metal. The noise startled Rapp but wasn't loud enough to be heard over the clamor of the drills. Rapp slid around the door, leading with the gun, careful to show only as much of his body as necessary.

Quickly, he jerked the pistol to the left and then the right, his eyes following. The room was empty. He approached the open door and took a quick peek down the hallway. Nothing. Taking a longer look this time, he looked up at the vent in an attempt to see Rielly. He was relieved to see that he couldn't. Returning his attention to the task at hand, he turned and looked for the source of his and many others' frustration.

There it sat, immediately to the left of the bunker door, touching the shiny polished steel. The black box was no bigger than a large stereo receiver. Rapp stepped over a toolbox and around another. Dropping down to one knee, he looked at the control panel and studied the dials and digital readout. The unit was manufactured by one of Westinghouse's little-known subsidiaries who just happened to do a lot of work with the CIA, FBI, and Secret Service. Aziz had taken this baby from the Secret Service's arsenal. Rapp pulled the box away from the door so he could get at the wires and antenna in back. He grabbed a small pair of wire cutters from his web vest and lowered the arm of the lip mike on his headset. Rapp snipped the wire that lead to the antenna.

"Milt, can you hear me? Milt can you hear me?" Rapp waited a couple seconds. After failing to raise Adams a second time, Rapp flipped the jammer onto its front and looked at the perforated black metal on the back. Through the cooling slats, he could see several bound groups of wire. Turning the thing off wouldn't work. He had to disable it. The key was to make it look as if it were still on.

Rapp plunged the wire cutter in between two of the cooling slats. The pointy nose of the wire cutter bent the metal. Rapp twisted the tool back and forth several times to get more access, and then opened the snips. As he clamped down on the first group of wires, it never occurred to him to unplug the machine first. Rapp squeezed hard, and as soon as the metal jaws of the wire cutter broke the protective insulation of the wires, sparks shot up, and Rapp was knocked back onto his butt.

With tingles shooting up his right arm and feeling as if he'd lost all of the hair on his body, Rapp mumbled, "Shit." Shaking his right arm vigorously, he started to get back up. Over his headset he heard the voice of Milt Adams, and then someone else. A voice he didn't recognize.

IRENE KENNEDY sat at her elevated position in the control room with a phone to her ear. On the other end of the secure line, General Campbell was explaining Lt. Commander Harris's plan to send in a small team of demolition experts to clear the path for the strike teams. Kennedy was not excited about the plan at first, that was until Campbell explained to her that Harris and the three men he had chosen had all succeeded in accomplishing what seemed to be the most difficult aspect of the operation during a training operation with the Secret Service some eight years earlier. She still wasn't crazy about the idea, but the fact that they had already proven they could do it went a long way.

As Kennedy listened to the general fill her in on the other aspects of the plan, her concentration was broken by a flurry of motion and voices from the two rows in front of her. When she looked up, she almost dropped the phone. The monitors that were showing the pictures that Rapp had already provided were now crystal clear, and smack dab in the middle of the big board was a picture of a shiny silver door that could be nothing other than the one to the president's bunker.

Campbell repeatedly called Kennedy's name. After the third or fourth time it registered, and she said into the phone, "He did it."

"Who did it?" asked a slightly irritated Campbell.

"Mitch did. We have a picture of the bunker on the board." Kennedy paused for a second while one of her people pointed to his own headset and spoke to her. Kennedy clutched the phone and said, "You'd better get back here right away. We have Mitch on full audio from his Motorola, not the field radio. I think he's taken out the jammer. Hustle back. I have to let Thomas know." Without waiting for a response from Campbell, Kennedy hung up the phone and quickly dialed the extension for her boss. At the same time she rifled through a stack of papers.

Stansfield answered on the second ring, and Kennedy could barely contain her excitement. "Thomas, Mitchell has taken out the jammer. We have him on full audio, and we've picked up two more surveillance feeds."

"I'll be there in a minute," Stansfield calmly replied.

Kennedy hung up the phone and put on her headset as she called out Rapp's code name over the microphone hanging in front of her lips. She came across the document she was looking for, a list of numbers provided by Secret Service Director Tracy.

45

PRESIDENT HAYES LOOKED at his watch. It was nearing five o'-clock. "Are you sure we shouldn't wait until it's dark?"

Jack Warch shook his head. "I'd like to, but we don't know how much time we have."

All of the agents were either sitting or standing around the group of couches in the middle of the room. Warch had convinced the president that their chances for survival were better if they made the break. Valerie Jones had also agreed. Not that it made a huge difference, but at this crucial juncture the less dissent the better. After getting Jones out of the way, Warch had brought the agents in, and they were now finalizing the plan.

Warch looked up at Pat Cowley. Cowley was hands down the best shot of the group with either a pistol or submachine gun. The former Supreme Court police officer had just finished a four-year stint with the Secret Service's Counter Assault Team, where he had spent the majority of his time riding around in the back of the old, black, armor-plated Suburban that followed the president's limousine wherever it went. These were the men that carried the big hardware. If the motorcade came under attack, it was their job to, first, cover the president's evacuation and, second, neutralize the threat if possible. Their basic doctrine was to carry enough firepower that they could enfilade the threat with a volley of bullets while the president was evacuated from the area.

Warch continued going through the agents' assignments one by one. He picked two agents to leapfrog behind the point as they moved, and assigned Ellen Morton and three other agents to stay with the president at all times. The last agent was to provide a rear guard if needed. Warch himself would stay fluid and try lead as they moved.

After all questions were answered and the evacuation routes were decided on, Warch got the troops lined up. Five of the nine agents carried MP-5 submachine guns along with their SIG-Sauer pistols. The others, including Warch, were armed with their pistols only. With weapons checked and ready, Warch turned to Ellen Morton and said, "Take the president and Valerie and put them in the bathroom. When we give you the all clear, you bring them out, and we move."

As Warch turned for the door, he was interrupted by a noise he had been waiting to hear for more than two days. Simultaneously, every head in the room snapped toward the small kitchen table. On the second ring, Warch bolted toward the noise. Reaching out, he snatched his digital phone and pressed the send button.

"Hello!"

"Jack, it's Irene Kennedy."

Warch's heart was in his throat. "Thank God!"

Kennedy spoke quickly, her eyes staring at the monitor in the center of the big board. "How's the president?"

"He's fine . . . but somebody's drilling through the bunker door. What in the hell's going on?"

Kennedy took a deep breath and started in. "Jack, we don't have a lot of time, so I'll give you the short version. Rafique Aziz and a group of terrorists have taken over the White House. They are holding hostages, and we know they are trying to break into the bunker."

Warch was a little surprised that Kennedy knew about the assault on the door. The president was now coming toward him from across the room. "Well, what are you guys doing about it?"

"We're working on it, but we need to speak to the president first."

"Sure, he's right here." Warch handed Hayes the phone, saying, "It's Irene Kennedy."

Hayes took the small gray phone and held it to his ear. "Dr. Kennedy?"

"Yes, Mr. President. How are you doing?"

"Good!" exclaimed a relieved Hayes. "It's great to hear your voice."

"It's nice to hear yours too, sir, but we have a lot to cover, and we're short on time, so I'm going to hand the phone over to Director Stansfield."

Stansfield and General Flood had just entered the room. Kennedy had her chair turned around, and as the men hurriedly approached their seats, she held up three fingers.

Stansfield grabbed his phone and pressed line three. In his normal businesslike tone he said, "Mr. President, I apologize for taking so long to get through to you, but we've been experiencing some difficulties."

"What in the hell has been going on?" asked Hayes.

Stansfield started from the top and moved through the highlights of what had happened over the last three days. He covered the demands that had been made and met, and those that were in the process of being met. He told the president of the murder of his national security adviser and his secretary, and the subsequent mental breakdown of his attorney general.

He intentionally stressed certain events and exchanges that hinted at Vice President Baxter's incompetence. Stansfield gave him the soft sell. It was better to let Hayes come to his own conclusions than to hit him over the head with the obvious.

The president, for his part, let Stansfield brief him without interruption. President Hayes was not happy about much of what he heard. The only bright spot thus far was the news that Stansfield had managed to get someone inside the White House. And not just anyone, but the man he had just learned of several days earlier. The man the president knew only as Iron Man. A man that had been billed as the absolute best Thomas Stansfield had ever seen.

When the director of the CIA explained the vice president's reaction to the news that Aziz was in the process of extracting the president from his bunker, Hayes lost it.

"He told you to do what?" Hayes's face was tense with anger.

"He told us that before he would risk the hostages' lives by ordering a raid, we would have to present him with more precise information."

Hayes shook his head. "It sure as hell sounds to me like you had pretty good information."

"Yes," replied Stansfield. "We felt so, sir."

"Well, get him on the phone so I can give him irrefutable information that he's an idiot."

Now came the time for Stansfield's calm vision. His ability to slow things down when they seemed to be speeding up for everybody else had been one of his greatest assets over the years—that and his ability to approach a situation like a grand master and plot his moves far in advance. Stansfield was pretty confident where this entire situation was headed, and for now he knew it was best to keep the knowledge of their contact with the president to a bare minimum.

In regard to putting the president in touch with his next in command, Stansfield said, "I would advise against that right now, sir."

"Why?"

"We have suffered several leaks from the vice president's camp thus far." Stansfield paused, giving the president time to digest the innuendo. "We know that Aziz is monitoring the news, and I would not want it to leak out that we are in contact with you. We need to let Aziz continue to think that he has the upper hand. General Flood and General Campbell are in the process of putting the final touches on an assault plan. As soon as they are ready, and you give the order, we can end this."

Hayes thought about the decision. His mind was made up almost instantaneously, and then he paused, wondering why Baxter hadn't given the approval. Turning his back to the group of agents and his chief of staff, he asked, "Why hasn't the vice president given this order?"

"I'm not sure, sir. I have some ideas, but I don't think you're going to like them."

"Try me."

"I think it would be best if waited to discuss them face to face."

Hayes nodded. "All right." Then moving on to practical matters, he said, "I'm assuming that the powers of my office have been transferred to the vice president."

"That's correct, sir."

"Well, if I remember my Constitution correctly, we have some procedural issues to take care of."

"Such as?"

"We need to inform both the president pro tempore of the Senate and the Speaker of the House that I am able to resume my duties. Technically, unless we do that, the transfer of power is not complete."

Stansfield exhaled an uncharacteristic sigh. To someone who had spent years trying to skirt, bend, and sometimes break laws, this technicality seemed to be utterly trivial. He reminded himself that President Hayes was both a lawyer and an amateur presidential historian. Stifling the temptation to tell Hayes that it was a waste of time to discuss such a point, Stansfield instead said, "Sir, you are the president. The powers of your office were transferred to the vice president for the sole reason that we could not communicate with you. That is no longer the case. General Flood and I are going to take our orders from you. If you feel that it is absolutely imperative to inform the vice president and the Speaker of the House that you are once again able to discharge your duties, we can do that in the minutes just prior to the raid."

Hayes thought about it. Always a stickler for detail, he wanted to make sure everything would be legitimate. "That sounds fine to me. I just want to make sure those calls are made."

"We can do that, sir."

Hayes turned and looked at the bunker door, the humming sound of intruders just on the other side. "Thomas, what are we to do if they breach the door before the strike teams are ready?"

Stansfield paused for a moment and looked at Kennedy. Kennedy was listening in on the call, and she pointed to herself. Stansfield nodded for her to go ahead.

"Mr. President, it's Dr. Kennedy again. We are monitoring your situation and have both audio and video surveillance of the bunker door. Iron Man is very close by. If it appears that they are about to get the bunker door open, we can order him to prevent that. In addition, the FBI's Hostage Rescue Team is deployed across the street at the Executive Office Building. They have a pretty good idea of where the hostages are being held and"—Kennedy sounded less than enthusiastic—"if we really need to rush it, they can be inside the West Wing within thirty seconds of the execute order."

Hayes picked up on Kennedy's tone and said, "I get the feeling you have some reservations, Doctor."

"Aziz brought a lot of explosives with him, and he has threatened to bring the whole building down if there is any rescue attempt."

Hayes thought about this new, disturbing piece of information. "Any chance he's bluffing?"

"None at all, sir."

"Can we handle this?"

Kennedy looked up at her boss and General Flood. "We're working on it, sir."

THE SUN WAS falling in the western sky, and from the east a solid wall of gray was approaching. Salim Rusan stood near the tailgate of his ambulance and looked in both directions. A deeply superstitious man, he did not like the foreboding change in the weather. One of the other ambulance drivers had stopped by and introduced himself, and as luck would have it, the man was gay. Instead of the disguise working as a repellent, it had done the opposite.

After several moments of idle chitchat, Rusan made up the excuse that he needed to run and make a phone call. When the other ambulance driver offered his cell phone, Rusan declined and stated that in addition to having to call his boyfriend, he also had to use the bathroom.

He turned and started walking to the east down Pennsylvania Avenue. Just a dozen paces later he approached two D.C. cops manning the barricade at Fourteenth Street.

"Excuse me, Officers," he asked. "Can you tell me where I can get a bite to eat?"

One of the officers eyed him with a frown while the other paused for a moment and then pointed down the street. "If you head down E Street here, you'll run into a deli and a couple fast-food joints."

Rusan smiled and said thank you as he passed the two men. Then turning, he asked, "Will I have any problem getting back to my ambulance?"

"No, we'll be here for a while."

Rusan turned on his toes. He ducked under the blue sawhorse at the far end of the intersection; he was immediately pleased with the volume of people. After pressing his way through the crowd, he found that it ran about ten people deep and then loosened up. A large concrete trash can, overflowing with trash, sat behind the crowd. There must have been a McDonald's nearby because eight or so their bags stuffed with cups and spent french-fry containers littered the immediate area around the receptacle. All the better, since the bomb would do more damage lying on the sidewalk than in the garbage can.

He pulled one of the cans of diet Coke from his fanny pack and bent over. Taking one of the spent McDonald's bags, he wedged the can in with the rest of the refuse and set the whole package back on the ground. He positioned the bag so the majority of the blast would be directed toward the crowd.

Rusan stood and started down the sidewalk again. He would come back the same way and make sure the bag was still there. Up ahead on his right, he could make out the ugly brown surface of the Hoover Building. He wouldn't go that far, although it was very tempting. There were too many cameras and too many professionals with a trained eye. Rusan would play it safe for now. There was no need to risk exposure.

46

THE CONFERENCE ROOM at the Counterterrorism Center at Langley was bustling with action. The room was actually a room within a room. Built several feet off the floor and surrounded on four sides by glass, it was enveloped in an electromagnetic field that made eavesdropping impossible. Irene Kennedy stood at the front of the room with General Campbell as the meeting attendees filed in.

Director Roach and Special Agent Skip McMahon of the FBI entered the room with Thomas Stansfield holding on to each man's elbow. The elderly director of the Central Intelligence Agency led them to where Kennedy was standing.

Stansfield released his grip on the men and said, "Irene, I was just filling in Brian and Skip on Iron Man." After hanging up with the president, Stansfield had sealed off the control room. No one was to breathe a word that they had reestablished contact with the president. Stansfield, Flood, Campbell, and Kennedy were the only people outside the control room that knew. The men from the FBI would be informed of this piece of information by the president himself.

Kennedy was half ready to have Skip McMahon chew her head off, until Stansfield said, "I was telling Skip and Brian that you had wanted to let them in on what we were doing with Iron Man. I take full responsibility for this, gentlemen, and I have good reasons for doing so."

"Such as?" asked an edgy Skip McMahon.

Stansfield played his old man status for all it was worth. Reaching out, he patted McMahon's large forearm and said, "That's why I like you, Skip. Always vigilant, always pressing for the whole story."

"That's right. So let's hear it."

"I'm afraid that will have to happen during a later conversation. Right now I have something I think you will be far more interested in. Now, if you will please take your seats, we need to get started." Stansfield gestured to two chairs near Kennedy, and McMahon and Roach sat. Stansfield turned to Kennedy and said, "Let's get started." The director walked to the far end of the table and sat next to General Flood.

The attendees at the meeting were chosen on a need-to-know basis.

The secretaries of state and defense were bypassed, as were several other high-ranking officials. Stansfield, Flood, and the president had agreed that, for now, only a select few would be told that contact had been made with the president and that his life was in danger. Those selected, other than those already mentioned, were the commanders of HRT, Delta Force, and SEAL Team Six.

One of Kennedy's people closed the airtight door to the conference room, and Kennedy pressed a switch that lowered dark blinds over the glass walls. Standing at the front of the room next to General Campbell, Kennedy started off by saying, "Gentlemen, what General Campbell and I are about to tell you doesn't leave this room. You don't tell the people on your teams, you don't tell your bosses, you don't tell your wives."

General Campbell stepped forward. "I can promise all of you"— Campbell eyeballed the three commanders of the elite counterterrorist strike teams—"if I find out you breathed a word of this information to anyone, I will make sure your career is ended." Campbell waited to get a nod from each of the three commanders.

Behind Kennedy and Campbell were five TVs. Four twenty-five-inchers and one thirty-six-incher. Kennedy dimmed the overhead lights, and then with a remote control she turned on the TVs. Dead center, on the thirty-six-inch TV, was the live feed of the bunker door.

"As all of you know, the president was evacuated to his bunker in the initial minutes of the assault. Shortly thereafter, we lost the ability to communicate with him due to the fact that Aziz was using a state-of-the-art mobile jamming unit that he conveniently borrowed from the Secret Service's arsenal. Yesterday evening we were able to sneak two individuals into the White House. One is a civilian with intimate knowledge of the White House, and the second is a counterterrorism specialist who for our purposes we will refer to as Iron Man. The images that you see on the screens behind me are provided from surveillance units they have in place in the White House."

Kennedy turned around and pointed at the middle screen. "For those of you who haven't figured it out, this is a shot of the door that leads to the president's bunker. This slovenly man that you see moving about is Mustafa Yassin, an Iraqi who specializes in breaking into vaults. These three objects you see attached to the door are drills. We have no idea how far along they are in this process, but we are not going to wait around for them to succeed." Kennedy pressed a button on the remote, and a white screen lowered from the ceiling. On it was an overhead view of the White House compound. Turning to General Campbell, she signaled for him to take over.

Campbell pointed to the West Wing and said, "The bulk of the hostages are being held in the White House mess on the ground floor. Intelligence from the FBI and the NSA leads us to believe that there is a second, smaller group of hostages being held in the Roosevelt Room on the main floor. Iron Man thinks this second group of hostages consists of any Secret Service or military personnel that are still alive. Dr. Kennedy and I agree."

Sid Slater, the special agent in charge of the FBI's Hostage Rescue Team, raised his hand. The general looked at him and said, "Sid?"

"Do we have any video on the hostages?"

"I'm afraid not. At least not at this point. We don't have a lot of time, which brings me to my next point. H-hour is set for twenty-thirty."

"Whoa," proclaimed Director Roach of the FBI. "The order's been given to go in?"

"That's affirmative," said General Flood from the other end of the room.

Roach looked at his watch. It was several minutes past five in the evening. "Baxter gave you the go-ahead?" asked the skeptical head of the FBI.

From the overhead speaker system a very familiar voice answered Roach's question. "No, I did."

Half of the faces in the room looked up toward the heavens as if God were speaking to them. President Hayes cleared his throat and said, "Men, I know we're not giving you a lot of time, but I have an immense amount of faith in you. Now, if I may make a suggestion, I think we should all keep a lid on any questions until General Campbell finishes briefing us. General, please continue."

Campbell looked up at the speakers in gratitude and then back at the group. "Gentlemen, we don't have much time, so we're gonna use the KISS rule. HRT"—Campbell tapped the left side of the screen—"the West Wing and the hostages are all yours. Sid, I know you and your people have been working on different scenarios. You are going to need a two-pronged assault at a minimum." Campbell held up his finger and cautioned the stocky head of the Hostage Rescue Team. "We have some ideas for entry, and I'll get to them in a minute."

With his usual precision Campbell did a left face and tapped the roof of the mansion. "Delta Force will be responsible for the mansion." Campbell looked at the unit's CO, Colonel Gray. "Billy, your boys are going in on the Little Birds, and they have to be ready to move lightning fast. Before I get to the master plan, I want to caution everybody that there is a real chance that we might not make it to H-hour. If we get an inkling that they are about to get that bunker door open, we have no choice but to move."

Campbell looked at the commanders for a moment and then held up a file. "What I have here is Commander Harris's briefback." Campbell shook his head. "This is one of the finest, most thorough briefbacks I have ever read. I have to compliment you, Commander Harris, on doing such a fine job on such short notice." Campbell shook the file and looked at the rest of the group. "This thing is a doozy. If Lieutenant Commander Harris hadn't already performed part of this, there is no way he could have sold me on it, but he did." Campbell shook his head. "Here it goes. Almost eight years ago, Commander Harris and three of his fellow SEALs jumped out of a MC-130 Combat Talon in the middle of the night and parachuted onto the roof of the White House undetected by the Secret Service. This was no stunt; it was an exercise that the Secret Service wanted the Navy to help them conduct. The results have been confirmed."

Campbell paused and looked at the group. "I'm sure some of you are wondering why I am even considering a crazy James Bond maneuver like this, and here's my reason. Iron Man has verified that explosive devices have been planted in the mansion. We have separate intelligence that tells us Aziz brought along enough Semtex to level the whole building, which means that most likely any raid will result in the loss of all the hostages and most of the assault teams. Our only chance is to get a group of demolition experts into the building just prior to the assault and figure out a way to disable these bombs. This is what we were trying to do early this morning when one of the men on Commander Harris's team was killed."

Campbell paused for a moment and then said, "Here is how things will go if we make it to H-hour. Commander Harris and three of his men will do a HALO jump out of a Special Forces MC-One-Thirty Combat Talon. Our intel people think the rooftop cameras that monitor the grounds are still operational and being used. Because of this, all four men must land on the roof. Two of SEAL Team Six's best snipers have set up shop four blocks away from the White House in the bell tower of the Old Post Office. Just prior to the landing of the first element, the sentry in the rooftop guard booth will be taken out by the snipers. From there Commander Harris's team will be met by Iron Man, who will lead them via a tunnel that runs from the basement of the mansion over to the West Wing."

Campbell paused for a moment to backtrack. "Between now and H-hour, Iron Man will reconnoiter the West Wing and collect as much information as possible. His first priority will be to obtain video surveillance of both groups of hostages. His second task will be to scout out both primary and secondary assault lanes for the Hostage Rescue Team. Having taken care of the that in advance, he will lead Commander Harris's team to open at least one of those lanes, if not both. If Commander Harris and his team fail to open those, we have one other backup in place. Within thirty minutes an Air Force E-Three-A Sentry will be on station above the city. We have reason to believe that Aziz has the ability to detonate the bombs by remote control. We don't know if this remote is radio, cellular, or digital, and we can't take a chance on guessing, so if the order is given, the AWACS will shower the area around the White House with a storm of disruption that will jam everything except the stuff that we are using."

Looking at the commanders of HRT and Delta, Campbell said, "We considered lighting up the area from the get-go but decided against it. The break in communication may tip them off and allow them to manually detonate the bombs."

There were several moments of silence, and then Slater and Gray looked at each other. They both knew it would do no good to start asking questions. There wasn't enough time to really plan and practice. This would be one of those times that they had talked about during their countless training exercises. This would be one of those times they had feared. A time when they would throw the playbook out the window.

The commander of JSOC looked around the room. After a moment of silence he focused on the warriors to his left. The men who would be going into battle. Speaking as one commando to another, he said, "A thousand things could go wrong at any stage of this operation." The three commanders acknowledged the warning given to them from a decorated soldier with a knowing look. Campbell frowned, biting his lower lip, and then added, "Stay loose . . . Pick your best shooters . . . This one is going to be all instinct and reaction. There's no time to rehearse."

RAPP AND ADAMS were back in the tiny elevator with all of their equipment, descending to lower levels of the White House. The stash room had served them well, but now they needed to be closer to the action. Before heading up to retrieve their gear, Rapp had affixed one of the surveillance units to the bottom of a fire extinguisher in the hallway. With the jamming unit out of action, Rapp could now speak clearly with the control room at Langley and bypass sticking the fiber-optic snake under the door to check and see if everything was all right.

As the elevator came to a stop, Rapp spoke into his lip mike, "Iron Man to control. We're back in the basement. Give me a check on the hallway."

A monotone male voice came back. "The hallway is clear. Over."

Rapp nodded for Adams to open the door. When Adams did so, Rapp stepped out into the hallway, his MP-10 sweeping from left to right. Adams joined him, and, after closing the outer door to the elevator, they moved quickly down the hall.

With key in hand, the wiry old engineer opened the door to the china storage room, and the two of them entered. Anna Rielly looked up, relieved they were back.

"How did it go?"

"Fine," answered Rapp as he set his weapon down and started to take the heavy backpack off. "Except Milt had to go to the bathroom again."

"Again?" asked Rielly.

Adams stood there looking the miniature version of Rapp, with his matching black baseball cap and black Nomex coveralls. Placing his hands on his hips, he shook his head and said, "You two, just wait. I'd like to see you try and do this secret-agent junk when you're my age."

Rapp laughed. "If I could only be lucky enough to live that long."

The statement sobered up Rielly in a snap. She realized that although he had said his statement with levity, he was serious.

Rapp moved his gear to the floor and said, "Milt and I are going to go over to the West Wing and check some things out while you wait right here."

"Why can't I come with you?" Rielly asked.

"Because"—Rapp kept a level tone—"this could get real hairy, Anna, and I'm going to have a hard enough time keeping an eye on Milt."

"I promise I won't get in your way. In fact, I could probably be a help."

Rapp shook his head. "It's not going to happen, Anna. And I don't have the time to sit around and discuss it with you. I've been ordered to find out what is going on in the West Wing, and I need to do it quick. Because of the situation with the president, we might be forced to launch a raid at any minute."

Rielly nodded reluctantly. "Is there anything I can do while you're gone?"

"If things proceed as I think they might, there's a chance I might need your help with something later. Okay? For now, just sit here and look pretty."

She gave a fake smile. "Thanks."

"Well"—Rapp stood—"it shouldn't be very hard for you to do." Turning to Adams, he said, "Milt, come here." Adams walked over, and Rapp affixed a small object to the side of his headset. The camera was about three inches long and an inch in diameter, with a lens at the front and a cord at the back that was hooked up to a transmitter. Rapp tucked the transmitter into a pocket on the back of Adams's combat vest, then arranged another camera on his own headset.

Rapp adjusted his lip mike and said, "Iron Man to control. You should have two more feeds from the head-mounted cameras. Can you confirm?"

The reply came over their headsets a second later. "That's affirmative, Iron Man. We are receiving both feeds."

With his baseball cap on backward, Rapp swung the arm of his headset up above his forehead and grabbed one of the fanny packs. After strapping it around Adams's waist, he said, "There are ten of the surveillance units in here. We'll decide where to put them when we get over there. Are you ready?"

He nodded.

"All right." Turning back to Rielly, he said, "You should be safe here until we get back."

"What if someone shows up?"

Rapp put a hand on his hip and thought about it. There was a chance he and Adams might not make it back. Grabbing for his thigh holster, he drew his silenced 9-mm Beretta. "You told me your dad taught you how to shoot?"

"Yep."

Rapp checked to make sure the weapon was on safety and then handed it to Rielly. He pointed to a spot on the far wall almost thirty feet away. "You see that scuff mark just above the shelf?"

Rielly nodded.

"She's locked and loaded. One in the chamber and fifteen more in the magazine. Take her off safety, and squeeze one off at the scuff mark." Rapp always felt that you could learn a lot about someone by watching how they handled a firearm.

Rielly held the weapon in both hands confidently. Keeping it pointed down range, she turned it slightly, and with the thumb of her right hand, she flicked off the safety. She stood with her feet a shoulder width apart and took aim. The silencer made the gun nose heavy, forcing her to adjust for the weight. When she had the scuff mark lined up in the sights, she squeezed the trigger.

There was a spitting noise from the end of the gun, and a split second later the louder noise of the bullet hitting the smooth concrete wall. A chunk the size of a quarter broke free and fell to the floor. Rielly's shot missed the mark by about twelve inches, low and right.

She put the gun back on safety and said, "The silencer makes it heavy."

"But nice and quiet," replied Rapp.

"Yeah." Rielly looked at the smooth black weapon.

"That's not a bad shot. My advice is for you to sit right over there." Rapp pointed toward the door that led into the hallway. "If anyone comes in that door dressed in green fatigues and carrying an AK-74, you put a bullet in his head and ask questions later."

Rielly licked her lips and nodded.

Rapp started back toward the door that led to the tunnel. "Whatever you do, Anna, don't come looking for us. If we're not back within an hour, that means something has gone wrong. You're better off waiting right here until someone from our side comes and gets you."

Rapp turned to Adams, who had the outer door open, and said, "Let's go."

Adams punched the code into the reinforced tunnel door and pushed it in. Rapp followed him into the tunnel and turned to give Rielly a smile and a nod. Then they were gone, the door closed, on their way to the West Wing.

47

AZIZ LOOKED UP at the digital clocks on the wall to his left. The clock closest to him gave him the East Coast time. It was 6:29 P.M. He took the remote control and turned the main TV from CNN to NBC. The nightly national news was about to start, and he wanted to feel the force of America's number one news network announcing another victory for him and his jihad.

When the overly dramatic music announced the start of the program, Aziz grinned with anticipation as the logo flashed across the screen, followed quickly by the words "White House Crisis—Day Three."

Tom Brokaw came on and, after a brief lead-in, he cut to the United Nations in New York. The network's correspondent clutched her microphone and passionately retold the late-breaking news. The UN Security Council had unanimously voted to lift all economic sanctions against Iraq except those involving military imports and technology. The reporter went on to tell how Israel was the only UN member to protest the vote, but since they were not a permanent member of the Security Council, they could do nothing to prevent the lifting of sanctions.

Aziz stood and smiled triumphantly. He had won again. Now all he needed was the president and he would have complete victory. Aziz grabbed his radio and barked the name of his little thief. "Mustafa!" Aziz repeated himself two more times, and then one of his other men answered.

"Rafique, it is Ragib." The man was standing watch in the basement by the door to the boiler room. "I don't think he can hear you because of the drills. Do you want me to get him?"

"Yes."

Ragib let his radio fall to his side, and he walked down the hallway toward the bunker. When he rounded the corner, he yelled, "Mustafa!" The plump man appeared from behind the door and peered down the hallway. Ragib held up his radio and yelled, "Rafique wants to talk to you."

Mustafa Yassin nodded and started walking toward Ragib. After taking his ear protectors off, he brought his radio to his mouth and said,

"Rafique, I am here." The plump little man kept walking. The farther away he got from the drills the better he could hear.

Back in the Situation Room, Aziz watched the UN story unfold on the TV and asked, "What is your progress?"

"I think it will take me about an hour."

"Are you sure?"

"I think so. The drills are getting close. Once they have reached their mark, all I have to do is take them off the door and . . . and then it should take me another ten to twenty minutes of tinkering and it should be ready."

"Call me when you are ready to take the drills off the door, and I will come over."

Yassin wasn't sure he heard him correctly and yelled into the radio, "You want me to call you when I'm ready to take the drills off the door?"

"Yes."

"Okay." The dumpy safecracker turned and walked back down the hallway toward the bunker.

IRENE KENNEDY AND General Campbell were back in the control room getting ready to monitor Rapp's foray into the West Wing. Director Stansfield and Chairman of the Joint Chiefs General Flood were sitting quietly one row behind, watching and waiting to offer their approval or opinion if needed.

General Campbell turned to one of his staffers sitting to his right and covered the mike on his headset. "Do another check on the communication links with Commander Harris, Delta, and HRT, and make sure we have backups in place." The aide nodded and went about following the order.

On the big board at the front of the room several new shots from within the White House had been added. The two that Kennedy and Campbell were most interested in were the images provided by the head cams mounted on Rapp and Adams. They had made it to the other end of the tunnel and were in position to open the door and enter the hidden hallway that led into Horsepower and up a flight of stairs to the Oval Office. The danger, of course, was their inability to check what was on the other side of the gasket-sealed door.

Back at Langley a piece of intel had been collected that was creating quit a stir. Mustafa Yassin's conversation with Aziz had been picked up by the tiny surveillance unit that Anna Rielly had placed in the ventilation shaft. Kennedy immediately ordered Rapp and Adams into a holding pattern while they reviewed the tape.

The words of Mustafa Yassin were replayed. When the segment was over, General Campbell looked to Kennedy and said, "That's it. We're not going to make it. We have to move H-hour up." Kennedy agreed, and Campbell turned to the colonel on his right and said, "Reset H-hour for nineteen-thirty, and notify all commands."

Campbell then stood to join Kennedy, who was conferring with Flood and Stansfield. The commander of JSOC listened to Kennedy explain the new time constraints.

"We need to get Iron Man moving. We have less than an hour to collect and disseminate any information he can gather."

"I disagree." Campbell shook his head. "I think we should put Iron Man in a holding pattern until just before the strike."

"Why?" asked a frowning Kennedy.

"Commander Harris and his team will be in a position to jump within twenty minutes. I don't think it's worth risking a confrontation until we have everything in place. When we're ready to move, we do so with complete surprise and overwhelming force."

Flood nodded in agreement. "And we make sure there is no chance Aziz can get his hands on the president."

"Absolutely." Campbell pointed to the monitor on the board that showed the bunker door. "With our surveillance we can guarantee to stop him before that happens."

Kennedy folded her arms stubbornly across her chest. "I disagree. I think we need to collect the intelligence. We can't send HRT in blind, or it will be a slaughter."

Flood looked to Director Stansfield. "Thomas?"

Stansfield stared at the big board for a half dozen seconds and then said, "Let's consult Mitch. He's on-site, and I'd like to get his opinion."

Without waiting for agreement, Kennedy turned around and grabbed the headset off her desk. Holding it over one ear, she adjusted the lip mike and said, "Control to Iron Man. Come in."

Rapp was leaning against the wall by the reinforced steel door, waiting impatiently. His thoughts had drifted back to putting a bullet in the center of Aziz's forehead. Again, he had not shared this with the people back at Langley, and he wasn't about to, but if the chance came up, he was going to do it. Tactically it made the most sense to him. Kill the leader and watch the others flounder. The voice of his boss interrupted his pleasant thought.

Rapp pushed away from the wall and said, "I'm here. Go ahead."

"It appears they will have the bunker door open in about sixty minutes." There was a pause, and Kennedy added, "We're not going to make it to H-hour."

"Well, I'd better get moving then."

"We ah . . ."—Kennedy looked at the three men—"have some dissension on how to proceed."

Rapp rolled his eyes. "I'm listening."

"The new H-hour is set for nineteen-thirty."

Rapp looked at his watch. "That only gives me about forty-eight minutes. Like I said . . . I'd better get moving."

General Campbell had grabbed his headset and was standing next to Kennedy. "Iron Man, we will have Six's element in place in approximately twenty minutes. We don't want to risk precipitating a confrontation until we have everything in place."

"But we have absolutely no idea what we're up against there."

Campbell looked at Flood and said, "Right now we think it's better that we retain the element of surprise."

Rapp was getting pissed. Milt Adams stood from where he had been sitting and asked, "What now?"

Rapp waved him off and said into his lip mike, "I disagree. If we don't find out where the bombs are, and what we're up against, this is a suicide operation." Rapp listened for a response, but got none. He knew they were conferring with each other. Not wanting them to come to a decision without his input, he asked, "Why are we talking about changing the plan?"

Kennedy fielded the question. "The surveillance unit you placed in the ventilation shaft picked up a radio conversation between Yassin and, we think, Aziz. Yassin told him that he would be done with the drills in about an hour. After that it would take him anywhere from ten to twenty minutes to get the door open."

"Anything else?"

"Only that Aziz wants Yassin to call him when he takes the drills off the door."

Rapp thought about the number of terrorists. The information they had gotten from Harut told them there were eleven. He had personally reduced that number by one, leaving ten to be dealt with. Rapp tried to guess how Aziz would proceed with the next part of his plan, focusing on the operational aspect of how Aziz would have to extract the president. That was when it hit him.

"Aziz is going to want to be there when Yassin gets the door open, right?"

Campbell answered. "I suppose."

"Not only will he want to be there, he'll have to be there. He knows the president has Secret Service agents with him, right?"

"Probably."

"Whether he wants the president dead or alive, he's going to have to bring some firepower with him to deal with those agents."

"Where are you going with this?" asked Campbell.

"He's going to have to split his force. Our intel tells us Aziz went in with eleven people, including himself. He's down to ten. One of those ten is on the roof and two more are in the basement by the bunker." The plan crystallized in Rapp's mind. "The way we attack this is we wait for Aziz to split his force. When they shut the drills down, we'll have a minimum of a ten-minute window of opportunity to strike. During that time, the number of terrorists guarding the hostages will be no more than six . . . maybe less if Aziz brings more men over to back him up."

Back at Langley the plan was gaining ground. Especially with General Flood, a military tactician who loved the idea of dividing his enemy's forces. "Iron Man, I like the idea. Sit tight for a minute while we run this one by the president." General Flood set down his headset and looked at Stansfield. "What do you think?"

48

VICE PRESIDENT BAXTER sat behind the desk in his study and stared blankly at the TV. The images were nothing more than a blur and the voices a hum of background noises. He was immersed in the thought of becoming president. It was so tantalizing, so tempting, it had drawn him into a fantasy world. Since early childhood he could remember dreaming of being president one day, and now with it so close, he had some reservations. Not reservations about assuming the office, but how it would play if word leaked that he had been given information that the terrorists were working on getting President Hayes out of the bunker.

Baxter started to think angles. He started to think PR. First, he had been in New York when the whole mess started. He wasn't the one that had invited these terrorists into the White House for coffee. Second, he would somehow have to let it be known that the Pentagon's best and brightest had sworn the president was untouchable in his new bunker. General Flood's information that the terrorists might be attempting to extricate the president would have to be downplayed. They would have to say the information was vague and incomplete. On top of that they could spin the story of the two SEALs getting caught in the ventilation shaft, and Aziz's subsequent warnings.

Dallas King would be proven right, though. Eventually, they would have to rely on the morally superior premise that they acted in the interest of saving the hostages. That in good conscience, he could not have risked the lives of all of those people just to make sure the president was safe when, in fact, the information to the contrary was incomplete at best.

Dallas King entered the room eating a banana. He said, "We need to talk about something." King continued walking across the large study. He sat in one of the two chairs sitting in front of the vice president's desk and took another bite.

Vice President Baxter picked up the remote control for the TV and hit the mute button. "What now?"

"Everything went off great at the UN, but I'm a little nervous about tomorrow."

"Why?" Baxter placed his right elbow on the chair's armrest and rested his chin on his hand.

"I was just talking to Ted." King was referring to the vice president's national security adviser, Ted Nelson. "He says Israel is starting to make waves." King sat back and took the last bite of his banana.

"What's their problem now?"

"They think they know what Aziz's final demand is, and they want it to be known that they will refuse to cooperate."

"What do they think the last demand will be?"

"They think he will ask the U.S. and the UN to recognize a free and autonomous Palestinian state."

"And?" Baxter shrugged as if it was no big deal.

"Israel has sent word that they will not be bullied into any such agreement. Ted says his sources are telling him that in four hours the Israeli defense forces will go on alert, and if Aziz demands a free and autonomous Palestinian state, the Israelis will occupy the territories."

Baxter swung forward in his chair. "Damn it. You get their ambassador on the line, and tell him if they do any such thing, I'll make sure their aid from us dries up to nothing."

King shook his head. "You can't do that, and they know you can't. There are too many senators and congressmen that would come to their aid."

Baxter's temper flared. "The hell I can't."

King looked at his temperamental boss and waited for him to calm. After several moments he continued. "Picking a battle with Israel is bad politics. . . . It plays horrible in New York and even worse with our big donors out in Hollywood. I have an idea that might keep everybody happy." King sat back with a grin and crossed his legs.

On edge, Baxter blurted, "Well, out with it. I don't have all day."

"I think it's time to broker a backroom deal with them. We tell them to protest loudly if the demand is made, but to take no military action. In return, we promise that as soon as this next group of hostages are released, we'll retake the building."

"I thought we didn't want to do that."

"I thought so at first," King said cautiously. "The more I think about it, though, you don't want to be seen as too big a wimp. If you can succeed in getting two-thirds of the hostages released and then give the order to retake the building . . ." King smiled. "You will be seen as someone who was not just a good diplomat but someone who can get tough when it's called for." To himself King added, *and you'll solve my problem in the process.*

"Maybe." Baxter frowned while he thought about this new strategy. Then, looking at his watch, he asked, "Why hasn't Director Stansfield or General Flood come to me with this information?" King shrugged. "If Ted knows about this, they sure as hell do."

"I don't know. Maybe Ted has a better source."

"Come on," scoffed Baxter. "Better than Thomas Stansfield . . . I doubt it." Baxter reached for his phone and then realized he didn't know where either Flood or Stansfield was. One of the minions could take care of that. He had more important things to do with his time. Looking across his large desk, he said, "Get General Flood and Director Stansfield on the line for me."

STANSFIELD HAD DECIDED it would be better if they called the president from the conference room, so he, Flood, Campbell, and Kennedy left the control room and entered the glass-enclosed bubble. In under a minute both Rapp and President Hayes were on the line.

General Flood gave the president a brief overview of Rapp's plan to wait until the last possible moment before launching the assault. President Hayes listened intently.

The first question out of his mouth was, "What's the downside if our timing is off and we wait too long?" Hayes had an inkling of what the result would be.

"If we miscalculate, sir"—General Campbell paused for a second—"we might jeopardize all of you."

"General Campbell." It was Rapp on the line. "Delta Force is handling the mansion, correct?"

"Correct."

"How much time will it take to get them from the forward staging area to the White House . . . assuming the skids are warmed up and the shooters are locked and loaded?"

"Colonel Gray tells me he can put twelve operators on the roof in under two minutes, and have twelve more on-site within the next thirty seconds."

"Excuse me for asking"—back in the bunker President Hayes was frowning—"but if we can put that many people on the roof by helicopter, then why in the hell are we screwing around with parachuting these SEALs onto the roof?"

General Flood fielded the question. "Element of surprise, sir. If we start moving the troops in by helicopter, the media and the thousands of people downtown will see them. We hope to land the SEALs and get them into the mansion without anyone noticing. It's risky, but it's the only

chance we have of defusing some of the bombs so we can get the HRT in
to save the hostages in the West Wing."

Rapp grabbed the chance to drive his plan home. "And my point, Mr.
President, is if we wait for Aziz and an unknown number of terrorists to
head over to get you out of the bunker, we will significantly increase the
chances of successfully rescuing the hostages."

General Flood liked the idea and added, "It's a sound plan, Mr. President. We divide their forces at a time when you are still safe in your
bunker, and our main concern is saving the hostages over in the West
Wing. Instead of having to deal with eight Tangos, we'll only have to
worry about five or six."

"So you're telling me it will increase our chances of saving hostages."

"Yes."

Hayes didn't pause for a second. "Then let's do it."

There was a knock on the conference room door, and then one of
General Flood's aides entered. "Excuse me, General. The vice president is
on the line and he wishes to speak to you and Director Stansfield immediately. If you'd like, I can have the call patched through to you here."

President Hayes's voice floated down from the overhead speaker system. "I think it's time we let Vice President Baxter know that he's no
longer running the show."

Flood turned to his aide. "Patch the call through."

Ten seconds later one of the lines on the main telecommunications
console started to ring. Irene Kennedy punched the proper buttons and
brought the newest party into the teleconference. She nodded to her boss
and Flood to let them know the line was up.

Flood called out in his deep voice, "Vice President Baxter?"

A woman's voice answered and told them to hold the line while she
got the vice president. For more than a minute the group sat in silence,
waiting for the man who had initiated the call to join them. No one
spoke. They all waited with anticipation to witness the ensuing confrontation between the two biggest players in American politics.

When Baxter finally came on the line, he said, "General Flood, are
you there?"

"Yes, I'm here with Director Stansfield."

"Good," replied Baxter in voice that implied anything but. "I just received some troubling information." Baxter paused, waiting for them to
ask him what it was. No one bit on his lead, so Baxter expanded. "My national security adviser just informed me that Israel has been making certain threats."

Baxter stopped again, waiting for Stansfield or Flood to respond. The two men looked at each other and said nothing. If it weren't for the tense situation, they probably would have been smiling, taking the time to enjoy the impending moment.

Baxter started again, frustration showing in his voice. "Have either of you heard any of these rumors?"

"Yes," replied General Flood. "We have."

"Well, why haven't you bothered to tell me?"

Flood looked up at the speakers, wondering when the president would decide to join the conversation. "We've been busy, sir."

"Busy." Baxter mocked General Flood. "Too busy to pick up the phone and inform the commander in chief of a crucial development."

"Commander in chief." President Hayes's voice floated down, neither angry nor calm, just supremely confident. "I don't think so, Sherman."

Only Stansfield kept a straight face. Flood, Campbell, and Kennedy all grinned with satisfaction. There was a long moment of silence before Baxter responded. When he did, it came forth with a combination of insincere relief and fear.

"Robert, is that you?"

"Yes, it is, Sherman."

"How did . . . What happened . . . How did we get ahold of you?"

"Never mind, Sherman. I hear you've done a super job setting our foreign policy and national security back a half a century."

"I don't know what you've been hearing"—Baxter sounded panicked—"but this has been no easy task, trying to save American lives and balance our foreign-policy concerns. We have been working very hard to ensure—"

President Hayes cut him off by saying, "I have been fully briefed on what you, Marge Tutwiler, and your lapdog Dallas King have been up to, and I don't like one bit of it. I don't have the time, the patience, or the energy to deal with you right now, but when I get out of here, you are going to have some explaining to do."

"But, Robert"—Baxter's voice was cracking from the tension—"I think you have it all wrong. I don't know what General Flood and Director Stansfield have been telling you, but I'm sure I can explain. I have had the best of intentions in every decision I have made during this crisis."

"I'm sure you have," replied a skeptical President Hayes. "You've had your chance to sit on the throne, and you've screwed things up miserably. Now it's time to get the hell out of the way and let the professionals handle things."

"But, Robert . . ."

"But nothing, Sherman! This conversation is over!"

All that was heard from the vice president was the click of his phone hanging up. After a couple of long moments of silence, the president's voice floated back down, asking, "Now, where were we?"

49

THE AIR FORCE MC-130 Combat Talon cruised through the skies over Washington, D.C., at ten thousand feet. Part of the 1st Special Operations Wing, the Combat Talon was a unique asset in the delivery and retrieval of Special Forces operators. Lt. Commander Harris stood in the back of the modified C-130, looking out the open ramp and down at the city. The wind whistled through the back of the cargo area, and the four engines outside rumbled in the evening air, making communication difficult. To Harris's right, the bright orange orb of the sun was falling beneath the horizon. To his left, storm clouds were moving in. The first was a good sign—darkness was something that he welcomed—but the second was not. Wind and rain did not go well with parachuting.

The pilots were flying up and down a fifteen-mile corridor five miles east of the White House. Harris and his fellow SEALs had made every jump there was. He'd done both high-altitude, high-opening (HAHO) and high altitude, low opening (HALO) jumps, as well as static-line jumps from five hundred feet all the way up to thirty thousand plus. Eight years earlier, when he had participated in the exercise for the Secret Service, he and his men had conducted a HAHO jump out of the back of an Air Force C-141 StarLifter. At an altitude of twenty-five thousand feet the men leapt from the plane and popped their chutes. From almost five miles up, Harris and his team expertly guided their double-canopy parachutes over a forty-five-mile distance and set themselves down gently on the roof of the Executive Mansion. At first the Secret Service was shocked by the results. But, after they sat with the SEALs and realized the years of training and high level of skill that such a jump required, they ruled the possibility of a terrorist group successfully conducting such an operation all but impossible.

Harris and his men were about to put all of their jumping skills to use. General Campbell had briefed him minutes earlier on the newest aspect of the plan, and it was creating a mathematical nightmare for the SEAL. No longer would they be able to choose their jump time. They would now have to wait for Aziz to make his move and then quickly get the plane into position.

Repeating the jump he had done eight years earlier was not an option. Jumping from that altitude would have required that he and his men, and the crew of the unpressurized aircraft, go on oxygen an hour before take-off. By the time his plan was approved, they had missed that window of opportunity. There wasn't enough time, so Harris had decided they would jump from ten thousand feet and go into a free-fall glide for the White House. At one thousand feet they would pop their chutes and float down the last leg.

Commander Harris moved away from the back of the ramp to inform his men of the impending rain. Inside, the bleak cargo area glowed with the red light to help the men gain their night vision. Harris had brought along the large Mick Reavers, who was serving as the jumpmaster, and Tony Clark and Jordan Rostein—two of Six's best shooters and demolitions experts. All four men were dressed in their black Nomex coveralls, balaclava hoods, and gloves. The fire-retardant material was a must in any operation, and even more so when dealing with explosives. Operating in a dry environment, all of the men were carrying 9-mm SIG-Sauer P226 pistols, integrally silenced MP-10s, and a bevy of extra magazines in their assault vests that fit snuggly over their Kevlar body armor. Radio checks had been completed on the ground. The four operators were using Motorola MX300 radios rigged with throat mikes and earpieces.

Harris approached his men and screamed over the wind, "That storm keeps coming in from the east, and it doesn't look good."

Clark shook his head at his CO. He'd known Harris for over a decade and knew the man to be just crazy enough to try to jump in the middle of a storm. Clark reached up and adjusted his goggles. While doing so, he leaned closer to Harris. Over the roar he yelled, "We ain't jumping in the rain, Harry."

Harris nodded, and then, turning back for the ramp, he muttered to himself, "We'll see."

Out the rear of the plane Harris saw the storm intensifying. Suddenly, a flash lightning lit up the sky and streaked toward the ground in two separate veins. The strike was followed by a crack that could be heard over the roar of the engines. Sheets of rain could be seen falling over the Chesapeake. The rain would continue to roll in across the Maryland countryside and envelop the capital. They had thirty minutes, tops, before the rain rendered the jump suicidal.

RAPP AND ADAMS were ready to go. They were at the door going over the final checklist. If things went sour, HRT was twenty seconds away from breaching the building and Delta Force could be on-site to secure the president in under two minutes. Now was the time to take risks and roll the dice.

Before telling him to punch in the code, Rapp asked Adams, "Are you good to go, Milt?"

Adams pulled off his baseball cap, and with a handkerchief, he wiped a layer of sweat from his bald, black head. Then with a nod, he said, "I'm ready."

Rapp did one last quick check of his equipment, and said, "Iron Man to control. We're going in. Over." Rapp then nodded to Adams, who punched in the code.

At the first sound of air escaping from the gasket-sealed door, Adams stepped back, allowing Rapp to move forward and take the lead. Rapp didn't know what to expect on the other side. The door could be booby-trapped; Aziz could have a guard posted on the other side—there was no way of knowing. Rapp had to guess. With a limited amount of resources, Rapp thought, Aziz wouldn't be able to afford to place a guard outside the door. And that was assuming he had found it.

The bigger concern was a bomb. Rapp pushed Adams against the wall closest to the door's hinges and placed his hand on the handle. After pausing for a moment, he turned his head away, pushed down on the handle, and pulled the door in two inches.

Hiding behind the heavy steel door, to protect him from the possible blast, Rapp listened for the telltale sound of a trip wire pulling a pin. He counted to three, then five, for good measure. With his left hand clutching his MP-10, he reached back with his right, and Adams handed him the snake. Rapp nosed the tiny fiber-optic camera around the corner. He scanned to the left, to the right, and then up. The shadowy images were being broadcast back to Langley.

Over his headset he heard the voice of General Campbell, "Everything looks good, Iron Man."

Rapp peeked around the door to get a better look. To his left was a set of steep concrete stairs. Rapp had half expected the passageway to be dark. Instead, the hidden staircase that led up to the Oval Office was dimly lit with only two bulbs. Straight ahead a sliver of light shone from underneath a door that led to Horsepower—the Secret Service's presidential detail command post. That was where the alarm systems and surveillance cameras were monitored. All video surveillance of both the grounds and the interior of the West Wing, Executive Mansion, and East Wing were monitored by the new Joint Operations Command, across the street in the EOB. Horsepower was concerned primarily with the president and watched only the areas of the compound where the president was. The

uniformed division was responsible for everything else. In Rapp's Secret
Service briefing they had explained that in the moments after the raid, the
interior cameras around the White House began to go off-line one by
one. The obvious reason was Aziz did not want the Secret Service to be
able to watch what he was doing. Rapp's responsibility was to discover
how much of the system was still on-line, and if any Tangos were monitoring it.

Stepping completely from behind the door, Rapp carefully edged forward into the small landing area just outside of Horsepower. Adams followed close behind, then slid the tiny lens under the door and began
working it from one side of the room to the other.

Rapp watched over his shoulder. A couple of old metal desks came
into view, and then they spotted something. Rapp gestured for Adams to
bring it back. There, all the way across the room, were the shoulders and
head of a man.

"Mark one Tango," said General Campbell over Rapp's headset.
"That's the control panel. Can you get us a better look at what he's watching?"

Adams zoomed the camera in on the man sitting behind the door. In
front of the terrorist were a dozen small black-and-white monitors
mounted in a metal rack. The bottom middle two were obscured by the
man's head, but the ten other monitors all appeared to be showing images
of the exterior of the White House.

Rapp turned away from the door and, in as soft a voice as possible,
asked, "You're recording this, right?"

"That's affirmative," replied Campbell.

"Good. We're going to plant a monitor here and move on." Rapp
fished one of the micro video-and-audio surveillance transmitters out of
his pocket and turned it on. Then, setting it on the floor, he edged the
unit's thin fiber-optic camera under door as far as it would go. Turning
away from the door again, he whispered, "Are you receiving the new signal?"

"That's affirmative."

Rapp tapped Adams on the shoulder and pointed up the stairs. Adams
retracted the snake and coiled it back into a loose loop. Before proceeding,
Rapp bent over and checked for any trip wires. After making sure it was
safe, he took the lead. At the top there was no landing, just the interior of
the wall panel that accessed the area between the Oval Office and the
president's private dining room.

Adams pointed to a latch and said, "It opens in." Rapp nodded. He
would have preferred to have quietly drilled a hole in the wall and inserted

a camera to see what was on the other side, but they were short on time. Rapp pressed the latch and held his MP-10 ready. The narrow section of the wall popped in. Pulling it open further, Rapp looked out across the hall at President Hayes's private study. Almost instantly his nostrils filled with a ripe stench.

The smell crawled into the stairwell, and Rapp started breathing through his mouth. Remembering Adams, he turned and whispered, "I think there are some dead bodies up here. Are you going to be all right?"

Adams nodded and waved Rapp forward.

Rapp pointed at Adams and then the ground, signaling for him to stay put for a second. Rapp moved to the right and hugged the wall. The failing evening light came through the windows. In the dining room ahead, the overhead light was lit as well as a table lamp. It was as if the building were stuck in time. Several half-filled coffee cups littered the table, and a tray filled with dishes was waiting to be carted away. To the right, the pantry door was open, and Rapp could see out into the main hallway. This caused him to pull back a step.

Everything Rapp saw, the people back at Langley saw. Campbell came over his headset. "Iron Man, there is a door on your left that leads out into the Rose Garden." Rapp's head swiveled toward the door, and the general said, "That's it. Let's check it for explosives."

"Roger." Looking back to make sure there was no one in the hallway, Rapp moved out around the left side of the dining room table. A large plant stood next to the door and behind was the same gray metal box Rapp had seen in the president's bedroom. From the side of the box a clear filament wire wove its way through a series of eyelet screws. The clear wire, really nothing more than fishing line, went across the base of the door, through another eyelet screw, up three feet, where it went through another looped eyelet and then began its horizontal course across the door again. Rapp followed it to the other side and stopped.

"Shit."

"What is it?" asked Campbell.

"You can't see the wire?"

"No."

"It runs across the base of the door, up three feet, and then back across. But the big problem is it doesn't stop." Rapp walked along the wall, eyeing the clear wire as he went. "It runs all along the wall, not just the door."

"That could be a problem." They had guessed that the doors would be wired, so the HRT was planning to blow mouse holes in the walls to enter the building. With wire running across the walls, that wouldn't work.

"I'm going to keep moving. We'd better hope those SEALs are good, or we're in a lot of trouble." Rapp walked quickly back toward the other end of the room. Instead of heading back into the short hallway, he cut into the pantry and carefully approached the door that led out into the main hallway of the first floor of the West Wing. Clutching the thick grip of his integral suppressor, he inched his way to the doorframe. His eyes were instantly drawn to the trails of dark dried blood that stained the hallway carpeting. The blood came from both directions, as if bodies had been dragged, and went into the room that was across the hall and to the right.

Rapp didn't want to think about what was behind the closed door, but believed it was probably what was causing the grotesque smell. As he checked up and down the hallway, he noticed another bomb to his left. Rapp cringed and tried to focus the head cam on the gray metal box. This was worse than he thought. Not only was there an outer layer of bombs, it appeared there was also an inner layer to contend with. Rapp retreated to join Adams.

"Did you get a bead on that second bomb and its location?"

"Affirmative. Was the discoloration on the carpeting what I thought it was?"

"It looked like it was dry blood," replied Rapp as he reached Milt Adams's position. Rapp continued past him two steps and poked his head into the Oval Office. Instantly, he saw the cause of the smell. The bloated body of a man lay between the two couches on the floor. His head had fallen next to the embroidered presidential seal and had deposited a large pool of blood. Rapp edged around the first sofa and tried to get a look at the man's face, but it did no good. His cheeks and neck were so swollen they looked as if they might break the binds of the dress shirt and necktie. The man's hands had suffered the same gross expansion.

Rapp moved on and checked the curved wall behind the president's desk. Near the door that led onto the Oval Colonnade, he found another bomb. The clear wire traversed the wall horizontally twice.

Exhaling, he said, "Same thing as the other room. I'm taking Milt, and we're going to check out the interior."

Adams was standing in the doorway, looking at the puffy body on the floor. As Rapp pulled close, he asked, "Do you recognize him?"

Adams shook his head.

Rapp jerked the barrel of his gun back in the direction from which they had come. As he walked into the dining room, he hugged the wall to his right and kept his gun up and leveled. He turned back to Adams and asked, "There's a door right across the hall here; where does it lead?"

"The Roosevelt Room."

"What's in there?"

"Just a big conference table."

Rapp nodded. "Okay. I'm going to cover you from this little room here. I want you to go across the hall to the Roosevelt Room and stick the snake under the door. And remember, stay on the left side of the door-frame. Don't stand in the middle."

Adams nodded his little head. Rapp had been adamant about where to stand so as not to get shot. Rapp moved out and stepped into the small pantry off the dining room. At the doorway to the main hall, he eased his head out and checked in both directions. His right hand came up by his shoulder, and he waved Adams forward.

Milt scampered through the pantry and across the hall. The door to the Roosevelt Room was just to his right, and the main door to the Oval Office was almost directly across the hall from it. Staying on the left side, as Rapp had told him, Adams eased the tip of the snake under the door and stared at the monitor. He wasn't sure at first what it was that he was looking at. There were lumps on the floor and the large conference table had been overturned and flipped against the far wall. Something moved, and that's when he figured out that the lumps on the floor were bodies. What had moved was a leg. A leg wearing blue trousers with a red stripe running down the side. Adams immediately recognized the pants as those belonging to a U.S. marine.

A pair of more discerning eyes were back at Langley, watching both the shots from the head cams and the fiber-optic snake. General Campbell's voice came over Adams's headset. "Milt, give me a full sweep nice and slow, and then pull back away from the door." Adams turned the dial with his thumb and slowly moved the snake from the left to the right and then back again. When he was done, Campbell told him, "That's good, now bug out." Adams withdrew the snake and went back across the hall to join Rapp.

Rapp whispered into his lip mike, "Control, what did you see? Over."

"One Tango at eleven o'clock, sitting in a chair facing your door, holding what appears to be an AK-74 in his lap." As Rapp listened, he could hear other voices in the background. Campbell came back seconds later. "I've been advised that there are two other entrances into the room, one of which is blocked. On the floor we appear to have at least a half dozen hostages, maybe more. They look to be tied and wearing hoods."

Adams, who was standing just behind Rapp, was hearing the same thing, and he added, "One of those men in there is a marine."

"That's affirmative. We are reviewing the tape to see what else we can get, but for now, it looks like we've found our missing hostages."

Rapp peeked back around the corner and then looked at the base of the door to the Roosevelt Room. Turning his head back toward Adams, he whispered, "Milt, fish out one of the surveillance units. Bend the lens at a right angle and stick it to the base of the door. I'll cover you."

Adams nodded, walked quietly across the hall, and placed the camera. Rapp asked, "Control, how does the new feed look?"

"Good, we've got about eighty percent of the room, and the Tango is in the picture."

Rapp turned back to Adams. "Rig me two of the black ones."

Adams readied the first one and handed it off to Rapp, who stepped out into the hallway. Immediately to his right was a small credenza with an arrangement of wilting flowers sitting in an ornate vase. Rapp reached behind the credenza and stuck the surveillance unit to the back of it. Stepping back into the pantry, he retrieved the second unit and placed it underneath the credenza at an angle that would cover the hallway as it went in the other direction.

50

MUSTAFA YASSIN WAS proud of his work. He double-checked his progress again and grinned. With satisfaction, he flipped off the power switches on all three drills and backed the bits out of their holes. He had reached the proper depth early. Yassin did not have the brawn of men like Aziz, but he was smarter than most. The little thief had learned from dealing with men like Saddam to pad his estimates and manage his superiors' expectations.

The main drill, and largest of the three, sat on a tripod. Yassin tugged at the base and pulled it back out of the way. The other two drills were magnetized. After wresting them from the door, he sat on his toolbox and lit up a cigarette. The plump man inhaled deeply and picked up his radio. He toggled the transmit button and called Aziz.

Aziz was snacking on a sandwich in the galley of the White House mess when he heard the call. Pulling his radio to his mouth, he said, "Mustafa, this is Rafique. What do you want?"

"I am ready for you."

Aziz set his sandwich down and wiped the crumbs from his fingers. "Say again."

"I am ready for you. When you arrive, I will proceed with the last part."

Aziz was elated. "I will be over shortly." Grabbing his MP-5 from the counter, he walked out into the mess and looked over the mass of huddled hostages. There was one person in particular he was looking for. Someone who would elicit the proper emotion from the president. Aziz circled the group looking for the face of Sally Burke, the president's secretary and mother of five. If the president's bodyguards chose to fight, Mrs. Burke would be used as a shield. Aziz found her sitting with a group of women. With his long thin finger, he gestured for her to join him.

Burke pointed to herself nervously and asked, "Me?"

"Yes, you, Mrs. Burke." Smiling, Aziz extended his hand to help the woman to her feet.

Burke reluctantly grabbed it and stood. "What do you want with me?"

"Don't worry. Everything will be all right; we just need you to talk to someone."

"Who?"

"Don't worry. Everything will be just fine." Aziz squeezed her shoulder and again told her not to worry. Then gently he turned her toward the door and led her from the room. Bringing his radio to his mouth, he said, "Muammar, meet me in the pressroom."

TO RAPP'S LEFT was the hall leading to the main entrance for the first floor. To his right was the pressroom and a door that led out onto the Colonnade. Rapp wanted to check both of them and see if they were as strongly defended as the doors in the president's dining room and the one in the Oval Office.

As Rapp headed for the pressroom, he heard an increase in the chatter over his headset. At the same time he heard voices from somewhere ahead. He began rapidly backpedaling down the hallway.

General Campbell came over the headset, his voice rushed. "Iron Man, we're out of time. They've stopped drilling and are getting ready to open the bunker door."

Rapp couldn't respond at the moment. He had more urgent things to worry about and didn't want to give himself away by making any more noise than he had to. He made it back to the pantry seconds later and ducked out of the hallway alongside Adams. He whispered into his headset, "Are you sure?"

"Yes."

"How much time do we have?" They cut through the dining room and into the hallway, where he pushed open the wall panel.

"We're not sure."

Rapp closed the wall behind him and gestured for Adams to start moving down the stairs. "What's our best guess?" he whispered.

There was some discussion on the other end and then, "Ten minutes, tops."

Rapp and Adams hit the landing outside of Horsepower, and Rapp pushed Adams into the tunnel. Once they were inside, Rapp closed the door so he could speak without worry of being heard. "Control, let's take it from the top. The place is wired to the gills, and we've only seen a quarter of it. Our only shot is to get these SEALs in here and have them defuse a point of entry for HRT."

"We've got another problem. We just discovered that one of the monitors in Horsepower is tuned to a rooftop camera."

Rapp thought about it quickly and came up with a solution. "I'll wait down here, and if the Tango in Horsepower sees them come in I'll take him out."

Rapp looked at Adams and waited for Campbell's reply. He quickly grew frustrated with being cut out of the discussion process on the other end. After more than ten seconds of waiting, he shouted into his lip mike, "Irene, are you there?"

"Yes."

"Keep me in the loop. I'm your only on-site asset, and we don't have time to debate every point."

General Flood came on the line. "Iron Man, we've got some logistical problems. We were off by almost thirty minutes on our last estimate, and we can't afford to be off by that much again. Not with the president's life on the line."

"Then bring Delta in quicker, but we have to get Harris and his boys going, or those hostages are all dead."

"They might be anyway," stated General Campbell. "I'd say right now the chances of getting HRT in that building are between slim and none. And if we do get them in, the chances of them coming out alive aren't much better."

Rapp was pissed. The minutes were ticking away and people were getting cold feet. "I need help. I can take out the Tango in Horsepower. I can maybe take out the Tango up in the Roosevelt Room, but there's no way I can contend with all of these bombs and take out the Tangos in the mess. We need to take some risks!"

Flood's deep voice came over the headset. "We don't want to see the hostages die either, but we're not about to send good men on a suicide mission."

"We're paid to take risks, General Flood. You've been out in the field, and if you were twenty years younger, you would want in, no matter how bad the odds. Put the question to Harris and his men, and I'll guarantee they'll want in."

There was a moment of silence, and then General Campbell said, "I agree. We have to try."

Kennedy and Stansfield agreed with Campbell, which put all the pressure on General Flood. It was a risky operation, but they had to try. Flood knew it. After a brief moment of reflection the chairman of the Joint Chiefs gave the approval. The second he did so, General Campbell turned around and started barking orders to the JSOC staff sitting in front of him. The officers in turn relayed the orders over secure lines.

*   *   *

THE MC-130 COMBAT Talon was three minutes away from the jump point when they received the go-ahead from JSOC. The navigator informed Commander Harris of the countdown, and the four SEALs moved to the back ramp with their bulky chutes and packs. Under their left arms, their suppressed Heckler & Koch MP-10 submachine guns were safely secured.

The four men stood in single file at the top of the ramp. Reavers, the jumpmaster, was first in line. He checked everyone's chute one last time and then took up his place in the number one slot.

Harris walked up to Reavers's side and looked out at the horizon. To the west the sun was now down, but the sky above it was still lit. To the east it looked as if the world were about to end. The sky was black from as far to the north and east as the eye could see. Looking down, Harris could see the Beltway running east to west, and to his right was the University of Maryland. Beyond the university, the city of Baltimore was getting pounded by the storm. The commander could tell from the trees below that it was gusting hard.

Mick Reavers yelled into his CO's ear, "Great weather to jump in. Who's the crazy bastard that came up with this plan?"

Harris smiled. "We've been in worse situations, Mick. Just make sure you hike up your skirt before you jump. We wouldn't want it to get caught on anything." Reavers gave his boss the bird. Harris smiled at the big slab of beef before him and slapped Reavers on the shoulder. Returning to his spot at the end of the stick, the commander checked the altimeter strapped to his left wrist and waited for the signal.

Through the eerie red light of the cabin, the green jump light began to flash. Almost instantly Reavers raised his right hand and gave the signal for the men to stand by. Seconds later, Reavers gave the go signal and leapt from the open ramp of the Combat Talon. Tony Clark came next, then Jordan Rostein, and lastly Dan Harris pivoted and leapt from the plane.

All four men turned one hundred eighty degrees in the air and assumed the free-fall position known as the frog—arms and legs extended and bent slightly upward. In the darkening sky, the luminescent tape on their helmets helped them keep track of each other and line up. Beneath them and to the south, the White House was easily identifiable.

RAPP WAS RECEIVING steady updates from Langley while he tried to think of potential problems. He had identified many, but there were two he could actually do something about.

He turned to Adams and asked, "Is that door to Horsepower locked?"

"Yes."

"Does the S-key open it?"

"Yep."

Rapp pointed to Adams. "Take the monitor off, quick." As Adams started to do so, Rapp grabbed his lip mike and said, "Control, I am sending Milt up to the roof to guide the team through the tunnel."

General Campbell came back, "Are you sure we need to do that? They've studied the blueprints."

"We can't afford any screw-ups. Milt knows the way." Rapp flipped his lip mike up. "Milt, bust your ass back over there and grab my silenced pistol from Anna. I don't want you using yours. Tell her to hurry back over here because I need her help. Then you get up to the back staircase that leads to the roof. Someone will be talking to you on the radio and telling you if the coast is clear. When you hear that the snipers have taken the shot at the terrorist in the guard booth, I want you to pop that hatch immediately. If that terrorist is still alive, you are to put him down. You cannot allow him to say anything over the radio."

Rapp grabbed the monitor from Adams and started him down the stairs. "Hurry up, Milt."

Adams raced down the stairs with amazing agility for his age and disappeared into the tunnel. Rapp checked his watch and listened to the radio chatter coming over his headset. Waiting for Rielly to get back, he tuned the monitor into the surveillance unit that was mounted just outside of Horsepower. The image of the back of the terrorist's head appeared on the screen.

Less than thirty seconds later, Anna Rielly hustled up the stairs, out of breath and holding her side.

Rapp looked at her and asked, "Is it your rib?"

Rielly nodded with a look of pain on her face.

"Just hang in there a little while longer. Here's what I need you to do." Rapp held up his S-key. "There's a door on the other side of this, and that key opens it. In that room one of the terrorists is watching surveillance monitors. We might need to take him out, but we don't want to unless we absolutely have to."

"So you want me to open the door with this?"

"Yes. I'm gonna open this door, and once I do that, we have to talk in whispers. Just do everything I tell you to do, when I tell you to do it, and we'll be fine." Rapp punched in the code for the door, leaned on the handle, and stepped into the landing area. He set the monitor and his MP-10 on the ground. Dropping to a knee, Rapp moistened the jagged end of the S-key with spit. When he had it wet enough, he grabbed the doorknob with one hand and brought the tip of the key to the lock. Looking back and forth between the monitor and the lock, he began to slide the key in. It was inserted a third of the way when Rapp stopped. The terrorist leaned back his chair and clasped his hands behind his neck. Rapp didn't move, didn't breathe for five seconds; then slowly, he slid the key the rest of the way in.

He leaned back and gestured for Rielly to join him on the ground. Pulling her close, he whispered into her ear, "When I give you the signal, I want you to grab the key and the doorknob. After that, if you hear me say the word 'Go,' open it as quickly as possible and then get out of the way."

THREE MD-530 LITTLE Bird helicopters worked their way up the Potomac River. The small, agile, and quiet helicopters were being flown by the elite pilots of the Army's 160th Special Operations Regiment—the Night Stalkers. Each helicopter carried four Delta Force operators. The commandos stood on the chopper's landing skids, two to a side.

The helicopters approached the group of bridges just to the south of the George Mason Memorial Bridge, skimming the windswept waters of the Potomac. Instead of climbing to fly over the bridges, the pilots of the 160th continued to hug the deck.

Under the four bridges they went, working their way north and closer to the White House. They were to stay out of sight until given the green light. The choppers closed on the Arlington Memorial Bridge and began to slow. When they reached it, the three choppers pulled in under the bridge and hovered. This was where they were to wait.

Meanwhile, a second flight of three Little Birds worked its way up the Anacostia River to the northeast. The three helicopters passed over the Frederick Douglass Bridge and turned north. Skimming over the roofs of apartment buildings and row houses, they cruised at an easy sixty knots, keeping the noise of their rotors and engines nice and quiet. The choppers passed around the east side of the Capitol so no one out on the National Mall would notice them. The wind buffeted them as they turned west and cruised over the roof of the Department of Labor. Dead ahead, five blocks away, was the monolithic structure of the Hoover Building. The choppers slid in over the rooftop and hovered just five feet above the structure. That was where they were to wait.

The operators standing on the skids were loaded for bear. Each man was outfitted with the latest in body armor, including ballistic Kevlar helmets and throat protectors. Gas masks were readily accessible in spare pockets, as were night-vision goggles. Ten of the twelve men carried suppressed MP-10s. The eleventh carried a Mossberg 12-gauge shotgun, and the twelfth carried the heavy 7.62-mm M60ES machine gun. All of them were confident they could overcome anything they met, with one exception: the bombs. If the SEALs didn't find a way around them, they would be in for a real nasty operation.

51

FOUR BLOCKS AWAY from the White House, in the bell tower of the Old Post Office, Charlie Wicker slid in behind his .50 caliber Barrett sniping rifle and was looking through his Leupold M1 Ultra 10x scope. On the wooden platform next to him his fellow SEAL sniper Mike Berg was doing the same thing with another of the exact same massive weapon.

The acoustic top was on the shooting platform. Constructed out of plywood and lined with foam, the covers would absorb ninety-five percent of the significant noise when the .50 caliber rifles were fired. Wicker was very confident the shot would work. So confident that he thought he would get the Tango on the first shot. If he didn't, he knew Berg would. The odds of them missing from this distance were almost zero.

The only thing that had made him nervous was the weather. Wind and rain did funny things to the flight of a bullet, things that he couldn't always control and that drove him nuts. The wind had been steadily increasing for the last several hours, but as if they had been given a gift from above, it had just died down. Unfortunately, Wicker knew, the reprieve would only be temporary. They were in the proverbial calm before the storm. The black sky was descending from east, and the relative calm would not last.

Wicker had been listening to the play-by-play as his team members jumped out of the back of the Combat Talon and was relieved the operation was under way. He would make the shot count.

Only Wicker could hear what was being said between Harris and the other three jumpers. Having too many operators on the radio created unneeded confusion. Berg was to take his shot after he heard Wicker take his. There would be no commands, no signals. Nothing to distract the second shot. Berg would shoot when he was ready.

The two snipers could clearly hear their spotters outside the blind calling out the descent of the four SEAL Team Six operators. Wicker focused entirely on the task at hand. His whole body was molded to the big .50 caliber rifle as the crosshairs of his scope stayed centered on the terrorist's head. Wicker felt no remorse over what he was about to do. The man he was about to kill had put himself in this situation, and he had miscalculated the skill of his opponent. He naively sat behind the bulletproof glass thinking he was safe.

AT ONE THOUSAND feet Mick Reavers pulled the rip cord on his parachute, and his rapid descent stopped. Looking up, he checked to make sure his double canopy had unfurled itself properly, then maneuvered himself into position for the short glide onto the roof of the White House. Reavers didn't bother to look to see if his team members were in position above him. His job was to stay on line so the others could follow.

Harris had also opened his chute as close to one thousand feet as possible. After he got himself sorted out, he did a quick count of the airfoils beneath him and moved in to line up behind Rostein. At the same time he looked over at the tall steeple of the Old Post Office and said, "Slick, this is Whiskey Four. Do you copy? Over."

"I copy, Whiskey Four."

"We're getting close."

"Just give me the bingo."

Harris floated down looking beyond his men at the street and traffic lights. Suddenly, he felt a gust of wind, and then a raindrop touched his cheek. Looking back to the east, he could see a wall of driving rain marching toward him. The heavy stuff looked to be less than a mile away. Harris looked down and tried to judge how close Reavers was to touchdown. Harris checked his altimeter and then looked back to the lead chute. He waited patiently, watching Reavers glide in from the darkness toward the roof of the White House.

Harris waited to the last possible moment and said, "Bingo, Slick. I repeat, Bingo!"

Wicker heard the call and began a slow, even exhale. He had already lowered his heart rate to fewer than forty beats a minute and was completely at ease. The terrorist was offering him a full-profile shot, and Wicker held the center of the crosshairs just above the man's ear. With a steady constant pressure, he began to squeeze the trigger, and with a loud report the bullet was away.

The recoil from the massive rifle jolted Wicker back several inches. Another round was chambered, and as he maneuvered his scope in an attempt to reacquire the target, he heard Berg's massive fifty launch its round at the target. Wicker brought his scope back in on the guard booth a second later, but there was nothing to shoot. The only thing in sight was a large hole in the bulletproof glass the size of a fist.

Reavers came in hot. He had felt the wind picking up and had adjusted accordingly, allowing himself to drop like a rock for thirty feet, and then at the last second, he pulled down on the risers and filled his chute with air. When his feet hit the roof, he opened the vents and got enough slack in his canopy to collapse one side of it. Clutching at his shoulder hooks, he pulled them from the main harness and wrestled the chute to the ground. Reavers bundled the chute quickly, threw it out of the way, all the while running for the guard booth.

On the way, he reached for his machine gun and said, "Whiskey One is down and on the move."

By the time Reavers got to the guard booth, his silenced MP-10 was up and ready. As he looked inside, he saw the semidecapitated body of a terrorist lying on the floor. Reporting his findings, he said, "Tango one is out of commission." Reavers looked up for a second to see how the others were doing and then began to check the guard booth for booby traps.

Clark and Rostein came in much the same as Reavers. There was a pattern that was developing, though, and as Reavers finished circling the guard booth, he grew alarmed. Each man overshot the previous man's landing area by a good twenty feet. Reavers looked up and saw his CO struggling to get down as the wind picked up. With no time to waste, Reavers began running toward the western edge of the roof. As he did so, the rain started to fall.

Commander Harris was allowing himself to drop at a dangerous rate in an effort to get down before he overshot the landing area. With less than fifteen feet to go, he pulled on his risers as hard as he could. The chute fluffed with air, and just as the commander's feet hit the roof, a forty-mile-an-hour gust grabbed the parachute and yanked Harris toward the edge.

RAPP KNELT OUTSIDE the door to Horsepower, intently watching his monitor. Rielly knelt next to him, afraid to speak. They had been sitting in silence for several minutes waiting when Rapp noticed her look of fear. A little bit of fear was a good thing, but too much could lead to freezing in the heat of battle, and they couldn't afford that right now.

Rapp pushed the lip mike of his headset up and leaned close to Rielly. Whispering in her ear, he said, "Don't worry, Anna. Everything is going to be fine." Rapp moved away and smiled.

Rielly looked at him with eyes filled with dread. She leaned in close and whispered in his ear, "I don't want you to die." Then she hugged him and kissed him on the cheek.

Rapp's heart fluttered, and he felt a feeling in his stomach that he hadn't felt in a long time. With a huge grin on his face, he pulled her close, touching his forehead to hers. "Don't worry about me. I've been in worse situations than this. Much worse." He felt like kissing her, but held back. "Besides, you owe me dinner."

This finally got a smile from her, and after a couple of seconds, she added, "All right. Just don't do anything stupid before I get a chance to pay you back."

Before Rapp could reply, he heard Commander Harris and Charlie Wicker talking on the headset. Rapp pulled his mike back down and pointed to the doorknob.

Rielly nervously put one hand on the knob and the other on the key. Rapp brought his silenced MP-10 up with both hands and clutched the extended stock firmly between his cheek and shoulder. With his eyes on the monitor, he kept the gun level and ready to fire. He listened to the news as the shot was taken and then the words that the first SEAL was down. Rapp looked for the slightest sign that the terrorist was onto something. The seconds passed by, and there was nothing. It appeared they had eliminated the Tango on the roof without alerting the others. Then came the news that the second and third SEALs were down. Rapp started to ease up just a bit. Amazingly, everything was going off as planned.

HARRIS WAS HELPLESS as the wind filled his chute and yanked him toward the edge. Passing by one of the chimney stacks, he reached out with his left hand. This slowed him for only a second as the force of the gale peeled him away from his temporary brick mooring. Several feet off the ground, he was again airborne and headed for the edge.

"Whiskey Four is in trouble," announced Reavers as he sprinted across the narrow flat section of the roof. Pumping his legs as fast as they would move, he saw his CO slow for a second and then start moving. Reavers gained on him, and when he thought he had a chance, he dropped his weapon clear and leapt, both hands extended.

Reavers caught Harris's right boot, and they came to a skidding halt. Only half of Harris's upper body was on the roof. The other half was dangling over the edge, the parachute fully inflated by the driving storm continuing to tug him from Reavers's grip.

With Reavers preventing him from floating away, Harris got enough play in one of the main straps to undo the clasp and let it go. The chute instantly flattened and began snapping in the wind. With the tension reduced, the other clasp was free and released in seconds. The parachute then floated away for about fifty feet until it hit the southeast corner of the West Wing. There it came to rest flapping in the wind, hugging the building.

*   *   *

RAPP HONESTLY THOUGHT they were about to pull off the infiltration without a hitch. And then he heard the call that Whiskey Four was
in trouble. His ears perked up, and his eyes intently watched the small
monitor at his feet. The terrorist on the screen was sitting with his back to
the door. Rapp could see the Tango's AK-74 leaning against the table
within arm's reach.

After several tense seconds it came over the radio that Whiskey Four
was okay and that the team was proceeding into the mansion. Rapp eased
a bit, and then he saw the Tango come forward in his chair. Rapp's body
shifted forward as he continued to watch the small screen at his feet. The
Tango had seen something on one of the monitors, but Rapp couldn't see
what it was. When the terrorist's left hand reached out, Rapp noticed
what looked like a radio sitting on the console.

"Go!" The word came from his mouth without any thought or pause.

Rielly turned the key, twisted the knob, and shoved the door open.
Rapp was moving through the opening instantly, his silenced MP-10
hugged tight, and his left eye boring down the sights. The terrorist's head
was framed perfectly. The radio was coming to his mouth. He had already
got the name Rafique out and was just starting to say something else.

Rapp squeezed the trigger once and held it for a second. Two rounds
spit from the end of the silencer and hit the Tango directly in the back of
the head. The hollow-point Glaser rounds breached the skull and released
a total of six hundred sixty lethal miniature projectiles. The terrorist was
propelled forward, his head landing on the console and his radio dropping
to the floor.

Rapp moved quickly for the terrorist's radio, saying over his lip mike,
"I need help. Get the Whiskey Team over here on the double." Keeping
his gun trained on the open door that led out into the hallway, he grabbed
the radio and brought it up to his ear. The voice he heard on the other end
caused Rapp's skin to crawl. It was Aziz.

Rapp had to think fast. Speaking into his own headset first, he said,
"Control, we may have to go with jamming. Be ready to do so on my
command." Rapp thought about how to play it. After just a second or two
he brought the radio to his mouth and hoped his clipped Farsi accent
would work. "Everything's all right. It was nothing."

There was silence for a moment, and then Aziz asked, "Who is this?"

Rapp hesitated for only a second. Into his lip mike, he said, "Control,
jam everything! I repeat, everything!"

52

AZIZ LOOKED AT the door to the president's bunker and then at the electronic device in his hand. He spoke into his radio for a third time and then held it to his ear. Nothing came back. Without having to be asked, Bengazi tried his radio. The result was the same. Aziz calmly checked the digital pager clipped to his hip and then looked at Bengazi.

"Take Ragib, check the stairwell, and try to reestablish radio contact." Aziz then turned to Yassin, who was sticking a long spikelike object through one of the holes he had drilled. "Keep working," he told the plump little man.

Aziz walked down the hallway, following his men, and when they reached the stairwell, he waited for them at the bottom. As Bengazi and Ragib disappeared into the stairwell, Aziz tried his radio again. It still didn't work. Now he began to get nervous. If the radios failed, that was one thing, but if the Americans were jamming them and they covered the frequencies of his digital pagers, that would be something entirely different. The countdown would begin on the bombs, and if the Americans did not stop jamming the signal, there was nothing he could do to stop them from going off. He had only several options, and he didn't have a lot of time to think them through.

RAPP STOOD NEXT to the main doorway of Horsepower looking down the hall, waiting for a Tango to come around the corner any second. Rielly had ventured into the room and was staring at the dead terrorist. Rapp brought his hand up and motioned for her to get behind him.

She didn't see his gesture, and Rapp said, "Anna, get over here, and stay behind me." Rapp looked back down the hall again and said, "Whiskey Four, where in the hell are you?"

"We're in the tunnel. We'll be there in a second."

"Hurry up."

Commander Harris, who was in the lead, passed a tired Milt Adams and sprinted up the stairs. He arrived in Horsepower with his weapon up and sweeping the room.

Rapp heard him enter and turned. "We need to take these guys out quick before they figure out what's going on."

"What about the bombs?" The other three black-clad SEALs entered the room.

"We pray they don't go off while we're shooting, and we worry about them later."

"Slow down a minute." General Campbell's voice came over their radios. "We need to make sure we know what we're doing first."

"We've got one Tango upstairs watching a half a dozen hostages or more." Rapp spoke rapidly. "We're blind in the mess, but we know there's at least three Tangos watching over the hostages. There's nothing else to discuss. These guys are going to get real antsy if they don't start hearing something on their radios. We need to move now."

"I agree." Harris backed up Rapp.

"What's the Tango in the Roosevelt Room doing?" asked Rapp.

"Nothing. He's just sitting in his chair, but Aziz and several others are on the move."

"Where's Delta?"

"They're on their way in."

Rapp looked at Harris. "The mess is down the hall, first left and then first right. Take your team and clear the room. I'll go upstairs and take care of loner."

"Why don't I give you Mick?"

Rapp shook his head. "Thanks, but I don't need him. I've got video on what he's doing. You're flying blind. You need the extra man more than I do." Rapp started to move for the other door. He grabbed Rielly's hand and said to Harris and the boys, "Good luck. I'll see you in about twenty seconds."

When Rapp reached the back steps, Milt Adams was slowly climbing the staircase from the tunnel. He looked exhausted. Turning to Rielly, Rapp said, "Wait here with Milt." Then on the way up the stairs to the Oval Office, he remembered all of the bombs. Into his lip mike he said, "Control, you'd better start thinking of a way to get us out of here."

BACK AT LANGLEY, Kennedy was already on the job. Things were moving along at a frantic pace. General Campbell's Joint Special Operations Command staff was busy monitoring every aspect of the mission and telling the general only the things he needed to be most concerned about. Fortunately, everyone in the room had received enough training and, in some cases, real-life experience that they knew to keep their mouths shut unless what they had to say was imperative. During a frenetic operation like this, it was easy to swamp the lines of communications.

Kennedy tapped Campbell on the arm. "I'll handle Iron Man. You worry about the Whiskey Team."

Campbell nodded his consent. Colonel Gray, the commander of Delta Force, was to his right and overseeing the actions of his Alpha and Bravo Teams. The Alpha Team was on the move and about to be inserted onto the roof. The Bravo Team had left its cover under the Arlington Bridge and was on its way in. General Flood and Director Stansfield sat in the back row and watched. They were both very careful not to interrupt.

Kennedy looked at the three monitors on the big board that most concerned Rapp. "Iron Man, you are all clear. There is no movement in the hallway, and the Tango is sitting with his gun resting on his lap." Kennedy squinted at the screen. "There's a chance he could be sleeping."

"ROGER THAT." Rapp climbed the steep concrete staircase that led to the Oval Office. When he reached the top, he pressed the latch and pulled the wall in toward him. He checked to his left first and then moved through the dining room and into the pantry. There he stopped and looked out at the door across the hallway.

"Whiskey Four, are you in position? Over."

Harris and his three SEALs were crouched against the wall just outside the White House mess. Having gone through this drill together countless times, they fell into their slots. Reavers was number one, followed by Clark, Rostein, and finally Harris—the same way they had jumped out of the plane.

"We're ready to go on your command, Iron Man."

Before moving, Rapp asked, "How does my Tango look, control?"

"No change in status," replied Kennedy.

"Roger that. All right, Harry, let's bag 'em on three. One . . ." Rapp moved across the hall. "Two . . ." He placed his right hand on the doorknob. "Three!" Rapp threw the door open and stayed in his crouch. The Tango looked up, and as he did so, the thick black suppressor of Rapp's submachine gun coughed twice.

Downstairs Mick Reavers raced into the White House mess in a crouch and peeled to his left, sweeping his area for targets. A split second into the room-clearing maneuver, he found one. The Tango was standing with his weapon cradled across his chest. Reavers placed two rounds directly in the center of the man's forehead and sent him to the ground. The next three SEALs came in right on top of Reavers, each man peeling away and searching their area. Tony Clark, the number two man in the train, found his target thirty feet away and directly across the room. The Tango was bringing his gun up to fire, but it never happened. Two bullets hit him right between the eyes and sent him back over a chair. As Jordan Rostein entered the room, he peeled further to the right and came up blank. He fought the urge to sweep further to his right and went back over his area again. Harris was right on his heels and pivoted ninety degrees to cover the area all the way to the right. No more than eight feet away, the snubbed muzzle of a shortened AK-74 was being brought to bear. Harris was quicker and sent two rounds into the man's face.

Reavers called clear, and he was followed in quick succession by the other team members. They heard Rapp's call over their radios, and then several of the hostages began to cry out for help. The SEALs ignored them and kept their weapons up as they searched the mass of hostages for any Tangos that might be using them for cover. Harris ordered Clark and Rostein to watch the hostages, and then he and Reavers moved out to secure the other areas of the room.

53

THE THREE LITTLE Bird helicopters moved out from their holding pattern and raced in over the White House. The rain was falling in sheets and the wind was howling. Most helicopter pilots had the common sense to stay on the ground during weather like this, but the pilots of the 160th Special Operations Regiment trained in the worst possible conditions for this exact reason.

The only adjustment they made was to loosen their formation a bit to allow for some error that might be caused by the gusting wind. The first Little Bird came in and hovered ten feet off the deck over the eastern end of the roof. The NOTAR system on the chopper's tail gave it unmatched hovering stability. All four troopers kicked free at the same time and rappelled the short distance to the rooftop. The men pulled their ropes from their rappelling clips and headed out for the guard booth. The second chopper came right behind the first, and then the third. The twelve operators of the Alpha Team immediately set out for their objective in the basement.

AZIZ WAS TRYING to figure out what to do when he heard the distinctive noise of an AK-74 being fired somewhere on the floors above. The noise caused him to freeze at first, and then he raced back to the anteroom of the bunker. Neither Yassin nor the woman had any idea that something was wrong. Aziz grabbed the woman by the arm and yanked her to her feet.

Pulling the woman down the hall, he yelled back to Yassin, "Get that door open."

As they neared the stairwell, shots could be heard again. Aziz opened the door and yelled for Bengazi. He waited a moment but got no reply. Furious at all this when he was so close, he grabbed the woman by the hair and shoved her into the stairwell. He had to get to the first basement or there would be no escape. Aziz pushed the woman before him as the noise of battle grew louder.

When they made it to the first basement, he pressed on. At the next landing they found Bengazi and Ragib. The two of them were firing furiously at the stairs above them. Brass shell casings came tumbling down the steps. A hail of bullets hit the plaster wall just in front of them, and chips of the wall flew in every direction.

Aziz began backing down the staircase, yelling to Bengazi, "Muammar, hold on for another minute and then meet me in the tunnel!"

Without turning, Bengazi yelled, "Go!"

As Aziz headed back down the stairs, there was a bright flash and a loud bang from above. He reached the door to the first basement and burst through it with the president's secretary. Using her as a shield, he checked both directions and then headed for the Treasury tunnel. He had to fight all of his urges to go back downstairs and see things through with the president, but he knew that would end only one way. This was it. He had been so close, but somehow the Americans had figured out what he was up to.

Aziz rounded the next corner to the left and stopped. Holding the woman up in front of him, he brought his fist back and then punched her with a right hook. The woman spun from the blow and went to the floor like a wet noodle. Aziz set his MP-5 down and began to tear off the green fatigues he'd been wearing for the last three days.

RAPP DID A quick search of the room and came up with nothing. One by one he pulled the canvas bags off the hostage's heads, counting nine of them. The room reeked of urine.

"Whiskey Four, what's your status?"

"We're golden. Three Tangos down, and all of the hostages are secured."

Rapp looked over at the bomb by the wall. Its red light was blinking. "We're not out of this yet. Get your boys working on these bombs."

Turning his attention back to the hostages, he said, "Don't worry. Everything is going to be fine." He took his knife and cut the first two uniformed Secret Service officers free. Then, giving his knife to them, he told them to free the others. Rapp spoke into his headset, "Control, what's the plan?"

Kennedy answered. "Start moving the hostages into the tunnel. If there's no other safe way out, we'll off-load them by helicopter from the roof."

"Roger that." Rapp looked back at the hostages, who were still trying to get up. "Can you people move?" A couple of them nodded, and Rapp said, "All right. Follow me, and don't touch anything. Those of you that can't move, I'll come back and get you."

Rapp led the first three out of the room and toward the hidden staircase. "Control, what's the update on Aziz?" Rapp waited but got no reply.

He repeated the question as he went back to grab a couple more hostages and was stopped cold in the hallway outside the Roosevelt Room. He had heard a beep and looked down at the bomb on the wall. The red light had stopped blinking and was now green. Beneath that, two red numbers appeared.

"Shit! We've got big problems! These bombs are counting down! Control, did you hear me? Whiskey Four, did you hear me?" Rapp ran back into the Roosevelt Room. "People we have to move fast. Who needs help?" One of the remaining six raised his hand. Rapp snatched the Secret Service officer from the ground like a rag doll and threw him over his shoulder.

"Say again?" General Campbell asked.

"These bombs are counting down. Something went wrong. Get the Alpha Team back up to the roof." Rapp headed out of the room. "Let's go! Everyone, follow me." As Rapp raced across the hall and into president's dining room, he yelled, "Harry, move everybody into the tunnel fast. It's our only chance."

Rapp cut through the short hallway and started down the steep stairs. When he reached the bottom, he handed the wounded Secret Service officer off to several other hostages and told Anna and Milt to head down into the tunnel and keep people moving. Rapp then ran into Horsepower, where he saw the first of the hostages coming his way. Rapp screamed, "Come on, people! Move! Hurry up!"

The line slowed for a second, and Rapp backed up to the door and screamed, "Get your asses moving! This whole building is wired to blow!"

The line instantly surged forward. Rapp checked his watch. He had no idea how much time they had left, but it couldn't be much. Harris and the other three SEALs finally appeared. Reavers was carrying a hostage in each arm. Clark, Rostein, and Harris appeared within seconds, each of them helping a hostage.

"Is anyone else left?"

"No." Harris passed Rapp and said, "Get your ass in the tunnel."

Rapp didn't need to be told. He was right on Harris's heels and slamming the heavy steel door closed behind him. Rapp yelled over his headset, "Milt, make sure the door on the other end is closed."

AZIZ PEAKED AROUND the corner to see if Bengazi was coming. The gunfire had stopped, and he took it as a bad sign. The Americans would have silenced weapons, and if he could not hear shots, that meant Ragib and Bengazi had been overpowered. The Americans would be arriving shortly.

Looking at his pager, he smiled. The Americans were in for a big surprise. The pager had gone into countdown mode. The system was foolproof. He had designed and tested it himself. With the laptop jammed, the pagers didn't receive their codes. Now they were in countdown mode, and in sixteen seconds they would start to blow.

The green fatigues were off. Underneath them Aziz had been wearing black coveralls similar to those worn by the FBI's Hostage Rescue Team. The black assault vest he wore over it had *FBI* printed in yellow across the back. The plan was a long shot, but in the confusion created by the bombs going off, it just might work. The Secret Service MP-5 submachine gun, the black gas mask he would put on once the explosions occurred, the coveralls—they would all help him blend in.

Aziz looked around the corner again, expecting to see members of the Hostage Rescue Team working their way down the hall. There was no one. It was completely silent. He checked the pager one last time and pulled his gas mask down.

The first explosion was a rumble in the distance. It was followed by a quick succession of explosions, each one getting a little louder. The building began to shake, dust and plaster started to fall from the ceiling, the lights fluttered several times and then failed completely. All of the sudden a huge blast came from the left, where the entrance to the Treasury tunnel was located. The concussion knocked Aziz to the floor, where he landed on the president's unconscious secretary.

Aziz pushed himself up, spitting the dust from his mouth and shaking it from his hair. His hearing had been rendered useless from the explosion. Commanding himself to get up, he stood and found the small flashlight in his assault vest. Aziz turned it on and tried to regain his sense of direction. The air was thick with dust and smoke, preventing him from seeing more than five feet in any direction.

He was pretty sure the tunnel was to his left. Grabbing the woman, he threw her over his shoulder, picked up his gun, and felt his way along the wall for the tunnel. At the next corner he went right, and several steps later he stumbled over chunks of concrete that had been knocked loose from the blast. In front of him was a mound. He started to climb into the tunnel. For a moment he was fearful the entire structure might have collapsed, but then the rubble began to dissipate.

Breathing through the gas mask was difficult. It didn't give him oxygen; it just helped filter the dust and smoke from the air. Carrying the woman was proving to be more tiring than he had anticipated. He stopped for a moment to gather himself. The dust started to settle, and his breathing became slightly easier. The visibility grew better with each passing step, and it motivated him to pick up the pace.

All of the sudden he was out of the tunnel. He was immediately met by several figures wearing dark coveralls like his. Aziz did not want to have to use the weapon unless he had to. They were trying to talk to him as he continued forward, but they were not pointing their weapons at him.

When Aziz was within several feet, he yelled through his gas mask, "Ambulance! I have to get her to an ambulance!"

One of the men grabbed him by the arm and started to jog with him up the ramp. As they stepped out from under the covered part of the Treasury garage, they were hit with the rain. The man kept trying to talk to Aziz.

Finally, Aziz yelled, "I'm deaf from the explosions! I can't hear a thing!"

When they reached the top of the ramp, a stream of fire trucks raced past them and onto the south grounds of the White House. Aziz turned to the left and started jogging. Dead ahead on the other side of Fifteenth Street was where Salim was supposed to be. Emergency vehicles were lined up, their lights flashing in the pouring rain. Every second counted. Aziz pressed on. He desperately wanted to take the gas mask off, but it was too big a risk to show his face.

When they reached the intersection of Fifteenth Street and Hamilton, just a half a block away from the White House, another explosion occurred. The circular lid on the concrete trash receptacle across the street shot up in the air almost fifty feet and then came spinning back to earth. It landed with a thud in the middle of the intersection and lay smoldering in the rain.

The few people that were out in the deluge were now running for cover. Aziz continued through the rain. The man that had been with him stayed behind, fearing more explosions, which Aziz assumed, if Salim had done his job, were occurring all around the area.

Aziz made it across the street and ran down the sidewalk. He couldn't take the mask any longer. It was too hard to breathe, and it was fogging up. He yanked the mask up onto his forehead and took his first real breath of air in minutes. It felt incredible in his burning lungs. Aziz pressed on, looking in the windows of the ambulances for a white head of hair. As he neared the end of the row of vehicles, he began to worry that Salim had abandoned him, but there, in the last ambulance, he spotted him.

Aziz ran around the back and pulled open the doors. He quickly climbed in and dropped the woman on the gurney. Before the door was shut, he yelled, "Get us the hell out of here!"

Salim threw the vehicle into reverse and hit the emergency lights on the roof. He spun the wheel and yanked it into drive, stepping on the gas. The wheels spun for a moment on the rain-soaked street and then caught. Salim hit the siren as the ambulance raced forward. The police at the next intersection hustled to move the barricades just in time for the ambulance to pass through.

VICE PRESIDENT BAXTER had just finished bawling out Dallas King. Less than thirty minutes earlier, Baxter had been blindsided by the information that President Hayes was no longer out of the loop and that he himself was no longer in charge. After being humiliated like never before in his life, Baxter had gotten off the phone and started screaming at Dallas King. The vice president went into a tirade, blaming his chief of staff for the entire mess, belaboring the point that he should never have listened to a word of King's advice.

King had taken the verbal beating without a fight. Secretly he was relieved. Baxter not becoming president wouldn't end his career, but Abu Hasan making it out of the White House and telling his story to the FBI or media would. With Hayes back in charge, the odds were a raid would be ordered.

King let his boss vent until there was nothing left and then turned the tables. Methodically, he made his case, pointing out that they had saved the lives of twenty-five people and had sacrificed what? Some money that wasn't even theirs and some sanctions that weren't even working. King stressed to Baxter that there was no way they could have played it any better. And then in an attempt to help bolster his boss's ego, King proclaimed that history would judge his three days as president as some of the most difficult ever served by the nation's chief executive. That history would re-. member him as someone who put the lives of Americans above money and a failed foreign policy.

"Remember, it ain't over till it's over." King was building strength in his position. With each passing minute, he could see that he was getting to Baxter. King paced back and forth in front of the desk, and then suddenly stopped. "This is perfect. Absolutely perfect."

"What is?"

"Hayes may have just done you the biggest favor of his career." King clapped his hands together. "You're off the hook, and the timing couldn't be better. So far you've only had to deal with the little demands. Tomorrow, Aziz is going to ask for something big, and you are not going to have to be the one to say yes or no." King was grinning ear to ear. "They are going to have to storm the White House, and Hayes is going to have to give the order."

The vice president began to see the bright side. "There just might be a way out of this."

The door to the study suddenly burst open, and one of the vice president's staffers rushed in yelling, "Turn on the TV! The White House is on fire!"

Baxter sprang from his chair and grabbed the remote control from his desk. The TV came on almost instantly. Within seconds, images of fire engines racing through the White House's gates appeared. In the background flames could be seen shooting out of windows. Baxter turned up the volume. The anchor was saying that people on the scene were telling him that as of yet no survivors had been seen coming out of the building.

As soon as the anchor said the words "no survivors," Dallas King ushered the aide back out of the room and closed the door. The two of them stood for several minutes, watching the live coverage. There were flames everywhere. Firemen were manning hoses from the ground and from the top of hook-and-ladder trucks.

King turned to his boss, unable to hide the smile on his face. "No one is going to make it out of there alive."

All Baxter could do was shake his head.

King stared at the TV for a while longer and then said, "We need to let the media know that you are not responsible for this disaster." King pointed to the screen. "Hayes is responsible for this mess, and we have to make sure everyone knows that." King felt as if he were floating on air. He was going to get away with it.

Baxter looked at his chief of staff and said, "Dallas, this is a tragedy."

"Life is a tragedy, Sherman. Thirty thousand people a year die in car accidents, another hundred thousand from cigarettes." King pointed to his boss. "Now, that's a real tragedy. This is not good. Don't get me wrong. Some people might consider it a tragedy, but it's my job to make sure they don't think you caused it." King picked up the phone on his boss's desk and punched in a phone number. When he got the person's voice mail, he pressed zero and got the operator on the line. "I need to speak to Sheila Dunn immediately! Tell her Dallas King, the vice president's chief of staff, is on the line."

King was put on hold. Standing next to his boss, he watched the White House burn on the TV. In the back of his mind, he was chanting, *Burn, baby, burn.*

54

PRESIDENT HAYES STOOD in front of the White House, bathed in the early morning sunlight. Reporters shouted questions from beyond the fence line, and he ignored them. The important thing was that the nation see he was alive and well. He would make a formal speech in the evening and explain the tragic events of the last four days.

Special Agent Jack Warch stood at his side along with a half dozen other Secret Service agents, all of them wearing sunglasses. President Hayes held his hand over his eyes and gazed up at the proud, old building, amazed she was still standing. FBI agents were sifting through the carnage collecting evidence. Virtually all of the windows were blown out, and there were holes punched in the stone exterior where the bombs had exploded. Fortunately the fire had not burned uncontrolled. Between the heavy downpour and the firefighters, the blaze had been kept in check and was prevented from engulfing the structure. Priceless national treasures had been damaged beyond repair and lost forever, but the important thing was that the hostages were alive.

Jack Warch reached out and tapped the president on the arm. President Hayes looked down at his watch and nodded. The troop then moved out across the lawn for the northwest gate.

The president looked to Warch and said, "I bet your wife and kids were happy to see you this morning."

Warch smiled. "Yep. Lots of hugs and kisses."

Hayes grinned and slapped Warch on the back as they crossed Pennsylvania Avenue. Several large limousines were parked in the street. One of them, Hayes recognized, belonged to the vice president. The entourage walked up the steps of Blair House, where a U.S. marine opened the door for the president and saluted. Hayes returned the salute and entered the foyer of his new home. Several reporters from the White House press pool were inside with their notepads ready.

The president paused to take a look around and pronounced, "If it was good enough for Harry Truman, it's good enough for me." The reporters laughed and wrote down the quote.

The president's chief of staff appeared from the parlor and said, "Everybody's here, Mr. President."

Hayes tugged on his white shirtsleeves and entered the room with Warch and Jones. All of the attendees stood, some more enthusiastically than others. The president had called the meeting several hours earlier and had put together the list carefully. Stansfield, Kennedy, Flood, and Campbell were all seated on of one the room's two large couches. Sitting across from them was Vice President Baxter and Dallas King. Despite the extra room on the couch, Anna Rielly and Milt Adams had chosen to stand.

The president walked to the front of the room and looked at the only two people he didn't know. "I'm looking forward to meeting both of you, but we have some business to take care of first." Hayes looked around the room for a second and then to Director Stansfield. "We're missing someone."

"He'll be along shortly, Mr. President."

Hayes nodded and brought his hands together in a tight grip. "All right, let's get down to business. First things first." Hayes's gaze fell on Dallas King. "We are going to set the record straight, and we're going to make things right. Dallas, I've been told you made quite an ass out of yourself over the last several days." Hayes paused. "Anything you would like to say in your defense?"

King shifted uncomfortably on the couch and was rapidly trying to think of a defense when the parlor doors opened and in stepped Mitch Rapp. Rapp walked across the room to where Rielly and Adams were standing.

"I'm sorry I'm late, Mr. President."

"That's quite all right, Mr. Kruse. We were just getting ready to hear Dallas King explain his behavior over the last several days."

King was sweating bullets.

The president extended his hand and Valerie Jones deposited a copy of *The Washington Post* in it. Hayes held it up for everyone to see. The headlines read, "President Hayes Orders Failed Raid." Hayes handed the copy back to Jones and said, "The *Post* rushed to press with this story last night and wound up with a lot of egg on their face this morning. I won't even get into the specifics of the article, other than to say that almost all of it is false." Hayes watched King for a moment. "Dallas, do you have any idea how the *Post* came up with a headline like this?"

At first King only shrugged and then muttered some unintelligible words. Inside, he was relieved. For a moment he had thought Hayes had found out about his late-night tour of the White House.

"Let me see if I can refresh your memory." Hayes extended his hand, and this time Stansfield placed several documents in it. "I have phone records here showing that someone called the *Post* last night from the vice president's house. I have other records showing that over the last several days someone has been calling a reporter at the *Post* from your mobile phone and your home phone." Hayes held the phone records up for all to see.

King squirmed on the couch and looked to his boss for support. He got none. Afraid to look the president in the eye, he answered with great discomfort. "Ah . . . I made them."

"I thought so." Hayes handed the phone records back to Stansfield and turned to Jones. She handed him a folder and a pen. Hayes crossed over to King and dropped the pen and folder in his lap. "We took the liberty of typing your resignation for you. Sign both copies, and keep one for yourself."

Hayes watched King sign the two sheets and took one of them back. "You may leave now."

It was silent as the vice president's chief of staff got up to leave. King was more relieved than any of the others in the room could know. He could handle a quiet resignation. The truth, however, would ruin him.

Hayes turned his attention next to Vice President Baxter. "How do you like foreign travel, Sherman?"

Baxter looked up at Hayes and said nothing.

Hayes went on. "I hope you like it a lot because for the next three years I'm going to send you to every third-world country I can think of." The president turned and walked to the front of the room. It was obvious to all that he was trying to keep his temper in check. "You have set our foreign policy and national security back a decade. I would fire you if I could, but the harsh truth is that I can't. So I'm stuck with you for the rest of the term, and then, Sherman, as everyone in this room is my witness, you will choose not to run." Hayes's cheeks were flushed. For good measure, he added, "Don't press me on this, or I swear to God, I'll have Director Stansfield start leaking your CIA file to the media. Now get out of here, and keep your mouth shut." Hayes pointed to the door.

When the door was closed, Director Stansfield looked around and said, "Mr. President, I don't have a file on the vice president."

Hayes winked and said, "I know that, but he doesn't."

The president grabbed a glass of water and took a sip. Turning back to the group, he said, "I can't thank all of you enough for the job you did. It was truly unbelievable. I'm going to start with you, Mr. Adams." Hayes walked over and shook his hand. "I am indebted to you for what you did.

The risks you took, when you clearly didn't have to get involved, speak volumes about your character."

Adams was uncomfortable with all of the praise. "I was just doing my duty, Mr. President."

Hayes grabbed his shoulder and squeezed. "We need more people like you, Milt. If there is anything I can do for you, just let me know and I will take care of it."

"There is one thing that I can think of, sir."

"What's that?"

"This retirement thing isn't all it's cracked up to be, and I was thinking that since your house is in dire need of repair, I could come back and help supervise the rebuilding."

"Absolutely. That's a great idea, Milt. I will have it taken care of immediately. Anything else?"

"Nope."

"Well then, Valerie will walk you to the door and get all of the information. I can't thank you enough."

Adams finished shaking the president's hand and turned to Rielly. Milt reached out and kissed her on the cheek. "Watch out for this guy here." Adams let go and shook Rapp's hand. "Well, Mr. Secret Agent Man, I suppose this is the last I'll see of you."

"You never know." Rapp pulled Adams over and gave him a hug. "I'll make it a point to stop by and see you."

"Yeah, you do that. Just don't come asking me to join you for any more crazy missions. I'm too old for this stuff."

Adams started for the door and turned back. "You two make a cute couple. Maybe you should stop by some night, and I'll make you dinner."

"We'll have to do that." Rapp turned to Rielly and laughed.

After Adams left, the president focused his attention on Rielly. "Young lady, your first day at the White House turned out to be a doozy."

"Yes, you could say that."

"Are you going to stay on, or has this experience soured you?"

"Stay on?"

"At the White House."

"Of course."

"Good." Hayes smiled. "I asked you here this morning for two reasons. The first was to thank you for all of your help. I've been told you played a crucial role in helping Mr. Kruse here pull this thing off."

"A very small one." Rielly blushed.

"Well, thank you. Your sacrifice is very much appreciated." Hayes looked over at Rapp for a second and then back to Rielly. "Can you guess what the second reason is?"

Rielly folded her arms across her chest. "You wanted to talk to me about how much of my story I plan on telling." She intentionally chose the word "my."

"Precisely." Hayes backed up a bit. "How many reporters do you think have witnessed an exchange between the president and the vice president like the one you just witnessed here this morning?"

"Probably none."

"That's right." Hayes gestured to the four people sitting on the couch. "These four fine individuals think I should pressure you into signing a bunch of documents that will bind you legally from publishing anything we think a threat to certain security interests. But I have assured them that there is a better way to handle this."

Hayes paused to give Rielly a moment to reflect on the first option. Walking back to the front of the room, he continued. "The other way, the better way, is for you and I to make a deal." Hayes raised his eyebrows. "In exchange for your voluntary cooperation in regard to keeping certain aspects of the most recent events secret, I will give you a head start on certain events of importance."

Rielly could barely believe she was even in this meeting let alone receiving such an offer from the president. She told herself to play it cool and asked, "What types of things will you want to censor from my story?"

Hayes looked to the four on the couch. Kennedy spoke first. "If you leave out Mr. Kruse and any direct involvement by the CIA, we're fine."

"Am I all right if I say you were involved in intelligence gathering and planning?"

"As long as you stay vague, we won't have a problem."

Rielly raised a skeptical eyebrow. "Define 'vague.'"

Hayes stepped forward and waved his hands in the air. "Hold on. I have a better idea. Ms. Rielly, how would you like to get the scoop on a huge part of this story?" Hayes looked her in the eye. "At noon FBI Director Roach is going to hold a press conference, and the cat will be out of the bag. I can give you that story right now, and you can head out to NBC and break it to the world. You will scoop everybody."

Rielly was interested. Very interested. This could turn out to be a nice arrangement. She nodded and said, "I'll play ball."

"Good. Here's the deal. The FBI has searched the White House, and they can't find one of the terrorists. We have reports that last night after the explosion someone from the FBI carried a wounded woman out of the Treasury tunnel. That woman turned out to be my secretary. She was found in a ditch in rural Maryland at six this morning, barely conscious. She was last seen with Aziz right before the explosions took place outside of my bunker." The president paused, giving Rielly a second to pull it together. "Oh, and one other thing. There were no FBI agents in the building when the bombs went off."

Rielly's eyes got big. "So you're saying Aziz escaped."

"It looks that way."

Rielly looked to Rapp, who reluctantly nodded. After shaking her head, she said, "Wow."

Hayes walked over and placed his hand on her shoulder. "I'm serious about our arrangement." The president turned her toward the door and started walking with her. "You've earned this, Anna. Thank you for everything you've done."

Rielly didn't know what to say. She didn't feel as if she had done all that much. "Thank you, sir."

"No—thank you." Smiling, Hayes squeezed both of her shoulders. "I almost forgot. I have one other thing for you. Director Tracy of the Secret Service is expecting a call from you. It appears he has some information on Dallas King that you might find interesting. Now, if you'll excuse us, we need to discuss certain things involving Mr. Aziz. Stop by next week, and we'll talk more." Hayes turned Rielly toward the door and opened it for her.

Rapp sat watching the exchange, and as Rielly left the room, he felt a sinking feeling in his stomach. He wanted to talk to her. With a frown Rapp looked back across the room.

President Hayes came walking back toward the fireplace saying, "I don't care who we have to bribe, who we have to threaten—I want Aziz's head on a silver platter. I want him taken out, and I want us to seriously explore our options for dealing with Saddam Hussein."

Hayes turned to Rapp. "I can't thank you enough; this country can't thank you enough." The president shook his head. "It's a shame they'll never know the contributions and sacrifices you've made."

Rapp grinned. "That's all right, sir. I didn't exactly get into this line of work for accolades and recognition."

"I know you didn't, but I just wish there was a better way to repay you and properly show our gratitude."

"Just let me be the one to punch Aziz's ticket, and that'll be payment enough."

"I plan on it. Which brings me to my next point." Hayes looked away from Rapp for a second and focused on the others. "I want every intelligence asset we can spare focusing on tracking down Aziz. Call in every marker we have. As I said a second ago, we are not going to play by the rules on this one. I want him caught." Hayes turned back to Rapp. "I want you to go home, and I want you to get some rest." The president began to walk Rapp toward the door. "If we find him, I want you fresh."

"Yes, sir." Rapp shook the president's hand and left the room. He walked out onto the front stoop of Blair House. Bringing his hand up over his eyes, he shielded them from the light and searched the crowd. Nothing. He turned to his right and left but came up empty again.

"Can I help you find something, Mr. Kruse?"

Rapp looked down. Directly in front of him, leaning against the president's limo, was the beautiful Anna Rielly.

Rapp walked down the steps and said, "I thought you'd be hustling off to your station to break the story."

Rielly pushed herself away from the limo. With a grin she said, "I have some time." Reaching her hand out, she added, "Besides, I wanted to say good-bye." She grabbed Rapp's hand and squeezed it tight. Pointing down the street, she said, "Why don't you walk me down to the corner so I can catch a cab."

"Sure." The two of them started walking toward Seventeenth Street hand in hand.

Rielly leaned away from him and asked, "So, are you ever going to tell me your real name?"

"Maybe." Rapp took a couple more steps and smiled. "Someday after you earn my trust."

They walked in silence for a while, and then Rielly asked, "So about this life story of yours, when am I going to get a chance to hear it?"

"Whenever you want."

"I'd imagine you're going to be pretty busy for a while."

"Who knows." They reached the corner and stopped. "I'm thinking of taking some time off."

"Really?"

"Why do you sound so surprised?"

Rielly studied him for a second. "You don't seem like the type of person that takes time off."

Rapp shrugged his shoulders. "You'd be surprised."

"I think there are probably a lot of things about you that might surprise me."

Rapp shook his head. "I doubt it. I'm pretty boring when it comes down to it."

Rielly looked down at their hands and rubbed her thumb along his finger. Peeking up at him, she said, "We need to set our dinner date."

Her thumb rubbing up and down on his finger made his heart race. "Any time you can fit me into your schedule."

"How about sometime next week."

"I was thinking about something a little earlier."

Rielly looked up with her green eyes, a soft smile spreading across her face. Rapp reached down and grabbed her chin. Pulling his mouth to hers, he kissed her and said, "How about tonight?"

Epilogue

THE OLD MAN shuffled down the busy street. It was almost midnight, and the crowds were thinning. He picked his way through the people, his posture hunched, his eyes scanning their faces. He wore a pair of dirty, cracked tennis shoes, and his jeans were several inches too short. Matted clumps of dirty gray and black hair adorned his head and a film of dirt covered every inch of exposed skin. In some cities he might have stood out, but not in Sao Paulo, Brazil. With over twenty million people, five million of whom lived in utter poverty, he was just another lost soul.

He stepped past a fellow homeless person who had curled up in a storefront doorway for the night. He was in Bom Retiro, the ethnic enclave of the massive city that was home to almost a million Palestinian, Lebanese, Iranian, and Arab immigrants. His arrival in this city, of all the cities in the world, was a feat in and of itself. It had been prompted by one small piece of information.

Muttering in semiconscious delirium, Fara Harut had unwittingly given them their clue. Within minutes, a massive electronic gathering operation by the National Security Agency was under way. A KH-12 Keyhole Satellite was moved into geosynchronous orbit over the city of Sao Paulo and began recording phone conversations from the Bom Retiro neighborhood. The NSA's supercomputers at Fort Mead, Maryland, sifted through the thousands of calls and kicked out the ones that matched pre-assigned profiles for content, tone, and voice signature. It had taken three weeks and a day, but the analysts finally found what they were looking for.

The old man continued weaving his way through the crowd, his dirty canvas bag draped over his shoulder. He marked the faces of the people he had seen on his previous visits. He looked at their eyes and checked their waists for the telltale bulge of a weapon. That was how he had found this street the night before last. It started with one man standing in a doorway smoking a cigarette. He had shifted his weight from one foot to the other, and when his unzipped leather jacket opened, it revealed the black steel of a pistol.

Rafique Aziz was near. Rapp could feel it. When he passed the man standing guard in the doorway, he kept his head down and looked the man over closely. A few steps later, Rapp stopped and bent over to pick up a bottle cap he had dropped on a previous pass. When he stood, he looked through the small crack at the bottom of the window shade and spied two men sitting on a couch watching TV. Twenty minutes earlier, Rapp had watched a sedan pull up in front of the row house and deposit a prostitute.

Rapp continued down the street and turned into the alley. He pulled the top off a garbage can and pretended to go through it. Fifty feet away in the darkness of the alley, the hot red tip of a cigarette glowed. Rapp had been adamant about one thing: he would go in alone. No contact with the Brazilian authorities, no electronic-surveillance vans, and no hit squads. Nothing to spook Aziz into running. Commander Harris and twelve of his SEALs were on station—waiting in two sedans a mile to the east and two more to the west. Rapp had convinced his bosses and the president to give him a week. It had taken just three days for his trained eyes to discover what all the expensive surveillance equipment in the CIA's arsenal would have missed. The simple bulge on a man's hip.

With each passing garbage can, the alley grew darker and the rats more plentiful. Rapp threw a bottle in his canvas bag and looked up at the second story of the house. The shade glowed a soft yellow as a candle flickered behind it. A figure briefly moved in front of the shade. Rapp licked away the dryness on his lips and felt his heart quicken as he neared the back door.

The bodyguard was only twenty feet away, and Rapp could feel the man watching him. Glancing to the side, he looked for the guard's hands. One was resting on his right hip and the other on the butt end of the cigarette. Rapp stepped carefully. He was close now, just under ten feet away. He heard the guard's pistol slide out of its holster and kept about his business. The guard spoke to him in Arabic, telling him to move on. Rapp looked up and acted as if he didn't understand the man. His hand was still in the worn canvas bag, a firm grasp on the familiar grip of his silenced Beretta 9-mm pistol.

Rapp looked at the barrel of the guard's pistol. It was pointed at the far end of the alley. Wrong move, Rapp thought to himself, as he squeezed the trigger of the Beretta. A single bullet spat from the end of the gun and hit the guard between his thick black eyebrows.

Rapp rushed the next three steps, grabbed onto the falling man, and eased him to the ground. From his bag, he pulled out a small radio and said, "I'm entering the house." Leaving the bag next to the body, he slowly stepped into the kitchen. There was laughter from down the hall and voices could be heard from the TV. Rapp closed the door behind him and crossed the kitchen. Straight ahead and down the hall was the front door. To his left, the stairs that led to the second floor, and to his right the two men watching TV with their back to him.

Every second counted. Rapp stepped into the room and leveled his Beretta. The man on the left sensed something and spun around. Rapp immediately connected the face with a name. It was Salim Rusan, the man who had stood on the roof of the Washington Hotel a month earlier and killed a dozen Secret Service officers. Rapp put a bullet in the back of the second man's head, then hit a surprised Rusan between the eyes. The silencer barely made a noise. Rapp stepped to the dead man on the right and took the remote control from his hand. After turning up the volume on the TV, he started for the stairs. Into his radio, he whispered, "Three Tangos down. Proceeding to second floor." He checked the stairs quickly and then started up them two at a time. Stopping just short of the top, he listened. From the door straight ahead and to the left came the passionate purrs of a young woman moaning. Rapp took a deep breath; it had come down to this. He grabbed the doorknob with his right hand and pushed.

Rapp rushed the room, his gun sweeping from left to right. To the right was motion. Two bodies intertwined, lying flat. An arm extended above both heads, reaching for something. Rapp took aim and fired. The bullet slammed into Aziz's elbow, shattering the joint.

Rapp did not hesitate. He moved his gun in an effort to find a more vital target. The woman was in the way, and Aziz was rolling to use her as a shield. Rapp found Aziz's hip, fired his weapon, and started to close. The second arm was now reaching for the pillow. Rapp hit him in the other elbow. Blood geysered from the fresh wound, and Aziz let out a low, guttural moan.

Rapp yanked the woman off the bed. He took off his wig and spat out his fake teeth. He looked down at Aziz, lying on the bed and bleeding in three places, his arms useless. With the silencer pointed at Aziz's forehead, Rapp asked, "Do you remember me?"

Aziz looked up in pain, no recognition on his face.

Rapp turned his head to the side. "You cut me in Paris, remember?"

Aziz's face froze as he searched his memory. After a moment a thin smile creased his lips.

Rapp backed up a step. With great satisfaction he squeezed the trigger one more time, closing a very bad chapter in his life.

"Four Tangos down. I'm on my way out," Rapp muttered into his radio. He herded the prostitute down the hall and to the first floor. At the back door he told her to get lost and watched her stumble into the darkness. Rapp reached into his bag and grabbed a block of C-4 plastique, setting the timer for twenty seconds. He threw it into the kitchen and closed the door.

Rapp walked casually to the end of the alley, where a four-door Mercedes sedan skidded to a halt. The back door flew open, and Rapp got in next to Commander Harris.

As the driver hit the gas, there was a loud explosion and the dark alley erupted into a fiery ball.

About the Author

VINCE FLYNN is a graduate of the University of St. Thomas in St. Paul, Minnesota. His previous book, *Term Limits,* is currently available in paperback from Pocket Books. He lives in the Twin Cities, where he is working on a series of political thrillers.